# NIKHOLAI PULLED HER HEAD BACK AND TOOK HER MOUTH WITH HIS IN A HARD, BRUISING KISS . . .

He pressed her against the horse until she was conscious of the stirrup in her back. His beard stubble chafed her cheeks, and his body was hard, powerful, and overwhelming to Elise.

It was the intimacy of the kiss that frightened her the most. He forced her mouth open with his tongue and assaulted her lips, teeth, and tongue. . . . She blocked his intruding tongue with her own and tried to twist away. He continued to take the liberties he wanted. He stroked her shoulder and slipped a hand over one breast. Elise trembled.

When he took his mouth from hers, he continued to hold her close. He whispered into her ear so that it looked to the other Cossacks as if he were nibbling it. His breath was warm and tingling.

"Understand, you will not defy me and win." Then he brushed his unshaven cheek against hers. "You taste like apples, Green Eyes. Sweet and tangy. I'll be back for more." Without another look at her, he led the mare away.

Indignantly, Elise realized that he had done to her exactly what she had threatened to do to him and more . . .

Most Pocket Books are available at special quantity discounts for bulk purchases for sales promotions, premiums or fund raising. Special books or book excerpts can also be created to fit specific needs.

For details write the office of the Vice President of Special Markets, Pocket Books, 1230 Avenue of the Americas, New York, New York 10020.

# Sweet Ransom

## Linda Madl

POCKET BOOKS

New York   London   Toronto   Sydney   Tokyo

"Volga, Volga" from Collection of Folk Songs (Botsford), copyright© G. Schirmer Inc. Used by permission.

An *Original* Publication of POCKET BOOKS

POCKET BOOKS, a division of Simon & Schuster Inc.
1230 Avenue of the Americas, New York, NY 10020

ISBN: 0-671-66943-5

First Pocket Books printing October 1989

10  9  8  7  6  5  4  3  2  1

To my daughter, Lori

# Acknowledgments

Thanks to all the people who supported my writing in general and this project in particular—Babette Morgan, Judy Moresi, Susanna Bullock, Carm Utz—and to my writing teachers who may wish to remain unidentified.

Special thanks to those who helped me with the map—John Flaherty and Kevin Williams.

# Historical Note

Cossacks are one of the many peoples of the Russias. They possess their own language, cultural traditions, and fascinating history. These farmer-warriors were among those who helped the Romanov family to the throne of Russia in 1613.

At the time of this novel, fall 1669, Tsar Alexis Romanov—father of Peter the Great—like the tsars of Great Russia before him, recognized the Cossacks as an independent, self-governing people. They were considered allies and received on an ambassadorial status in the Muscovite court.

# Sweet Ransom

Nikholai Fomin's
Country
1669

# ❧ Prologue ❧
# Dnieper River, Fall 1669

The first Tartar arrow thudded into the coach wall next to Elise Polonsky's cheek just as she dozed off. Hawkins screamed. Elise blinked awake.

"Keep down," she ordered, reaching for her sister, Anna. Hastily Hawkins dropped to the floor and pulled the child along with her.

Count Oscar Polonsky snatched aside the coach window curtain to see what was happening.

"What the devil?" he demanded. But the Polish aristocrat's words were cut short by the shrill war cries of the Krim Tartars descending on the coach and its small contingent of Polish cavalry.

With her hand still on her sister's back to keep her down, Elise peered over her husband's shoulder to see Tartars with flashing sabers and cocked crossbows swarm down on them.

Already some of the Polish soldiers reached for their crossbows, but the experienced ones pulled out their sabers and rode directly at the shrieking Asian horsemen.

Nine-year-old Anna whimpered.

"It will be all right, dear. William will take care of us," Elise comforted her with a confidence in her voice that she didn't feel.

1

The coach lurched to a halt. Elise and the count were thrown to the floor on top of Hawkins and Anna. Elise heard the injured coach horses scream and thrash against each other. The coach rocked dangerously in hub-deep water. The count pulled himself up from the floor and leaned out the window.

"No!" exclaimed Elise. She reached for her husband's arm to pull him back. Before she could warn him, his body jerked twice, then slumped over the edge of the opening.

"Oh, my lady," cried Hawkins, who peered out the window.

"Oscar?" Elise reached for her husband.

Hawkins pushed her and Anna away from the body and drew them down onto the floor. "We can't do anything for him now, Miss Elise," Hawkins said. "He was an old man. He had a long life."

Stunned, Elise took Anna into her arms and huddled on the floor next to Hawkins. She ignored her sudden emptiness and rising panic to speak soothingly to her young sister. "William will be here shortly, dear. He'll get us out of this."

The coach rocked again, then toppled over onto its side. Elise fell against her dead husband. Hawkins slid down on top of Anna, who quickly became drenched in the muddy river water that gushed through the coach windows. The golden-haired child began to choke and cry. Elise struggled to her feet first. Then she pulled her sister from the water as Hawkins scrambled to her own feet.

No longer willing to wait for rescue, Elise grabbed the count's silver-headed walking stick. With her other hand she stretched up along the red velvet seat to the door above her. Just as her fingers closed around the brass handle, it was jerked from her grip. A grim round Oriental face peered down at her.

When the Tartar saw the two women and a child crouched in the overturned coach, he grinned. He called something over his shoulder, then reached for Elise. She poked him in the face with the walking stick's silver head, struck him with as much strength as she could manage from her position. The Tartar howled in rage and pain, drew back for a moment to wipe his bloody nose on his sleeve, then lunged for her. Before she could strike him soundly on the head, he was yanked from the doorway. She heard a body hit the underside of the coach. Another thud and a pistol shot, then William filled the doorway and looked down at her.

"Come, Elise," he ordered, and reached for her. His tall hat was gone, a lock of blond hair fell across his forehead, and a button had been ripped off his uniform. But William was his usual unruffled self. Relieved, Elise grasped her brother's strong hand and climbed out of the overturned coach. Then she turned back for Anna. Hawkins lifted the girl to Elise, who handed her to William.

"Where's the count?"

"He's dead, Master William," Hawkins said as she climbed from the coach. William looked at Elise questioningly. She shook her head, too numb to speak. Part of her still didn't believe any of this was happening.

"I'm sorry. Are you all right?" he asked.

"Yes. Let's get Anna away from here," Elise said as she jumped down from the side of the coach. She hurried, aware that soldiers were fighting hand-to-hand with the Tartars to protect the women while they escaped from the stranded vehicle.

She pulled Anna behind her skirts to protect her and block her view. She looked around to see that someone had cut the uninjured coach horses from their traces. A dead Tartar lay spread-eagled on a slowly rotating coach wheel. Blood-streaked water swirled around her knees.

She watched in horror as a saber-swinging Tartar rode down on an unmounted Polish soldier armed only with a sword. Their blades rang on impact. The wild-eyed Tartar pony shied from the flashing steel. The Pole grabbed the Tartar by his caftan and yanked him from the uncontrolled horse. They both fell into the river, grappling for life and death.

William vaulted from the coach and pulled the women closer into the protection of the vehicle's muddy underside.

"Run for the east riverbank," he said. "The men will cover us. I'll carry Anna. Go, Elise." He spoke rapidly to Elise in their native English.

The women gathered their skirts about their knees, William tucked Anna under his arm like a sack of grain, and they all bolted for the east bank.

Matchlocks flashed. Arrows whirred past them. Elise could hear clearly the cries of dying men and the grunts of wounded horses.

The river sand sucked at her feet. She wanted to run faster, but her feet moved sluggishly through the water. Twice Elise looked back to make sure that William and Anna were still with them. Each time, Hawkins urged her on.

When they finally reached the protection of the golden poplar trees, Elise turned to see the fighting men following them across the river. The coach and the count's body had been left deserted in the middle of the ford.

Oscar was dead. Elise forced herself to face that. They would never play chess again or enter a palace salon side by side. Her kind, gentle husband was dead.

The churning river glittered in the harsh fall sunlight. On the opposite riverbank several riderless horses, bridle reins dragging in the water, shied from the noisy confusion of battle.

"Listen to me carefully," William instructed as he put Anna down. He tugged at Elise's sleeve to gain her attention. Around them the surviving Polish soldiers took cover behind the trees and continued to fight.

"You *must* follow my directions," William said. Elise didn't miss the emphasis on "must." He stopped to shout orders in Polish to some of the men. When he faced Elise again, he returned to English.

"The men and I will create a diversion near the coach. When I give the signal, I want you, Anna, and Hawkins to ride out of here, east down the riverbank, then up onto the steppe. Stay on the road if you can, until you come upon help. The tsar's negotiator should have sent out streltsy to escort us from the border."

William drew his sisters down farther against him as another arrow whisked over their heads. He pulled Elise's handkerchief from her fur cuff, where she had tucked it earlier in the afternoon. "I want you to take Commander," he said. "He responds well to you. He'll get you through this."

"How are you and the men going to get out?"

"Don't worry about us," William said. "Remember what

4

Father always said? You must obey orders. Do you understand?"

Elise nodded, only too aware of what William's evasion meant.

"Stay here," he ordered as he disappeared around one of the trees. He returned leading a huge white stallion, Commander, and a smaller, well-muscled black gelding. He motioned Hawkins toward the black.

"Mr. William, you know I don't ride," Hawkins protested with a shake of her gray head.

"I think this is an excellent time for you to learn," said the young officer with a distracted smile. He linked his fingers together to give a leg up to the aging maid.

"Well, I don't know," she said. "It isn't proper to ride astride, for me or Lady Elise."

A blast from a matchlock splintered bark from the poplar tree above Hawkins. Yellow leaves rained down on her head. She gasped. With a look of pure determination, she went to her young master, hiked up her muddy skirt, and put her foot into his waiting hands.

Turning to Elise, William said, "You're the more experienced rider, so you take Anna." He gave Elise a leg up on Commander. The enormous stallion snorted and pranced, but Elise was steady.

William picked up Anna. Her small white ermine muff swung from a velvet cord around her wrist, and a matching hat sat atop her golden curls. He kissed the child's pale cheek before he placed her on the saddle before Elise.

"There must be another way," Elise protested. She looked around, casting for ideas. She would not let this happen.

William grasped Elise's arm urgently. "Remember, ride out when I give you the signal. Don't look back. When you reach the Russians, demand diplomatic immunity. Make it clear you were with the count on a peaceful mission, negotiating the Andrusovo treaty. Don't stop until you reach help."

"William?"

"For once in your life, follow orders," he said. "These men's deaths will be for nothing if you don't."

Elise looked down at her fair-haired brother. Of her three older brothers, William had always been the one to get her out of trouble, to keep watch. She could always count on him to back her against James's outrageous schemes and Thomas' ridicule. This was a nightmare and she wanted to wake up safe now, with everyone alive and well.

"I won't do it," Elise cried. "There must be another way."

"Think of Anna. If not yourself, think of her. When I wave your handkerchief from the end of my saber," William reminded her. "Good-bye, sisters." He squeezed her hand, then turned to shout orders in Polish to his remaining men.

Elise disobeyed William's orders. She looked back as Commander carried her from the riverbank to the edge of the steppe. She blocked Anna's view. Elise saw the men leave the shelter of the trees to fight the Tartars in the open, on the riverbank, and in the water. Their horses were dead, wounded, or strayed. The Polish men fought on foot against mounted Tartars. William carried his pistol in one hand and his sword in the other. He downed one Tartar with his pistol, then threw it aside to use his sword. He was defending one of his wounded men against a warrior on foot when a mounted Tartar attacked him.

William unhorsed the Tartar, but his foe, a bearded man garbed in yellow, raised his saber above William. The blade flashed in the autumn sun as it swung down on William's neck and shoulder, nearly cleaving his strong body in two.

Commander gave Elise no time to cry out, no time to be sick with grief. She wasn't even given the choice of turning back. The giant white horse plunged from the riverbank up onto the open steppe and reached out, eager to cover the treeless distance that stretched before them. The valiant black gelding followed, with Hawkins helplessly clutching the saddle pommel.

Cold wind stung Elise's face, bringing her senses back to her. Expertly she brought the white horse's headlong gallop under control and held Anna more securely in the saddle before her. Over her shoulder she could see Hawkins, but the gelding was already beginning to lag behind.

The dignified English maid had lost her black velvet hat, so her gray hair streamed loose down her back. Her black cloak flapped about her narrow shoulders and the gelding's flanks, and her lips were tight. Under other circumstances Elise would have found Hawkins an amusing sight. Even now she felt a laugh rise to her lips. Hysteria was taking over, she realized. She hugged Anna against her body and asked God to give her the courage to hold them all together through whatever was to come.

She looked over her other shoulder in time to see a small group of Tartar horsemen closing in.

Ahead, Elise saw nothing but empty steppe, a rolling, endless sea of grass stretching to the eastern horizon. She hoped to ride closer to the main road they had been following in the coach. Hawkins followed, still astride the black.

Elise had little hope of reaching help. She doubted the Russians had sent an escort. She and her husband had already discussed that omission in the coach. It was one more way the Russians had found to insult the Poles, with whom they were secretly negotiating for territory and a port on the Baltic Sea. Tsar Alexis was determined to take a Polish seaport to provide Russia with a direct connection to the west.

She heard the scream of an injured horse and turned to see the black gelding go down with an arrow in its neck. Hawkins was thrown clear and landed in a flapping heap of skirts and cloak.

Without breaking the stallion's pace, Elise pulled Commander around in a large circle and started back toward Hawkins.

The great white horse headed for the floundering black gelding and the struggling heap of a woman. The Tartars reached Hawkins first. Curious, they jumped from their ponies and watched the huge white horse descend upon them. The thundering hooves didn't hesitate as the horse neared the staring men. With yelps of surprise, the warriors scattered before the charging horse like ducks before a fox. As he passed, the white stretched out and viciously bit the arm of a fleeing Tartar. Another warrior took aim with his matchlock rifle, but the stocky Tartar in yellow shoved the gun barrel aside.

Still at a safe distance from them, Elise reined in the white, turned toward them, and halted. The Tartars surrounded Hawkins again.

"Go on, my lady. I'll be all right. Ow! Oh! Take Miss Anna

7

and go. Don't worry about me," called Hawkins as two warriors pulled her to her feet.

The chief shouted at Elise and waved a pistol at Hawkins' head. Elise understood the language well enough to know that the yellow-clad Tartar demanded her surrender for Hawkins' life. He would sell them into slavery, if they were lucky, she concluded. But he wanted the white horse for himself.

The white snorted and switched his tail.

"I don't think Commander likes the smell of them," said Anna. The child coughed several times before she was able to go on. "We aren't going to leave Hawkins, are we?"

Elise glanced toward the eastern horizon. Freedom was still possible, she thought. As William had reminded her, she had to think of Anna. But Elise already regretted leaving her brother behind. She shook her head.

"No, we're not leaving anyone else," Elise promised, and hugged her sister against her.

## ❧ 1 ❧

# Pirates on Horseback

In the fall of 1669, revolution brewed on the Russian steppe.

Russian serfs longed for freedom. Law bound them to their landlords like cattle to farmers. In the villages and cities along the Don and Volga rivers, Tsar Alexis' appointed voevodas, or governors, levied heavy taxes on merchants and tradesmen to finance Russia's recent war against Poland.

Along the southern border, vicious bands of Krim Tartars, loyal to the Turkish sultan, terrorized villages. They murdered farmers and clergy, burned Christian churches, and dragged women and children away to the slave markets.

Only the courageous proud Cossack brotherhoods challenged the infidels. Tsar Alexis promised the Cossacks grain and gunpowder in exchange for their defense against the heathens. But often the promised food and supplies never arrived or were never sent.

So the Cossacks resorted to whatever means necessary—raids on merchant caravans, on river barges, or on ships at sea—to provide for their families and to defend the steppe, the rivers, and the freedom they loved.

\* \* \*
9

"Moisy Tokin is dead," Ataman Nikholai Fomin said as he knelt beside his dead warrior. "That makes two we've lost.

"Bury them on the steppe with honor. Throw the Tartar dead into the river," the ataman ordered crisply. The trading party on the river barge had been a rich one, just as the Cossacks had been told, but the ataman didn't like losing two good men. He stood up and glanced at his anxious lieutenant. "What is it?"

"Vikola Panko and Ostap Koltso have found a fair European woman with the Tartars' slaves. They're fighting over her."

"A European woman? This was supposed to be a trading party."

"She is a problem, Ataman," Kasyan Cherevik insisted.

"For two warriors? Where are they?" Annoyed with this unexpected development, Nikholai strode across the ravine with Kasyan. Around them the air still stung with the odor of gunpowder. At Kasyan's order, Don Cossacks in wide, full pants belted with bright sashes began to drag dead Tartars to the river's edge. Unceremoniously they threw the bodies of the infidels into the swift water of the Volga. Already, vultures circled lazily overhead.

Other Cossacks tied prisoners to trees and rounded up the Tartar horses. Not far away, the burlaki, the river men, silently watched from beside their morning campfire. Survivors of other raids, they knew they would be unharmed as long as they did not defend the merchants' barges.

When the two Cossacks reached the far side of the ravine, just beyond a small grove of leafless maples, Nikholai saw an injured white horse. Lying on its side, the animal grunted and groaned in pain and fear. The stallion's left hind leg, broken just below the hock, swung from a pink-and-white sinew. Blood soaked the ground beneath the dangling leg.

Then Nikholai saw a blond woman standing protectively over the great white's head. She stood nearly as tall as the two Cossack warriors she faced. She was dressed in a tattered green fur-trimmed traveling dress. The rich brown fur collar and cuffs of her dress contrasted with her creamy white neck and hands. Her young face was smudged with dirt, and her pale lips were set in a grim expression. Golden hair covered her proud head. From the cut of her costume and the elegance of her bearing, Nikholai could see that she was a European lady of quality.

She brandished a long leather whip in her right hand, a river man's whip used in driving the teams of oxen that towed the barges upriver. Facing two armed Cossacks didn't seem to daunt her. She shook the whip at Ostap and addressed him in a stream of words foreign to Nikholai. But the rage in her voice made it clear: Ostap should prepare to defend himself.

Then she turned on Vikola, a Zaporozhie and the fiercest of Nikholai's warriors. In elegant, well-spoken Polish she threatened, "You killed my friend—I saw you. Don't come near Commander, you blasted, bloody Cossack."

Vikola stood to her right and Ostap to her left, just beyond the reach of her whip. Menacingly Vikola waved the matchlock pistol in his hand and shouted at her. He took a step forward and leveled the pistol at the horse. Without hesitation the woman leapt over the horse's head and lashed Vikola across the face with the whip. The Zaporozhie staggered back a step. Immediately she whirled to attack Ostap. The chubby Cossack backed away. Enraged, Vikola had recovered and now leveled his gun at her back.

"Stop," Nikholai commanded. "What's going on here?"

Disconcerted, the two Cossack warriors turned to their ataman. Reluctantly Vikola lowered his pistol. Ostap sputtered.

"Ataman Nikholai Fomin, I have captured this woman and her horse. But the horse is injured and must be destroyed. The silly woman won't let me get a good shot at the head," Ostap complained.

"I saw her first, Ataman," Vikola objected as he rubbed the growing welt on his cheek. "She mounted the horse and broke away just as we attacked. She was here with the shore party."

The Cossacks glared at each other. The woman watched Nikholai.

He stepped closer to her. She drew the whip back. He held his hands open before him to show himself unarmed.

11

"Your horse is in pain," Nikholai said in Polish. He spoke soothingly. He hated to see animals in pain too, and he let his sympathy come through in his tone.

Surprised, the young woman lowered the whip. She tilted her head questioningly. Nikholai repeated his words in Polish.

The woman pushed a lock of honey-gold hair from her face. She glanced at the horse's broken leg, then back to Nikholai again. She did not hesitate to look him in the eye. Her level gaze unsettled him. It had been a long time since he had faced a European woman who regarded herself as a man's social equal.

"He is a fine stallion, but he must be destroyed."

The tall woman, with large green eyes, continued to regard Nikholai fearlessly. He was fascinated by the color and had to resist the urge to move closer to peer more deeply into them. He had never seen such a rich, living green except in the very finest jade from Cathay: not the muddy green stone of cheap work, but the fine, lustrous, polished jade carved by only the best artisans. Smooth, almost liquid, yet solid with contours and depth, and surprisingly warm and sensuous to the touch. Her green eyes were fringed with thick dark lashes, and her brow had a wonderful arch.

Her bold courage in the face of two veteran Cossack warriors was impressive but unwise. Nikholai admired her bravery, but he wouldn't let her or his men see that.

The horse groaned again and struggled to rise. Nikholai watched as the woman lowered the whip and turned to the horse. With a natural grace she sat down on the ground and placed the animal's huge head on her lap.

The white horse trembled from head to foot, but submitted to her comfort. The woman bent over the horse and spoke softly.

"That's no Tartar horse," Vikola said, tucking his long dark scalp lock behind his ear. "Look at those long legs and the full crest and deep chest. And the saddle. Probably Polish."

"Give me your pistol," Nikholai ordered without taking his gaze from the woman.

Vikola placed his brass-trimmed matchlock pistol in Nikholai's outstretched hand. Nikholai took it and walked

12

around to the woman's side. He reached down to help her up, but she merely continued to stroke the stallion's powerful neck. She looked up at Nikholai in stubborn refusal.

"These foreign women never know how to behave properly," Vikola snapped. "She doesn't even know to keep her gaze lowered in respect. If she were mine, I'd make sure she knew how to behave."

Nikholai ignored the older Cossack's obvious ploy to win the woman. He knelt next to her. She patted the horse's neck again and gently rested his head on the ground. She moved away only far enough to allow Nikholai to kneel next to the stallion's head. All the while, she stroked the great white's trembling neck and spoke comfortingly to the frightened animal.

Nikholai put the pistol against the back of the white's noble head. Quickly he cocked the gun and fired. The horse's body jerked, then fell still, the trembling gone, the dark eyes unseeing. Slowly, but without tears, the woman crossed herself. She stroked the broad white forehead tenderly and continued to talk softly to the brave animal.

Then Nikholai saw one huge tear spill down her cheek, but her face was calm. He reached out to help her up. But she turned on him with a closed look that forbade him to invade her grief.

"Silly woman, all this fuss over a horse," Ostap said in disgust. "And did you see how she crossed herself? Roman Catholic. You're probably right, Vikola, a Lyakh."

Nikholai stood up and returned Vikola's pistol. "I think the horse was her friend," he said. "It seems that even Poles can be loyal to their comrades."

The kneeling woman looked up at Nikholai briefly, almost as if she had understood his defense of her, spoken in Cossack. But she quickly turned away and rose from her knees. She wiped the tear from her face with the back of her hand. Wearily she walked around the horse and began to remove the saddle.

"Vikola, you take the saddle," Nikholai said. "Ostap, you take the hide. The woman should bring a good ransom. When we get it, you both will be honored with an extra share. Until then, she is under my protection."

"Thank you, Little Father," Ostap replied.

Vikola seemed about to object, but on second thought he pushed the woman aside and began to remove the finely tooled leather saddle.

Nikholai reached for the animal's bridle at the same time as the woman did, but both stopped before their hands touched. For a moment they regarded each other warily, without moving. Nikholai noticed that her small, delicate hands were rough and scratched and that on her left hand was an indentation where a ring had been, a wedding ring. The Tartars would have taken it from her. He saw her hand tremble. And when she straightened, she winced.

"Are you hurt?" he asked her.

She shook her head as if she didn't understand him.

"Are you hurt?" he asked again in Polish.

"No," she responded. She stood back as he removed Commander's bridle. A look of concern crossed her features when he turned to hand it to Vikola. She reached for the bridle too. Pointedly Nikholai held it just out of her reach until Vikola took it. Nikholai watched her closely as the Zaporozhie shot her a victorious look. Vikola picked up the saddle and started back toward the riverbank.

"What is he doing with my saddle? I want my saddle," the woman demanded. When Nikholai saw Ostap pull out his knife to take the hide, he seized her wrist and dragged her away.

"It's Vikola Panko's now."

"It's mine," the woman called after him. She was having difficulty matching his strides, but he didn't slow down.

"It belongs to Vikola now," he repeated over his shoulder.

"You can't do that. You can't just take it from me like that," she insisted, hiking up her skirts with her free hand to avoid stumbling over a fallen tree limb.

Nikholai turned to her abruptly. As fascinating as she was, he had no time for a woman intent on making trouble. The Muscovites could be down on them at any time. They had to work fast. He yanked her to him and grabbed her by the shoulders. Despite her height, he found her surprisingly light. Her shoulders felt thin and bony beneath his hands. He shoved her roughly against the trunk of a maple tree. She swallowed a groan of pain.

"I can do what I like, Green Eyes. I'm ataman here. That

14

saddle is part of the spoils of this raid, just as you and the other slave women are. You'll do as you're told, or you'll go into the river with the dead Tartars."

"I'm too valuable to throw into the river, Ataman. You know that. My family will pay you a sizable ransom," the woman said, bravely looking him in the eye again, her voice tight with pain.

"If the Muscovites catch us here, we'll all suffer at the end of their lances," he told her. "They won't stop to ask you if your family offers a ransom. You are a Pole in Russia. Your people have been their enemy for the last twenty years. They will care about little else."

The woman stared at him, obviously weighing his words. Her high round forehead was clear and smooth. Her softly pointed chin just completed the perfect oval of her face. Her nose was classically formed, and her mouth . . . Nikholai found the shape of her bottom lip particularly inviting.

Despite the dirty hair, he thought, despite the smudged face and the weariness around her eyes, she was a beauty. Those jade-green eyes set in that lovely face were unforgettable. Just her nearness made him think of apple blossoms; he wondered if that bottom lip would taste of apples.

Finally she nodded. Nikholai released her.

"All right," he said. "You will cause no more trouble among the men. You will keep your eyes lowered and stay at my side unless I tell you otherwise. And be quiet."

The woman nodded again, but she did not cower. Nor did she draw away from him or shift her gaze. She was lovely, but she was trouble, Nikholai decided. Perhaps even more trouble than she was worth. Angrily he seized her wrist and started off toward the riverbank with her in tow.

Resentfully Elise let the ataman pull her along. Her chance for escape was gone. She had come so close to being free to return for Anna. Now she was a captive once again—this time a Cossack captive.

She had watched and waited for days for a chance to break away from her captors. Then she had won the sympathy of a slave merchant, who bought her from the Tartars. She had managed to persuade the kind but greedy old eunuch to take her to Moscow and ransom her to the English ambassador.

15

She had told him she was worth more as a hostage than as a slave, and he had agreed. But she hadn't trusted him entirely and had managed to remain with the shore party, near the horses. Then she had seen the burlaki around the campfire become restless after receiving a message. A chance for escape was near, she had suspected. She had no food, no water, and no weapons, but she had to take the chance. Once free, she would find some way to go back for Anna.

So she lay wrapped in the rug she used for a bed and waited. Where the water lapped at the riverbank, the barges were tied together, and the Tartar mercenaries paced the decks. They did not trouble to patrol the riverbank where the burlaki camped and Elise and the old eunuch slept.

Chilled, sore, and still aching from the beating at the hands of the yellow Tartar, Elise had finally drifted into a light doze. But it was only a brief rest. She awakened as the first light of dawn stole across the river. Still sleepy, she lay quietly, watching the soothing flow of the water. Through the mist she saw reeds where she didn't remember reeds. They floated silently downriver toward the barges. She realized what was happening only a moment before gunfire erupted from the reeds.

Behind her she heard the hoofbeats of the first charge on the camp by the mounted Cossacks. She had watched in horror as the old merchant who had purchased her from the Tartars was murdered: shot in the back by the same Zaporozhie who later took William's saddle.

In the confusion of that first wave of attack, she had made her way to Commander. The Tartar who first captured her had been unable to bring himself to destroy the beautiful but belligerent stallion. He had driven a hard bargain when he sold Elise and the horse to the slave merchant.

In seconds she tightened Commander's saddle girth, vaulted onto his back. Lying close to his neck, she wove through the maple grove toward the steppe. Commander had given her all he had to give, but in the vague light of dawn he had stumbled in the rocky ravine and broken his leg. Elise was thrown clear of the horse and into the Cossacks' hands.

Frustrated, angry, and frightened more than she allowed

herself to realize, she would have gladly beat the ugly Cossack to death with the whip she had found. She blamed him for the merchant's death, for Commander's injury, and for her failure to reach freedom. Certainly one of them would have died if the ataman hadn't interrupted their confrontation.

"Stand here," the ataman said. "Eyes down." Then he turned to issue orders to the men.

Elise watched him covertly. He was a big man, at least a head taller than most of his warriors and herself. He was lean and moved easily. She noted his penetrating gray eyes. His full dark mustache was a rich charcoal brown like his short curly hair. His brows were dark and expressive, his jawline strong and firm. On either side of his mustache small lines hinted at a broad smile and a ready laugh. Did a Cossack ataman laugh? she wondered inanely. She thought him a young man for a leader, but he was comfortable with his authority, and so were his men.

Elise had already guessed that her steady gaze unsettled him. And she refused to speak to him in Cossack, just as she had refused with the Zaporozhie. It had surprised her when the ataman, obviously a Don Cossack, spoke to her in Polish. Cossack words sounded too much like Tartar, and she hated the Tartars. She refused to utter a single sound of the Cossack language, though she understood it perfectly. Let the ataman speak to her in Polish. It sounded like a comforting old friend after these nightmarish days with the Asian horsemen.

Elise turned to watch the rapid unloading of the barge and the loading of the packhorses. Then she looked at the ataman again. He would be no one's fool, she decided. He had not been taken in by his warriors' conflicting stories about her capture. Under his eye, escape would be even more difficult. Elise chewed her lip in frustration.

"How does it look?" Nikholai asked Kasyan as the lieutenant came away from one packhorse.

"Good," Kasyan replied. "Almost everything is unloaded, and we've started packing the horses. Several of the barrels we've opened were filled with wheat flour, and there are some barrels of vodka and gunpowder too."

"Work fast," Nikholai warned as he nodded approval. "The scouts signal it's clear, but let's not waste time."

Work continued. As Nikholai gazed upriver, looking for smoke signals, he felt the woman move away from him. Without a glance at her, he grasped her fur-covered wrist and drew her back to his side. He was unable to dismiss the need to keep her near.

Then, impatient with himself, he set her to work beside the five captured Christian women. Still, he caught himself gazing at her from time to time.

The six women captives folded the confiscated Turkish fabric and stuffed it into bags to be carried by the Don ponies. Tall and lithe, golden and creamy white, the woman moved like an elegant swan amid common brown ducks. The peasant women bobbed about their work. The European woman moved with grace, each movement smooth and flowing. For some reason, she stopped and looked directly at him. When their gazes met, Nikholai had the strange feeling that she was taking his measure just as a warrior would—but he didn't like it from a woman. With a frown, he motioned her to return to her work.

Grateful for rescue from the hands of the heathen Tartars, the other women willingly did the Cossacks' bidding. Nikholai noticed that two of the women were already casting flirtatious glances over their shoulders. They were not ransom captives, but they would offer their own kind of reward to his men.

When the packing was finished, Elise watched unmoved as the Cossacks disposed of the Tartars and Turks in the river.

The roar of the river faded behind them as they rode up the ravine toward the steppe. It was quickly replaced by the swish of the tall steppe grass parted by the horses. Elise rode between the ataman and his lieutenant at the head of parallel columns of Cossacks. As they emerged onto the open steppe, they passed a pair of fresh graves marked with Cossacks' lances. Elise wondered for the first time if Oscar and William had received any kind of burial, or had they been left to the birds of the sky and the fish of the river as the Turks and Tartars had been. She pushed the thought away;

18

she could do nothing for them—but she would find Anna again.

Trotting, the wiry little horses could travel for hours on end. The Cossacks rode silently under a gray-veiled sky.

Elise shifted her weight in the saddle to ease the dull pain that jarred through her with each step of the horse. The pain had been with her so long now she was able to ignore it at times. At other times she wanted to scream with the agonizing frustration of its constant presence. She could have fared worse at the hands of the Tartars, she knew. She was thankful for both the small things and great that had saved her thus far. Many had paid with their lives so that she could be here, and at times she didn't even want to go on. The exhaustion was too great, the responsibility too overwhelming. But she had promised William, and she had promised Anna.

For a moment, when the ataman had seized her wrist while he issued orders, she was afraid he had read her thoughts and knew she plotted escape again. *Blast him and his Cossacks!* she cursed. Freedom had been so close.

The wind flapped the dark burkas across the riders' backs and whipped the horses' tails around their flanks. Bridles jingled and horses snorted, but the Cossacks rode in silence. They rode all day with only one stop to relieve themselves and to water the horses. After dark they slowed their pace to a walk only until the moon peeked from among the eastern clouds and the steppe became light once again.

The ataman or Kasyan periodically dropped out of line to ride back along the column. Once the ataman surprised her. Totally exhausted, she had fallen into a light doze. Suddenly she felt a tug and jumped, causing the pain to knife through her side. She sucked in her breath sharply.

"We will camp soon. You can rest there," he said in Polish, and eyed her with concern.

She nodded and shifted in the saddle, determined to keep him from knowing how weak she was.

As the moon set, the Cossacks began to descend into another small, shallow river valley. The group formed a triangle, a defensive formation. In the center they built a huge fire; the flames leapt into the black night sky. Casks of vodka were lifted from the packhorses' backs. At Kasyan's direction, a freshly killed saga antelope was set to roast over the fire by the captive women.

Elise found she wasn't hungry. Eating seemed a waste of energy. She wanted to rest and to ease the pain in her side. She settled herself on the ground with her back against a barrel and wrapped the burka around her. She watched as handleless wooden cups were dipped into the vodka casks. Playing cards appeared from caftan pockets, and a Cossack warrior put a gudok to his mouth. The strains of music turned the warriors to dancers.

Nikholai found the woman huddled inside her burka near the packhorses, so far from the fire that the light did not penetrate the shadow cast across her face.

She started as he sat down next to her and offered her a cup of vodka. She refused. Nikholai was curious about her refusal to eat and concerned that she might become too weak to keep up.

He took a sip. "Now we will discuss who you are and how much ransom you will bring," he said, speaking in Polish. "But, first, tell me how you came to be with merchants bound for Moscow." He did not return her stare.

When she turned away to watch the fire, she said, "I was with my husband on a diplomatic mission. We were attacked by the Tartars at a river ford. My husband and my brother were killed."

"Who was your husband?" he prompted.

She was silent again, but he heard her take in a deep breath as if preparing herself for something unpleasant. "My husband was Count Oscar Polonsky, diplomat and negotiator for the newly elected King Michael of the Kingdom of Poland."

Nikholai had not heard the count's name in years, and he was surprised at how the sound of it made the fury rise in him. The old count's face was suddenly clear in his mind— long and narrow, with a thin beard that never quite covered the hollow-cheeked, greedy appearance of the old man. He turned to stare at her. Here was the count's young wife in his possession. This had the taste of irony about it that would please the old river spirits. Nikholai turned away from the woman so that she would not see the hatred and the pleasure in his face.

"You know of my husband?" she asked.

"Yes, but I can't say that I'm sorry for your loss." Nikholai turned back to her. How deeply did she mourn? he wondered. "So the old man finally took a wife?" he said aloud. "Have you given him heirs?"

"No." She hesitated again, as if she were about to say something painful. "We were married only two years. We were not blessed with children."

Nikholai peered at her over the edge of his cup. He could see no reason why the old count should have had difficulty planting his seed in this fertile ground. Finally he asked, "Where were you attacked?"

"On the Dnieper between Pereyaslav and Kaniev. We were not crossing at the better-known fords."

"Ah, a secret mission. Have the Muscovites finally decided to betray us to you Poles?"

"I'm not Polish," she snapped. "I'm English."

Not entirely surprised, Nikholai set the empty cup on the ground. "How did you come to be married to Count Polonsky?"

The countess told him that the count and her father, an English diplomat in Poland, had been friends for years. Her father had appointed the count her guardian. "When my father died, it seemed wisest to be married," she concluded.

How fortunate for the count, Nikholai thought. She was so young, it was possible she knew little of her husband and his feud with the Cossacks. But for Nikholai, her story raised more questions than it answered.

"You've come a long way from the Dnieper," he said. "How long ago was this?"

She shook her head. "I can't be sure. We rode across country for days. Then I was sold to the merchant." Impatiently she shifted her position and let the hood fall away from her face. She frowned at some unpleasant thought.

"No one was with you?" Nikholai asked.

The countess turned to look at him again with that resentful expression. Nikholai found her impertinence irritating. He was certain she was not telling the entire story, and she dared to look at him as if he had no right to ask.

Her gaze never wavered. "I traveled with my maid, Hawkins."

Nikholai stared back openly. Despite her unwavering gaze, he could see she was soft and feminine. He wondered if her skin would feel as smooth as an apple blossom. He would know in time. After all, she was a married woman already initiated into the pleasures of the marriage bed. She would succumb eventually.

Nikholai picked up his cup to take another drink of vodka. He needed something to calm the sudden desire for her that quickened his blood, but his cup was empty.

Winter would make the ransom process slow and tedious —long weeks, even months for the Polonsky family to live with the knowledge that Nikholai Fomin held the countess. He would need time. She was no coy maid who would simper when handled roughly or giggle when her hindquarter was pinched. She was a lady, a countess. He looked at her directly again. This conquest would not be accomplished quickly, but it would be most satisfying.

The countess remained silent, motionless, her gaze transfixed by the dancing red flames of the campfire.

Around the fire, three wild Cossacks danced in a circle, arms crossed in front of their bodies. They quickened their steps as the musician speeded up the music. They danced bare-chested, their sheepskin hats and embroidered caftans thrown onto the ground. One dancing warrior clipped a feather in his hair and, with a flourish, wrapped the turban fabric around his waist.

"How long will it take to ransom me?" she suddenly demanded.

"It will take some time to get word through to the Don Host and on to Warsaw and your family."

"How long?" she repeated, turning on him with a ferocity that took him by surprise. "Tell me. How long? Weeks? Months?"

"I don't know. It depends on the winter weather—"

"Weeks? Months?" She leaned forward insistently.

"Months. Why? What difference does it make?" replied

Nikholai, annoyed with her once again. Then a disturbing thought occurred to him. "You aren't with child, are you?"

The countess shook her head dismally. She put her hand to her face. An ermine muff dangled on a velvet cord from her wrist.

"What's this?" Nikholai asked, reaching for the small piece of ermine, more aware than ever of the nagging sense that she had told him only part of the story.

"That's mine," the countess said as she jerked the piece of fur away. "You took the saddle. You won't take this." She tucked the ermine beneath her burka and refused to look at him.

Astonished, Nikholai stared at her. This defiance could not be allowed. He reached for the ermine piece again, but she anticipated him and twisted away. Her gaze never left his face.

"Do that again, and I will make such a scene your men will laugh about it for days," she threatened in a deadly whisper. "Their ataman defied by a mere woman. For a silly piece of fur."

For the first time during the evening, he could see the green of her eyes flash at him from beneath the burka hood.

They faced each other coldly, each aware that Nikholai could overpower her easily. And he knew she was counting on his reluctance to damage valuable goods or to be embarrassed before his men for her protection. Nikholai looked away first, irritated and yet amused. He wondered what was in the muff. Jewels? Coins? Whatever it was, he would have it eventually.

"Are you sure you want to play this game with me, Countess?"

"This is no game, Ataman. It is life or death for me and my family." Then the countess pulled the burka around her and withdrew into its shadows. He longed to peer into those green eyes again, but she had turned away to watch the dancing warriors.

Nikholai watched one of the women captives sit down in Vikola's lap and twirl his dark scalp lock in her fingers. The welt from the countess's whip still branded Vikola's cheek. Nikholai had overheard the Zaporozhie explain to one of

23

his comrades that he had been scratched by a tree limb. Nikholai also noticed the other women had found Cossack warriors to drink and dance with. One couple disappeared into the darkness as he watched. It pleased him to think that in a few months there would be more babies and weddings in Vazka.

Nikholai rose to leave the countess. He would take care of her impertinence tomorrow. As he stood, she whispered to him, "And I will have my brother's saddle back too."

Without a reply, he left her, the ermine still tucked inside her burka.

# ❧ 2 ❧
# The First Attempt

When the Cossacks were unable to celebrate any longer, they slept where they fell. Then, at the first gray light of dawn, they silently packed up camp and soberly moved out in the standard two-column formation. They turned their horses south and east to continue the false trail for the tsar's troops. The Don Cossacks were counting on their fierce brothers, the Yaik Cossacks in the east, to discourage the Muscovites' pursuit.

Elise understood what they were about. Once, the day before, she had looked back to see that only a streak of trampled grass marked their passage. It was just enough to lead the streltsy away from the Don Cossacks' home and into danger.

She had slept on the ground with a cushiony Cossack saddle for a pillow and the grease-covered burka for bed and covers. Mounted on the bay mare again, she ached everywhere. The pain in her side had not eased. Although her mind worked busily on escape plans, her emotions were still numbed with sadness for Commander, worry for Anna, and grief for William and Oscar.

The Cossack chief glanced at her just once as he issued

25

instructions to the scouts. His eyes were icy gray. Elise decided to be compliant, at least for a while.

Under a colorless sky they rode for six hours. The Cossacks stopped once for a short, silent rest, then doubled back in a southwesterly direction. The steppe that stretched away from them on all sides offered no landmarks or trails. Elise knew the Cossacks navigated by the sun and stars and read the hills, rocks, and gullies to find sources of water.

Occasionally Kasyan rode back along the line to check the packhorses. Once he offered her water from his goatskin. She accepted.

Elise tried to doze in the saddle, but without success. Although the horse and burka kept her legs and body warm, her nose and her toes ached with the cold. Late in the afternoon they reached the Volga River again where it gouged its way through the steppe. A few yellow-leafed poplars marked the bank that stretched out into the broad gray river toward the sandy western bank. The rutted trail to the riverbank indicated that this was a well-used crossing. She thought she remembered making camp there with the Tartars only two or three nights ago.

Somewhere along the Cossack column the order to halt and dismount had been given. Cossacks swung down from their horses as if they had been in the saddle for only a few moments. Elise looked at the ground and wiggled her cold toes. She anticipated the shafts of pain that would shoot up through her shins and into her side when her feet hit the dry sand. She wasn't sure her knees would hold her.

Slowly she swung her right leg over the cantle and held herself there, leaning over the saddle, braced on her arms. She closed her eyes and gritted her teeth against the coming pain. She let herself down as slowly as she could, but her arms were tired and gave way.

"Easy," came the ataman's deep voice from behind her. He grasped her about the waist before her feet touched the ground. He set her gently on the sand. "There. Can you stand?"

"Yes, I'm all right." Elise tried to pull away, and turned her back to the mare to face him. He let her turn, but he did not release his painful grip on her waist. The mare stood firm.

"Thank you," Elise said as she looked up at him to search his face for traces of anger. She saw none. But he didn't release her.

He met her gaze openly, his gray eyes light against the dark tan of his face. His short dark hair curled up and over the edge of his black Persian-lamb cap.

"We're on the Volga, just above Tsaritsyn, aren't we?" Elise asked, looking over his shoulder at the river and the tow road along the bank. Still he didn't release her, and warriors had begun to watch them.

"Yes." Surprise was evident in the ataman's tone—he didn't expect her to know where they were. "Our village is on the Don just after it turns west away from the Volga. We'll be there by dark the day after tomorrow."

"What's the name of your village?" Elise asked as she pushed a strand of golden hair behind her ear. She felt ridiculous making idle conversation with him. When was he going to let her go? She placed her hand against his broad, solid chest casually to push him away without making a scene.

He refused to be moved, and in fact leaned closer to her. So he played a game.

"Vazka," he said as he pulled her even closer until her forearms pressed against his chest, her breasts against her arms, and she had to tilt her head back to look at him. He watched her, his face still expressionless. Little by little, he forced one of his red-booted feet between her two small ones, until even through her skirts she felt his knee rub against her thigh. He held her gaze with his. She was embarrassingly conscious of his hard male body intimately pressed against hers. She felt suddenly breathless, weak, and frightened. He grasped the back of her head in one hand so that she couldn't turn away.

Over his shoulder she saw Ostap point to them and say something to another warrior. Horrified, she watched as the warrior replied with a knowing nod. Both men laughed lewdly. One reached into his pocket for coins to make a wager.

The ataman pulled her head back and took her mouth with his in a hard, bruising kiss. He pressed her against the horse until she was conscious of the stirrup in her back.

27

Before it became painful, he slipped his hand up her back and covered the cold metal. His mustache tickled her nose, his beard stubble chafed her cheeks, and his body was hard, powerful, and overwhelming.

It was the intimacy of the kiss that frightened her most. He forced her mouth open with his tongue and assaulted her lips, teeth, and tongue. This was no wet, slobbering kiss of a loathsome Tartar. She had suffered that with detached contempt. This Cossack she had to fight. She blocked his intruding tongue with her own and tried to twist away. Escape was impossible, and he seemed to enjoy her struggle. He continued to take the liberties he wanted. He stroked her shoulder and slipped a hand over one breast. Elise trembled.

When the ataman took his mouth from hers, he continued to hold her close. He whispered into her ear so that it looked to the other Cossacks as if he were nibbling it. His breath was warm and tingling.

"Understand, you will not defy me and win." Then he brushed his unshaven cheek against hers. "You do taste like apples, Green Eyes. Sweet and tangy. I'll be back for more."

Elise covered her throbbing lips with the back of her hand. Wide-eyed, she stared up at him, too stunned to even think of striking back. She trembled with confusion, humiliation, and anger. Without another look at her, he led the mare away.

Ostap and his friend howled with laughter and slapped each other's backs. Ostap counted out some coins for the other. Elise felt a fiery blush stain her chafed cheeks.

Hurriedly she walked among the men as they settled themselves on the ground next to their comrades to eat their rations. She would have run if she hadn't thought it would make her humiliation too plain. As it was, soft, knowing chuckles followed her across the camp. She lifted her chin proudly and quickened her pace to find anonymity among the other women.

Elise realized that the ataman had done to her exactly what she had threatened to do to him, and more. She had sensed last night when he left her that she had gone too far. But the idea of parting with the only things she had left of her family was unbearable. William's saddle. Anna's muff.

They would bring him a few coins, but they were priceless to her.

She sat down on a log, a water-worn tree trunk, near the other women. To sit on something that wasn't in constant motion was a relief. Despite her riding experience, she was so saddlesore she momentarily forgot about the pain in her side. The women were eating their rations. She noticed that a couple of them had already found protectors. She knew what they had given for the protection. Must she do that too? Surely that could be no worse than what she had suffered at the hands of the murdering Tartar. The skin on the back of her neck prickled, and she felt suddenly nauseated. She covered her face with her hands and tried to control her stomach.

She was concerned about more than just herself. The days were slipping away. Time. She was upset that she could no longer remember how many days had passed since the attack . . . since her sale to the slave merchant. And each day that passed put more distance between her and Anna.

At the sound of footsteps, Elise looked up to find Kasyan offering her hard black bread and tough dried fish. She managed to smile at him. He reminded her of William. His sandy-brown hair was not as light as William's, his eyes were dark hazel instead of blue, but she was drawn to his quiet, unassuming authority, so like William's. With a shake of her head she refused the food. She felt no hunger, and had no energy left to attempt to eat. He frowned at her refusal. Abruptly he left, but soon returned.

"Here, eat this, Countess." This time he offered her a piece of precious white bread. Elise looked at it, then up at him. He spoke in Cossack, but his meaning was plain enough.

"Take it," he said, offering the bread again. "This will be easier for you to eat than the fish. The ataman sent it. He says we don't need to have a woman fall from the saddle for lack of food."

Fall from the saddle in a faint, indeed, thought Elise. She had never fallen from the saddle for any reason. If the ataman had been standing before her instead of Kasyan, she would have thrown the bread back in his bloody Cossack face. She looked beyond Kasyan in the direction he pointed, only to see the ataman watching her, a small, derisive smile upon his lips.

The peasant women turned to look at the ataman too, then back at Elise, and twittered among themselves. They obviously envied Elise the attention she would have gladly done without.

Elise took the bread and cup of vodka from Kasyan. The offer of white bread was a generous one, but she refused to acknowledge it. After all, the ataman only wanted to be sure he didn't have a woman fall from the saddle. She took a small bite of the dry bread.

Kasyan shook his head and squatted on his heels before her. "No, Countess. Like this," he explained in Cossack. "Soak the bread in the vodka. It makes the bread softer and takes the sting out of the drink." Gently he took the bread and vodka from her. He dunked the bread and handed it back to her. "There. See if that isn't better. When we get to Vazka, Aunt Natalia will fill you with a good meal."

Elise found the bread did taste better soaked in vodka, and wondered why her brothers' Cossack military trainer had never shown her and her brothers this manner of eating. She discovered she was hungry after all, and began to eat in earnest. Satisfied, Kasyan returned to his ataman.

She saw the young lieutenant speak briefly to his chief. The ataman glanced at her over Kasyan's shoulder, then returned to tending the blood bay.

She reflected again on the ataman's kiss and his promise: "I'll come back for more." And that derisive smile was a warning, she was sure. She closed her eyes, and her skin crawled as she remembered the feel of the Tartar's greasy hands upon her skin, his wet lips across her face and shoulders, the sound of ripping cloth, and the pain. She shuddered. There had to be a way out. Once in the ataman's fortified village, or stanitsa, escape would be even more difficult. She had to do something before they reached Vazka. All she needed was a horse and a weapon.

Elise's energy returned with that thought. Where was the ataman? she wondered. She looked up to see him watching her again over Kasyan's shoulder. Quickly she looked away, remembering too well how her eyes always gave her away to her brothers. Laughing, they insisted that her eyes literally flashed when she was about to do something especially outrageous.

Just then a scout on horseback splashed across the river ford and pulled up near the ataman and Kasyan. He lurched off the winded horse and immediately told the ataman his news, which the ataman appeared not to like.

She finished the bread, swallowed the rest of the vodka, and licked her fingers as she watched the three men. She was unable to hear them, but the scout was agitated.

The ensuing confusion was just the diversion Elise needed. The peasant women were hastily gathered up by their escorts, and Kasyan brought Elise her bay mare. She gestured for his help in mounting. Surprised because she had not asked for help before, he hesitated before he offered her a leg up. Awkwardly, Elise's foot missed his proffered hand and she stumbled into him, giving a cry of dismay. Innately a gentleman, Kasyan steadied her. Feigning embarrassment, Elise thanked him. The second attempt to mount went more smoothly, and he handed her the reins and turned to other duties.

Elise carefully wound the braided horsehair reins through her fingers the way she liked them, then willed herself to remain calm until the best opportunity presented itself. She waited and listened to the Cossack commands and orders issued around her, orders she wasn't supposed to understand.

Elise had always possessed an unusual facility with languages, but she considered it no more special than her brother Thomas' ability to touch his nose with his tongue. If she didn't know a language, she could learn it easily just by hearing it over a period of days and weeks. While she was a Tartar captive she had learned more Tartar than she ever intended to speak.

When Elise was only four, her mother had discovered to her horror that her daughter spoke the Gaelic language of her Welsh nurse as fluently as the Chathams' own native English. The nurse was immediately replaced with a French governess. Elise charmed the French court with her fluent

French when she was only six. At age ten she had begun to ask about the dusty Latin and Greek texts in her father's library. So Elise was included in her brothers' lessons.

She proved to be an apt pupil and a stimulating influence. Neither James, nor William, nor Thomas would let his little sister best him. The competition was tough. Elise gave little quarter in the classroom. Her brothers gave little quarter on the field.

When her father brought the family to Poland, eight-year-old Elise easily conquered Polish within a few weeks, much to the embarrassment of her three older brothers. Then she absorbed Cossack from the Terek Cossack Yergov, hired as her brothers' military instructor. The wiry little Cossack had resented training a girl with the boys at first, but the foursome was not to be parted.

Nikholai had seen the green flash in the countess's eyes. He wondered about it, but the word from the scouts was serious, and it distracted him from the unique expression the countess had cast his way. He ordered Kasyan to see to her, then returned to questioning the scout. Later, when he was satisfied that they were ready to move out on the last leg of the journey, he realized he hadn't seen the countess among the riders. He turned to Kasyan. His lieutenant turned to him.

The two men said nothing as their gazes met. Kasyan's expression revealed his chagrin. Nikholai realized they had both underestimated their golden-haired captive. He shook his head. The streltsy was about to ride over the horizon, and the countess had just ridden off in another direction.

"Would she take the tow road?" Kasyan asked.

"Someone would have seen her," Nikholai said. "Look for her trail on the side of the road. She would head south." He turned his blood bay south on the road. Now he knew why she had asked where they were and how far south Tsaritsyn was. It was the only city of any size in the area. And she would tell the people of Tsaritsyn all about the pirates of Vazka who had captured her. Alexander Rostov, the streltsy captain, would sniff out that piece of information quickly enough.

Nikholai pressed the blood bay on. The woman could bring them reward, but she could bring them disaster too.

Kasyan picked up her trail on the tow road just around the river bend. They rode about a verst farther downriver, then lost the trail. Kasyan rode in circle after circle around the point where he had lost the bay mare's tracks. He could find no indication of which way the countess had gone.

They rode up the nearby hillside to a bluff for a better view of the tow road. She was not on it, but they did spot her to the east, riding rapidly across the open steppe. They set out after her. The ataman's blood bay, Sultan, easily took the lead and closed the distance between him and the countess.

Nikholai saw her urge the bay mare on when she looked over her shoulder and saw them closing in on her. When she purposely swerved the little horse across Sultan's path and caused the big stallion to break his stride and lose speed, Nikholai knew she hadn't been taught to ride in some polite female academy. Every time he rode close enough to grab the reins of the mare, the countess maneuvered the animal away. Nikholai even reached for her once, and she ducked. Clearly she was determined to avoid being recaptured. With a curse, Nikholai wished he had his lasso with him.

The lathered horses plunged down a rocky ravine, through a grove of trees, then out onto the steppe. Kasyan followed.

Nikholai decided on what he had to do. He saw no other way to stop her before she ran both horses into the ground. He slipped his feet from the stirrups. Riding up beside her once more, he launched himself at her before she could swerve away. He knocked her from the galloping horse. They both landed clear of the horses' hooves and rolled down the hillside, coming to rest against a tall clump of swaying grass. Momentarily stunned from the fall, neither moved. When the countess did stir, she groaned and clutched her side.

Concerned that she had been injured in the fall, Nikholai released her. Instantly she scrambled to her feet and started away. Angrily Nikholai grabbed her ankle. She fell, almost yelping with pain, but she didn't stop fighting. She rolled over and kicked at him with her free foot. The first kick missed. The second caught him in the upper thigh, just missing his groin. The pain was enough to make him loosen his hold. She jumped up and almost collided with Kasyan, who ducked away from her. At first Nikholai didn't understand why; then he saw a small knife in her hand.

"How'd she get that?" he demanded as he got to his feet.

Kasyan reached for the four-inch utility knife he carried in his sash, as did every Cossack. His was gone. He glanced at his ataman.

Nikholai made no comment. He watched the countess carefully. He didn't like what he saw.

Her face was pale, unnaturally white, and her breathing was ragged, strained. She was almost panting. Nikholai found the sound oddly disturbing. He was certain now that she was injured in some way and that the injury had not happened in the fall from the horse. He had taken the impact of that fall on his shoulder. He rubbed it thoughtfully. For the first time, he began to wonder what she had suffered at the hands of the Tartars.

He wasn't too concerned about overcoming her with the knife, but he didn't want to worsen any injury that might render her unable to ride. What concerned him most was the thought that she might turn the knife on herself.

She had probably heard frightening tales of Cossack rape and murder of women, but the truth was that women were scarce on the frontier. He knew the Yaik Cossacks—when they'd been at the vodka jug too long—sometimes still rode out to steal women.

"Countess, give me the knife," he ordered. He held out his hand for the weapon.

Her face remained impassive. She backed away but said nothing. Pain and desperation were plain in her eyes. Her hair had come loose from the knot at the back of her neck and floated in a gold-wrought nimbus about her shoulders. Despite the knife and her height, she seemed small and vulnerable to Nikholai.

He searched for something reassuring to say but could think of nothing. He had to end this quickly.

"Countess, there are two of us. We can take the knife from you if we have to. We might hurt you. Don't make us add to your pain." He stepped toward her. Kasyan began to move to her right.

"Stop that. Stay together," she demanded. She backed

34

away. Nothing but open steppe spread out behind her. Nikholai was thankful there was no place for her to retreat or hide.

"Oh, damn," she said in a language Nikholai thought must be her native English. "You, Ataman, especially you, stay away from me." She waved the blade in his direction.

Nikholai halted. But Kasyan continued to walk slowly around to her side, closer and closer. Nikholai remained before her, forcing her to divide her attention between them.

"This is not fair, Ataman." Her voice was a tight whisper now, and she had begun to favor her right side.

"Ah, but you haven't played fair either, Countess."

"Anything is fair for a woman against one hundred Cossacks, Ataman."

"Give me the knife."

Kasyan had stopped only an arm's length from her, but she still held Nikholai's gaze. Her green eyes were glazed with pain, but he knew she wasn't about to do what he had asked.

She started to speak again, then groaned. With obvious effort she made herself stand up straight. She squared her shoulders.

"Don't," she commanded when she saw the slight movement of Kasyan's attempt to take the knife from her.

She turned back to Nikholai. "The knife is Kasyan's. I took it by deception. I will only surrender it to him."

Nikholai paused before he nodded his consent. But when she turned to Kasyan, an unfamiliar shaft of jealousy shot through the Cossack chief. In a gesture of formal surrender, she placed the knife, handle first, into Kasyan's broad hand. Then, almost in an appeal for help, she reached for the lieutenant's arm with her other hand. Kasyan caught it and prevented her from collapsing.

With tremendous self-control Nikholai made his face remain expressionless while inside he wanted to roar his anger and jealousy. The emotions were unreasonable—he had never begrudged his lieutenant and friend anything. Not Daria, not even the flirtation with Aksinia. But now Nikholai wanted the countess to turn to him, not Kasyan. He wanted her to reach for him, not his lieutenant. He wanted Count Oscar Polonsky's wife to surrender to him.

The ataman's anger didn't surprise Elise, but she was aware that his behavior upset Kasyan. She was in too much pain and despair to care. She had failed again. Another chance for escape might never come. Dispiritedly she held her hands before her when the ataman demanded she be tied. His growl at the sight of the raw flesh on her wrists, which had been hidden by the fur cuffs of her dress, startled her. He muttered something as he stuffed the hobble rope back into his trouser pocket. She closed her eyes to concentrate on overcoming the pain in her side, her wrists still stretched toward him. Then she felt the sudden silken caress of his sash upon her wrists. He said no more, tied the sash firmly, and led her to her horse.

They rejoined the Cossacks at the ford and rode west at a hurried pace. At times, Elise was aware of the ataman near her, at other times of Kasyan giving her water. She had slipped into a stupor of pain and cared about little except falling off her horse.

Then, about two hours before sunset, she gradually became aware of her surroundings again. The unvarying steppe still spread out before and behind them, but she discovered that her hands had been untied and her chafed wrists covered with a pungent salve. Probably something they used on the horses, she realized, but it felt good. She looked up as the ataman halted the column at the foot of a steep ridge. One of the scouts was riding toward them.

Elise was unable to overhear all that the scout reported. They had outridden the Muscovite threat on the Volga, but it seemed the Muscovite streltsy had been to the ataman's village. The confrontation there had been tense. She could hear the scout's news hum rapidly along the column of Cossacks.

"I told you we shouldn't have gone on this raid now," Vikola said as he drew his horse up in front of Elise and the ataman. "Rostov was in Vazka while we were gone and the women unprotected."

"Bogdan Cherevik and the elders are there," the ataman reminded him.

"What can those old men do?" said Ostap, who had ridden up to join his friend.

"It's plain Rostov is out to get us if we don't do something," insisted Vikola. "Take a strong stand." He pulled at his long string mustache, which reminded Elise of one she had seen on a Chinese man in an illustrated volume of Oriental poetry.

"This is not the time or place for that discussion, Vikola Panko," the ataman said.

Vikola ignored him. "And what about her? What if Rostov sees us with a Lyakh captive? What will he do to us then?"

"He'd take her and ransom her, just as we are going to do," Nikholai replied evenly.

"And we'd get no thanks for it. But he'd take his pleasure with her first"—Vikola leered at Elise—"just as you plan to do, Ataman."

Kasyan had ridden to the top of the ridge, and Elise looked up at him in an effort to pretend she didn't understand Vikola's words. She bit the inside of her lip and tried to breathe normally. But her mare pranced nervously.

The ataman took hold of the mare's bridle to calm the horse. "My only plans, Vikola Panko, are to unload the goods and get us back to Vazka to learn what happened. You have your orders."

On the other side of the ridge lay the Don river valley. They forded the river just below a rocky bluff. Though they rode in silence, the splashing of the horses startled a flock of swans in the marsh on the west bank. The regal white birds rose high above the cliff. The late-afternoon sunlight caught in their white feathers so that they glowed like pearls against the deep-blue evening sky.

To Elise's surprise, at the base of the rocky bluff the Cossacks halted. From a shadowy grove of maple and oak trees a group of older Cossacks appeared. A tall, thin man with white hair and beard came forward to greet first the ataman, then Kasyan. All of the Cossacks dismounted. They began to unload stolen goods from the packhorses, then disappeared into the dark grove. Empty-handed, they reappeared to carry more booty off into darkness at the base of the bluff. Elise suspected that the casks and barrels were being stashed in a hidden cave. The village must be close by.

Kasyan walked back to Elise.

"Who is she, Kasyan?" asked a girl who had appeared from amidst the group of older men. Her dark curly hair was worn loose. Something in the sway of her red skirts, the tilt of her head, and the darkness of her eyes made Elise think of a Gypsy.

"Daria. You came with Father?" Kasyan asked. He was surprised but pleased to see the dark-haired girl. "Oh, she is a captive. English, Nikholai said. He has talked to her in Polish. He thinks we can get ransom for her."

"She's pretty. Whose captive is she?"

"Nikholai's," Kasyan said, turning to her. "I brought something for you, Daria." Elise saw that the young lieutenant was unable to keep his eyes from the rich colors in Daria's embroidered blouse or the shine of her gold earrings.

"What is it?" Daria smiled and stepped closer to him.

"Not now. Later," Kasyan whispered. He softened his voice when he saw Nikholai walking in their direction.

Suddenly Elise found herself surrounded by a curious crowd of men. Fearlessly she lifted her chin and faced the ataman, Kasyan, and the group of Cossacks behind them. No matter how much her side hurt, no matter how exhausted she was, she wasn't going to let them think she was frightened.

The Gypsy stood to one side and watched the ataman intently. Even in the shadows as the sun sank behind the bluff, Elise saw jealousy gleam in the girl's dark eyes. With a jolt, Elise realized the jealousy was for the ataman, not Kasyan.

"So, Ataman, the unloading is done. What do we do with this green-eyed Lyakh?" demanded Vikola. He walked through the group to Nikholai. "She is really mine, you know," Vikola said with his fists set arrogantly on his hips.

"That's not so," objected Ostap.

Uncertainly Elise glanced at the ataman. She did not like being his captive, but she was not eager to become Vikola's either. The ataman watched her but remained silent.

Before it was clear to Elise what Vikola was doing, he seized her about the waist and dragged her from the horse. Too surprised to anticipate his move, she was unable to protect her side. The instant pain plunged her into a whirling, dark-fringed world. It knifed through her side and across her chest and shoulder. She struck at Vikola and gulped for air. She refused to be at the mercy of anyone, especially the Zaporozhie. She fought the unconsciousness closing over her. But the darkness won.

# 3

# The Ravished Countess

Elise awoke gradually. She had vague memories of Vikola's offending hands being replaced by a warm embrace, of being cushioned in strong arms. Before the darkness was complete, she thought she remembered the ataman's face above hers, his gray eyes dark with concern.

She tried to focus on some familiar object, but the candlelight flickered on unfamiliar timbers overhead. The somber drone of a foreign language spoken by serious men came from the next room. She attempted to sit up, but pain everywhere persuaded her to sink back against the pillows.

"So you're awake, Countess." Heavy skirts rustled as a small woman sat down on a stool next to the large, intricately carved bed on which Elise was lying.

"I'm Natalia. My nephew Nikholai tells me you're a countess. Here, try some of this." The birdlike woman leaned over Elise. She spoke Polish in a small voice. On her head she wore the traditional head covering, and over her skirt she had tied a bright embroidered apron. Reassuringly, Natalia patted Elise's leg through the down comforter. Then she picked up a bowl of soup and coaxingly offered Elise a spoonful.

"Nikholai ordered me to fatten you," the little woman

told Elise. "He said you're too thin. This good fish soup will bring back your strength."

Elise's stomach turned over when she smelled the fish soup. She resisted the urge to push the spoon away only because she liked Natalia. She didn't care what the ataman wanted. But if this were his aunt, then Elise must be his captive still, not Vikola's. She felt a wave of relief wash over her.

She turned to Natalia with renewed interest and tried to sit up again. Her body ached everywhere as she pulled herself up into sitting position. The comforter fell away from her shoulders, and she discovered she wore only her chemise.

"I decided you'd be more comfortable out of those dirty clothes," Natalia explained. "Here, now, you must eat."

From the fading daylight streaming through the cottage window, Elise realized she had slept for only a short time, but she did feel refreshed. She took the spoonful of soup offered to her. To her surprise, she found it tasty. Eagerly she reached for the bowl. "I can manage, thank you," she said.

Natalia nodded her satisfaction and left.

While Elise ate the soup from the fine porcelain bowl with a wooden spoon, she looked at the room around her. The rough wood floor was well-swept. A damask rug lay at the bedside. The whitewashed walls were hung with a mixture of Cossack household goods: a golden curb bit hung next to bird and fish nets, riding whips, iron pots, and sabers. A fire crackled in the central clay oven that warmed both the lower rooms and a partial loft overhead.

Elise lay upon a carved gold, gilt-edged bed; nearby stood a crudely made trestle table with benches. Burning candles in an ornate silver candlestick on a shelf by the door lit the room. Other shelves were laden with leather-bound books, flasks, and flagons of green and blue glass. On a corner shelf a votive candle burned before an icon of the Madonna and Christ Child framed in silver filigree. Elise knew that no Cossack home was complete without this tribute.

She continued to sip her soup and tried to concentrate on the men's conversation in the next room.

"I tell you, Nikholai, it was uncanny how Alexander Rostov knew that you were gone on a raid. He just laughed at the story that you were helping our neighbors catch the horses." Elise recognized the voice as belonging to the man with the white hair and beard.

"How could he know we were gone?" Kasyan asked.

"Could he know how we get our information from downriver?" suggested the white-bearded man.

"I don't think so," the ataman said. "Even if Rostov stopped him, Grishaka would never tell the Muscovites the truth. Alexander Rostov knows that. If he actually knew we had ridden out, why didn't he come after us? Why come to Vazka? Unless he didn't know where we were, but was trying to frighten us."

"Maybe he learned too late to be able to follow us." Vikola's raspy voice was unmistakable. "Is it possible that a peddler overheard something? Perhaps one of them is a spy, or someone in Vazka is betraying us to the streltsy."

"Perhaps," the ataman said reluctantly.

"We have two new families in the stanitsa since last spring, Nikholai," Kasyan said. "They said they were fleeing the serf law. But who knows what the truth is. They could be spies."

"It's possible, of course," the ataman said. "But both families have worked hard to make homes here." He paused, then added, "It's too late in the fall to try another raid. Let's work at persuading Rostov that our only activities are the regular patrols along the border."

"What about the Lyakh woman?" Vikola asked. "What if Rostov comes around and sees her or hears something about her? And Don Host Ataman Kornil Iakovlev won't be happy with how we took her. He has warned against pirating. Is she worth the risk?"

"You thought her worth enough risk to challenge my protection of her, Vikola Panko," the ataman replied. Elise heard the shuffling of feet, and uneasy coughs drifted through the door between the two rooms.

"Ataman Iakovlev issued the warning against pirating only to please the tsar," the ataman continued. "He knows our situation here. I have learned that the woman is the daughter of an English military adviser and wife of our old friend Count Oscar Polonsky."

The cottage was filled with another silence.

Elise felt Natalia turn from her cooking to look at her with renewed curiosity. Elise wondered what her gentle husband had done to offend these people. She realized that she knew little of her husband's affairs. Beyond their social obligations and some of his diplomatic negotiations, the count had made her privy to few things. And those items he had shared with her only because he needed her as an interpreter.

The ataman went on, "Both Polish and English officials will be interested in her safe return. I think she is definitely worth the risk. Kasyan, select a messenger to send to the Don Host, and tell him to be ready to ride at dawn. We'll ask the Host to contact both Polish and English officials, but we won't tell them where she is. We'll deliver the countess to their representative in Cherkassk for a reward. We'll take the best offer. I want to inform Iakovlev of Rostov's activities too."

"They'll want proof that we have the countess," said Kasyan.

"True," the ataman agreed. He called to Natalia and asked her to bring the countess into the room.

Elise had finished her soup and sat on the edge of the bed in her worn, dirty chemise. The bodice and skirt of her fur-trimmed green brocade traveling costume lay on the table next to Anna's muff.

"We'll be right there, Nikholai," Natalia said as she motioned for Elise to put on a long blue caftan she had laid out. As Elise pulled on the garment, she tried to think of what to say to these men her husband had offended. She needed to ensure her own safety. Was there any way to win their sympathy or appeal to their greed? Natalia brushed Elise's trembling fingers away from the caftan's tiny buttons and fastened them for her. The rich fabric felt clean and smooth against Elise's skin, and it smelled softly of sandalwood. Natalia helped her put on a pair of pointed-toe velvet slippers and handed her a brush. Hurriedly Elise tried to groom her golden curls, but she dropped the brush.

"Leave it," whispered Natalia. She tossed a lock over Elise's shoulder. "It will be all right, Little One. I'll be there with you." Natalia squeezed Elise's hand. Elise found herself smiling at the tiny woman's name for her. Elise was

43

as tall as most of the Cossack warriors, and she towered over Natalia.

The room where the Cossack men were gathered was larger than the bedroom. In the center stood another long trestle table with benches. From the doorway Elise could see that the table was laden with parchments, an inkstand with quills, and maps. Many candles in a tall bronze candlestick on the table lit the room. The krug, or councilmen of the village, sat on the benches along the cottage wall. The ataman, with his arms folded across his chest, stood at the opposite end of the table.

For a moment Elise surveyed the circle of warriors. Then she summoned her courage and walked into the room as if she were entering a palace salon.

"Good evening, sir knights," she greeted in Polish. "Where would you like for me to sit, Ataman?" she asked, looking at the bench next to the littered table. Her side ached from the effort to stand straight and tall.

"Stand where you are, Countess. We have only a few questions for you," the ataman replied. He left the head of the table to walk around her. Elise realized he wanted her to be uncomfortable.

His shadow darkened the walls as he circled her. He had replaced the red silk sash that he had bound around her wrists. His coarse peasant shirt was open at the neck, revealing just a little of the dark hair upon his chest.

"She is not well, Nikholai. I hope you are not going to keep her long," said Natalia, who watched from the doorway.

The ataman said nothing, and returned to the head of the table. When he turned toward Elise again, he looked at her directly. Steadily she returned his gaze and held it. With obvious irritation, he looked away first.

"This is Countess Polonsky, widow of the illustrious Count Oscar Polonsky so many of us once knew in the Ukraine," the ataman explained in Cossack. "Unfortunately, the countess informs me, the count died at the hands of the Tartars who took her prisoner."

"Too bad," said Vikola in Polish. "I wish he could be here to see what we will do with his wife." The ugly Zaporozhie stared lewdly at Elise, taunting her purposely. She stared back.

"I've always known my husband to be a kind, fair man, sir. What did he do to offend you so?" she asked.

"Of course, a young wife would play the innocent. No doubt you have enjoyed the profits of his *offense,* as you call it," Vikola said sarcastically in Polish. But he squirmed in his seat on the bench, and Elise relished the knowledge that he was uncomfortable under her direct gaze.

"She is very young, Vikola Panko," Natalia interrupted. "It is possible she knows nothing of these things."

But Vikola pressed on. "The farm your husband took from me had been in our family for over one hundred years. You don't think I've always worn the scalp lock of a Zaporozhie, do you? I was once a rich Cossack like the Fomins. But your husband was a friend of Prince Ieremia Vishnevetsky. They profited handsomely from the Cossack rebellion in the Ukraine. They confiscated two fine estates from Ataman Nikholai Fomin's family, eh, Nikholai?"

With sudden understanding, Elise turned to the ataman. So, it was more than ransom he wanted from her.

He had not moved from the end of the table. Impassively he returned her startled gaze, his gray eyes icy. This time it was Elise who looked away first. There would be no winning him as a protector, she thought.

"It's true, I don't know much about your struggle against the Poles," Elise said. "But it must have been painful for you to lose your family homes like that. My family too lost a home in a civil war." Genuine sorrow was in her voice. She looked down at her hands clasped before her.

"We don't want your pity, Countess," Vikola snapped.

Elise raised her head again. "Then, of course, I won't offer it," she replied arrogantly, then wondered what had happened to her diplomatic tongue. Turning to the ataman, she demanded with a little more softness, "Just what is it you *do* want from me?"

"Proof that you are in our hands," the ataman said.

Elise saw him draw something from his sash as he advanced toward her. She realized he had unsheathed his knife and was ready to use it. With all the courage she possessed, she forced herself to stand where she was and to hold her head high.

His hand brushed against her shoulder as he seized a handful of her hair and began to cut. Her scalp tingled. Elise held her breath and did not move. She was very aware of him, of his size, his strength, and his touch. Anger emanated from him like heat from a fire. If he touched her, she knew her skin would burn. She did not attempt to look at him. He seemed to cut on her hair for an eternity, so she was surprised when he moved away and handed only a small curl to Kasyan.

"Wrap this in paper to be included in the dispatch to the Host," the ataman ordered. "Natalia, bring me her dress."

"I don't like this, Ataman," said Ostap. "Women can be bad luck, even the wife of an enemy like the count. She is too bold, too lacking in proper humility. I think that we should get rid of her now. It is too easy for her to give us away. She has already attempted escape once."

"What if she is a Muscovite spy?" Vikola added.

"A spy would not make such a determined attempt to escape," the ataman said. He reached for the garment Natalia brought him.

"Have you foreseen anything or had a vision about the countess, Mistress Natalia Fomina?" the white-bearded Bogdan asked.

"No, I have not," the little woman admitted. "But no good can come of hurting her. She is a mere girl. She couldn't have been out of her mother's nursery when the count did his deeds. Leave her to me."

Several men in the room shrugged and nodded. Only the village dolduna, or witch, would be given the respect Natalia received from the krug, Elise realized at last.

"We will keep her for ransom," the ataman asserted. "We need the money, and the Polonskys owe us already."

Elise saw Natalia frown at her nephew, who stood at the table scowling at the garment. In a quick motion he ripped three of the silver filigree buttons and the fur collar from the bodice and handed them to Kasyan. "Enclose those with the lock of hair," he ordered crisply.

Natalia led Elise from the room and carried the damaged

bodice with her. She shook her head regretfully as she held the green brocade garment up for Elise to see.

"I will help you repair it," she whispered in Polish. "I think I have some small brass buttons. Wash now. Don't let the men bother you. They will get used to the idea of having you here." Natalia turned to the chest to find the buttons.

Elise's hands shook as she began to wash. The reality of her helplessness was becoming too clear. They could ransom her or kill her. At least Cossacks didn't deal in slaves, Elise thought, but that was small comfort.

The krug meeting broke up as Elise finished washing. She was dressed only in a clean chemise when the ataman walked into the bedroom. She didn't even have time to turn her back. Her damp curls were piled on top of her head so that she could dress. The small rough towel held to her breast was a poor shield. She had been too involved in eavesdropping on the krug conversation; it hadn't occurred to her that the ataman might walk in on her before she finished dressing.

Also surprised, the ataman stopped and stared.

"She is a lovely woman, Nikholai," commented Natalia from the corner of the room, where she sorted clothes from a wooden chest. "You're right. A little thin right now, but very lovely. Your Maria's clothes fit her well.

"Tapering waist and fine breasts. Good for a baby or for a man," Natalia said, grinning. She watched the ataman for a moment, then closed the chest. Elise wanted them both to stop staring.

"She reminds you of Maria, doesn't she?" Natalia asked.

"Yes," the ataman replied, his voice husky. They both spoke in Cossack.

"She's not anything like Maria," Natalia said. "Oh, they are about the same size, and she has blond hair, but she's nothing like Maria. Those eyes, for one thing. Such warmth!"

Confused and embarrassed by his intense gaze, Elise clutched the small towel closer against her breasts and looked down at the washbasin. She turned her shoulder toward the Cossack chief. Despite the clean, fine undergarments she wore, she felt naked and uncovered before him, especially after Natalia's frank comments.

47

With an easy, casual step, the ataman crossed the room and walked around her. She felt him touch her shoulder with a finger. Then slowly, lingeringly, he drew an invisible line across her back, from one shoulder to the other. His touch was light and teasing. Elise shivered.

"Are you cold, Countess?" he asked in Polish. He spoke softly, in an amused whisper, into her ear, his breath warm and brandy-scented.

He smelled of horses and pipe tobacco, odors that Elise had grown accustomed to on her brothers. Now they stirred her in a new and disquieting way. She didn't know how to fight the feeling.

Without speaking, Natalia helped Elise into the blue caftan. Gratefully Elise grasped it at her throat and waist, all the while refusing to look up at the ataman. She wanted him to move away, but he stood fast.

"Better?" he asked in a whisper. He leaned toward her so that his lips almost touched her ear. The dark hair of his great mustache tickled her cheek. Elise almost gasped.

"Nushka," scolded Natalia again in Cossack. "Enough. No doubt she's heard all sorts of stories of Cossacks who ravish and murder helpless women. Even if you do intend to ransom her, she will be given the respect due a guest in our home. So behave as the gentleman you were brought up to be."

The ataman lingered a moment longer. Elise felt his warm breath on her neck. Then, finally, he moved away from her and sat down at the table.

"I like to watch her, to see how she reacts," he said, continuing to speak to his aunt in Cossack. "Have you noticed she smells of apple blossoms?"

"She will trouble you, Nikholai," Natalia said. "You always prefer fair women. That's why the poor mamas in this village haven't a chance of marrying one of their plain daughters to you." Natalia put away the porcelain washbowl and pitcher.

"Please, Little Firebird, don't start on that again. You said she is not well. What is it?"

"You must think of the future, Nikholai," Natalia said. "About the countess—she suffers with one, maybe two cracked ribs. Also, she has some ugly bruises and marks, but they appear to be healing. She needs rest. Two days of hard riding didn't help her. Nikholai, she has been terribly uncomfortable."

"What are these other marks, Little Firebird?"

Elise felt his gaze on her back. She stared into the flames that licked around the oven door, forcing her mind to go blank, to ignore Natalia's words. She refused to recall how she had suffered her injuries. Something in her reaction must have alerted the ataman, because he was suddenly standing before her.

"Show me the marks on your body," he ordered in Polish.

"What?"

But he didn't wait for her to comply. He pulled her from the bench, jerked the caftan off her shoulders, and began to untie the ribbons of her chemise. Despite her protest, she was suddenly nude to the waist. Incensed and frightened, she tried to push his hands away. He merely caught her wrists and ordered her to be still. Then he began to run his hands over her body with the practiced touch of a stockman inspecting an animal for trade. There was no passion in his touch. She forced herself to stop resisting, and stared at the wall beyond his shoulder.

His hand brushed lightly over her injured ribs, and she shivered. When he saw a bite mark on the side of one breast, his roar rang in her ears.

"Who did this?" he demanded angrily. "Tartars? Only a devil dog does this." After he found several more bites on her, he harshly muttered something she was unable to understand.

"Count Polonsky's wife or not, you will treat her kindly, Nikholai," Natalia said in a tone of voice that sounded very like the ataman's when he issued orders. "She's been through enough."

"Ump," was all he said before he went back to his cup of vodka. He was silent for a long time, his back to the women. Elise hastily began to dress herself. Natalia gave her a reassuring smile as she helped.

"I want to know more," the ataman said in Cossack, his back still turned. "She's not telling us something."

49

"Nikholai, don't make her speak of it. The marks are probably a week old. They are healing well. Let her forget," Natalia said in Cossack to her nephew.

He turned and switched to Polish. "What I'd really like to know more about is this muff." He picked it up from the table. He glared tauntingly at Elise. She reached for the small piece of fur, but he held it just beyond her reach.

"Tell me about the muff, Countess," he teased. "What's in it—the family jewels perhaps? Or a little extra gold? What is so special about it that you would threaten to make me a fool before my men?"

"Nikholai, don't be cruel," Natalia scolded.

Elise took a deep breath and tried to compose herself. She stared across the table at him with all of the hatred she could muster. Putting her defenseless before a council of angry men wasn't enough. Stripping her naked wasn't enough. Now he baited her with the last token of her family that she possessed. Her hands shook and her throat ached with angry tears, but she refused to allow herself to break down. Especially before him.

To tell him of Anna would only expose the child to whatever vengeful scheme he was planning. Elise expected little sympathy or help from him. And if he did help, no doubt he would bargain for more ransom. Yet, she thought, if there was any chance he might help find Anna, she would gladly pay the price. Winter was coming.

The ataman was watching her closely. "What's in this muff, Countess? Tell me the whole story."

"Nikholai, you are being cruel," Natalia protested.

The ataman began to pull at the white satin lining of the elegant little fur piece. With an angry rip, he pulled out a small doll and held it up victoriously.

Natalia began to giggle. "You would have indeed looked foolish before your men when you pulled that out," she gasped.

The ataman turned to look at Elise accusingly. "You told me there were no children."

Choked with feelings of loss, dread, and anger, Elise could only look at him and shake her head.

"Tell me now. Whose is this?" he demanded.

"My sister's. This is my sister Anna's muff."

Recovered from her giggles, Natalia took the doll from the ataman. Elise saw some silent agreement pass between them.

Natalia straightened the doll's clothes gently. Then she asked, "Where is Anna? She's not dead, is she?"

Elise shook her head. "I hope not."

Somehow she felt relieved that Natalia now held the doll. A sudden wave of weakness overcame her, and she was aware of the ache in her side again. Elise sat down on the bench. "She was sold to . . . What are they? A tribe of the Wild Country. Kalmyks? We camped with them one night, and they were fascinated by our light hair. They asked for both of us, but the Tartars sold her." Elise's throat hurt. But there were no tears. Natalia and the ataman waited for her to finish the story.

"And I couldn't stop them. I couldn't keep us together. I promised her we would never leave anyone behind. But the Tartars decided to take me to the slave market. Anna's cough had grown worse, and they thought she was too weak to travel that far. I couldn't make them keep all of us together." Elise's strength was exhausted, and she hiccuped in place of a sob.

"Another woman traveled with you?" the ataman asked.

"Yes, Hawkins, our maid. She's been with the family since I was a child," Elise said. "The Tartars let her stay with Anna because they thought she had little value on the auction block. I must find them. Anna is frail. She won't survive the winter with the Kalmyks. Will you help me, Ataman Nikholai Fomin? Please help me find my sister."

"We can help her, can't we?" Natalia asked in Cossack.

"Why should we help Count Polonsky's wife?"

Natalia turned to her nephew with a look of surprise. "To make the count pay for a wrong is one thing, Nikholai. To refuse to help an innocent child is another."

"We can't help her now," he said with a shrug. "The Kalmyks stay either in the south or east of the Volga most of the time. We're not making any more trips beyond our regular patrol routes this fall." His face was solemn.

Natalia turned to Elise and translated.

"If it's more ransom you want, I'll see that you're paid whatever price you name," Elise offered. "Anna's so very young, only nine." Encouraged by Natalia's sympathy, Elise turned to Nikholai. She let hope shine in her eyes.

The ataman looked at Elise, picked up the ermine muff from the table, and in Polish told her, "It's not a matter of ransom. I don't have enough men to search the steppe for a child. We have to be concerned about Tartars ourselves. Nor can we afford to do anything suspicious with Alexander Rostov watching us."

"Nikholai, there must be something we can do," Natalia appealed in Cossack.

But the ataman shook his head and refused to be pulled out of Polish. "I must think of the village first."

Elise looked away to hide her disappointment.

The ataman went to a shelf to find his pipe.

Rising from the bench, Natalia finally said, "I think she should sleep in your bed, Nikholai, until those ribs are healed. I don't think she should be climbing to the loft."

The ataman lit his pipe thoughtfully. "Fine," he said. "I'll sleep in the stable to keep an eye on the black mare that's about to foal. But I have one more question for our fair countess." He took a long reflective draw on his pipe.

"How much Cossack do you understand?" he asked in Polish, looking directly at Elise. "Before you deny that you understand any, let me remind you of how you made the mare prance when Vikola talked of the Muscovites taking you."

Elise stared back at the ataman in openmouthed dismay. Quickly she realized it was too late to cover the error.

"I . . . I understand some things," she lied in Polish. "Maybe about half. There are many words I don't know."

"Continue with that deception if you wish, Countess, but be prepared to hear things that make you uncomfortable," he said as he rose from the table. "I have dispatches to write."

Elise lay wide-awake in the ataman's bed and stared at the dark timbers overhead. She could hear him move about in the next room. When he sat at the table, the bench creaked under his weight. Then she heard the scratch of his quill pen on parchment as he wrote out his message to the Don Host. Sometimes his shadow crossed the open doorway.

Natalia had put her to bed and left the cottage to comfort the widows of the two warriors lost in the pirate raid. Elise turned over restlessly. All of a mother's dreads danced grotesquely in the dark, and she found sleep impossible. Because of their mother's long illness, Elise had been the only mother Anna had ever known. Only twelve when Anna was born, Elise had mothered her baby sister through all of childhood's illnesses and joys. Anna's first teeth, her first steps, her first words, her first fall from a pony. Anna was a child of Elise's heart if not her body. She loved her little blond sister, feared for her, and longed to have her safe in her arms as a mother longs for her firstborn.

The delicious scent of the ataman's pipe tobacco drifted to Elise. It relaxed her and reminded her of her father, of his study. Then she heard someone enter, and Kasyan's voice.

The two men discussed the dispatches and the sale of the stolen goods in Voronezh. Elise heard the young lieutenant pace the room.

"What else is on your mind, my friend?" the ataman asked.

"Nikholai, do you think there's a spy in the stanitsa?"

"I don't know. I know the news of Razin's victorious return has stirred some of the men. They feel Razin can solve our problems with the Muscovites. But I don't know if that unrest is connected with Alexander Rostov's source of information. To be divided among ourselves now is very dangerous."

"Rostov would like to catch us," Kasyan said. "He would like to catch *you*. He blames you for his fall from favor."

"I know." Elise heard the ataman tap his pipe into a bowl.

"If we chose to follow Razin, we'd have allies," Kasyan suggested. "Rostov would not be so eager to attack us."

Elise listened to the thoughtful silence. Then the ataman continued, "Razin is not to be trusted either. If we have a spy among us, we will discover him soon. And when we do, I will take pleasure in cutting his throat myself. Now go, Kasyan, and see to the dispatches."

Silence settled over the cottage again, but Elise's body ached, and thoughts of Anna still kept her from sleep. She rolled onto her side and found that she could peer through the open doorway between the two rooms.

The ataman was silent, apparently studying the parchment map stretched out on the table. Elise remembered that its corners were held down by two leather-bound books, a silver goblet, and a jug of brandy. Then Elise heard a soft knock on the cottage door. Curiosity banished her drowsiness.

The ataman went to the door, but did not admit the visitor at first. Elise heard the whispered words of a woman.

"Oh, Nikholai, why not? Isn't this why you sent Kasyan out tonight? So we could be together?"

Elise saw Daria's full skirts swish through the cottage door, past the ataman. Elise could see them face each other just inside the door. His face was grim.

Daria smiled up at him. "You were thinking of me, weren't you, Nikholai, when you gave Kasyan this necklace?" Daria held out a gold chain-mesh collar with a large tear-shaped pearl swinging from it.

"I gave it to Kasyan because I knew he would like to give it to you," the ataman said, turning away from Daria and moving out of Elise's sight.

"It's beautiful," Daria said. "I wonder what Turkish princess has worn it. Help me with it," Daria asked as she followed Nikholai into the room beyond Elise's range of vision. Silence. Then Elise saw Daria's bright blouse hit the door and fall to the floor. It seemed the ataman was wasting no time.

"Stop it, Daria," Elise heard him say in a tight voice.

Then she heard the soft whisper of Daria's felt boots dancing across the wood floor. The Gypsy stopped dancing in the doorway into Elise's room and whirled to face the ataman. She was nude to the waist, her heavy breasts profiled against the candlelight. Only the rich gold collar glittered across her throat and shoulders. The tear-shaped pearl shone from the hollow between her large breasts. She turned slightly with hands on hips, inviting the ataman to take in the beauty of the golden collar and her body.

"What do you think?" she asked him. "Do you like it on me? Is this how you imagined it would look?" She lifted her thick black curls off her shoulders and piled them on top of her head. She danced, swayed, and turned. Her breasts undulated with her rhythmic movement, and her nipples became tight and pointed.

Elise heard no sound from the ataman. She imagined him avidly taking in Daria's tempting body as he had her own earlier.

Daria looked down. "Pearls are so smooth to touch. Smooth against the skin," she said as she lifted the tear-shaped gem for the ataman to see. Then she moved toward him, out of Elise's sight.

"Touch it. See? So smooth," Elise heard Daria say invitingly.

With quick, determined steps the ataman reached the door. He picked up the blouse and held it out to Daria. Elise could see only his back.

"Get out, Daria, before Kasyan returns." The ataman spoke in such low, tight tones that Elise could barely understand him.

"Oh, Nikholai, don't be like this," Daria pleaded. "I wouldn't be Kasyan's betrothed if you hadn't forced me to make the promise before Brother Ivan."

"Out, Daria," the ataman ordered. "I won't have you spreading your favors around the village and causing problems among the men. You are Kasyan's betrothed now. Behave accordingly."

"But I want you, and you want me." Daria threw her arms around his neck and kissed him soundly. Before he could react, she said, "Come," and took his hand. She led him into the bedroom where Elise lay.

Elise had seen some brazen flirtations in the French court, but she had never seen a woman act as Daria had. And a betrothed woman, too. Besides that, Elise liked Kasyan and certainly wasn't going to help the ataman cuckold him.

Daria stopped abruptly when she saw Elise rise from the ataman's bed. Elise fluttered her eyelashes as if she had just awakened. She sat up, pushed her hair from her face, licked her lips, and let the blue caftan fall open, revealing the round curve of her breast. She looked up at Daria and the ataman in sleepy wonder. She hoped the Gypsy spoke Polish. Even a little would be enough.

"Back again so soon, Ataman?" Elise asked. "And you want two of us this time?" Elise held up two fingers to make sure that Daria understood, then covered her mouth as she gave them both a sleepy yawn.

Immediately Daria released the ataman's hand, and her mouth fell open. She looked over her shoulder at the ataman, who backed away, his face expressionless.

"You and her? Already?" Daria said in Cossack. "And you think I would join you?"

Elise hoped the Gypsy would slap the ataman, but she only started for the door. The ataman handed her her blouse as she passed him. She shoved her arms through the sleeves and banged the door behind her as she left.

Elise did not move, nor did the ataman. She held her breath. In the darkness she was unable to read his face. She couldn't decide whether she was disappointed or relieved that he had been uninterested in Daria's offer.

Nervously Elise watched him stroll to the footboard and lean against the gilt-edged post. He folded his arms across his chest. Elise was still unable to read his face, but she thought she heard just a hint of amusement in his voice when he spoke.

"Very clever, Countess, but how could you know I wasn't going to do what you just suggested? Both you and Daria—an intriguing prospect."

"Daria has no intention of sharing you with anyone," she said. "That's obvious. How is it that she is Kasyan's betrothed when it's you she wants?"

"You understood all that?" The ataman shrugged. Then he unfolded his arms and sat down on the edge of the bed. "Kasyan wanted Daria, so I encouraged her to agree to the betrothal."

Slowly he put his hand upon the back of Elise's neck. She tried to pull away, but he did not release her.

"There's no one here to see us now, Green Eyes," he said. "There's no performance you must give. This is between us. Look at me." She tried to turn away, but he lifted her chin with his finger. "I think I could grow to like this Western custom of gazing at one another," he said. Then he kissed her.

He did not invade her this time. When she resisted his effort to open her mouth, he tantalizingly ran his tongue along her lower lip, teasing one corner of her mouth, then the other. He dropped his hand from her chin to her throat. Patiently he stroked her neck and her shoulder, all the time teasing her lower lip with his tongue.

As frightening as his touch was for Elise, she did not find it repulsive as the Tartar's had been. A sweet thrill coursed from her throat through her middle. She felt breathless and not entirely sure she wanted him to stop. At the same time, she was very aware of how vulnerable she was. Without Natalia in the cottage, there was little to restrain him. With that chilling thought, she managed to push him away, only to realize that he had been the one to pull away.

"I bid you a dreamless and restful sleep, Green Eyes," he said softly, and left her abruptly.

Nikholai closed the door behind him this time. He had to put at least that much between them. He had dispatches to write, and he didn't want any more distractions, even ones as lovely as the countess.

As soon as Daria had drawn him into the bedroom, he had recognized the flash in the countess's eyes. And he had known something was about to happen. She had regarded them with heavy-lidded eyes, the blush of sleep still in her cheeks, her hair disarrayed about her shoulders. Her blue caftan stretched tantalizingly across her breasts, and she had allowed it to fall open just enough to give a glimpse of her creamy throat and rounded breasts.

But she had made his decision for him when she had licked her bottom lip. She had looked very much like a recently ravished and very satisfied countess. Nikholai had instantly longed to be the man who had ravished and satisfied her. Even now he still bore the painful reminder of his desire for her. He would have her, he decided, as if there had been any question. He would have the Countess Polonsky. But he would wait until she was in better condition—he couldn't satisfactorily ravish a woman with cracked ribs. No wonder she had favored her side. How had she ridden for two days in that pain? He would expect that of a warrior, but not a woman.

She had resisted him, yet her response to his kiss had proved that she had passion. He sat down at the table, humming the tune of the Russian song "Dark Eyes." But he had already revised the words to "Green Eyes."

# 4

# No Ransom for the Persian Princess

Elise threw another handful of dusty grain to the ducks and geese at her feet. But her mind was on the old minstrel entering Vazka's gate.

The fowl gathered about her skirts to peck at the grain. They had come to recognize her as their friend in the last two weeks. And she had come to know the individuals among them.

"Stop that. Let the young one eat too," she scolded. The flock scattered in a flurry of honks, quacks, and flapping wings.

She shook the last of the precious grain out of her apron and wiped her hands. She still wore her tattered traveling costume, which Natalia had helped her wash and mend. Gone were the remaining silver buttons, replaced by the brass ones. The silver ones left untouched by the ataman had been put to good use. She now had William's saddle. She had nearly turned the village upside down in winning it. And she had angered the ataman, but she had William's saddle. Elise smiled to herself.

She looked up again to watch Kasyan and the old minstrel at the gate. The minstrel, a thin, fuzzy-bearded man dressed in a long, tattered caftan, walked next to his two-wheeled kibitka. He wore a tall, dusty black sheepskin cap, and he carried a long walking staff used to prod the bullock. Elise watched the minstrel and Vazka's lieutenant greet each other.

The village dogs' barking brought the ataman out of the sod-roofed stable.

"How are you, Minstrel Fydor Astahkov? What news of the world do you bring us?" Elise heard the ataman ask as he joined Kasyan and the old minstrel at the stanitsa gate.

Kasyan pulled on the bullock's yoke to keep the animal moving past the wooden watchtower and into the village. Just inside the gate, the three men stopped for a moment, deep in conversation. Elise could not overhear it.

Elise knew the people of the steppe gleaned their news from Cossack messengers, peddlers, and wandering minstrels, the same way Europeans learned their news from town criers. Like Fydor Astahkov, the minstrels were often old, infirm, or nearly blind. But their memories were sharp and accurate. The only other source of news might be friendly burlaki camped overnight on the river. In these days of pirates, the river men were sometimes unwilling to talk to the riverside villagers. Elise wondered what news the minstrel would bring. She knew there had been no response to the dispatches the ataman had sent to the Don Host.

She had slept for two days after that first evening in Vazka. Natalia had awakened her only twice to feed her. "And when you finish the soup, I have some apples and dumplings sweetened with honey and seasoned with tansy for you," the little woman told her.

Elise's appetite returned, and she gladly submitted to Natalia's care. The bruises faded, the aches disappeared, and each morning she awoke less stiff and more eager to face the day. Always the ataman lingered in the background. He seldom spoke. He just smoked his pipe and watched.

After a week of rest, Elise began to help Natalia with simple chores. She worked willingly. To be busy made the days pass more quickly and kept her mind from dark thoughts of Anna's fate.

Daily Elise watched ragged V's of wild geese and ducks fly south over the village. They followed the Don River to the warmer shores of the Black Sea. She noted that the Cossack ponies were becoming soft and fuzzy with their winter coats. On the cold fall mornings, frost clung to the hairs on their noses, and their breath snorted forth like smoke from great hoary beasts.

Fourteen days had passed since the messenger was sent to the Don Host. How long would it take to reach her brothers? she wondered. Too long. Anna needed her now.

Day to day there were small routine exchanges between her and the ataman. Sometimes he even touched her lightly, casually. He had spoken to her only a few times since her first night in the village.

"It would be best for you to be dressed as the other women," the ataman told her on the fifth day with the Cossacks. "Keep a head covering over your fair hair. Don't call attention to yourself. Wear the clothes in the chest."

Natalia had shown Elise the clothes carefully packed in the chest. All the chemises, petticoats, and nightgowns were of the finest lawn and linen available in eastern Europe. The three-part skirt, or ponyova, quilted caftans, embroidered blouses and aprons, and full, flowing sarafans, or jumpers, were well-made of heavy cotton, and some in wool or satin, in the traditional style of a Cossack woman's costume. They were very nearly her size, just a little short. She had refused to wear any of them except the chemise, one warm ribbon-trimmed nightdress, and the quilted blue satin caftan Natalia had given her that first night.

Later that morning, when Elise started to leave the cottage to feed the fowl, Natalia handed her the blue scarf the ataman had asked her to wear. Elise put it on, folded as narrowly as possible, allowing her hair to flow loosely down her back. She ignored Natalia's frown.

The autumn-morning air was brisk and crisp, and a sparkling white mist rose from the river below the village. Soft quacks and honks greeted her as the ducks and geese gathered expectantly about her skirts. She was talking to the gabbling flock when suddenly, from behind, the head covering was yanked from her. Elise grabbed at the knot that threatened to cut off her breath. She dropped the grain.

Geese and ducks flapped, honked, and fluttered about her as she stumbled backward into hard arms that whirled her about to face an angry Cossack ataman.

"What do you think you're doing?" he demanded. He grasped both her upper arms and gave her a shake.

Elise clutched her throat and tried to catch her breath. Tears of pain threatened. She gasped again for breath and looked up into his angry gray eyes, dark as a summer thunderstorm.

"I'm feeding the fowl," she said with a choke.

"No, I mean this." He released her and reached for the knot at her throat. She winced and pulled away. He restrained her with one hand on her shoulder.

"That's not the way it's worn," he said in a low, controlled voice.

"Daria doesn't wear a head covering," she complained.

"Daria is an unmarried maiden," he said, taking the scarf from her head.

"Maiden, indeed!" Elise huffed. She thought she saw a glimmer of humor in his eyes.

"You will dress properly as a married woman unless you wish to be as free with your favors as Daria is," he said without a smile. "She's Kasyan's responsibility."

The ataman freed the scarf and folded it the way he wanted. "You'll wear it like this," he said as he placed it over her head and held the corners with his fingers beneath her jaw.

She could feel the wide triangle tight on her loose gold hair, from her hairline, over her ears, and down her back. With a touch to the top of her head, the ataman adjusted it the way he thought proper and stepped back to inspect his work.

"That's better," he said. "Don't flash those green eyes at me. If you value your life, you'll do as you're told." Without another word, he left her.

Before long Elise noticed that when she was not with Natalia, Kasyan appeared at her side. His manner with her was always open and friendly, but proper. They learned to communicate through a combination of hand signals, and Elise discovered he understood some Polish words. If she had to have a guard, she was glad it was the calm, fair Cossack who reminded her of William.

The second time Elise earned the ataman's wrath, she and Kasyan were trying to discuss chess as they strolled along the church square toward a bench where a chess game was always in progress. That day several idle men had gathered around the board. Elise saw wagers exchanged. One player was a young warrior named Filip, and the other was the new owner of William's saddle, the Zaporozhie, Vikola.

The circle of warriors parted for Elise only when they saw she was in the company of Kasyan. Elise kept her gaze lowered, watched the game closely, and fingered the three remaining silver buttons in her pocket.

When Vikola won, Elise spoke in Polish and gestured to Kasyan. "Ask him if I may play."

He understood her request but shook his head and frowned. Women didn't enter into the men's games, he was warning her.

"If you won't ask him, then I will," Elise said. "You understand my Polish, sir knight, Vikola Panko?"

The ugly Zaporozhie refused to acknowledge her. Elise reined hard on her temper.

"I will wager these silver buttons against the new saddle that I can defeat you," she said as she pulled the buttons from her pocket. "Your new girl, the one with the turned-up nose, Teresa? She has admired these."

The filigree buttons sparkled in the late-fall sunlight as they rolled in the palm of Elise's hand.

Kasyan frowned his disapproval. Vikola's eyes turned greedy at the sight of the buttons. He glanced up at Elise, then back at the buttons. He laughed as he told the Cossacks standing around him that the countess had tried to buy the saddle from him for the buttons and that he had refused. Now he could win the buttons for Teresa and keep the saddle too. They all laughed. What did a woman know about chess? Elise said nothing.

Vikola gave a curt nod. Filip left his seat at the board, and Kasyan motioned to Elise to sit down.

"May we have a practice game before we play for the wagers?" Elise asked. Vikola agreed. With hands trembling, she lost the first game. Her opponent grinned at her over the board. Then he looked up at the circle of fellow Cossacks around them. They laughed together as though they were part of a conspiracy.

Kasyan frowned and motioned to her that she could still back out. Elise shook her head and placed the silver buttons on the bench next to the board.

"Where is the saddle?" she asked. Vikola sent one of the observers for it and the bridle. When he returned with it, Elise saw that the leather reins had been replaced with ones made of horsehair. But she didn't care.

The second game went more slowly, with Elise taking her time to play for control of the center of the board. When she took Vikola's queen and checkmated him three moves later, he stared at the board as if he couldn't believe what had happened. In cold silence the Cossacks who had crowded around also stared at the board. Elise stood and reached for the saddle.

Vikola jumped to his feet and barred her from the saddle. Kasyan was suddenly at her side.

"She won," the young lieutenant ordered. "The saddle is hers."

Without warning, Vikola slugged Kasyan; then the ugly Zaporozhie turned to Elise. She braced herself for the blow. She would not give ground to this bad-tempered man. But Kasyan had already recovered. He punched Vikola in the nose. As Vikola went down, Ostap started after Kasyan.

"What's going on here?" demanded the ataman as he pushed his way through the Cossacks.

Kasyan picked up his cap. He motioned to Elise to get the saddle. "I was just persuading Vikola Panko to honor his wager with the countess."

"The saddle is mine, Ataman," Elise declared, and took it from the Cossack who had brought it to the game.

The ataman ignored her and looked from his lieutenant to the Zaporozhie warrior, who was wiping blood from his nose. Then he studied the chessboard and glanced briefly at the countess. No one left the group or said a word. Elise felt every man in the group watching her and the ataman.

In Polish he finally said to her, "I don't suppose you told them that the count was a chess master and that you were one of his better students?"

64

"Vikola Panko seems to know my husband's history well," Elise said. "Why should I remind him?" She shrugged and hugged the saddle closer.

The ataman's expression was hard and closed. "You agreed to the wager with the countess, Vikola Panko?"

"Yes, I agreed." Vikola stood straight and proud. His vanity wouldn't allow him to say she had led him to think that she barely knew one piece from another.

With a free hand, she picked up the silver buttons from the bench and held them out to Vikola. He shook his head angrily, refusing them.

Calmly Elise laid the buttons onto the middle of the chessboard. "Then, Vikola Panko, if you do not wish to accept them, please do me the honor of presenting them to Teresa as a gift from me."

The ataman took her elbow and led her away. "We will talk," he said under his breath. She thought he was going to pull her arm from its socket, but she clutched the saddle before her and did her best to keep up with his long strides. She smiled to herself in satisfaction: she had William's saddle.

The ataman slammed the door of the stable tack room behind him. "What do you think you are doing, woman?" he nearly shouted. "By purposely drawing Vikola into that game and defeating him, you made enemies of every warrior out there."

"Oh, did I take unfair advantage of one of your warriors?" Elise asked, regarding him with her most challenging gaze. She was satisfied when he looked away first and shook his head.

"You embarrassed a respected warrior before his fellow warriors," he said. "You must understand that wagering with a Cossack warrior is not like gaming at some nobleman's ball."

"I'll play a rematch if you insist, but his chess really does need some work," Elise explained in her defense. The saddle was becoming heavy, and she shifted it against her. "He plays with many weaknesses, and I will win again. William's saddle is all I have of him—I didn't even say good-bye to him." She hugged the saddle against her body even more tightly and blinked back tears. She turned her back to the ataman, stroking the leather, which was smooth and worn, but well-cared-for.

The Cossack frowned at her, a furrow between his brows.

"Your men gamble all the time," she said. "They even place wagers on who will be the first one to get falling-down drunk every time someone brings out a vodka jug."

"But they don't gamble against women."

"What does that mean? Is there some Cossack law against women gambling with men?"

"It's bad luck."

"I don't know your rules, and I won't learn them." Angry now, Elise turned on him. He regarded her in silence. "Is there a place for this saddle here, or shall I keep it in the loft with me?" she asked.

He gestured to a space on the rack for a saddle. He leaned against the door and, without an offer to help, watched her lift the heavy leather tack onto the rack. She managed to place the saddle where he had indicated. Then she lifted the bridle to examine it.

"Vikola couldn't make use of this bridle anyway," she said. "The headstall is much too large for any of the horses here, except maybe for your Sultan." Elise stopped for a moment, regretting that slip. She hung the bridle next to the saddle.

The ataman remained silent, his arms still crossed before him.

"Well, is there something else, Ataman?" Elise asked. He obviously was not ready to release her.

"Do you realize the effect you have had on this village in just ten days?" he asked. "It's important for you to understand that the fact that you are a ransom captive doesn't protect you from all harm."

"Why?"

"Because these people fear someone who is different, someone they can't explain, someone they don't understand," he said. "You are all of those things to the men and women who have spent their whole lives in this village. They are superstitious of strangers. You continue to remind them you don't belong."

"I want to remind them," she said. "I'm a countess."

"That's not wise here, Green Eyes," the ataman said.

"Perhaps I should turn you over to Alexander Rostov. It would be interesting to see if you can turn his Muscovite discipline upside down in ten days too."

At that moment his words seemed a threat. Elise had no desire to become a Muscovite captive. In a menacing voice she replied, "Turn me over to the Muscovites, and I'll take them to the cave where the pirate booty is hidden."

Instantly he straightened to his full height, his eyes and his expression dark. Elise felt chills cascade down her spine like cold water. Before she could move, he seized her by the throat and shoved her against the wall.

"Betray Vazka to the Muscovites, and I'll personally slit your throat if I have to climb down off the gibbet to do it."

He nearly lifted Elise off the floor with one hand and shook her. She clutched at his arm and at the hand that almost cut off her air. Her toes barely touched the floor.

Immediately he let go of her. She covered her throat with both hands and stared up at him, too dazed and shocked to be frightened. When he stepped back from her, she thought he looked almost as shocked as she felt. Then he left the tack room.

Elise's knees gave way, and she let herself sink to the dirt floor. Her hands shook, and she was breathing in short gasps. She wondered whether her throat was bruised. His hold on her had been brief but savage. When was she going to learn not to threaten him? It worked with her brothers, but it did not work with the Cossack ataman. He did not play her kind of game.

"Countess. Shake out your apron and come," Natalia invited in Polish. "Fydor Astahkov, the minstrel, is about to sing for us." Elise looked at the small woman, suddenly aware that she had been lost in thought. She let the little Cossack dolduna lead her from the ducks and geese toward the village square.

The men were laying a huge fire of wood and fagots, and women carried babies and baskets of food. Some stood, some brought stools to sit on, some rolled up barrels for seats, and the children sat on the ground.

The sunlight faded, leaving golden crescents of light on the contours of the highest church domes. Around the fire in the purple shadow of the building, orange flames warmed the circle of faces gathered to hear the minstrel.

Natalia seated herself on a stool she carried, and Elise stood at her side. Vikola frowned at her as he walked by with his Teresa. But Teresa, the turned-up-nose captive who had taken a fancy to Vikola, smiled at Elise and put her hand to the shiny silver buttons sewn onto her sarafan.

Since the gift of the buttons, Teresa had been friendly to Elise. Others were not. Unaware that she understood their language, the women talked freely around her when she went to the spring for water. The remarks were sometimes cruel. They thought her to be vain and proud, without morals, and possibly an evil witch—no woman had been able to make the ataman watch her as he did the green-eyed countess. Surely she had cast some spell.

Most of the time Elise held her head high and ignored them. But at times, when she was tired or when Anna had been on her mind, she wanted to hide in the loft, where she slept with Natalia, never facing any of them until her brothers came for her.

Elise saw the ataman opposite her in the fireside circle. With a relaxed expression he joked and laughed with Kasyan, and several warriors passed along vodka jugs. The ataman did have appealing laugh lines on either side of his mouth, Elise noted. And his smile was white and even, his laugh hearty.

Olga Umana walked by with a crying babe in each arm. The young mother's face was drawn with dark circles around her eyes. Her head covering was tied askew. Without another thought, Elise held out her arms for one of the babes. The exhausted mother of twins hesitated for a moment. Natalia turned and nodded to her. Gratefully Olga handed Elise one of the whimpering children. Elise smiled her thanks and cradled the infant in her arms, and magically, he quieted.

"Tell us about Razin, old man," shouted Vikola. "Has he truly returned from Persia victorious?" The crowd murmured agreement and applauded.

"Surely he has, and he brought riches with him and a princess," replied the old minstrel as he tuned up his guitarlike instrument, the bandura.

"Tell us that part first," begged a boy sitting on the ground near the front. "Don't sing the whole thing now."

"All right, young warrior," agreed Fydor with a chuckle. "I'll sing the most recent part first." The minstrel began to sing a version of the Cossack folk song "Volga, Volga," and Natalia, at Elise's side, translated for her:

> From the quiet island inlet
> Out where the stream flows deep,
> Stenka Razin's painted galleys
> Through the waters boldly sweep.
>
> Stenka in the foremost galley
> Has his princess at his side,
> Drunk with wine and mirth together
> As he clasps his new-won bride.
>
> Sullen murmurs rise behind them:
> "Chucked us for a wench! Why, true,
> Just one night with her and Stenka
> Has become a woman too!"
>
> Swelling now the angry mutter
> Surges round the headman's ears,
> And he holds his Persian beauty
> All the closer at their jeers.
>
> But his brows are scowling darkly.
> Now a storm begins to rise.
> There are swift and savage lightnings
> In the headman's bloodshot eyes.
>
> "Volga, Volga, Mother Volga,
> Russian river, look upon
> This my gift: you've not yet seen one
> From a Cossack of the Don.
>
> "In a fellowship of freemen
> Never shall a quarrel rise.
> Volga, Volga, Mother Volga,
> Take the beauty as your prize!"

High he lifts the lovely princess,
With his great arm's mighty sweep
Forth he hurls her, without looking,
Forth into the hungry deep.

There was more, but Elise didn't hear it. Her blood turned cold in her veins. Was this what the ataman had tried to warn her of? How many enemies had she made among the warriors of Vazka? She looked about the gathering of Cossacks. Vikola had every reason to dislike her. And, of course, Daria was jealous of her. How badly did Vazka need or want her ransom money? she wondered. No doubt the Persian princess could have been ransomed for a fortune if Razin had wanted to do so. Countess or not, she could be thrown into the river as easily as the Persian princess.

Elise looked across the roaring fire at the ataman. He returned her gaze as if he read her thoughts. She wanted to run from the circle and hide in the dark cottage loft. She cuddled the sleeping baby against her breast and tucked the blanket about his feet. Silently she vowed she would not show her fear.

"Tell us more of his return to Astrakhan," someone prompted from the shadows. "We would know more of how the great Razin made the voevoda bow before him."

So Fydor strummed his bandura and continued with his song of the great Don Cossack. He sang of how Razin, dressed in rich Persian robes, had received Prince Prozorovsky, voevoda of Astrakhan, aboard one of the Cossacks' seagoing vessels. He told how Razin had made a gift of the unfortunate princess's brother to the voevoda. Razin shared some of the forty-one brass cannon he had captured with the Prince Prozorovsky. And the Cossacks' captured wealth in silk, jewels, and spices had been sold at incredibly low prices to the Astrakhan merchants. The Muscovite city, on the Caspian Sea at the mouth of the Volga, had fallen in love with Stenka Razin.

Then Elise heard the minstrel mention the Kalmyks. The unfortunate Persian princess was forgotten, and she listened closely to the minstrel's tale of the Cossack rebel.

Razin was building a city called Kagalnik on an island in the Don only two days' ride to the south. There, serfs,

Cossacks, Tartars, and Kalmyks joined him to live a free life. Kalmyks!

The minstrel went on to sing songs of betrothals and weddings taking place in other Cossack villages. Ganna and Filip were pushed to the front of the group before the old minstrel, who began to sing a lusty song of the marriage bed.

Elise returned the sleeping baby to his mother and quietly slipped away from the firelit circle. She fled to the dark side of the church, toward the river, away from the festive group of Cossacks and villagers. Above the mist, a waning moon lit the night sky.

In the quiet darkness Elise allowed the river mist to wrap itself about her feet and drift up around her face to steal the heat from her cheeks. She breathed deeply of the sobering coolness and pressed her forehead against the damp weathered wood of the church wall.

The ataman had been right. Insisting that she wear his wife's clothes wasn't just his effort to make her into something she wasn't. He was protecting her from Ostap, who had wanted to get "rid of her."

The ataman owed her nothing. All of Vazka thought she was his mistress. Daria had been quick to let it be known she had seen the countess in the ataman's bed. Elise smiled ruefully. But in the end, even that alliance with Razin had been no protection for the poor Persian princess. It would be none for her either.

Elise wrapped her arms around herself for warmth and turned to face the moon, her back to the church wall. She slid down against the wall to sit on the cold ground, her knees pulled up beneath her chin. For Anna's sake, she realized, she had to be careful. She'd wear some Cossack clothes, she decided. After all, it would be for only a little while longer. Kagalnik was only a two-day ride to the south. Two days from the Kalmyks.

Elise heard footsteps, quick and light. She didn't move. She was certain the fog hid her, but she shrank closer to the wall.

"Vikola?" It was Daria.

"Here."

"Who's that with you?"

"It's me, Ostap."

Elise remained silent.

"Did you talk with Alexander Rostov in Voronezh?" she asked.

"No, I talked with his agent."

"What did he say about the Englishwoman?" Daria demanded.

"I didn't tell him about her," Ostap admitted.

"Listen to me," Daria hissed. "The Englishwoman is proof that Nikholai is a pirate. Rostov would put Vikola Panko in charge. Tell him, Vikola."

"I want to be elected to office," Vikola said. "I want the warriors of Vazka to make me ataman, not some Muscovite dog."

"But if Rostov knew that Nikholai Fomin was the pirate leader, he would gibbet the ataman," the Gypsy said. "And you would be elected. Tell me, what did the agent say?"

"He said there was nothing in our booty to prove it was pirated," Ostap said. "It could have come from the Silk Road."

"Then we must talk to Rostov and tell him the woman is here," Daria repeated. "She is the proof he needs."

"I don't like it," Vikola said. "If we do give him actual proof, he could use it to destroy the whole village. I want him to make Ataman Nikholai Fomin look bad. Then we'll take care of Rostov in our own time, with Razin as our ally."

"But Vazka's warriors trust Nikholai Fomin," Ostap added. "They must see him as a fool before they will lose faith in him."

"Then have Rostov take the Englishwoman from the stanitsa so that we don't get the rich ransom Nikholai has promised us," Daria proposed. "If Rostov rode into the village and demanded her, wouldn't the ataman have to give her up? Wouldn't he look the fool? The people would gladly give her over to Rostov."

Elise couldn't believe that Daria was so quick to relish the ataman's loss of position. Surely his rank was part of his attraction for a woman like her. Or was this Daria's kind of revenge for his rejection of her? Elise heard one of the men pace toward her. She pulled her knees closer under her chin and prayed they wouldn't stumble over her there in the dark mist.

"It might weaken Fomin's position enough to make the warriors look to a new leader," said Vikola thoughtfully. "Right now, hardly a man or woman in the village would mind seeing the countess gone. She thinks too well of herself, the women say. And she addresses the ataman and the warriors as if she is their equal. The ataman insists on keeping her for a ransom, he says."

Elise could practically hear their silent agreement.

"When can we communicate with Rostov again?" Vikola asked.

"Next week," said Ostap. "A barge is coming up the river, and an agent will be among the burlaki."

"Then tell him about the woman," Daria said. "Tell him she is valuable. He can get a good ransom for her in Moscow."

"Quiet, woman. I'll decide what we tell Rostov," ordered Vikola. "Go back to the dancing, Daria. Ostap and I will lay our plans now. And you'll say nothing about this to anyone."

"Of course not," Daria said. "But I look forward to being a good friend of our next ataman." She turned then, and Elise heard her quick, light step and the swish of her skirts fade around the other corner of the church.

"What do you think, Vikola?" Ostap asked. "Should we do as she said?"

"It's a good plan," Vikola said. "Next week when the barge comes, tell the agent about the Englishwoman. If Alexander Rostov demands we give her up before the entire village, the ataman can't refuse. No one will fight to keep her. The ataman will lose face before all the warriors."

"I shall do it."

"Now, let's find that jug of vodka we need, eh?"

Elise heard the men walk past her in the direction of Vikola's cottage. Stiffly she rose to her feet and tried to think what to do. The gibbet. She knew about that. A hook in the ribs, the man left to hang by it and die an agonizing, ignominious death. Should she warn the ataman? He should know that traitors plotted his overthrow and endangered the village. Would the ataman believe her? The situation could be turned on her. What if Vikola accused her of being a traitor? Her violent encounter with the ataman in the tack room was still fresh in her mind. Perhaps silence was the wisest course.

Still undecided, Elise wanted to slip back to the cottage to think. Just as she turned the church corner, she collided with a small body.

"Oh, there you are, Countess," Natalia said as she took Elise's hand. "I thought I saw you come this way. Nikholai has been asked to sing. Come, you will enjoy it."

Voices were raised in rousing song when Natalia and Elise returned to the firelit circle. Vazka's citizens, Cossacks and peasants, clapped their hands in rhythm as they sang along with their ataman and the minstrel.

The Cossack chief appeared to enjoy sharing the attention with the minstrel, and played the bandura as well as the minstrel did. The night air was filled with song, laughter, and good feelings.

After one song, Natalia left to talk with a friend. Elise settled herself on Natalia's vacated stool and waited for the ataman and the minstrel to decide on their next song.

The ataman's shirt was unbuttoned at the neck, and his lambskin cap was set far back on his curly head. His color was high, probably from drinking, Elise thought. But nothing else in his demeanor revealed that. His red satin sash was snugly tied about his waist, and despite the blousing of his shirttail and the fullness of the wide Cossack trousers, it was evident that his legs were long and his hips lean. He was a fine figure of a man, Elise admitted to herself. And it was no great wonder that Daria would throw herself at him.

He began to sing softly. As Elise watched him, he turned to her. His gray eyes were clear and serene. It was obvious he liked to sing. Then she noticed the crowd had become very quiet, and they were all looking at her too. As she listened to the Russian words of the song he sang, their meaning became clear to her. He was singing "Green Eyes" to the old Russian song "Dark Eyes."

When the ataman laid aside his bandura but continued his song, Elise's instincts told her to bolt. She rose from her seat, but the women around her shamed her with their fingers. Laughing, they took her arms and held her as the ataman advanced on her.

# 5

# The Gentling

Helpless, Elise watched the singing ataman approach her. The giggling women still refused to release her. She was unsure of what was happening, but knew it couldn't be good.

Still singing, he took her hands and drew her into the open circle. Slowly at first, then faster and faster, he swung her around and around until she was too dizzy to protest when he reached for her and threw her over his shoulder. The circle of Cossacks and peasants shouted with laughter and applauded.

The wind was knocked from Elise when her middle made contact with his shoulder. That didn't bother her as much as the dizziness. She closed her eyes and tried to right the world. When she opened them again, she realized the ataman had carried her from the circle and was striding purposefully through the darkness. Elise pushed against his back and kicked.

He laughed and playfully swatted her upturned bottom. "Be quiet, Countess. You're not hurt."

"Put me down. Now. I insist. Put me down."

The ataman swung her down into his arms so that she was cradled against him like a baby. He carried her through the low cottage door and dropped her onto the bed. Before Elise could recover her senses, the ataman flung his leg over hers. He grabbed both her wrists as she struck at him, and she felt his body press hers into the feather mattress. In the darkness, he felt strong, hard, and warm. Elise prayed he wouldn't hurt her as the Tartar had.

He shifted his hold on her wrists to one hand and pulled off her head covering with the other. He drew a sheaf of golden curls over her shoulder and buried his face in it. Then he teased her ear with his tongue. Elise shivered.

"No, Ataman. Don't, please."

He kissed her despite her efforts to turn away from him, holding her still with a hand in her hair. His kiss was insistent, searching, hot. When he released her from it, he began to rip open her bodice with his free hand. The brass buttons popped off.

"No." Elise started to struggle again.

"I'm just getting rid of this thing, Green Eyes," he said. "It's too tattered for you to wear." He pulled the bodice open and regarded her chemise-covered body for a long moment.

Elise closed her eyes and willed herself to remain calm, not to tremble or scream. This couldn't be as bad as being assaulted by the Tartar, she told herself. He smelled better, for one thing. And his smile—surely there was some kindness in a man who smiled like that.

She clenched her teeth when she felt the sudden warmth of his hand over her midriff. Spread wide just above her navel, his fingers lightly touched her ribs, and his palm pressed upon her stomach. He seemed to be savoring the feel of her. Maybe if she was very still he would go away.

"Look at me," he ordered, his voice low and husky.

She obeyed, too uncertain to do anything else.

"Do your ribs pain you now?"

"Only when a Cossack ataman throws me over his shoulder," she snapped.

He chuckled as he lightly drew his fingers across her ribs. Then he bent over her. She felt his breath on her ribs through the chemise. He slipped his free hand beneath her lower back and pulled her body against his lips. Elise gasped and tried to pull away. His hold on her was secure. When his lips touched her belly, she felt that sweet thrill again. The same thrill she had known when he kissed her that first night. She sensed he felt it too.

Encouraged, he moved to her throat. She realized he was untying the ribbons of her chemise with his teeth. Fearful of the pain to come, she put more effort in her struggle. No use.

His mustache tickled as he nuzzled the fine fabric away from her breasts. Without hesitation he covered her sensitive fullness with dozens of little kisses. He paid no heed to her struggles, and he never touched her swollen nipples.

Exhausted, Elise stopped fighting. She closed her eyes and steeled herself against the violence she was sure would come. Relentlessly he nuzzled her breasts and belly. She waited. The warmth of his lips and hands seeped deep into her. No pain.

Her fear eased, but she remained alert. He spread his hand across her belly again and stroked her soothingly. Her tension faded. He kissed her shoulder, her throat, then her chin. His breath was vodka-scented and his kisses tender. She drew a deep breath and waited for his lips to touch hers again.

"Nikholai! What are you doing? Stop that."

The room was suddenly filled with candlelight. Elise opened her eyes just as Natalia pulled the ataman's lambskin cap from his head and hit him with it. The ataman winced, then looked up at his aunt and grinned. At the same time, he released Elise and tossed the corner of the comforter over her.

"Nikholai, I told you to be a gentleman with her," Natalia scolded in Cossack.

"I know, but I want her," the ataman said with a lecherous grin at Elise. She held the comforter against herself and moved to the far corner of the bed.

"Think, Nikholai," Natalia said. "Use that drunken brain of yours. You paw at her like a cat playing with a mouse. You terrify her. She is young. She had an old man for a husband. Then there were the Tartars. Her experience is limited and unpleasant at best."

The ataman regarded Elise quietly for a moment. "That may be true. She doesn't even know how to kiss."

Elise flashed him a defiant look.

"But does that look like a mistreated woman?" he asked, lightly touching a finger to Elise's lips. "You understood what I said about kissing, too, didn't you, Green Eyes?"

"Nikholai! You must stop this. What are you thinking of? Do you intend to send her back to her brothers with a belly full of your babe? What would you do if someone did that to one of your sisters?"

A new light appeared in the ataman's eyes as he turned back to Elise. "Natalia, do you think she would throw green-eyed babes?"

"Oh, Nikholai! You have been breeding horses too long," Natalia said with exasperation. "If you need a woman so badly, go to the widow Aksinia Stockmana in Cherkassk. She always welcomes your company."

"I want the countess, Natalia."

"I know, and she will be yours—in time," Natalia told her nephew. "She will pass all of your tests, and she will come to you willingly and place her life in your hands, Nikholai. You must be wise enough to trust her. Until then, be patient."

Nikholai stared at his aunt. "You have seen this?"

"Yes," the dolduna said.

"What does it mean?" Nikholai asked.

"I wish I knew," Natalia said with a shake of her head. "I can only tell you to be patient and to trust her."

She placed the ataman's cap back on his head as he sat on the edge of the bed and returned his gaze to Elise.

"Sleep here tonight, Green Eyes," he said. "I'll sleep in the barn and dream of you in my bed." Before he left, he took her hand and bent over it as if to kiss it in a gentlemanly farewell. Instead, he kissed her palm. Silently he held her gaze with his own, promising to finish what he had started.

Elise knew she could never depend on Natalia's interference to save her again.

Alone in the dark Elise trembled. Tender, passionate kisses from an admirer were a new experience. She had never lacked for dance partners at a ball or compliments from the bold. But she felt that those attentions were part of the diplomatic life and no special tribute to her. She had received neither the stolen kisses nor the declarations of love from an ardent suitor that her friends whispered of.

She assumed her lack of suitors was due to her height and her unruly hair. She had no idea of how infectious were her smiles or how devastating her green eyes. Or how intimidating three brothers in uniform could be.

But she did know that her brothers were relieved when she and the count announced they would marry. Marriage to her legal guardian sealed the commitment and removed any hint of impropriety. The count was a longtime friend of their father's and like an uncle to their family. Oscar had been kind, but she had known no passion with him.

The brutal Tartar had been intent on satisfying his own lust. Elise learned to distance herself from the pain. But the ataman's expression of desire was strange and terrifying. She sensed that he wanted something more than the pleasure of her pain.

She closed her eyes and recalled the strength of his embrace, the demands of his mouth, lips, tongue, hands. The pressure of his thighs against hers. His hand on her back. She had never been held like that.

Damn him. He refused her freedom. He refused to help her find Anna. Then he had made her long for his touch: the tickle of his mustache against her cheek, the caress of his hands. Was this his vengeance? she wondered.

The frightening promise in his eyes as he had bent over the palm of her hand made it plain she was not safe. She had to put her plan into action soon.

She turned over, plumped her pillow, and tried to sleep, but she found her mind on her brothers—James, William, and Thomas. They had always included her in their adventures because she could speak so many languages. They soon learned to dress her as a boy. No one threatened four brothers together. And the common people from whom they asked for directions or for water for their horses were eager to talk with the angel-faced young brother rather than the three arrogant youths at his side.

James, Elise's eldest brother, was the leader and planner of their adventures. He always knew of the events to attend or the places to see, and was always looking for maps of the New World.

Thomas was Elise's youngest and only dark-haired brother. He was the one who courteously introduced himself to all her dance partners and dinner-table companions. With a genial smile, he worked a few comments into the conversation about his fine marksmanship.

And William. Elise brushed away the tear that rolled down her cheek. Dear William, his quick thinking had rescued them more than once from irate merchants, suspicious police, and their father's anger. She wished he was here now to help plan her escape from the Cossack.

The next morning dawned sunny, clear, and unusually mild for early November. Only mud remained to remind the village of the night's rain.

Energetically Elise helped Natalia carry a basket of soiled clothes and linens to the spring below the village, not far from Natalia's young apple orchard.

The women at the spring gossiped and laughed over their baskets of clothes. They took turns tending one another's children and rinsing and pounding things on the stones at the edge of the spring. Elise wanted to go to the children, but today she had to give her attention to another matter.

The sun was bright and the breeze gentle. Working at Natalia's side, Elise watched the others as they laundered husbands' and sons' caftans, shirts, wide black trousers, and bed linens. She was unable to decipher a system of determining ownership. Each woman apparently knew which clothes belonged to her family and which didn't.

This morning Elise had donned a large peasant overblouse and embroidered apron over her own skirt. She was discovering that the loose garments had great benefits.

A shadow fell across her work, and Elise looked up to see Daria standing over her and Natalia.

"So, Old One, I want to know about Nikholai's wife," demanded Daria, her hands planted upon her hips and her skirts still swaying.

Natalia regarded the Gypsy girl for a moment before she asked, "Why do you want to know about Nikholai's wife, Daria? Maria has been dead for many years."

Natalia handed Elise another of Nikholai's shirts to be wrung out and hung on a nearby bush to dry. Elise shook it loose and held it up. She was sure it was much too large for her. She hung it on a bush next to the shirts of Polya Zykova's son, then hurried back to hear what Natalia was telling Daria.

"I want to know why Nikholai has never remarried," Daria said. "Why has he never taken another wife to give him children and keep his house? He won't speak of her. Did he love her so much?"

"Yes, he loved her very much," Natalia replied. She rose from the spring bank and went to the basket for another garment.

Elise tried to work as if she didn't understand what was being said, but she too had wondered about Nikholai's wife. A Cossack leader his age with status in his village surely needed a wife.

Natalia dropped a nightgown into the clear water. "Perhaps you should know about Maria," said Natalia as she lifted the garment and plunged it into the water again. "She came from a Polish family, Ukrainian gentry. They were neighbors of ours for years. She had been gently raised, sent to a convent school so that she could learn to read and write. Nikholai is an educated man himself, and he admired that."

"What did she look like? Was she beautiful?" asked Daria. She knelt down next to Natalia and Elise, but she did not help with the washing.

"Oh, lovely. Blond like that one." Natalia gestured toward Elise, who silently watched the nightgown floating in the water.

"But smooth silky hair and blue eyes," Natalia said. "She was very young, but so was Nikholai. They'd been sweethearts since childhood. They believed their love could overcome the problems that were already growing around them."

"Like what?" Daria asked. "You were among the registered Cossacks and landowners, weren't you? Wasn't Nikholai's father a member of the privileged starshina? What could be a problem?"

"True, our families were good friends," Natalia said. "Then the trouble started. The Poles tried to limit the number of registered Cossacks. If you weren't a registered Cossack, you couldn't own land. Then they demanded our men at war during planting season. They tried to tie the wandering Cossacks to the land, to make them serfs to be bought and sold with the land like livestock, just as they have tried for years to tie your Gypsy people down to one place.

"Anyway, Maria and Nikholai were in love. They were wed in the village church. It was spring, and I remember the apple blossoms were huge that year, and fragrant. We had traveled there from our new home. Already, Fomins had lost their estates. The rebellion had begun two years earlier. There was a great celebration, even though her family was unhappy about the marriage. Nikholai and Maria had many friends. Music, dancing, and food were plentiful. Many toasts were made to the happy couple. But the Ukraine, Little Russia, would never be the same again."

Lost in memories, Natalia stared into the spring.

"She died in the rebellion, then?" prompted Daria.

"Oh, nothing that simple," Natalia said. "Like many Cossack families on the right bank of the Dnieper, we had moved east when our estates were confiscated by the Poles for our part in the rebellion. The countess's husband took some of them. Anyway, we knew we could join other Cossack brotherhoods along the rivers to the east. We left comfortable homes, with fine furnishings, and good farms, but we would have our freedom. We are not peasants or serfs. We have always been free and always will be. Tsar Alexis has even had to put it in writing.

"After our move, Nikholai was able to continue to see Maria. The Fomins were in disgrace with the Polish government, and Maria's family was unhappy with her continued affection for Nikholai. They even arranged another marriage for Maria, but Nikholai won her over. When he wants something, he gets it. He can be very patient that way. So they were wed.

"At first, Maria was excited by the prospect of the move east. And Nikholai had worked hard to prepare a modest home for her. I think she thought it was a great adventure. But adventures end, and this one did not. She had to leave many fine things behind when they went to Putivl.

"Nikholai was asked to serve as lieutenant to the ataman there. By then Maria was with child, their first. That first winter was very bleak. Nikholai did all he could for her comfort, but she hated it. She was very unhappy. She ranted at Nikholai, but he understood that she longed for her family, for the comforts she had left behind. In February there came a break in the weather, and some peddlers came to the stanitsa. Nikholai was away with a two-week patrol. She could not accept that Nikholai had to be away on patrols regularly. Without telling him or leaving word, she left with the peddlers."

Natalia wrung out the nightgown and handed it to Elise.

"Well, go on, old woman. What did he do?"

Elise shook out the garment and scurried to the nearest bush. She threw the nightgown on it and nearly ran back to Natalia so that she wouldn't miss more of the tale.

"Well, of course, Nikholai went after her as soon as he learned what had happened. They had almost four days' lead on him. When he caught up with them, she was already ill. Later, one of the peddlers told Fydor, the old minstrel, that she had refused to return with Nikholai for help. She died in his arms still carrying their child."

"So he's afraid to love again," Daria sniffed. "Is that why he made me become Kasyan's betrothed? He's afraid to love me?"

"No, Daria, I think he truly wants to please Kasyan."

"I want him," Daria said. "Help me, old woman. Give me a potion to make him look at me the way he looks at the countess." Daria stood up and stroked her skirt-covered thighs.

"I have no potion for that, Daria."

"The countess will be gone soon," Daria said. "You'll see. Maybe I don't need your help. Once she's gone, then Nikholai will look to me again."

Elise didn't like the malevolence in Daria's dark eyes. Purposely she rose from the spring and went to the bushes to check on the drying clothes.

Puddles marked the small paddock, and the air was redolent with the sweet, heavy smell of manure and sweating horses—comfortable, familiar smells to Elise. She smiled to herself, pleased with the morning's work and pleased that Kasyan had invited her to watch the gentling of a colt. She leaned against the fence next to the fair Cossack and watched the ataman lead the sorrel mare into the paddock. The mare was followed by her chestnut colt. The mare switched her tail, pricked her ears forward, and gently nuzzled the ataman. He rubbed her nose and gave her an apple. The colt, at his dam's side, leaned against her and looked at the faces gathered along the fence.

Elise watched the ataman walk across the paddock. She had attempted to have as little to do with him as possible since the night he assaulted her. At breakfast the next morning he had offered her the last honey-barley cake as a peacemaking gesture. She had refused it, until Natalia frowned her into submission. Living in the same cottage made it impossible to ignore the man. Daily they ate at the same table, sat by the same fire, passed through the same doorway. She was forced to be content that he had made no more advances.

In the paddock the warmth of the sun made the ataman pull his shirt off over his head and throw it across the wattle fence. Elise watched his muscles ripple. She had seen her brothers shirtless on occasion, but the ataman was different. He was tan and well-muscled to his waist. Dark, crisp hair curled across his chest and down the center of his flat stomach. Elise wondered how that hair would feel in her fingers. As he pulled an apple from his red sash, Elise noticed a rivulet of perspiration rolling down the side of his neck. She caught herself licking her lips and wondering whether it would taste salty. Guiltily she looked around the paddock to see if anyone had read her thoughts. She hoped she wasn't blushing. But all of the Cossacks were watching the ataman.

With a firm hand he stroked the mare's neck, then stepped toward the colt. The colt scented the apple and stretched his neck to find the prize. But he did not feel safe enough to go to the ataman's outstretched hand. The tall Cossack stepped closer, and the colt stretched farther. All the time, the ataman talked softly to the two animals, so softly that neither Elise nor anyone else could understand what he was saying. His voice was soothing, and both the mare and the colt were lulled by his calm words. Finally the colt reached the apple, and the ataman slid his other hand to the young horse's neck.

The desired apple between his teeth, the colt tried to pull away, but the ataman had a firm hold on the colt's ragged mane. Only a little fearful, the colt braced himself, leaned away from the ataman, and munched on the fruit. When he had finished, he rolled his eyes and pulled away again, but the ataman's grip was still firm. The colt nickered in panic. His unconcerned dam turned to her colt to find the source of alarm but saw none.

"Kasyan, why don't you come in here lest the mare gets upset?" asked the ataman without releasing his grip on the colt. Elise watched Kasyan climb the fence and go to the mare. The dam was nervous but showed no great fear.

The colt stood perfectly still, his ears laid back almost smooth against his head. His nostrils flared as he breathed, and his eyes showed white at the rim.

Elise was fascinated with the ataman's patience and strength. He never ceased talking reassuringly to the frightened animal, and his hold was firm and strong, never cruel. The touching and the stroking never stopped, steady, reassuring, gentle.

Throughout the next half-hour the young horse tossed his head, kicked up his heels, charged forward, and backed away, but he always found himself in Nikholai's firm embrace. By the end of an hour the colt had relaxed enough to allow Nikholai to stroke his silky rich brown back without a constant grip on the mane.

As she watched the ataman's big hands on the colt, Elise was reminded of the countless times he had touched her in the past weeks. Except for the night he had carried her to his bed, his touches were never improper, seemingly casual, often coming when Natalia was in the room. The brush of his shoulder against Elise's when they passed through the doorway. His hand lightly grazing hers when he handed her honey-barley cakes. The firmness of his fingers when he took her hand to help her up or down the loft ladder. Sometimes he put his hand lightly on her shoulder, and just once he had caressed her head.

At first his touches had frightened her, especially after the night he had thrown her down on the bed. With each touch she had become as rigid as the frightened colt. The ataman had never shown that he noticed. Little by little, she had learned to accept his nearness.

Now she understood that was what he had intended all along. He had been gentling her with his hands just as if she were one of his horses—feeding her honey-barley cakes as readily as he gave the colt an apple.

She had waited warily for him to advance on her as he had before. His subtle seduction had gone unnoticed. And he knew it. He refused her assistance in finding her sister, and offered her this deceit. Elise wanted to throw something at him. No, she wanted to sit on him and rub his face in the mud. He was playing with her, like a cat with a mouse, just as Natalia had said. The blasted, bloody Cossack.

Elise backed away from the fence. She hadn't thought the ataman knew she was there, but at that moment he looked directly at her.

"So what do we name this colt, Countess?" the ataman called to her across the paddock. He spoke in Polish.

Anger faded. Slowly Elise returned to the fence. Memories of great dark eyes and a velvet-soft muzzle choked her. She knew exactly what she would name the proud colt. When she found her voice, she answered, "I would call him Commander, in honor of my fallen friend, the great white stallion."

"Very fitting, Countess. Commander, it is," the ataman replied. Then he translated for the other Cossacks at the fence, who nodded their agreement.

"Then, Countess, come and properly bestow the name upon him," he invited.

Briefly Elise wondered what game the ataman played now. But she was unable to resist the invitation. Bogdan opened the gate for her. She had long ago given up her dainty slippers and adopted the practical felt boots the village women wore. Without hesitation she picked her way through the mud and manure to where the ataman held the chestnut colt in his large strong hands.

The colt had resigned himself to the ataman's touch. He switched his tail impatiently and stamped his small hooves from time to time.

Elise approached the colt so that he could see her, and she also spoke to him in soothing tones, calling him "Commander."

When she reached the ataman and the colt, she said, "He is a fine animal, Ataman. Thank you for giving me the honor of naming him."

"There is an apple in my sash if you would like to feed him," he told her.

She looked up at him, the colt between them, and wondered where the trap was. But the ataman was intent on holding the animal. She reached over the colt's back and into the bright red sash wound around the ataman's narrow waist. She was so near that she could see the beads of perspiration on his chest hair. She thought that she could feel his breath upon her neck for a moment.

His sash was damp with perspiration from the exertion of handling the colt. Elise took the apple and looked up at him. The warm male smell of him made her feel warm. He smiled at her, and she smiled back uncertainly.

With a trembling hand she gave the colt the apple. She stroked the small, narrow nose and announced, "I name you Commander, and I know that you will be as brave and honorable as your namesake."

Suddenly the colt tossed back his head and lunged against Elise, sending her flying backward through the air to an ignominious landing on her bottom in the mud and manure.

Every Cossack standing at the fence saw her sprawled in horse dung, with her skirts about her knees, her hands sunk up to her wrists in the mire, her braid dangling down her back into a puddle, and her face splattered with mud. Elise was very aware of her uncountesslike position.

Shocked, she looked up at the ataman. With the frozen silence growing around her, she saw the unspoken message clear in his gray eyes: What will you do now, Green Eyes?

Elise wasn't about to let him make a fool of her in front of Vazka's warriors. She threw back her head and laughed, a hearty contagious laugh that rang from deep inside. One by one every Cossack joined her. They slapped their knees and their friends' backs in delight at the sight of the countess sitting in mud and worse.

As the laughter died, Elise regally held out a filthy hand. "Sir knight, please help me up."

Silence. Now the warriors watched their ataman.

The ataman shook his head regretfully. "I'm sorry, Countess. As you can see, I'm not free to help you," he said, nodding to the colt he held.

Her back still toward most of the warriors at the fence, Elise lifted her chin and silently mouthed the Polish word for "coward."

The ataman only laughed. "I'm sure Bogdan will be glad to help you up, Countess."

Uncertainly Bogdan came forward. Elise flashed a reassuring smile at the white-bearded elder. He caught the fun of the game. Soberly he bowed before her with mock formality. Everyone, including Elise, laughed again. Daintily she held out her muddied hand, and with assumed dignity she accepted his assistance to her feet. She gave a curtsy to the men at the fence and the ataman. Then she made her dignified exit with her hand on Bogdan's arm. She still laughed with them. The laughter rang in her ears all the way to the cottage.

After that, Elise found that the women smiled at her and made room for her to put her bucket into the water next to theirs at the spring. She was sure that her toss into the mud and manure had provided some entertaining mealtime conversation. But she wasn't embarrassed—she was certain she had won that round, until she looked back at the ataman as she left the paddock. He smiled at her with satisfaction.

Nikholai watched Elise, aware that, as Natalia had said, he did eye the countess as a cat would a mouse. But he knew there was little chance the countess would be mistaken for a mouse. She was never that. In fact, she was seldom what he expected. Her attraction to children had surprised him. Yet, as he watched her, he admired how natural the affinity was.

It had become routine to see the countess striding about the village with a pool of children, ducks, and geese eddying around her skirts. All ages, boys and girls, sought her out. Language seemed to be no barrier. Sometimes she carried one of Olga Umana's twins on her hip.

Often in the evening the countess went to the church to

pray. He understood that she mourned the loss of her family. And he observed with satisfaction that she did not grieve for the count as a woman grieves for a lover.

What troubled Nikholai was her affection for Kasyan. Natalia had explained that Kasyan reminded the countess of her dead brother. In his mind, Nikholai understood. But in his heart, jealousy festered. The countess was comfortable in Kasyan's company. That was why Nikholai had ordered his friend to guard her. He also knew that Kasyan still wooed Daria. His lieutenant and the countess never appeared to be more than friends. Yet, jealousy stung Nikholai every time he saw them share a smile.

But something changed that day in the paddock; with the colt between them, Elise had taken the apple from his sash and looked up at him with a soft smile of confusion and gratitude. He had almost pushed the little chestnut away and dragged her into the stables for a tumble in the hay. And yet he didn't want to fight with her when he took her. Her bruises proved she could put up a valiant struggle. He intended for the count's family to suffer, not the countess.

Patience, Natalia had counseled. Now he had little doubt that patience would be rewarded.

That evening a cold wind came up. Bright stars pierced the hard black sky. The animals were bedded down for the night. The watch had been posted and their meal finished when Nikholai and Kasyan sat down to a game of chess. The fire crackled in the oven. The two friends poured themselves cups of vodka and talked over the events of the day and the direction of the colt's training as they set up the chessboard.

Bathed, and her hair freshly washed, the countess excused herself to go to the church. Nikholai watched Natalia give the countess a lantern with a new candle.

"Now, don't stay too long," Natalia warned. "It's turning colder. And the moon has not risen yet. It's too dark to be out and about. Here, wear this." Natalia wrapped her warmest shawl around the countess.

Nikholai didn't hear Natalia's words because he was admiring the way the countess's loose hair was tied back with a red scarf. Like a lacy veil of spun gold, her curls spread across her shoulders and down her back. She wore the traditional head covering improperly pulled back from her hairline so that gold tendrils feathered across her brow. One more gesture of defiance, Nikholai observed, but he liked the look of it and said nothing.

He turned to the chessboard and frowned at the thought of the countess kneeling alone on the hard church floor, yet he would not deny her the comfort of prayer. He found the village church a cold, empty place. Only widows went there now. The plague had taken the village priest a few years before Nikholai came to the village. The bishop had never sent them another. They had only Brother Ivan to perform the sacraments when he passed through Vazka.

The countess assured Natalia she would return soon.

"The countess spends a lot of time in the church now," commented Kasyan as he finished setting up the ebony-and-ivory-inlaid board. Nikholai was silent.

"Yes, the last week or so," replied Natalia. She stood at the corner of the table, her look thoughtful. "She is frightened for her sister. You've seen her with the children. Imagine how she must miss that child. She has terrible dreams at night."

Nikholai decided that he didn't want to discuss the countess's dreams. He leaned over the board and said, "Your move, Kasyan."

Outside, loud women's voices broke the silence of Kasyan's contemplation. Then a banging on the cottage door began.

"Ataman Nikholai Fomin. Ataman Nikholai, Polya Zykova and Tasha Pana wish to speak with you."

Nikholai recognized the voice of Kasyan's father. "Enter, Bogdan Cherevik," he replied as he shrugged in answer to Kasyan's questioning look. He rose from the table to admit Bogdan and the women.

Bogdan curtly greeted Nikholai. As village elder, he had been appointed by the ataman to settle minor differences in the stanitsa. He was also in charge of village affairs in Nikholai's or Kasyan's absence. The women of Vazka liked Bogdan, and he readily settled most problems.

Two women followed Bogdan into the cottage, bobbed a greeting, and pulled their wool shawls closer around them.

"What is it?" Nikholai asked, casting his most charming

smile at the women's sideways glances. But his gesture eased none of the tension.

"Today was washday, Ataman. And there are . . . well, some clothes are missing," Bogdan finished. The women nodded in agreement and peeked at Nikholai from under the edges of their shawls. Small women, rounded from years of childbearing, they fluttered on either side of Bogdan like a pair of brown sparrows.

"I see. This is a serious problem," Nikholai said. Theft seldom occurred in any form among the Cossacks. Nikholai dealt mostly with disputes among the men over wagers. "Tell me the story," he ordered.

The women told of collecting their clothes. One was missing a shirt and a sash for her son. The other could not find trousers for her son, and two towels were missing. Each was certain the other had taken the garments when the dry clothes were being collected. But each denied having the other's clothing.

Bogdan only shrugged when Nikholai looked to him for more information.

"Is anyone else missing anything?" Nikholai asked.

"Gregor Bulba complained that his new red leather boots are missing," Bogdan said.

Tasha Pana giggled and explained that she thought Gregor's dogs had dragged away the boots one night when Gregor was drunk.

"Perhaps another hungry pup is to blame for the clothes," Nikholai said.

The women twittered.

The ataman ordered Bogdan to open the stanitsa stores to replace the cloth necessary to make new clothing.

The women nodded their thanks and followed Bogdan out the door.

Nikholai returned to his seat across from Kasyan.

"Well, my friend, what is going on in this village?" Nikholai asked. "It seems we have a thief as well as a spy."

"Would it be some runaway serf too afraid to present himself to the village?" suggested Kasyan.

"Why would he steal a Cossack boy's clothes? And two towels?" Nikholai pondered. Then he shook his head. "The matter is settled to the women's satisfaction. Are you ready to face defeat once again, my friend?" he challenged over the chessboard.

"I will win tonight, Ataman," Kasyan declared, as always. He had won three times in as many years.

The November wind rattled the church windows and whined around the wood-shingled onion domes. The bare sanctuary smelled of the fresh pine boughs the Cossack women placed on the altar daily. Icons of oval-faced saints watched the golden-haired woman genuflect before them. St. Nikholas. St. Florus and St. Lavrus, patron saints of horses. The Blessed Mother and Child. Elise knelt alone in the wavering circle of altar lamplight.

She had finished the first part of her mission here, and now she prayed. She said prayers of thanks for being alive and well and not in the slave markets of Turkey. She said prayers for William, for the count, for her parents, for Anna and Hawkins, for courage and luck. She was going to need both soon.

"Oh, dear Lord, please don't let me lose Anna too," Elise prayed. "I must find Anna, and I have to do it alone. I can't stay here. Lord, please help me this time."

## ❧ 6 ❧

# The Storm Rises

Daily, Elise watched the sky. The weather was right for her plans, but the moon was wrong. Each evening when she walked to the church, the marble-white moon shone brightly, too brightly on the frosty steppe. She would be easy to follow even at night, so she had to be patient.

Elise waited and watched as the Cossacks readied the village for winter. To her surprise, the entire village continued to carry on its outside activities, even in the November weather.

"We will be forced inside for the long dark of hours of winter soon enough," Natalia explained as she carried her basket of fresh-water pearls outside to sit and work in the sun.

Some Cossacks worked along the river, preparing the boats and chopping firewood. Others sat in the sun and spat sunflower-seed shells on the ground as they repaired fishnets, built fish traps, or braided horsehair ropes. Elise overheard them tell unbelievable stories—wild tales of sturgeons so large they had to be pulled from the frozen river by teams of men and horses.

Small patrols of six warriors came and went regularly, but the Tartars seemed to be content to stay warm in the south.

93

Elise learned through eavesdropping that the stockade gate often remained open at night, with only a single guard on watch.

Natalia was full of plans for the coming wedding of Filip and Ganna. She began to sew a bridal crown of pearls. Brother Ivan had sent word at last that he would be in Vazka in a month. The whole village would celebrate the wedding. Natalia confided in Elise that she thought Kasyan was trying to persuade Daria to make that date their wedding day also, but she feared Daria still entertained ideas about the ataman.

"That girl is trouble," Natalia said, shaking her head. Elise nodded silent agreement. She and Daria had exchanged venomous looks nearly every day since the minstrel's visit.

A week after Elise had named the new colt, the moon was right for an escape. Elise decided as she lay on her pallet that morning that tonight would be the night. But as she fed the fowl, she spotted a storm looming on the western horizon. Her heart sank. The bank of black clouds reclined on the horizon at sunrise and rested until about noon. Then, gathering its strength, it rose across the western sky. Elise watched it as she searched for eggs. Her concern grew when the soft southern breeze shifted abruptly and a cold gust of westerly wind buffeted the village.

In the paddock the horses snorted and milled restlessly. They searched for the source of the wind so they could turn their tails to that direction and lower their heads out of the wind's reach.

Against the cottage walls, tall, faded sunflower stalks rattled in the wind, and dry willow leaves swirled from the trees along the river bluff and eddied across the church square.

Elise made a mental list of the things she still needed, and went to the church about midday. Later she helped Natalia stack a supply of wood just outside the cottage door. The westerly wind grew stronger and colder until it unceasingly whipped about Elise's and Natalia's skirts and tore at their head coverings.

By evening Elise's nerves were stretched as taut as the strings on the old minstrel's bandura. She forced herself to sit down by the oven fire next to Natalia, who was working on a crown of pearls.

Nikholai and Kasyan pondered the chessboard in their nightly game. The fire crackled comfortably in the oven and the wind whistled through the thatched roof.

Should she delay her plans because of the storm? Everything was ready. Unable to sit still any longer, Elise rose from the bench and paced by the table once. Then again.

"Checkmate," declared the ataman.

Kasyan groaned. But the two immediately set the board up to start another game.

"Are you going to play again?" Elise finally snapped. "I can't bear to watch you defeat Kasyan one more time." She didn't know why it bothered her that these two friends should enjoy this nightly ritual of triumph and defeat, but it did.

Both Kasyan and the ataman looked up at her in surprise. Although Kasyan had understood only some of her words, he had heard his name and the edge in her voice.

"It seems the countess tires of our nightly contest, friend," the ataman said with an amused smile at his lieutenant.

Before Kasyan could reply, Elise spoke again.

"Ask Kasyan if I may advise him." She smiled at Kasyan. The ataman frowned but translated for his lieutenant, who liked the idea and accepted the offer. Elise cast a smile of victory at the ataman and sat down on the bench next to the younger Cossack.

Using her favorite queen-sacrifice strategy, she helped Kasyan to victory. Only when the ataman had taken her queen and the series of moves had been completed did a look of understanding spread across the tall Cossack's face. Kasyan slapped his knees and laughed.

"You've grown complacent, Ataman," Elise quipped. Then, realizing that what she had said was undiplomatic, she looked down at the board and covered her mouth with her hand.

In the strained silence that followed, Kasyan hastily excused himself. "I've promised to see Daria tonight," he said. Elise watched him go out the door and felt strangely deserted.

To her surprise, the ataman began to laugh. "I think you're right, Countess. I have grown complacent. Another game?"

Hastily she rose from the table. "I have to go to the church now." She wiped her hands on her apron nervously and went to her brown caftan on a peg by the door. She had to do this tonight. Anna needed her.

"I'll get you a lantern," Natalia offered.

"No, Natalia. Don't bother. The wind will just blow it out. I know the way, and the altar lamp is always lit." Elise pulled on her caftan, then stopped and turned back to them. "I may be a while, so don't worry about me." She hesitated again, the large caftan clutched tightly around her slender body.

"Ataman?"

He looked up at her from his study of the board.

"Beware of Vikola. He means to take your place, you know." She had to give him some warning. She owed him that. Despite how he must feel about the wife of a man who took his family estates, he had not abused her as the Tartar had.

"I've suspected as much. Why?" The expression in the ataman's gray eyes became curious.

Alarmed, Elise tried to shrug innocently. "Just a thought. Good night, Natalia," she said, but hesitated a moment more. She longed to embrace the little dolduna and to thank her for her kindness. But she couldn't do that. She promised herself she would send Natalia something to repay her hospitality. With slow steps she turned and went out the door into the night.

Nikholai felt a strong urge to go after her. He wasn't sure why. Maybe it was because of the uncertain look on her face as she had said good night. Perhaps she thought he was angry about the game. He wasn't. The play had been stimulating, and he hoped she would offer to play another match. He would win next time.

Slowly he packed the finely carved ebony and ivory pieces away into their box. He rubbed the ivory queen and recalled the countess's skin, white and smooth as ivory, but warmer, softer. He remembered well her body's tremor the night he had thrown her down on his bed. It had not been a tremor of fear. He knew she did not desire him as he did her. But neither did she find him loathsome.

Natalia had risen from her sewing and was arranging things in her cupboard.

"Nushka, did you or Kasyan eat that loaf of bread I left on the cupboard this morning?" she asked. "My best knife was with it too, and it's gone. And that small jug of vodka."

"No, Little Firebird," Nikholai replied. "I did not see it, and I'm sure Kasyan would not take your best knife even if he did eat the bread. Has our thief struck again?" Thievery was not to be tolerated. He knew he should be more concerned about these thefts, but he wasn't. He went to the oven, opened the iron door, and began to throw more wood onto the fire. Visions of golden hair and green eyes danced in the flames.

Something about Elise was scratching at the back of his mind. She shouldn't be out on a night like this, he thought as he heard the wind whistle around the eaves of the cottage. On a night like this the devil and the witch Baba-Yaga herself walked the earth.

"I'm going to walk the countess back from the church," Nikholai called to Natalia.

He strode to the door and reached for his lambskin cap. He had hung it on the peg next to the countess's brown caftan.

"Where's my hat?" he asked, staring blankly at the bare peg.

Only then did the pieces fall into place. The stolen clothes. The missing boots. The bread. The hours alone in the church. His hat. The strange way she had said good night to Natalia. Sly as a fox. He knew now she had meant to say good-bye. She had plotted it all as cleverly as she had the queen sacrifice.

Nikholai yanked open the cottage door and ran toward the church, but he didn't expect to find her there.

Inside the church, Elise flipped the loose floorboard back into place and pulled the ataman's cap over her short blond curls. Taking the cap from under his nose had been a silly risk, she realized now. But she needed a hat, and she wanted his.

She started to blow out the candle she had lit before St. Nikholas' icon, then decided to leave it burning. Perhaps St. Nikholas would help her.

With one hand she picked up the sack of food she had collected, and with the other she grabbed the small vodka jug. She had learned that Gregor Bulba was on duty as lookout in the tower this evening, and she knew that he loved his vodka. She left the church by the side door and quietly ran across the square to the watchtower by the gate. Winter thunder rumbled in the distance.

Gregor accepted the jug with few questions. "Thanks, friend," he called after Elise as she retreated down the ladder of the watchtower. He had not recognized her.

She slipped silently inside the stable door and stopped to listen for voices. She couldn't be too careful, she had decided. She heard nothing. She was about to go to Sultan's stall when she heard the rustle of hay and low moans and whispers. She cocked her head to catch the sound more clearly. She was unsure whether these noises expressed pain or pleasure.

"Oh, Kasyan."

Then Elise heard the jangle of bracelets and the rustle of hay again. Even in the dark she felt a blush glow on her cheeks. She hadn't really given serious thought to what Daria and Kasyan would do once alone, but it was obvious now. How was she going to get Sultan out of the stable?

She listened intently, trying to locate in just which stall the lovers were. She stepped quietly down the corridor between the box stalls, making sure each was either occupied by a horse or empty. In front of Sultan's stall she realized that the lovers had discreetly chosen the one farthest from the stable door.

Elise released a silent sigh of relief. Carefully, to avoid startling the big blood bay, she slipped into his stall. The stallion's white blaze bobbed out of the darkness as he recognized her scent and moved toward her. Deftly she bridled the horse and started to lead him out of his stall.

"What was that?" Kasyan whispered.

"What?" Daria's voice was soft and dreamy.

"I heard something."

"Oh, Kasyan. You're off-duty now. Oh, do that again."

Elise stood motionless and listened. She held her breath, but her heart pounded so loudly that she was certain Kasyan would hear. With a snuffling noise, Sultan nosed her side in search of the apple he was sure she had brought.

"I don't hear it now," Kasyan said. Elise could tell from the sound of his voice that he had turned back to Daria.

Daria giggled, the hay rustled again, and the bracelets jangled. Elise headed for the door with Sultan in tow.

To the accompaniment of a rising duet of moans, she led the huge stallion from the stable and noiselessly latched the door behind her. None of the horses had betrayed her presence. Outside the tack-room door she heaved William's saddle onto Sultan's back and silently thanked James for making her saddle her own mount as a girl. Then she tied the cotton bag full of bread, dried fish, Natalia's knife, and Anna's muff to the back of the saddle. She vaulted into the saddle and rode for the gate.

Gregor was leaning on the watchtower railing as she approached the gate on Sultan. The jug dangled from his right hand.

"Who goes there?" he asked, his speech already slurred.

"A friend," Elise answered softly in Cossack.

"Go, friend, go." Gregor waved to her and lifted the jug to his lips again. "Off to see a sweetheart, I'll wager," the drunken Cossack said with a laugh.

And Elise was gone, out the gate and riding south along the ridge that paralleled the river. She was so elated to be free that she didn't feel the sting of the first raindrops on her face.

As Nikholai had suspected, the church was empty. One candle burned before the icon of St. Nikholas. It flickered in the drafts inspired by the winter wind whipping about the onion domes above.

Nikholai paced the length of the bare place, looking for some evidence. Why had she come to the church every evening? She had done more than pray here, he was sure. Another flicker of the candle betrayed the hastily replaced floorboard. He knelt and pulled it up. There were her clothes, his razor, and a mound of golden locks. He grabbed a handful of that silken shorn hair, then threw it down. Cursing, he slammed the board back into place.

He ran from the church across the square directly to the stables. He didn't notice the rain start to fall or feel the wind whip his shirt. He threw open the tack-room door. In the light from flashes of lightning he could see that William's saddle was gone. Then he threw open the door to the stable and strode down the corridor, looking into each box stall to discover which horse she had taken. Only Sultan's stall was empty, of course. He cursed out loud again. She would take his best horse. His fastest horse. Then she chose the worst night of the year to ride off into the dark. He cursed again.

"Ataman?"

Nikholai turned to see Kasyan standing in front of the last stall in the row. He was bare-chested and buttoning his trousers. Someone moved out of sight into the corner of the stall. Daria hid herself with a surprising concern for modesty, Nikholai thought.

"Have you been here all evening, since you left the cottage?" Nikholai demanded.

"Yes, what is it?"

"Did you hear anything?"

"No." Kasyan turned his head and looked over his shoulder at Daria. "Well, once I thought I heard something, but we decided it was just the horses moving around. What is it, Ataman?"

"Sultan's gone, and so is the countess."

"She took him?" Kasyan's face reflected his surprise.

"Didn't you hear her? She must have been in here just a few minutes ago."

Embarrassed, Kasyan shook his head. "I'll help you search for her," he offered, and reached back into the stall to get his shirt.

"No, help me saddle Sotnik," the ataman said. "You're in charge until I get back. She can't have that much of a start."

Nikholai was already in Sotnik's stall, muttering about a mere woman stealing his best horse out from under his lieutenant's nose. Kasyan ran to the tack room.

"But how did she get past the watchtower?" Kasyan asked as he settled the saddle onto the gelding's back.

Nikholai buckled the bridle. "I don't know. Who's on duty?"

"Gregor Bulba," Kasyan said, tightening the girth as the ataman took the reins and led the dun from the stall.

"That's probably where Natalia's missing jug of vodka went," Nikholai said with a disgusted glance in the direction of the stall where Daria hid. "Some vodka and a couple of women, and our defenses fall apart. Discipline Gregor Bulba and put a sober man in the watchtower."

Nikholai led the gelding from the stall.

Bound by the Cossack code of honesty, Gregor admitted to having had some vodka. "Our friend furnished it. A man needs some comfort on a cold night," he shouted with a grin from the watchtower to the ataman.

"Which way did our friend ride?" Nikholai asked. He held his temper with some difficulty.

"South, Ataman," Gregor said. "To see a sweetheart, don't you think?"

The countess was thorough, Nikholai thought. But why would she go south, deeper into Don Cossack territory? He was sure she had a reason, a plan.

Nikholai legged the gelding out the gate at a canter. Once in the open, heedless of the rain and mud, he urged Sotnik into a full gallop.

## ❧ 7 ❧

# The River Between Them

Nikholai urged Sotnik along the ridge and berated himself for realizing too late what his captive was up to. She had been quiet and docile for days. He should have known. "I'm going to tie her up and lock her in the tack room when I find her," he promised himself. The thought of her hands tied and the countess at his mercy was intriguing.

Elise glanced over her shoulder to see if she were being followed. She could not be sure, with only flashes of lightning for illumination. The trail was difficult to follow in the dark, and dangerous when muddy. She knew she wanted to bypass the fork that turned to the ford just below Vazka. She wanted to go farther south before she attempted to cross the river.

The ataman's map had indicated a ford several miles south. But Yergov had taught Elise that rivers were whimsical and could change course drastically in one season. She could only hope the ford was still there. She kept Sultan moving at an extended trot. He was easy to sit and in good condition. She hoped that they could keep up the pace for a long time.

The rain streamed down her face, and her caftan was already soaked. She regretted she hadn't thought to bring one of the smelly waterproof burkas she had seen in the tack room.

Farther along the trail she found another fork that descended toward the river. She hoped that this led to the ford she sought. At the bank she halted in dismay. The river was already running high, swollen and angry with the autumn rain. The flashes of lightning showed her two islands in the broad stream. She had located the ford she had found on Nikholai's map, she was sure, but this wasn't a good time to cross.

A sharp snap of lightning startled Sultan, and he wheeled around in fear. Elise struggled to calm him. Another flash of lightning, but a more distant rumble. Elise glanced up at the ridge just in time to see a rider silhouetted against the stormy sky. She knew it was the ataman. She had to ford now. She turned Sultan back to the river. Once the river was between them, she would be farther from the ataman and closer to freedom.

Elise urged Sultan into the churning river. The blood-bay stallion plunged in without hesitation. Flashes of lightning gave only brief views of the swirling black flood. The first island was near, but the current was strong. Sultan swam energetically. Elise kept him headed slightly upstream. Even swimming into the current, she knew the river would pull them to the southern tip of the island or drag them past it. But Sultan navigated well. His head well above the water, his ears pricked forward, he struck out powerfully. Reins in one hand, her other tightly entwined in Sultan's mane, she felt the current pull at her. She kept her seat. Muddy water splashed in her face, blurred her vision, and tugged at her quilted caftan.

Nikholai saw her hesitate before she commanded Sultan into the flood. He was certain she would have waited to cross if she hadn't seen him on the ridge. He pulled Sotnik up at the bank and uttered another profanity. A flash of lightning allowed him to glimpse a black-capped golden head and a horse nearing the southern end of the island. He started to press Sotnik into the river, then stopped, afraid he would be unable to see whether the countess and Sultan reached the island . . . or would need his help farther downstream.

Suddenly her head disappeared. Nikholai's heart stopped. Darkness and thunder. Then he glimpsed her on the downriver side of Sultan. The stallion kept swimming on course. The wind whipped rain into Nikholai's face. He wiped the water from his eyes and peered into the darkness. Lightning. He saw Sultan leap onto the southern bank of the island, his saddle empty. Then Nikholai saw Elise on the other side of the stallion. The blood bay dragged her from the river, her hand entwined in his mane. He saw her steady herself on her feet, then grab Sultan's reins and lead the stallion to the far side of the island. Only then did Nikholai and Sotnik plunge into the flooded river.

The current tore savagely at man and horse. Nikholai prodded Sotnik on and wondered at Elise's ability to make it. The crossing was nearly impossible. Sotnik struggled ashore just as Sultan had, near the southern tip of the island. Nikholai stopped only a moment to get his bearings. Then he spurred the dun around the eastern side of the island along the sandy bank toward the northern end. Willow bushes whipped frantically in the wind, and rain pelted him.

The island was little more than a large sandbar. Nikholai urged Sotnik along the island's eastern bank at as fast a pace as he dared. He rounded a clump of brush just in time to see the countess swing up onto Sultan again.

"Don't try it again," he ordered in Polish. He saw the flash of her green eyes in the fading light of the lightning. He mentally cursed himself for not thinking that an order was the last thing he should throw at this woman. Thunder rumbled overhead.

He made a dive to grab Sultan's reins, but she maneuvered the horse out of his reach. Lightning flashed again. She looked defiant and determined despite the water dripping from the end of her nose. Somehow she had managed to keep his hat on.

"I'm not going back with you," she shouted over the raging river and the roaring wind.

He swore in Cossack at the fates that had burdened him with a captive who could smile like an angel and ride like a Cossack.

"Don't throw your bloody curses at me, Ataman. I'm not

going back," she repeated in English; he didn't need a translation.

Lightning flashed, and Nikholai saw her urge Sultan into the river again. Just as she should, she tacked the blood bay upstream. Nikholai was familiar with this part of the river, and he was sure they had yet to cross the Don's main channel. This particular channel of the river, between the islands, was more shallow. But the water was slightly higher now, and Nikholai could see large tree limbs and brush tossed along by the swift current.

Again he resisted the urge to plunge in after her. He knew he could come to her aid better from where he was if she needed him. Still, he felt helpless. She insisted on taking her fate out of his hands.

He saw the limb well before she did, and he called a warning to her, but she was unable to hear him over the roar of the river. When she saw it, she tried to avoid the blow, but the branch swung around and caught her on the side of the head. She disappeared below the surface. So did Sultan.

Ignoring the sting of rain in his face, Nikholai legged Sotnik into a trot along the sandy bank in an effort to remain opposite the countess and Sultan in the river. Once, he saw Sultan come to the surface much farther downriver, still near the drifting limb. He was afraid the horse was entangled in the debris. Then he saw the countess come up almost directly across from him. He raced Sotnik ahead of her course and plunged down the bank into the river. He allowed the current to drag them toward her. She disappeared again, but when she came up, she was surprisingly close to him. Nikholai reached out and grabbed the collar of her caftan, praying she wouldn't slip out of the oversize garment. He urged Sotnik on across the channel. They had swum too far to turn back. When Sotnik's forelegs struck shore, Nikholai slipped off and pulled the countess up onto the bank. She was choking. He threw her over his shoulder, took Sotnik's reins, and carried her to the interior of the island.

This island rose from the river with a backbone of rock outcroppings and brush along its length. The rock offered shelter. Nikholai located a ledge for protection and set the countess down.

Then he led the horse into the shelter and knelt by the countess to look at her head.

"Sultan? Did you find Sultan?" she cried.

"No. Last time I saw him, he was far below the island."

The countess started to get up, as if she were going after the horse.

Nikholai pushed her down. "Sit," he ordered gruffly. "Let me look at your head."

The countess became quiet, but for only a moment. "I'm all right," she said, and pushed him away. "Just dizzy. I'll be all right. Where are we? Did we make it across?"

"No. There is one more channel to cross, the main channel," Nikholai said. "You haven't won this round yet, Countess." He rose abruptly and left her. He checked Sotnik for injuries, then climbed to the center of the island. Elise leaned out and looked around the rock shelter. A flash of distant lightning showed the ataman looking north, up the river.

Elise sat back down and stared at her hands. Strands of Sultan's black mane were still threaded between her fingers. "Oh, poor Sultan," she whispered.

The ataman returned. "The storm is dying, but I'm afraid the river is going to get higher yet." He sat on his heels next to Elise, who was seated on a rock. "We are below the ford you were trying for. There's a creek from the east flowing into the river just above us. That's why the water is rising so fast." He spoke in Cossack as he watched the sky. The rain was lighter and the thunder farther away.

"I don't know if we should wait for the storm to let up or try to cross now," he told her.

He paced to the head of the island again, then back to her. She saw his anger flare when his gaze fell upon his hat.

"You took this to mock me, didn't you?" he demanded in Polish. "You wanted me to know you'd won." He yanked the black cap off her head and put it on his.

His anger didn't startle her, but his accusation did. "I did not take it to mock you," she snapped. "I took it because I needed a hat to complete my disguise." Before he could react, she stood, snatched the hat off his head, and tugged it down over her ears. "And I took it because it was yours."

"That's the same thing."

106

"No, it's not," she insisted in Polish. Then she groaned from the pain of the sudden exertion. "Lord, my head hurts." It felt as heavy and swollen as a giant melon. She moaned and sat down again.

Suddenly the wind switched from the west to the north. Brush on the island whipped around in agitation, and a shower of rain from the trees fell upon them.

"I don't like this," the ataman said as he looked over his shoulder and upriver again. In a lightning flash they could both see that the island they had stood on only moments before was gone, covered with angry floodwater.

Elise looked back at the ataman, uncertain about his concern. Water dripped from the end of his mustache and from the curls plastered against his temple. "We've got to cross now," he said. "Come on." He pulled her to her feet. "Let's get this off before it drags you down again," he said as he pulled the soaked caftan off her shoulders. Then he pulled off his own burka and led her to Sotnik.

"What are we doing?"

The ataman mounted Sotnik, slipped his foot from the stirrup, and offered Elise a hand. "Get up behind me," he ordered again. "We can't stay on the island. The river is rising too fast."

She looked at the empty stirrup, then up at him. To climb to that precipitous height was impossible at the moment. "Just as soon as the dizziness goes away," she said. She leaned her head against the horse's warm wet flank and tried to control the wave of vertigo that overcame her. Then her stomach turned upside down, and her head throbbed.

"I don't think I can do it, Ataman. Just go on."

"Countess, are you going to turn into a helpless woman now? After all this, you're going to let a bump on the head stop you?" He offered his hand again.

"I'm not a helpless woman," she countered, but the assertion made her head throb.

"No Cossack warrior would whine about a little dizziness." He leaned over to reoffer his hand.

"Damn you, you bloody . . ." Elise mumbled in English. She took his hand, placed her foot in the stirrup, and swung up behind him. He pulled her arms around his waist and legged Sotnik around the island's backbone. Elise gave up trying to see where they were going or to understand his action. She rested her head against his back. His shirt was cold and wet, but the movement of his body underneath was vital and strong. Little by little, the heat of his body seeped through the fabric against her cheek. She hadn't realized that she was shivering and that her teeth were chattering until his warmth eased the cold tension in her body. She relaxed against him. His back was hard, and the muscles rippled effortlessly beneath the fabric as he directed Sotnik. He felt good to her. Reassuring. If she could just rest her aching head against him for a short time, if she could draw on his strength, she knew she would feel better.

She looked around the ataman's shoulder when he halted Sotnik on the northeastern end of the long, narrow island. The sandy bank was only a thin strip now as the water rose rapidly. They were still dependent on the storm for light. The lightning was farther away now, but from the distant flashes they could see the channel before them. The ataman pointed out the steep riverbank across from the island.

"We'll cross here," he said. "The current will be stronger here than before. Once across, we have to get up that bank. If we're not pulled too far south, we can get back up to that slope to the north. But if the water starts rising faster, we'll just have to get out where we are."

Elise's head had cleared somewhat, and she began to understand the urgency of the situation. The ataman was concerned about a flash flood from the eastern creek just above them.

He pulled her arms tighter around him. "Hang on. If you're pulled off, try to float and swim to the shore. I'll find you."

"I can't swim."

*"What?"*

"I never learned to swim."

"You mean your brothers never threw you in the Dnieper to make you swim?"

"No, but I'm sure they thought about it."

The ataman was silent for a moment. "Then whatever I do, stay with Sotnik."

The rain had stopped, but the wind was stronger and

colder. When they plunged into the river, the icy water took Elise's breath away. She clutched Nikholai's sash and tightened her legs around Sotnik. The Cossack urged on the less-powerful and less-experienced horse. Small debris swirled about them.

Sotnik struck something underwater and faltered. They went under but came up together. The horse whinnied in panic. Elise felt the ataman slide from the horse. She turned to him.

"Go on," he ordered. The current pulled at him on the downriver side of Elise and Sotnik, but he stayed near them. Elise realized he was holding on to the stirrup leather.

Sotnik recovered and began to swim again with confidence. Elise continued to prod the horse. He snorted and breathed heavily, but all his heart was in obeying her. With a jolt she felt his forelegs strike shore. He stumbled and went down. The swift current grabbed at them and washed them farther south. Elise clutched his mane with both hands and clamped his body with her legs. He got his feet under him again and lunged for shore. The ataman swung himself ashore only a few feet downriver. Without hesitation he pointed up the steep riverbank.

"Go on," he ordered over the roar of the river and the rain. Elise nodded and pressed Sotnik on up the bank before he lost momentum. She looked around once to see the ataman start to climb up the bank behind them. Sotnik sprang forward and cleared the edge of the bank, then stopped. Elise slipped from the exhausted horse and ran back to the ledge. She saw the top of the ataman's head and knelt down.

"Are you all right, Ataman?" she called to him.

He nodded and reached out. "I'm all right. Give me a hand."

The countess didn't move. He tried to find purchase for his right foot, but the sandy earth gave way. He slid back to the ledge.

"I need a hand," he called again, and looked up at her. She stared back. He reached for her. She moved back from the edge, just out of his reach. She looked over her shoulder at Sotnik. Then back at the ataman. Even in the dark

Nikholai saw the determination flash in her green eyes. With a sinking feeling he realized that she still had a chance at freedom and she intended to take it.

"Countess?"

She began to turn away from him. In her place, he would do the same thing, but he cursed softly as he watched her run to the horse.

He renewed his efforts to scale the crumbling bank, but his purchase slid away again. He looked up over the ledge once more to see if she had gone.

To his surprise, she was still there, peering into the darkness to the north. Had she heard something? He turned to see what had drawn her attention. The earth rumbled beneath them.

Upriver a wall of trees, sand, and boulders thundered out of the darkness. It stretched from bank to bank and would swallow him in an instant. Even the countess would be caught in the onslaught, he realized.

"Run," Nikholai shouted to her as he turned back to his climbing. Then he heard her above him.

"Ataman." She lay on her stomach, one hand stretched toward him, the other gripping a large bush as an anchor. He grasped her small wrist as she clasped his larger one. With strength that surprised both of them, the countess pulled Nikholai up as he braced a foot against the bank and vaulted over the edge. Without hesitation he jumped to his feet, dragged the countess to hers, and raced for high ground. She tried to pull free to get Sotnik. The frightened horse shied away from her.

"Leave him," Nikholai shouted over the roaring wind that washed before the wall of water. Nikholai pulled her up a small rise. Then, on the other side he pushed her down and fell on top of her with such force that he knocked the breath out of her. He tucked her head under his arm just as a shower of water, stones, and debris pelted them. The wall washed over them in a fraction of a second, but the roar seemed to go on and on.

When he thought it was safe, Nikholai rolled off the countess. They were covered with mud. The countess pulled herself up on her hands and knees and gasped to catch her breath again. Suddenly she flung herself at Nikholai, grabbed his shirt collar, and attempted to shake him.

"Damn you! You bloody, bleeding Cossack," she cursed over the roar. "I could have gone. I could have been free."

"Don't curse me, Countess." His anger flared again. He grabbed her fists and shook her. "You just drowned my best war horse, my best breeding stock. And now we've lost Sotnik too."

The rain renewed its fury in sheets that sliced the mud from their faces and clothes. The countess tried to pull free, but he gripped her wrist with little thought of cruelty and pulled her to her feet.

"Come on. I think there's shelter nearby," Nikholai said, nearly dragging her behind him. She resisted once, and he gave her arm a jerk. "Don't argue with me now, Countess," he warned. She had lost his hat, and the rain had plastered her short hair to her face. And her stolen boy's clothes clung to her body, but he was still unable to see her woman's shape. He wondered how she had managed that.

She looked back at him for a moment. Then surprise lit her face as she sighted something over his shoulder. She pointed. "There he is," she said, laughing delightedly as she pulled away. Certain that this was another trick, Nikholai clasped her wrist even more tightly, but when he looked ahead, he saw Sotnik. Sensing that her pleasure was in being reunited with the animal, not in the opportunity to escape, he released her.

She approached the frightened, exhausted horse quietly. With soothing words and another piece of apple from her sash, she lured him close enough to pick up his loose reins. Then she hugged the dun. Nikholai walked around the horse, looking for injuries. He saw no serious ones. He took the horse's reins from her and clasped her wrist once more.

"If we are where I think we should be, a shepherd's hut is near," he said, and led the way to shelter.

111

## ❧ 8 ❧

# The Bargain Is Struck

I'm not going back, Ataman," Elise said firmly in Cossack.

He stood at the door with his back to her. Water dripped into a puddle about his feet. She could feel his anger fill the tiny dugout. She really didn't care. She had done what she had to do, and she would do it again.

He walked to the primitive clay oven and wiped the rain from his face with a corner of a dry blanket. Elise had already started a fire in the oven while he put Sotnik in the adjoining covered stall. Rain pelted against the one small window. The wind rattled the leather-hinged door and sent a draft along the dirt floor to flicker the flames in the oven.

"I should have known you'd try this," he said aloud in Cossack as he turned to her. "You nearly got us killed. It was madness to attempt a river crossing in that flood. And you lost my best horse." He swore at her again.

Elise shivered and draped a dry blanket over herself. "I'm truly sorry about Sultan," she responded in Cossack again, without thinking. Dispiritedly she sat down on the chest where she had found the blankets and clothes and carefully cradled her throbbing head between her hands.

"Sultan was a gift from my father—I've spent years training him," the ataman said. "Now drowned in the river

112

because of a foolish woman." He gestured in the direction of the river for emphasis. Elise sat motionless.

"I'm beginning to think you're not worth a ransom," he said accusingly. "You lost my horse. You've corrupted my warriors. You ruined my razor when you cut your hair. You lost my favorite hat—it was just beginning to fit well."

"Your hat is right here," Elise interrupted. Anger warmed her blood. She pulled the black lambskin hat from inside her shirt and threw it at him. "I lost things too. I lost Anna's muff and William's saddle. I helped you when you needed help, and that's more than can be said of the help you've given me in finding my sister," she snapped at him, angrily fluent in his language. Water from her soaked hair trickled down her forehead and threatened to drip from her nose. She wiped it away with the back of her hand.

The ataman regarded her in silence. Slowly he sat down on a bench next to the oven. He leaned forward, elbows on knees, and studied her as he ran his fingers through his own dripping hair.

"You told me you only knew *some* Cossack," he said. "Now you speak with a Terek accent. You did not learn that from the children."

"I learned from Yergov," she said. "He's Terek, I believe." Elise shivered once more, then gripped the edges of the chest on either side of her and willed herself to be still. She didn't want him to think she was afraid.

"Yergov the Terek?" the ataman asked, surprise in his voice.

"You know of him?" she asked. She pulled the blanket over her head to dry her hair and hide her shivering. "He was my brothers' trainer."

The ataman eyed her intensely, as if making some reassessment, as if she looked different somehow. She ignored him and continued to dry her hair.

"So you played us for fools," he said at last.

"Played you for fools? Because I know more than I revealed to you?" Elise shook her head. "Oh, I see. Once again, I have taken advantage of Vazka's great ataman and his one hundred warriors, is that it? Is that what you're angry about?"

"We have never been dishonest with you, Countess."

"You've played your games with me, Ataman. Cat and mouse, just as Natalia said. Feeding me honey cakes as if I were some skittish filly to be broken."

He was silent, turning away from her to look at the fire, but Elise saw a smile quirk at the corners of his mouth, the smile of a boy caught at mischief he didn't really regret.

She took advantage of the respite to ask about the owner of the dugout. The ataman explained it belonged to shepherds who moved from pasture to pasture, often leaving supplies in their shelters. He found some dried fish and estimated that the firewood in the corner would see them through the night.

As Elise bent over the chest to get more dry clothes, her head began to throb again. She dropped the lid and turned to sit down before another wave of dizziness hit her. Tenderly she touched the growing purple bruise at her temple.

"Does it hurt much?"

"It's sore, and I think there is going to be a big lump."

"Let me look." He moved suddenly toward her. Afraid he would seize her, she jumped away. Silently he restrained her with a firm hand on her shoulder. Then he gently smoothed back her hair to look at the angry bruise.

"A towel soaked in cold rain will ease the pain," he said as he fingered her curls away from the injury. "Tell me, Countess, how do you make yourself flat like a boy?"

"I bind myself with towels." Elise blushed and pulled the blanket closer around her shoulders.

"Oh," was all he said as he appraised her body with a look that deepened her blush. "Your lips are as purple as your bruise. Get out of those clothes. I'll get some cold rainwater and check on Sotnik." He went out the door.

Elise looked around the hut quickly. She saw no weapons. The window was too small to crawl out of. Getting out the door unnoticed would be impossible because the covered stall was right outside. His anger had subsided, she thought. Perhaps she could appeal to his reason, make him see the danger in her returning to the village.

By the time he returned, she sat cross-legged on a dry pallet spread on the dirt floor before the oven. She had dried her hair and dressed herself in a coarse white shirt under a long quilted purple caftan. The dry clothes felt good against her skin. She looked up at him uncertainly, her cheeks rosy from the heat of the fire.

"I found the vodka jug and started some soup," she said. "And I put out some dry clothes for you." She gestured to the neatly folded clothes on top of the chest. He did not return her smile.

"Here, put this on the bruise," he said as he handed her a pottery bowl full of cold rainwater. "Pour me some vodka."

He turned his back to her and began to pull off his wet clothes.

Elise put the cold cloth to her temple as he instructed. Then she watched him, fascinated that he would undress before her after he had made a point of her privacy. He pulled his shirt over his head, revealing the corded muscles down his back. Elise felt an inexplicable urge to draw her fingertips down the valley of his back, along his backbone, all the way from his neck to his shoulder blades, down between his ribs to his lower back, and below. Instinctively she knew she would have great power over him if she did. Hands shaking, she turned away and poured the vodka.

She suspected that the only reason he hadn't taken what he wanted from her before now was out of respect for Natalia. And even though the first heat of his anger had faded, she still felt vulnerable.

She drained her vodka cup and filled it again.

"That's better," the ataman said as he sat down opposite her on the pallet. The white shirt hung open at his neck, revealing the silver chain of his St. Nikholas medal and a little of the crisp dark hair that stretched across his chest and down his torso. He wore dry black trousers, but he was barefoot, as she was.

"I'm afraid you're going to have a black eye, Green Eyes," he said as he reached out to touch the lump at her temple. With great effort he resisted the urge to kiss the lump and catch the scent of her. "Everyone in the village will think I beat you."

"I told you, I'm not going back to Vazka, Ataman," she said, avoiding his touch.

Nikholai drew his hand away. He frowned into his vodka cup. He had never met such a stubborn, single-minded woman.

"I'm not going back," she repeated softly. "I have to find Anna. Besides, my return to Vazka would mean danger for both of us."

"What kind of danger?"

"Vikola plots your overthrow," she said. She told him what she had overheard outside the church.

"When was this?"

"The night that you . . . The night the minstrel came to Vazka. So you see, it would benefit neither of us for me to return. In fact, I'm doing you a favor. When Rostov rides into Vazka, he'll find no one who doesn't belong. The villagers are wise enough to tell him nothing. And Vikola will have no grounds for demanding an election."

Nikholai thought about what she had said for a moment. Her story had the ring of truth. Vikola had been causing trouble by calling his decisions into question at every turn. The Zaporozhie was obviously gaining influence among the warriors and would demand an election soon. The countess understood the language and politics well enough to recognize the implications of what she had overheard. That Vikola might be the village spy and traitor was no great surprise. Yet . . .

Nikholai glanced at the countess, at her eyes intent upon him, and he wondered how far she would go to gain her freedom. Would she lie to him about his own warriors? He shook his head.

"I'm taking you back, Green Eyes," he said. "I can't let you ride off across the steppe to be recaptured by the Tartars."

He saw her eyes flash and knew the fight wasn't over.

"I'm going to find Anna," she said softly. Her gaze strayed to the door behind him briefly before she went on, "But I could use help. What if I promised to return to Vazka without resistance after I find Anna? You could send Kasyan with me."

Nikholai felt a familiar jealousy at her mention of Kasyan. He looked at his vodka cup and shook his head.

"Then come with me yourself," she pleaded. "You won't accept my offer of more ransom. What can I offer you?"

Nikholai studied her for a long time. It annoyed him that she offered herself to him like some kind of prize. He admired the halo of golden curls about her head, the soft smudge of her dark lashes against her cheek, and her even white teeth nibbling on her rosy lower lip. He wanted to chew on that full lip too. He saw her glance at the door again, then gaze back at him without wavering. He might be able to get her back to Vazka tied to the horse, but she would fight. If he were going to bargain with her, he'd make the most of it.

"I've never made any secret of what I want from you, Countess. Are you truly willing to exchange your favors for my help?"

She only blinked at him so calmly that he began to wonder if she had made similar bargains with others. She was a married woman who had lived in the French and Polish courts. She knew well enough how a woman went about getting what she wanted. He emptied his cup, and the vodka burned uncomfortably all the way down his throat.

"Isn't that what you are suggesting?" he asked. "I'll take you to Kagalnik to find your sister. You'll become my mistress. All Vazka thinks you are already. And you will return with me—whether we find your sister or not—without resistance."

She looked at him wide-eyed.

How could she offer herself to him, then look so damned innocent? he fumed.

He glimpsed something in her face. But she covered it. She looked down at her hands and played with her vodka cup. "And what happens when Rostov rides into Vazka?"

"You let me worry about that," Nikholai said.

She raised her gaze to his face and studied him somberly for a long moment. He saw no flash, no defiance, only wariness. He realized she was thinking of the Tartar.

A vision of the hideous marks on her blossom-scented skin flashed through his mind. He tensed with anger and the new realization that this might not be as easy for her as he had first thought. Impulsively he sat up and touched her cheek tenderly with the back of his hand.

"I won't hurt you, Green Eyes," he whispered. "I'm not a Tartar. I give pleasure where I take it."

She didn't pull away, but closed her eyes. The muscles in her jaw tightened as he drew his hand along her cheek.

He liked the sweet contrast between the courageous countess and the vulnerable Green Eyes. He found a delightful little mole just below her ear that he longed to touch and kiss. His loins ached. How did she manage to drive him from wanting to strangle her to the blinding need to hold her? With effort he moved away from her, determined to play this out in his own time.

"Do you agree to this bargain?" he asked.

"Yes," she answered breathlessly without looking at him.

"Then tell me, if I had not followed you tonight, where did you plan to go, and what did you plan to do on your own?"

He saw her take a deep breath. She gave him a curious glance, then began to explain how she had planned to ride into Kagalnik dressed as a boy and join Razin's forces. She would ask questions to learn about the Kalmyks, hoping to find some clue to the whereabouts of her sister.

"And if your sister is there? Then what?"

"I'm not sure," she said. "I'd have to make plans then. But at least we'd be together." Nikholai watched her stare into the cup of vodka. "I have to find her. We only have each other."

"If we travel as a boy and a warrior, no one would think a thing of it," he said finally. "But you must understand, Green Eyes, this gathering at Kagalnik is no harvest fair. It's the mustering of a rebel army. Misfits. Angry men. Dissatisfied townspeople. Men cocky and bloodthirsty from their adventures in Persia. If you can play your part well, it may be possible to get in and out of Kagalnik and learn what you can in a few days."

How much trouble could Vikola cause in a few days? If anyone could carry out this masquerade, the countess could. She had the courage. That was half of carrying off any disguise. Her horsemanship was adequate. On the river, she had proved herself a courageous and trustworthy comrade.

He couldn't keep the smile of satisfaction from spreading

across his face. "And when we return to Vazka, you'll no longer sleep in the loft with Natalia."

"What?"

"You've agreed to be my mistress," Nikholai said, then gave her the same wicked smile he had flashed her that night he had thrown her down on his bed and undressed her. "You didn't expect this to be for just one night, did you?"

Elise stared back at him in silence, her mouth open. She hadn't had time to consider all the possibilities this bargain opened up to the ataman. She had accepted the offer in desperation—anything to win the freedom to search for Anna. A nagging suspicion tugged at the back of her mind that he had won the game and was somehow taking advantage. But he had agreed to help her find Anna, she reminded herself.

"You will honor this bargain?" he asked.

"Yes. Yes." She nodded, but inside she felt less emphatic.

"Good. Now, I'm hungry," he said. "Where is this food you found?"

Was that all? she wondered. She had surrendered her body to him and he was hungry? He had methodically touched her and fed her for weeks in pursuit of her favors, and now he was hungry? She shrugged. She had grown up with three brothers, but she was sure she would never understand men.

She showed him her attempt at dried-fish soup that she had started while he was out with the horse. He made a face when she gave him a taste. Laughing, they both agreed it didn't match Natalia's fine fare, but it would do. They discussed the storm outside, but Elise was careful to stay away from any talk of the river and flood.

"How did you persuade a Cossack military trainer to teach a girl?" he asked. He had stretched out on the pallet again with his feet toward the oven. He reclined on one elbow and watched her, his gray eyes curious, warm.

Why was he taking his time about this? she wondered. Was he really interested? She could make this a very long story.

She set the dishes aside and began to explain how her brothers had taken her along because she could speak many languages. Yergov had come to see the benefit of the arrangement, so he named her Mitka, and she had been included in much of her brothers' training, except for the swimming lessons in the Dnieper.

The ataman laughed. Then he said seriously, "This will be no boys' prank. If your disguise is uncovered, you could be considered a spy."

"There is no other way to do this, Ataman. I have thought about it," Elise explained to his back as he took wood from a stack in the corner of the hut. "I can't go into a place like that as a woman. I would be treated as a camp follower, as an outsider. I would have more difficulty getting people to answer my questions. No, I must go as a boy. It will work."

The ataman knelt before the oven and put the wood in log by log. "You *must* be good at being a boy."

"I am good at it."

"Not too good, I hope." He left the oven and sat down behind Elise. He placed one leg on each side of her, then drew one knee up so that he could rest his elbow on it.

With great effort Elise resisted the urge to pull away from him. So this is how it is to begin, she thought. I will not fight, I will not fight, she repeated over and over to herself.

She could feel his breath on the back of her neck, and she was profoundly aware of his nearness and the intimacy of their contact—her buttocks against his groin.

"I see there are advantages to your new hair style," he whispered. His words tickled her neck. She felt a light brush of his lips against her hair. Then he leaned forward and kissed the back of her neck, a lingering, tender kiss. The warmth of his lips spread down her back, into her middle, and a strange tingling shimmered through her. She forced herself to lean back against him slowly. Still he did not touch her with his hands.

He kissed the back of her ear. Only when Elise gasped and shivered did he slip an arm around her waist and pull her back against his shoulder. He kissed her unbruised temple, her eyelid, and her cheek. Elise closed her eyes and let it happen. That was the bargain. But the need to resist was fading. She realized that he had accomplished what he had wished with his gentling of her. She found nothing frightening or offensive in his intimate touch.

He turned her face toward him and leaned her against his knee and kissed her fully on the mouth. This time she responded and was thrilled with his tender nibbling of her lower lip. She threaded her fingers through his brown curls and tugged on them. He groaned and stroked her throat with his thumb.

His fingers busily worked at the buttons of her caftan. She ached to feel his touch on her skin. He slipped the caftan off her shoulders so that only the coarse shirt covered her.

He rested his body close to hers, his hand spread across her abdomen, gently caressing. She liked the smell of him so close to her and the feel of his skilled hand on her. His other hand sought out one of her breasts and began to fondle it through the fabric. With his thumb he teased the nipple, and the sweet pain almost made Elise cry out.

She closed her eyes and savored the tickle of his mustache as he pulled her shirt off and kissed each bare shoulder. He slipped his arms around her again, cupped each of her bare breasts in his gentle hands. He forced her to lean toward him. Relentlessly he began to place hot tonguing kisses down her back as his fingers lightly teased her nipples.

Shattering waves of pleasure washed over Elise. His kisses moved steadily down her spine. With one last kiss to her back, the ataman pulled her against him and began to caress the insides of her thighs. Slowly he lowered her to the pallet. At last she could touch him as she had longed to on the day he asked her to name the colt. She combed her fingers through his crisp chest hair and shyly kissed his collarbone. With a muffled moan he took her hand in his and refused to let her explore him further.

Elise sensed the growing impatience within him. He began to stroke her thighs again, each stroke becoming more and more intimate. When his insistent fingers found her sensitive center, fear seized her. She gasped and tried to push him away.

He stopped. Then he embraced her, rocked her in his arms, and whispered soothing words. She fought her conflicting emotions. This intimate experience in no way resembled her experience with the Tartar. Still, the fear persisted. He leaned over her and offered her words of praise. Gazing into his soft gray eyes, she relaxed against him and surrendered her fear.

Slowly he renewed the stroking of her thighs. Again each stroke became more intimate, until the need to open to him became undeniable. She had never understood why a woman would want to open herself to a man, but now she did. He took full advantage of her surrender, exploring her completely, deliberately. She stretched against him, aware of the need to have him cover and fill her. Instead, without warning he pushed her away roughly, angrily.

"You're a virgin!" His breath was ragged, and he held her at arm's length, his grip on her shoulders painful.

Elise opened her eyes and stared at him without understanding his anger. Her body ached and longed for him to resume his caresses, for him to press his hard warmth against her, into her. She reached out to draw him close again.

"No games, Countess," he said in disgust, as if she should have known better. He rolled away from her, pulled the blanket over himself, and covered his eyes with his forearm.

Tears threatened. Elise wasn't sure whether she was angry, hurt, or relieved. She reached for the blanket to cover herself. The cold quickly began to creep into her limbs. She had so much at stake here. She didn't care if he used her for revenge. She needed him. She needed his help to find Anna. And she needed him to ease the ache he had so carefully nurtured in her.

"You were the count's wife," he said. She was unsure whether he made a statement or asked a question.

"Yes. But he never came to my bed," Elise admitted, and felt an old shame flicker inside her. She remembered how she had never joined the giggling young matrons as they shared the intimate discoveries marriage brought. She had admitted to no one that the count had never wanted her as a true wife.

"You agreed to this exchange, Ataman," she whispered. "The bargain is struck. An honest bargain. I did not deceive you."

He shook his head in disbelief this time. "The count never came to your bed?"

"Do you forsake your word, Ataman?"

122

"If you were a true married woman, few questions would be asked when you return home. But a virgin . . . How much do your brothers know about your marriage?"

"Nothing. Do you think I would tell my brothers that my husband didn't want me?"

She pulled the blanket tighter around her. She felt confused and foolish, small and cold. She blinked again to make the hot tears disappear. She swallowed hard. "The Tartars thought to get a rich price from my virginity."

"So you think to offer the prize to a Cossack to get what you want?" He took his arm from his face and glared at her.

Elise stared back at him, trying to understand why that offended him and how everything had so suddenly been turned upside down. Only a moment ago in his arms, she had known a pleasure she had never dreamed a man's touch could bring. She knew he had wanted her. Now he pushed her away as if she were tainted, as if she had done something wrong. He had suggested this outrageous bargain in the first place. Her temper flared.

"I think you're afraid of my brothers."

He turned to her, his gray eyes thunderously dark. He sat up suddenly, seized her by the shoulders, and forced her down on the pallet. "I have no fear of your brothers, Green Eyes. And I will honor my word."

His face was just above hers. Although he was angry and his grip on her shoulders was painful, she sensed that the spell of what had passed between them earlier was still alive. She gathered her courage and whispered, "Then touch me again. Like you did before. I will honor my word. I'm not afraid."

He hesitated only a moment before he yanked away the blankets and straddled her. He kissed her fiercely. His body pressed against her so that she could feel the long hardness of him against her belly. His heat flooded through her. She put her arms around his neck again and responded to the challenge of his kiss.

His fierceness waned, and he began to make love to her again, tenderly. Little by little he whispered warnings into her ear about the pain and the blood that would come with the first time.

When the pain came, it was greater than she expected. She

bit her lip to keep from crying out, but she could not hold back the tears that rolled across her cheeks and into her ears. She hoped he wouldn't notice. But he did. He stilled his movement and gently kissed away her tears, one by one. When his lips found hers again, she tasted her own saltiness on him. His lips and tongue played lightly across hers, and she forgot the pain. When he moved on her again, it was gone. Only a few moments later, she felt him shudder in his pleasure. Then he withdrew from her.

Immediately she pulled away to cover herself, but the ataman held her firmly, as if she were trying to escape from him. Silently he made her let him help her wash, using the rainwater in the bowl, now warmed by the fire. Every time she pulled away to cover herself, the ataman restrained her gently. Elise was embarrassed to allow him that intimacy, but he gave her no choice. She wondered what thoughts so absorbed him as he dabbed away the blood.

When he finished, he covered them both with blankets and kissed her temple.

"Rest now. Sleep and sweet dreams," he ordered, his breath soft and warm against her brow. Strangely, she felt secure in his arms. She felt no need to defy him. She closed her eyes and fell almost immediately into a deep, dreamless sleep.

Nikholai had the nightmare.

# ❦ 9 ❧
# Mitka's Hat

Nikholai shifted slightly to more easily cradle Elise against his body. As he gazed at her face, quiet and calm in sleep, he felt a shadow of regret creep across his pleasure. For him, she was no longer the Countess Polonsky. In truth, he realized, she had never been the countess. She was green-eyed Elise, who wanted to find her sister. The discovery both pleased and unsettled him. He had had a right to take Countess Polonsky. He had had no right to the maid Elise.

He lightly brushed her hair away from her bruised temple. He should have done the honorable thing, but he had wanted her too much. His need had been too great. It had been so easy to let her goad him into taking what he had desired.

Nikholai drifted off into a light sleep filled with visions of golden-haired, green-eyed children playing in the garden before the cottage. They smiled at him with smiles reminiscent of Elise's. Then they chased one another out into the square around the church. When they turned to him again, all but two had disappeared. Those two began to grow and grow until they were giant golden-haired, green-eyed, grim-faced men dressed in military uniform. Suddenly they

125

appeared at the village gate, fully armed and astride two huge white chargers. They were not men to be feared, but formidable men to be reckoned with. They demanded Elise. And she ran to them, smiling and laughing. She climbed aboard one of the horses behind her brother. They turned and rode away. Elise never looked back.

Nikholai awoke with a start. She still lay next to him, sound asleep. With a sigh of relief he pulled her closer. He tried to remember why it had been so important to get word to the Don Host about her right away. He wondered if sending a dispatch directly to the count's relatives had really been necessary. What had been the reason for his haste?

What woman's foolishness was this? he asked himself. It was just a dream. He had never set store by such things, not like Natalia and the village women did. But he could not deny that he understood its meaning: giving up the countess was going to be more difficult than he had thought.

Elise awoke slowly, aware of being warm and rested. When she opened her eyes to the early morning's light, she saw fine grass roots dangling overhead from the dugout's ceiling. A rekindled fire popped in the oven. She was alone with the blanket tucked well around her. She sat up, huddled in the warmth of the cover that still smelled of the ataman; she wondered where he had gone. The door opened.

"There you are. Where have you been so early?" She greeted him with a smile, but he did not return it. Sobered, Elise moved aside as he carried a bucket of water to the oven and set it down. Elise saw he was freshly shaved. He smelled of soap, and the curls across his brow were still damp. She smiled at him again, but let it die when she saw his eyes, as cold and hard as a Tartar's saber blade.

Elise checked an impulse to reach out and stroke his smooth cheek, for he obviously had no warm greeting for her. Had she dreamed his tenderness and desire for her last night? Or had she displeased him somehow?

"Kasyan is here," he said as he put more wood on the fire. "He brought food and some warm clothes. Wash quickly, I want to leave soon." He turned away from her to gather up their things.

"How did Kasyan find us?"

"He can track anyone, even after a rain. Wash now."

Elise looked at the bucket and the towels he had brought. "What I'd really like is a bath."

"I'll take you down to the river if you like, but we must be quick," he said without even looking over his shoulder at her.

"Bathe in the cold river!" Elise exclaimed.

"That's where everyone bathes."

"Even in the winter?"

"Until it is frozen solid," the ataman said. He turned to her and handed her a lump of soap. "Which will it be?"

"This is fine," she said, indicating the bucket but not moving from her seat on the pallet.

"Then get started," he urged. "Or do you want my help?" His question sounded taunting, so different from the night before.

"No. I'm waiting for you to leave," she replied, and clutched the blanket tighter about her. She didn't understand his coldness now, when he had been so solicitous only hours before.

He was about to say something, then thought better of it. "Eat this," he said as he offered her a piece of bread. "I'll be outside with Kasyan."

Elise washed as quickly as she could. Despite the warmth of the fire, she felt cold and small. What had she expected anyway? she scolded herself. There had been no trickery. No rape. She had understood from the beginning what he wanted of her. This was a bargain. An exchange of services. A business arrangement that made the act into something she didn't want to think about. It put her at the same level as camp followers. Of course, that must be how the ataman would see it, she realized.

A troublesome thought occurred to Elise as she began to bind herself with the towels. Was he considering going back on the bargain? He easily could. She had nothing to hold over him except a refusal to cooperate or some kind of bluff. A painful knot began to twist in her stomach.

She listened to the low tone of the men's voices as they worked with the horses in the adjacent stall. She knew

Cossacks were honorable with one another. An outsider was another matter. Would the ataman honor his word to her now?

Elise dressed more slowly as she turned this thought over in her mind. The blouse was dry and the trousers only slightly damp. Bemused, she forced herself to take a bite of bread before donning each garment. When she finished dressing, she wrapped the remaining bread in a cloth and tucked it in her sash. She had no comb. That was unimportant, she decided. She ran her fingers through her hair, then pulled on her oversize boots. The wadding was still in place in the toes to keep the boots from flopping when she walked.

"Countess?"

"Yes, I'm ready, Ataman." Elise rose, began to fold the blankets and pallets, and ignored the tightness in her stomach. Carefully she replaced the linens in the wooden chest. All the time, she tried to think of some way to hold him to their bargain.

Kasyan must have been watching the door, because he turned to her immediately when she opened it.

"Are you all right?" he asked in a hushed voice.

The ataman appeared from behind Sotnik and gave them both an angry look. "Of course she's all right. Does my own lieutenant think I eat maidens for breakfast?"

Elise blushed as Kasyan looked over his shoulder at the ataman, then even more curiously at her. This time his gaze was fastened on her temple.

"I can speak for myself, Ataman," Elise asserted, praying the blush would fade soon. She touched her temple and explained, "I'm fine, Kasyan. Something in the water struck me, that's all."

Kasyan cast an accusing look at his ataman. "What did you do to her?"

The ataman appeared from around the horse so quickly that Elise thought he was going to strike the fair Cossack. She knew she was the cause of tension between them, but she did not understand why. Instinctively she put herself between them.

"Stop it," she ordered in her best mothering voice. "You should be grateful to see each other again. There is no need for trouble on my part."

The two men regarded each other sullenly. Then the ataman turned away. Elise sighed almost audibly.

Kasyan stared at her. "Nikholai, she is speaking Cossack."

"I know." The ataman returned to saddling the blood bay.

"Countess, you speak Cossack?" Kasyan asked as the obvious dawned on him. "You've understood all along? You mean we went through all those gestures, and you really understood?"

"I'm sorry, Kasyan. I meant no offense."

"She just meant to deceive us," the ataman added as he buckled the bridle on Sultan. Elise recalled that he had been more sympathetic to her cause the night before.

Then recognition came. "Sultan!" Elise nearly shouted. She would have recognized him sooner if the ataman hadn't distracted her with his bad temper. "Where did you come from, you big red brute?" She put her arms around the stallion's neck. With a surprising show of patience the ataman stood back to let her greet the horse.

"He came home about midnight, just after the storm let up," Kasyan explained. "He bears only a couple of scratches. And he was still wearing his tack. Natalia is drying out the muff and saddle for you, Countess."

"Oh, we thought we had lost you," Elise said, embracing the horse again. He nuzzled her, and she gave him the bread she had tucked in her sash.

"You spoil my horses, Green Eyes," the ataman berated her softly. "If we are to make Kagalnik by the end of the day, we must be gone soon." He pulled a red felt cap from his sash and held it out to Elise. "Natalia sent this. She said you must have your own hat. Put it on."

Elise pulled it on silently, her gaze locked on him. Did this mean he was going to honor his word?

"You need it to cover your light hair and so that I can spot you easily in a crowd," he explained. "We won't be able to stay together. But I want to be able to locate you easily."

"Yes, sir," Elise replied as if she were an obedient warrior. She glanced over at Kasyan, who said nothing. The knot in her stomach began to loosen.

The ataman stared at her for a long moment. Roughly he tugged a piece of her hair down over each ear. "Keep your earlobes covered so that no one notices that they're pierced for earrings."

"Of course," she replied, and pulled at the hair herself. Anything, she'd do anything as long as he was going to take her to Razin's camp.

"You will be my nephew, and I will ask you to act as a groom. I assume you can tack up and care for the horses without help?"

"Of course."

"Nikholai, perhaps I should go with you," Kasyan offered. "It will be very rough there. I can look after her, Nikholai, while you talk with Razin."

"No, Kasyan, I need you and your father to look after Vazka while we're gone."

Kasyan nodded with an uncertain look in Elise's direction.

"I can do it. Don't worry," she said, touching the fair Cossack's arm reassuringly.

After a few more instructions the ataman sent his lieutenant back to Vazka. Then he turned to Elise. His face was shadowed so she could not read his expression, but the voice she heard when he spoke was deceptively soft and without threat. "I have one last word of warning for you, Countess. I take you to Kagalnik today as we agreed in our bargain. There is no escape. You gave your word that you would return to Vazka with me. Your word is good, isn't it?"

"My word is as good as yours, Ataman," she replied, still attempting to meet his gaze, her chin held high.

Her statement was met with silence.

She knew by the sudden tilt of his head that he had raised a sardonic brow at her before he turned away. He understood.

"Let's be on our way," the ataman said as he led the way out into the cold gray day.

Nikholai had no illusions about Elise's determination. It amazed him, but he was satisfied she played no woman's game as Daria did. The countess had no intention of coming between him and Kasyan. She wanted to find her sister.

Nevertheless, this foray into Razin's encampment was against his better judgment. A woman, especially a beautiful woman like the countess, who loved to play with babies and knew instinctively how to hold a man, had no place masquerading as a boy in a rebel Cossack camp. He had nothing to gain from a talk with Razin, and he doubted she would find any trace of her sister in the camp.

But he had known when he kissed the sweet, salty tears from her face that he was bound to honor his part of the bargain.

As he had bathed in the river and shaved that morning, he considered sending her back to Vazka with Kasyan and making the trip to Kagalnik on his own. He probably could learn as much about her sister as she.

But her response to his warning about keeping her word had finally persuaded him to carry out his part of the bargain. If he didn't take her to Kagalnik, he was certain she would try to escape again. And another escape attempt like the last would kill them both.

# ❧ 10 ❧
# Skull and Tales

"There is Kagalnik," the ataman said, pointing downriver as they rounded a bend in the road and halted.

Razin had wisely chosen to build his settlement high on a large island in the middle of the Don River. The portage road to Tsaritsyn was easily watched from the ridge above and from the island. The steppe on the west bank offered no cover.

On both sides of the river root-twined tree stumps littered the banks, and mud-covered reeds lay combed against the earth. Otherwise the rocky, wooded isle appeared to have suffered little from the storm of the night before.

The settlement was larger than Elise had expected, but it was little more than a sprawling encampment, with none of the simple, tidy grace of Vazka—few cottages and no proud onion-domed church.

"This Stenka Razin is your friend?" Elise asked as she viewed Kagalnik.

The ataman shrugged. "We first met in the Sech years ago. I rode with a detachment of Cossacks commanded by him in 'sixty-three. We joined with the Zaporozhie in raids against the Tartars to the south. Both he and his brother were there at the time." The ataman turned to look at her.

132

"His brother, like my father, was killed in the war with Poland. Only his brother was executed by the Muscovites for disobeying orders. My father died because of a Muscovite coward."

After a moment of silence he added, "Razin and I disliked each other from the first day we met. Don't expect a warm reception from him in my company."

"Is that why you won't pledge Vazka's warriors to him?" Elise asked. "Because you dislike him?"

"Comradeship has nothing to do with it. Razin is emotional, unreliable. Like a woman. I would not trust him to fight at my back. I will not entrust the future of Vazka to him."

She decided to ignore the comment about women. But she was trying to understand what the ataman held against a man who had obviously made such a charismatic impression on others.

"Razin camped a few versts north of here two years ago at a place called Panshin," the ataman told her. "That was before he led his rabble down the Volga to the Caspian Sea and Persia. He needed supplies then, so he requested donations. 'Donation' was his word—'toll' was ours. He controlled the river. He demanded lead and gunpowder from cities like Voronezh. We of Vazka sent him six mares, three of them in foal, just to get some barrels of flour and a bale of tobacco. Our drove wasn't going to last long at that kind of exchange. And the Muscovite officials of Voronezh weren't in any position to help us."

"So you started pirating on the Volga?" Elise asked.

"I wasn't about to let Vazka starve because the Muscovites wouldn't pay us or because the Don Host ataman, Kornil Iakovlev, couldn't control his godson. Iakovlev and others finally supplied Razin with barkas and arms for an expedition to Persia, just to get him away from the Don."

"Razin is the Don Host ataman's godson?" Elise asked incredulously. "Then he knows people with influence. Surely he doesn't need to be an outlaw, a pirate." She turned to ponder the strange island encampment before them.

"Eventually Iakovlev had to resign because of the resulting rift in the Host. Now, two years later, Iakovlev is back in power, and Razin has returned rich from Persia with shares of booty for his supporters. But some say his six-thousand-man force numbers only three thousand. And Razin is seeking a pardon from the tsar for his crimes against Persia," the ataman said, finishing his story. "Beware, Stenka Razin is not what he seems to be."

Elise considered this in silence and wondered what kind of man Razin would be. Bitter? Vengeful?

The ataman also gazed at the strange island village. He sat on Sultan between her and Kagalnik, his brow furrowed again and his eyes dark, but not an angry dark. An impenetrable gray. He turned back to her. She didn't understand his reluctance.

"We will not speak Polish in the camp, and I will address you as Mitka," he warned her. He hesitated a moment more. Then he took off his lambskin cap and pulled the silver chain with the St. Nikholas medal from around his neck. "Wear this," he ordered, and put it over her head.

The long, delicate chain slipped easily around her neck, and the oval medal slipped inside the binding and dropped between her breasts. The silver still carried the warmth of his body.

"Why?" Without thinking, Elise pressed the medal against her breast. The ataman watched her gesture before he met her gaze.

"Because St. Nikholas watches over every Cossack," he explained. "And now he knows to watch over you too. Pull your hair down over your ears," he ordered. Then he led them across the wide channel of the Don River.

There was a ferry to the island, but the crossing was shallow. Sotnik never had to swim, and the water reached only to Elise's knees.

To her surprise, the ataman was greeted by name by several Cossacks. He returned the greeting and asked the way to Razin's kuren. A big kuren with a standard before it was pointed out. Elise could not take her gaze from the skull as they rode through the encampment.

"It's just Razin's standard," the ataman said as he put a steadying hand on Sotnik's bridle. "The skull and horsetails. The ancient symbol of the khans."

Tied to the bleached white skull, nine black horsetails

drifted ominously in the light breeze. The grisly symbol was mounted on a pole taller than a man on a horse—tall enough to be easily visible on the battlefield. Now it marked the door of an imposing kuren, where it was easily visible to all on the isle.

The ataman dismounted and tossed the reins to Elise as if she were a mere groom. "Tie the horses there, Mitka, before you come in," he ordered as he strode into the kuren. Elise suppressed her anger and did as she was told.

At the kuren door, Elise halted to allow her eyes to adjust to the darkness. Only a pale light filtered through the hemp-cloth roof. After a few moments she could see that the huge single room was lit by two feebly burning oil lamps hung from log rafters. Cushiony softness beneath her boots made Elise look down to see that she walked on a Persian rug fit for a shah's palace. She heard the music of a bandura badly played and the drone of many male voices. Tobacco smoke flavored the air.

"Ho, Ataman Nikholai Fomin," boomed a huge, deep voice from the opposite end of the kuren. "Look who is here, friends. Welcome, Nikholai."

Elise looked up beyond the ataman to see a bear of a man rise from a fur-covered chair. He opened his arms wide and strode from the dais toward the ataman and Elise. His costly khalat of gold cloth billowed behind him.

"Friend," the man declared, and he embraced the ataman. He kissed Vazka's leader first on the right cheek, then on the left, then on the right again in the traditional greeting to a welcome friend. In the big man's woolly embrace, the ataman's tall, well-proportioned body looked lean and slender.

The giant Cossack's brown hair frizzed about the collar of his khalat and over his ears. His intent dark brown eyes were set deep beneath his bushy brows. One of his front teeth was broken. His face was pockmarked, and one nostril had been split. Elise speculated that Razin had once been a handsome man—many battles ago.

As did most of his brother Don Cossacks, Razin wore a great mustache, but the ends of his drooped well below his mouth and curled at the ends from incessant twisting between his forefinger and thumb. A heavy gold chain set with rubies hung from his neck, and a gold loop flashed in his earlobe. Like the ataman, he was clean and wore his rich clothes with a casual masculine strength and swagger. Elise was certain she would never again be able to look at a court gentleman in silk stockings, curled wig, and silver-buckled shoes without thinking him anything but a fop.

"I was just telling my captains about our glorious days at the Sech, when we raided south with our brothers, the Zaporozhie," Razin said. "Was that only six years ago? Those devil's dogs, the Tartars, they didn't dare think of blocking us from the Black Sea then." Razin looked to his captains, who muttered their agreement.

"Ah, those were great days in the Sech, were they not, Nikholai Fomin? Too bad we lost your cousins. You were hardly more than boys, but good warriors all. We learned to call you 'Wolf.' And who is this cub? I didn't know you had sons."

The enormous Cossack seized Elise by both shoulders and shook her until she had to grab her cap.

"Mitka Stetskov, my sister's son from the right bank of the Dnieper. The cub wants to ride the steppe," the ataman explained. "Take off your cap, boy," he ordered gruffly. Elise obeyed immediately, but shot a look of annoyance at the ataman.

"Ah, you brought him to the right place, Ataman," Razin said. "We can use another fine horseman. Here, things are good for Cossacks, boy. As a horse has four legs, each of us Cossacks has four things: meat, brandy, good boots, and St. Nikholas to watch over us. Tell them it is true, Filka. Nikholai Fomin, have you met my lieutenant, Filka? And my general, Alena?"

A thin, twisted Gypsylike man appeared from the throng of men in the kuren. He nodded to the ataman curtly but said nothing. His nose was long and pointed, his eyes small. He had no chin. Mitka was reminded of a jumpy, secretive creature—a ferret.

With him walked a tall, stocky woman, modestly dressed except for the large gold earrings she wore. Down her back trailed the single braid of an unmarried maiden. Elise had seen her jest lewdly with the men in the room, but she turned an adoring look on Razin when he spoke to her.

"Alena brought me three thousand peasants. That's why I call her my general," Razin said with a laugh. "And I hope you brought the allegiance of Vazka with you, Ataman. Your warriors are always well-mounted on your Vazka-bred horses. That red stud makes your horses among the best on the steppe. Come, have some vodka with us, Wolf. And tell us how things fare for Vazka and for the pirates on the Volga. I hear you have given Rostov the slip one more time."

Razin draped his arm over the ataman's shoulder in a comradely fashion as they walked together toward the dais.

Elise followed with the growing awareness that the rebel's cordiality stemmed from wanting Vazka and the ataman's allegiance. Razin called him Wolf? She shivered.

Next to the dais stood a table crowded with stoneware jugs of vodka, gold goblets, and some of the finest rock-crystal vessels she had ever seen. The rebel Cossack poured a golden goblet full of vodka and pointed to richly woven rugs from Rasht. Brocade and damask tapestries from Baku hung on the walls. Brass and golden goblets and plates from Derbent sat on the table and the floor. All were from the great cities on the shores of the Caspian Sea. Razin bragged that the finely carved ebony chair on the dais had been taken from the personal flagship of Admiral Manady-khan of Persia.

Briefly Razin told them how his fleet of maneuverable Cossack barkas had defeated the admiral's fleet by sailing up to the great wooden ships and hacking holes in the sides of the vessels at the waterline. They had taken the admiral's son and daughter as prisoners. The doomed Persian princess, Elise realized. She was relieved when the ataman interrupted to ask about the fur robe draped over the chair—sable that even a tsar would envy. Elise wanted to touch it, but she resisted. Razin dismissed it as part of the loot taken from a city on the Yaik River.

Razin followed Elise's gaze. "The filigree lamps are from the mosque in Farah-abad," he told them. He waved an intricately carved ivory staff he carried. "Those infidels held many Christian slaves. They deserved no quarter. It was a grand adventure. You should have come along, Ataman Nikholai Fomin. There was enough treasure for every man to return rich. And women! Grateful women." Razin laughed, then drank from the golden goblet.

Elise wondered how grateful the poor Persian princess had been when Razin had thrown her into the Volga.

"And what do you know of women, cub? Look at those green eyes. I'll wager the maids envy you those eyes. You haven't even begun a mustache yet!" Razin exclaimed.

The rebel Cossack drew a big finger across Elise's upper lip. She stood frozen. Would the softness of her skin give her away? The ataman remained next to the table of vodka and brandy jugs, slightly behind Razin so that the rebel could not see him. He appeared to have little interest in their conversation, and he nodded a greeting to a Cossack across the room. Since he offered Elise no assistance, she decided the only thing to do was to brazen her way through.

"I know almost as much about women as my uncle," she replied without embarrassment. With an arched eyebrow the ataman glanced at her over Razin's shoulder.

"Ho, how much is that?" Razin asked.

"I know that Gypsy girls like to wear gold necklaces better than clothes," Mitka said. Over Razin's shoulder the ataman gave her a narrow-eyed look of warning. Elise disregarded it. He deserved repayment for her humiliation of sitting in the mud before Vazka's warriors. She wadded her felt cap in her hands.

"And Gypsies like to dance," Elise added with a wiggle of her shoulders. "They move all their body parts. I saw that. My uncle is partial to black-browed Gypsies."

"Ho, what say you, Nikholai Fomin?" Razin said, turning to the ataman. "You let the boy watch you with a Gypsy? And we thought you favored fair women. There are some fine Gypsy girls on the east bank, Ataman."

"I say that Mitka still has much to learn about keeping a tight rein on his mouth," the ataman said. He scowled at Elise.

Razin slapped Elise on the back and declared, "I like the boy, Nikholai Fomin. Tell me what you can do, cub."

"I'm a good rider, and I can fish." Then with a quick glance in the direction of the ataman, Elise added, "And I play a good game of chess and a good hand of cards. Kasyan Cherevik taught me to play the game fool."

"Can you swim upstream against the current across the river like a true Cossack warrior?" Razin demanded, now sober-faced with interest.

Her throat had become scratchy from the effort to keep her voice pitched low. She coughed, and when she spoke again, her voice cracked. "I'm good with horses."

Razin tossed back his head and laughed. Elise wasn't sure whether Razin laughed at her words or her cracked voice, but he said, "It's a start, cub. We'll make a Cossack warrior out of you. I do like the cub, Nikholai Fomin. We're glad you brought him. You are training him to ride with you when you strike at Rostov?"

Razin again turned his attention to the ataman, taking the gray-eyed Cossack by the arm and leading him to the chairs on the dais. He continued to talk in a low voice. Elise followed them and seated herself on the edge of the platform as the two men settled into the chairs. Word seemed to travel fast on the steppe, but she wondered how Razin knew so much about Vazka's affairs.

"You are a good leader, Nikholai Fomin, and your raids on the Volga have been well-timed and executed. But think what you could do to Rostov if you joined Vazka's forces with mine. How many mounted warriors have you? Almost a hundred, a full sotnia. Join with me. Cossacks join us daily—Yaiks, Dons, Zaporozhies, and Tereks. Some Kalmyks have pledged allegiance, and a small number of Cheremiss have joined us. They will serve as excellent guides when we move north next spring. We can take control of the rivers and the steppe."

Elise listened intently at the mention of Kalmyks.

The ataman spoke innocently. "Why do you plan to move north? We heard you had come here to live peacefully with the pardon of Tsar Alexis." His voice was even, but to Elise's ear there was an edge to it. The ataman disliked being pressured.

"The tsar has imprisoned the Holy Father of our church," Razin cried. Indignation rang in the rebel's voice. The crowded kuren grew silent. "Can you believe it? I sent word to his holiness, Patriarch Nikon, last year that we would rescue him from exile. We need only his assent, and we will deliver him from prison and place him on his true seat of power."

Elise turned slightly from her place on the edge of the dais so that she could see the ataman. His face was as inscrutable as it was when he played a particularly interesting game of chess.

"I did not realize your cause was a religious one, Little Father," he said evenly.

"My cause is that of poor Christian people," Razin said. "Many are concerned over this shameful state of affairs." The rebel leader turned to the others in the kuren and raised his hands, imploring a response. They cheered.

Satisfied, Razin turned to Vazka's ataman. "Give Rostov something to really send him packing back to Muscovy in shame," he said, hissing in the ataman's ear. "Make the tsar see that Cossacks are still a power to contend with. Show him that he can't ignore us like poor relatives."

"What says your godfather, Host Ataman Kornil Iakovlev, about these plans?" the ataman asked.

"Bah, the Host ataman has become an old woman," Razin said with a shake of his head. "He only wishes to protect his riches and dress his wife in fine cloth. He doesn't see the people starving here on the steppe as you and I do. Join us, Nikholai Fomin. We'll show the Muscovite dogs that Cossacks are to be respected."

"Your words paint an inspiring picture, Little Father," the ataman replied. "Indeed, many in Vazka would like to teach the tsar and the boyars a lesson, but I must think on it before I pledge Vazka's allegiance."

"What is to consider?" Razin asked. "The tsar wants your Cossacks to defend Russia's southern border, but he does not send your pay. Families starve. He demands your horses in payment for taxes to finance his war with Poland and Sweden. I heard how you paid the voevoda of Voronezh with three beautiful horses, all with the stamina of a fat goose." Razin slapped his knee and roared his approval in laughter.

Vazka's ataman shrugged modestly. "His tax collector didn't know much about horseflesh."

Razin leaned forward in his chair. With his elbows on his

knees he spoke quietly and earnestly to Nikholai. Elise was the only other person in the kuren who could hear his words. "We must fight this, Ataman. We are a free people. We must be free of this kind of domination from the boyars. They tell the tsar untrue stories about Cossacks, about our Holy Father, about me. The boyars side with the Persians against me and exaggerate the damage of my deeds. They describe them as great crimes. We must make the tsar see us as loyal defenders of the faith and of Russia. We set Christian slaves free. We are worthy of his respect."

"I will consider these things, Little Father."

"Pledge your allegiance now, Ataman Nikholai Fomin, and help us lay plans to rescue the Holy Father."

Elise started as a sudden commotion near the kuren entrance drew Stenka Razin's attention away from Nikholai. The giant Cossack stood up. "Oh, it's my messenger from Moscow," he said. "Perhaps the tsar has signed my pardon. We'll talk more of Vazka later, Ataman." He strode off in the direction of the exhausted, mud-covered Cossack who had just appeared at the door.

Elise remained seated on the dais, closely observing the men whom Razin had chosen to command under him. She saw several pipe-smoking Don Cossacks and a few Zaporozhies, recognizable from their shaven heads and long, bound scalp locks. But she gasped audibly and jumped to her feet when she saw two small slant-eyed warriors seated on a bench. The Tartars, with a chessboard between them, were absorbed in their game. Elise easily recognized them dressed in close-fitting clothes uncharacteristic of the Cossacks, as the kind of warriors who had attacked her family. She felt the ataman move to her side and turned to him in red fury.

"There are Tartars here," she hissed. "Why?" The others in the room had turned to the messenger and did not see the angry Cossack boy.

"They are Nogai Tartars, Mitka," the ataman explained in a low voice. "They have pledged their allegiance to Stenka Razin. They are allies just as the Kalmyks and the Cheremiss. Razin's mother is part Nogai." He added, "It was most likely Krims who attacked you."

Before she could say more, the ataman led the way out of

the kuren, past Stenka Razin and Filka, who still talked excitedly to the disheveled messenger.

Outside, in the fresh fall air, Elise's breath became even again, but her hand trembled as she reached to stroke Sotnik's nose. The horse's soft velvety warmth was somehow comforting and brought her back from the brink of panic.

"The Tartars in there aren't the only unpleasant surprise you may encounter here," the ataman warned as they stood near the horses. "Do you want to leave?"

"No," Elise answered firmly. "I was accepted as a boy, wasn't I?" But her hand still trembled as she stroked the gelding's nose. For the first time she understood the ataman's reluctance for this expedition. It was no boyish prank, no game. Discovery would mean angering a pirate, a rebel, a Cossack whose allies were the murderers of her brother and husband—men who had sold Anna into slavery.

The ataman shrugged. "I can tell Razin no, I will not pledge Vazka's allegiance, and we'll leave. Or I can appear to be considering the idea, and we'll stay for a few days."

"We stay."

## ✣ 11 ✣

## Love Is Like a River

By the end of the third day in Kagalnik, Nikholai had to admit to himself that the countess played a convincing boy. He watched her join a group of boys near the paddock. In the wide pants and loose shirt, red boots and cap, she took on the swagger and arrogance of a smooth-cheeked youth. How effortlessly she had slipped into the part of a Cossack boy when she had refused to accept the ways of Vazka's women, Nikholai recalled.

He had found lodging for them in the Lemkovs' loft. With the friendship of Cossack Lemkov's son, Pavel, "Mitka" was willingly accepted into the boys' activities. The Cossack youths challenged the older warriors to races, fished in the river, beleaguered the blushing girls as they helped their mothers with chores, and bedeviled one another with outrageous dares.

From time to time, Nikholai would see Elise join a small group or strike up a conversation with an individual. No one noticed that she spoke only a few words in a low, husky voice. They responded to her without suspicion. Even Nikholai, who knew how eager she was to find her sister, was sometimes deceived by the lazy comments she used to draw information from people.

The notion that Elise might be a spy troubled Nikholai again. But once more he rejected the thought. Why send a woman dressed as a boy to Razin's camp when a man disguised as a simple merchant or a shepherd would do? Yet she had been so obsessed with entering Razin's camp, and so eager for information.

At first Nikholai had watched her closely. He noticed that she avoided swimming dares, but she joined in the boys' teasing and imitated their obscene gestures. During her first horse race, he had uneasily watched her gallop out of sight across the steppe—free. His suspicion was shadowed by concern. Winning a Cossack race sometimes called for more than a fast horse. The races could become rough. And there was a tow road south and a merchants' road west. But she returned laughing with the others, her cap knocked askew. She was neither victor nor vanquished. She had called no attention to herself with her performance. Elise had great good sense for a woman, Nikholai thought. He wondered with a chuckle what her brothers would think if they knew they had trained their little blond sister to ride through a Cossack rebel's camp without being noticed.

Nikholai leaned against the corner of the stable and watched her look about for him. He was satisfied that during these three days she had been honest with him. She did not want to escape. She truly wanted to find her sister. That realization put him at ease. Even after the tense interview with Razin, Nikholai found he was enjoying this interlude with her more than anything he had done in many years.

The atmosphere of Kagalnik was festive, and Nikholai enjoyed being part of a community without the responsibility of leadership. The subterfuge of Elise's disguise added just enough excitement to make this an adventure.

The days were full of hunting, fishing, debate, and, always, horse racing. The evenings were filled with singing and dancing, storytelling, drinking, and gambling. And when the bonfire died, Nikholai had come to look forward to lying beside her in the Lemkovs' loft and sharing their observations in whispered words. She had heard nothing of her sister yet, but she always had amusing comments to make about the people she had met and the things she had learned about Cossacks.

He had thought it would be easier to resist touching her when she was dressed as a boy. It wasn't. He lay in the dark, talking and laughing with her, when all the while he ached to hold her again.

But she always kept him at a distance with her questions.

"Why are you called Wolf? I have heard that name used among the boys too. They call you the Wolf Pirate."

He could hear the concern in her tone. The nickname troubled her. "In truth, I don't know why I am called Wolf. It may come from my burka." He pulled the garment closer about them. "It is lined with wolfskin. Pelts from a mated pair my father and I killed long ago." He yielded then to the urge to caress her hip. Playfully she slapped away his seeking hand.

"There are people below," she reminded him with a smile. Then she turned over and went to sleep.

As Nikholai watched Elise with the boys in the paddock, she turned in his direction and spied him. A smile lit her face, and Nikholai felt the beat of his heart quicken. How could only a smile do that? he wondered. He motioned for her to join him. She nodded and bade farewell to her friends, who were bent on catching one of the wilder horses in the enclosure. Agilely she climbed the fence and joined Nikholai.

"Have you raced enough today?" he asked. With effort he resisted the urge to run his fingers through the ringlets at the base of her neck.

"Yes, Ataman, Sotnik is weary," Elise said. "I heard you made a fine kill today, and we will dine on fresh antelope tonight."

The hunt had gone well that morning, and he was pleased with himself. Although his responsibilities as Vazka's little father had prevented him from hunting for almost a year, that morning he had brought down a large antelope buck with his first arrow. It had been a clean kill, and his accuracy had impressed the other warriors.

Elise leaned closer, asking, "Will I like antelope?"

"You've had it before, but I think it is better prepared here." Nikholai looked away from her, remembering that she had been given antelope her first night with his Cossacks. He didn't want to remind her.

"I've learned something from the dolduna's daughter," Elise said as she turned to walk away from the paddock.

"About your sister?"

"Not exactly. She said that her mother had been taken to see a sick woman in a Kalmyk yurt beyond the ravine. She said that her mother thought the woman was European. It might be Hawkins."

"Or some other unfortunate woman. Is there more?"

Elise shook her head. "She said the woman was very ill and was living with an old Kalmyk warrior and his three wives. She saw no children around the yurt. Only a baby."

Nikholai heard horses gallop to a halt behind him as he said, "We will go talk to her after our meal." He started in the direction of the Lemkov cottage, then realized Elise wasn't following him.

When he turned back to her, he saw her staring in frozen terror at the three riders who had just dismounted at the paddock fence. Instinctively he walked back and put himself between her and the three newcomers. Her gaze was locked on the men, and her whole body was stiff. Yet her desire to run was almost palpable to Nikholai.

With his back to them, he asked, "Do you recognize them?"

She nodded. Her gaze never left the three men. Nikholai casually glanced over his shoulder. He saw the Krim Tartar who had ridden into the village that morning to pledge his allegiance to Razin. The other two were the Nogai Tartars who had been in the village when he and Elise arrived. The newcomer had just won a race against the two Nogais, and he loudly demanded settlement of his wager.

"That's him," Elise said. "He's the one. He killed William. Struck him from behind." She stepped forward. Nikholai caught her shoulder and forced her to turn away and walk beside him.

"We must not call attention to ourselves," he said. He refused to take his hand from her shoulder when she tried to shrug it off. But he allowed her to draw him in the direction of the river.

"How can he be here?"

146

Nikholai said nothing. He knew her urge to run was just barely restrained by his grip on her shoulder. He sensed that her initial panic had passed, but her terror remained. They left the cluster of two-wheeled carts and dugout dwellings behind them and entered the dark underbrush along the riverbank.

Across the Don, pink twilight softly rimmed the western hills and mirrored itself in the quiet river.

Visions of welts on Elise's back and oozing rope burns on her wrists slipped into Nikholai's mind as he kept pace with the trembling Elise. Only a Tartar's hinged whip would leave those kinds of welts and bruises. He remembered the way she had winced and sucked in her breath when he had touched the ugly bruise on her ribs. He was sure that injury had been the result of a booted foot. But the memory of the ugly teeth marks on her shoulder and breast was what made him want to roar with rage. Nikholai's mind refused to envision how she had received those teeth marks. He couldn't bear the thought of another man putting his hands or mouth on her. She would have fought. And that scum of a beggar's pot would have beaten her more viciously.

They were well clear of the village when he seized her roughly by both shoulders and whirled her around to face him.

"Why did you fight?" he demanded, shaking her. "You could have saved yourself and your sister with that damned bargain."

The panic cleared from Elise's eyes for a moment. Then Nikholai glimpsed disbelief and pain. In that instant he would have gladly choked himself with his foolish words.

"How can you say that, Ataman?" she cried. "You of all men?" Clouds of outrage and anger darkened the green depths of her eyes. Always stronger than he expected her to be, she twisted free and turned to run.

"No." He grabbed her wrist before she was beyond his reach. "Strike me if you must," he said, "but don't run away."

She turned on him. He braced himself for the slap. She doubled her fist and hit him in the stomach with all of her strength. His breath whooshed from him. He staggered back a step. Still he clutched her wrist. He saw her draw back to swing again. This time he caught her free arm, whirled her around to pin her against his chest, and clasped her hands firmly in his. He took a step back to steady his stance. She struggled only briefly. He could feel the angry throbbing of her heart and the tautness of her body.

Both of them gasped for breath. "I deserve your blows, Green Eyes, but let's not be so eager to deliver them," he said into her ear. He took a deep, painful breath and tried to regain control of his own anger and frustration.

"I shouldn't have said those words. I didn't mean them," he murmured soothingly in her ear. "Believe me, Green Eyes."

He felt some of the tension ease from her, and the trembling lessened.

After a moment of silence without struggling, Elise said, "Let me go, Ataman. I want to walk by the river."

Nikholai hesitated. He brushed his lips against her ear and pulled her more firmly against him. The boy's clothes and binding of her breasts and waist had done nothing to take away the apple-blossom scent of her.

She tensed again.

Slowly, reluctantly, he released her. Her wrists first. Then he rested his hands lightly upon her shoulders for a moment.

"I'll be right here, Green Eyes," he said. "Walk along the river. But don't leave my sight. I won't let the Tartar hurt you again."

She nodded without looking at him, and walked calmly through the knee-high brush to the water's edge.

As he watched her, Nikholai sat down on an outcrop. He pulled off his hat and ran his fingers through his hair. He hoped she was calm enough to consider that his words had been spoken in anger. He rubbed his sore midsection. He wasn't sure if the pain had come with the strength of her blow or the sudden realization that he loved her. He watched her idly pick up rocks to skip across the calm surface of the river. One, two, three. Four skips on the next one. The rocks barely marred the smooth surface of the quiet water.

The recognition of his feelings for Elise made him forget his anger. He marveled at how in that moment when he had seen the pain in her eyes he had known he loved her. He loved the countess. Somewhere between the time he had first looked into her green eyes over the injured white stallion and the moment he had seen the pain in her face, he had come to love her. Her pain was his. Her safety was his. Her pleasure was his. Her happiness was his. And this love he felt for her was as true, inevitable, and eternal as the river before them.

He watched her walk along the bank again, upriver a little farther. Her hands were clasped behind her back, and she stared at her red-booted feet on the wet sand.

Recognizing the Tartar had truly enraged and frightened her. Nikholai realized that he knew little about what had happened to her before she came to him. When he had first seen her injuries, he had concluded she had been raped. Now he knew that wasn't true. But a man could force other kinds of violation on a woman. Nikholai pulled his hat on. The Tartar would die, he decided.

Elise looked out across the river and refused to remember the things she had suffered at the hands of the Tartar. She thought she had wiped him from her mind if not her dreams. Then, there he was in Kagalnik—not as large as he was in her nightmares, but the fear and terror he stirred in her were just as enormous.

Every time she took a breath, she felt hollowness where her stomach was supposed to be. She had come to Kagalnik to find Anna. Instead she had found the Tartar.

She shivered inside. Would this nightmare never end? Would her life never be the same? Oscar and William were dead. Even if she found Anna and Hawkins, nothing would ever be the same.

She picked up a smaller rock and threw it into the river. She made no effort to skip it. She found no delight in creating ripples across the smooth water now. She wanted a big splash, a big crash. She wanted to hear the gun's explosion, see the fire, and watch the flat-faced yellow monster fall into a shattered heap. Maybe it was un-Christian, maybe it was unwomanly, but she wished him dead.

And the ataman? How dared he force a bargain on her, then mock her with it? Was he her ally or not?

She rubbed her hand across her eyes. Could she stay in

Kagalnik while the Tartar was there? Oh, Lord! The heathen might recognize her. He might realize that Mitka wasn't Mitka. The Cossacks believed her to be a boy, but that was partly because they had never seen her as a woman. Would the Tartar take notice of the boys and recognize her? She was so close to learning something about her sister, she couldn't just ride off into the dark. She had to know who that European woman was.

She glanced back at the ataman. He had seated himself on a rock, taken off his cap, then replaced it. Elise looked back down at the sand and dug a hole with her silver heel. Idly she watched water fill the hole. She wondered if he really regretted his words. There had been moments when she liked him, and she had thought they were becoming friends. But now she wasn't sure. She was only certain that he desired her body as the Tartar had. The only difference was that the ataman mysteriously made it possible for her to yield to him.

Nikholai watched Elise stare at the western horizon, the direction of home. She had made it plain that she wanted to find her sister and to return to her brothers. She didn't love him. She would never expect words of love from him, and he would never speak them.

When the time was right, he would give her up—when he was ready to part with her—but only to someone he could trust. To her brothers or someone who would see her safely back to Warsaw. He was relieved that there was no word from her brothers yet. At the same time, he was annoyed that they had not responded. Didn't they care about their sister? What kind of brothers would marry her off to an old man who didn't even care enough for her to introduce her to womanhood? Of course, it was he who had benefited. Perhaps old Polonsky had repaid his debt to the Fomins after all. But that debt wasn't so important to Nikholai as it once had been.

The first star of evening twinkled in the west as Elise stood on the riverbank gazing toward home. Nikholai joined her. They stood side by side, but apart, and gazed across the river.

"Do you think he recognized me?" she asked finally.

"Who?"

"The Tartar," she said impatiently. "Did he see me? Do you think he recognized me?"

"No, he didn't see you," Nikholai said. He glanced at her, relieved that his foolish words were forgotten.

"Is it safe to go on with our plans?"

"Just stay clear of him until I've killed him."

"Until what?" Elise turned to him.

"I'll kill him," Nikholai explained simply. "That will solve the problem."

They walked to the edge of the encampment on the east bank and turned to face each other. Her serious green eyes searched his face.

"No," she protested. "You know what happens to murderers—they are buried alive with their victims."

"It won't be murder. There are all kinds of ways for a Tartar to die in a Cossack camp."

"No. Promise me," Elise demanded. "Do not kill him." She seized both his arms and squeezed them.

"You would ask mercy for that infidel?" Nikholai asked. "Why should that devil's dog live? Besides, we can't take the chance that he will recognize you," he reminded her. The conflict he saw in the depths of her eyes confused him.

"I'll stay out of his way," she assured him. She turned away abruptly, releasing him. She walked on toward the village. Torches were being lit. The flames' reflection licked across the river toward them.

Nikholai caught up with her and drew her into the shadow of a wagon. "Why should the Tartar live?" he demanded.

She met his gaze steadily. "It's not the Tartar I want to live. Vazka needs you. Natalia needs you. To risk your life to kill one Tartar would be foolish."

Nikholai regarded her in silence. He found her answer both satisfying and disappointing. As he studied her, he was suddenly unsure of what to do about the Tartar. Her objections made him realize that if something happened to him, she would be endangered. He didn't want to take the chance she would have to fend for herself in Kagalnik.

"Let's get something to eat," he suggested, looking toward the noisy torchlit village again. Then he looked back at her to check her disguise before they emerged among the throng of Cossack men and boys around the nightly bonfire. She was pale, but still she looked the part of Mitka. He realized for the first time that she had never cried out her grief and loss. She had spent long hours in Vazka's church in prayer. Yet no tears. She had come upon the man who had been responsible for the death of her brother, her husband, sold her sister into slavery, and abused her. But no tears. Her restraint troubled him.

"Is something wrong?" she asked, and touched her red felt cap.

"No," he said. He wanted to reassure her. "Tomorrow you will talk to the European woman," he said. "And you will stay clear of the Tartar. I'll help you know where he is."

Despite the winter chill in the air, the serious card games and wagering were soon under way around one fire, and the veteran storytellers were drawing a crowd at another fire.

Nikholai sent Elise to their loft early and joined her after he had checked on the horses. He brought food and two cups of vodka he pressed her to drink so she would sleep. Nikholai was tempted to go out again and find the Tartar, but he refrained. He was uneasy about her calm after her first panic.

Well after midnight, sudden awareness that Elise's breathing had become ragged awoke him. She began to toss in her sleep, and turned away from him on her own pallet. He sat up to listen to the other sounds in the cottage. He heard only the deep breathing, snorts, snuffles, and snores of the sleeping Cossack family below. Still asleep, Elise moaned in protest. She tossed again, this time toward him. Her eyes were closed, but her brow was furrowed in distress. She raised her hand to ward off a blow. Quickly Nikholai leaned over her and put his hand over her mouth to muffle her scream. She came awake with a grab at his hand and a kick in the direction of her assailant. Nikholai caught her leg in his free hand and leaned across her to still her thrashing.

"It's all right, Green Eyes," he whispered in her ear. "It's just a dream. It's all right." But he didn't remove his hand from her mouth. Even though her eyes were wide open, he wasn't sure she was awake.

He felt her hesitate for a moment as she tried to make sense of what he had said and where she was. Then she relaxed back against the pallet, and great tears rolled from her closed eyes. She sobbed loudly just as Nikholai took his hand away from her mouth to brush away the tears on her temples. She stopped and held her breath, her own hand over her mouth and her eyes wide with the fear she would awaken the others.

"It's all right," Nikholai reassured her, and pulled her against his shoulder to muffle the next sob. In his arms, she cried as he had not seen her cry since they captured her on the river. He found the sound of her sobs painful. He could do nothing to ease her grief but hold her. Finally she was mourning her loss and crying for home.

# ❧ 12 ❧

# A Roll of the Dice

Elise awoke in the ataman's arms. Abruptly she pushed herself away from him. She threw off his fur-lined burka and retreated to her own sheepskin pallet. Her head ached and her eyes felt gritty. She was weak and shaken, yet somehow relieved.

The ataman reached out and touched her cheek gently. She did not withdraw, but she could not meet his gaze.

"Go see the foreign woman today," he said softly. "I will watch the Tartar."

He pulled on his boots and went to the ladder. "Mistress Lemkova, it seems Mitka drank too much last night," he said as he descended. "May we have some water up here?"

A bowl of water, a fresh cloth, and a pewter plate of barley cakes appeared at the edge of the loft by the ladder. Shortly after that, Elise heard the family go outside into the cold winter sunshine. She nibbled at a barley cake and wondered how to thank the ataman for his understanding. Then she prepared herself to find Hawkins.

Elise had learned that the Kalmyks were nomads who ranged with the seasons across the Wild Country from the shores of the Black Sea east to the Caspian Sea and north to the Ural Mountains. They lived in low round tents, or yurts. She had noticed on her first day in Kagalnik that the Kalmyks walked nowhere. They crawled astride a horse to travel the length of the village or to the kuren across the way.

Elise confessed to the dolduna and her daughter that she was curious about the Kalmyks' camp, about the inside, of a yurt, and about the language of a European. They took Elise at her word and asked her to accompany them on their visit.

The dolduna and her daughter bent down to enter through the flap of one of the Kalmyk yurts on the edge of Razin's camp. Near the entrance squatted a grizzled Kalmyk warrior. In one hand he held the reins of a small Roman-nosed pony that nuzzled the dusty earth in search of a mouthful of grass. The old warrior sat on a white horsehide, a mark of distinction, the dolduna told Elise. Slowly, with respect, the old warrior rose at the sight of a Cossack warrior, even a young one, and nodded a greeting. He was bowlegged and nearly a hand shorter than Elise. Nothing about him was familiar to her. She didn't think this was the same group of Kalmyks that the Tartars had traded Anna and Hawkins to, but her memory of those days was vague. Elise returned the warrior's greeting and followed the dolduna and her daughter into the yurt.

Inside, rank smoke from a fagot fire and the aroma of poorly cured skins hung heavily in the air. The floor of the yurt was layered with furs and well-worn Oriental rugs. Elise stood near the flap while her eyes became accustomed to the dimness. Near the fire a dark-haired Kalmyk woman leaned over an infant she held to her breast. She smiled a toothless grin at Elise.

The short, round dolduna and her skinny daughter went straight to the far side of the yurt and knelt near a low pile of skins. When the pile of skins moved and moaned, Elise realized that this was the ill woman the girl had told her of. Elise knelt apart from them so that she could observe without being seen.

"No, no. Take that evil stuff away," the reclining figure ordered in a weak whisper. "I'll live or die by God's will, not by your foul-smelling concoctions."

Elise recognized the words as distinctly English. She leaned closer to see the woman. The dolduna and her daughter went on with their efforts to straighten the furs, rugs, and pillows the woman lay on. Then they offered her water.

In the dim light, Elise could see the woman's face as the dolduna raised her head to put the cup to her lips. She was pale; her breathing was noisy and labored, her eyes closed and sunken well into her brow. With great effort she tried to drink. Elise recognized Hawkins, and she choked back the ache that rose in her throat.

Elise asked to speak to the woman, and the dolduna nodded and withdrew with her daughter.

"Hawkins?" Elise wasn't sure whether in this weakened state her faithful maid would recognize her.

Hawkins slowly opened her eyes and tried to focus on the face and voice beside her. "Who is it? Who calls me by my English name?"

"It's me, Hawkins. Elise." Elise bent low over her maid.

Hawkins' eyes widened, and she reached up to touch Elise's short golden curls. "Elise, my lady Elise. Oh, is it you or one of those strange dreams their medicine gives me?"

"It's me, Hawkins. What ails you?"

"Oh, Miss Elise, your brothers have dressed you up like a boy again. Are they here?" Hawkins asked as she tugged at one of Elise's short curls. "You are safe?"

"I am safe, Hawkins. Tell me how you fare. And where's Anna?"

"It's my lungs," Hawkins said. "But never mind that. There are things you must know. I am dying." She grabbed at Elise's sheepskin vest with both hands. "About Miss Anna."

"You're not dying, Hawkins," Elise replied calmly, and took Hawkins' cool dry hands in hers. She ignored the tearful ache in her throat. "We'll get you out of here, and you'll be well again soon. But where is Anna?"

"They traded her away like they did me," Hawkins said. "Those first people. They traded us to the old man here." The effort to talk was already beginning to tell on the servant. Her breathing had become more labored; the blue around her lips became darker and her face paler.

"Traded her away?" Elise choked back more questions as Hawkins began to cough. Comfortingly Elise rubbed the gnarled fingers of her servant's well-worn hand between her own. Hawkins was like family. As far as Elise knew, Hawkins had no kinsmen of her own. The plain woman had made the Chatham children hers. She had always remembered her place—more or less—but she had been a member of the family as long as Elise could remember. Steadfast as the cliffs of Dover, Hawkins had weathered nannies, housekeepers, tutors, and one governess who had been hired in an unsuccessful attempt to separate Elise from her brothers. Elise squeezed Hawkins' hands.

"It's all right. Take your time."

With great effort, Hawkins cleared her throat and went on. "The old man here traded her to another tribe of heathens. A big tribe with lots of horses. A herd as far as you could see." Hawkins stopped again to catch her breath. Tears rolled from her cloudy blue eyes. "I don't think the old man wanted to do it. He seemed to think Anna was good luck or something, but I think he was afraid of the other people. This other tribe, they carried a staff thing with feathers on it."

"A standard?"

"I guess. Yes, like a standard. A sort of eagle-wing standard. And some of their tents were set on wagons so that they never had to put them up or take them down." She paused. "May I have some water?"

"Of course, Hawkins. Here." Elise picked up a nearby cup and held it for the sick woman. "Are you getting enough to eat? Here, take this barley cake." Elise took the last of her morning meal from her vest pocket, where she had put it before she left the cottage. She held it out to Hawkins.

"No, I don't need food," Hawkins said. "You must find Anna, Miss Elise. It's always so cold. And Miss Anna isn't strong, not like you. You must find her." Hawkins' head rolled to one side. "So tired," she muttered.

"Sleep, then," Elise said. She leaned over the old woman, tucked the gnarled hands beneath the fur cover, and smoothed the gray hair and tears from the lined face. She placed the cake on a brass tray near Hawkins. She was reassured when she heard the shallow but regular breathing. "Rest," she whispered, and kissed the old servant's cheek.

* * *

Elise tried to quell the sense of urgency that dominated her as she ran toward the stables. A horse race was under way when she reached the sod structure. The day was bright and clear, with an invigorating, cheek-stinging breeze from the west. A plume of dust drifted on the crest of the hill where the racers had just disappeared.

When Elise didn't see the blood bay in the paddock, she suspected the ataman had finally given in to the desire to race. She thought he had refrained from racing so he wouldn't call attention to them after his strained interview with Razin. But if the ataman were involved in the race now, she had no way of knowing where the Tartar was. She looked about; no one noticed her.

Her good sense told her to go back to the cottage and wait for the ataman there, but Hawkins needed help soon.

Then she saw racers break over the crest of the far hill and gallop headlong down the slope. Sultan was at the head of a pack, and the Tartar rode behind the ataman. The heathen's high, short-stirruped seat made him easily distinguishable from the Cossacks. Elise joined the crowd that had formed to cheer the riders on. She watched only long enough to see that the ataman's seat was deep in his heels and his weight solid on Sultan's back. He was holding the blood bay back. As the horses raced up the hill to the stable, Sultan fell behind. The Tartar won.

Elise disappeared back into the crowd. She watched from a distance as the Tartar was congratulated with many hearty slaps on the back. The ataman was good-humoredly berated for his loss.

Elise watched the ataman rein Sultan toward the river. Before he turned that way, he cast a glance across the crowd of Cossacks. She took off her red cap and set it back on her head in their agreed-upon signal. Hers wasn't the only red cap in the camp, but it was the only one set atop golden curls. Satisfied he had seen her, Elise took a parallel path toward the river.

She found them walking along a sandbar, Sultan at last settled and resigned to losing this race, and the ataman quiet and preoccupied. She fell into step beside the stallion and gave his nose a brief sympathetic stroke.

"Poor Sultan. You denied him an easy victory, and you lost money for some of your fellow Cossacks."

The ataman gave a philosophic shrug. He remained mounted and urged Sultan on for a thorough cool-down. "Did you learn who the European woman is?"

"It is Hawkins and she is very ill," Elise said. "We need to get her out of here and to Natalia, who is more skilled."

"Can Hawkins ride?" the ataman asked.

"She's too weak," Elise replied. "Can we take her north by boat?"

He frowned, dismounted and led Sultan to the water's edge. The blood bay noisily sucked water through his velvet-soft lips. "She is that weak?" he asked.

"I won't leave her to die among strangers," Elise insisted.

The ataman gave an exasperated shake of his head, but when he turned back to her, she could see that his face had softened.

"Tell me what you learned of your sister."

Elise told him the story Hawkins had told her of the great tribe of Kalmyks with herds of horses as far as the eye could see. And she described the eagle-wing standard. "Do you know of them?"

"Yes, they usually stay far to the south or move east to the Urals in the summer. In the past they have sometimes joined with the Cossacks when the Tartars were too troublesome. They do not recognize the tsar or any other man as having power over them."

"How can we learn where to find them?"

"The Host usually has a good idea of their whereabouts."

"Then as soon as we have taken care of Hawkins, we'll go south to Cherkassk to learn of these Kalmyks," Elise said as she walked along the sandbar.

"Whoa, Countess. You make me feel as if I'm on a runaway horse," the ataman said with a laugh. "Our bargain was to come to Kagalnik in search of Anna and Hawkins. Then to return to Vazka." He pulled Sultan away from the water.

"But you said you would help me find Hawkins and Anna in return for . . ." Elise waved her hand vaguely in the air, then gave up the search for a proper-sounding phrase. "And now we have found Hawkins. And I thank you for your help, Ataman, but we still must find Anna."

"I agreed to bring you to Kagalnik," the ataman said. "And I promised not to turn you over to the Muscovites. I will honor that agreement." He led Sultan toward the stable.

"But the search can't end here," Elise said. "If we don't pursue this, Anna may die or be lost on the steppe forever."

"You have to face the possibility that your little sister may already be dead or dying, like Hawkins," the ataman said as he stopped to make some invisible adjustment to Sultan's bridle.

Stunned, Elise was silent. What he said was true, of course, but she had never allowed herself to consider it.

"Already you have learned more than I thought possible, but we're not going on to Cherkassk now," he said. "It's too late in the fall to travel that distance. Since the tsar is holding Host Ataman Iakovlev and the krug responsible for Razin's raids in Persia, the Host will be in a turmoil and won't be much help. And remember, we haven't left Kagalnik safely yet."

In the silence that followed, the ataman held out the reins to her. "Take Sultan to the paddock and unsaddle him for me."

Anger almost overwhelmed Elise, and she was about to declare what she thought of his bargain when she heard someone approaching.

"Ho, there. Ataman Nikholai Fomin?"

Elise and Nikholai turned at the same instant to see the Krim Tartar hail them from the riverbank.

The Tartar spoke in a jumble of Cossack and Tartar, but he was understandable. He led his stubby brown horse toward them.

"A race well run, Cossack," the Tartar said. "Too bad you didn't win. Perhaps we will ride against each other another day." He stopped before them.

Shorter than the ataman, he was sturdily built, with a strong, wide body, long arms, and bandy legs. He wore a turban-style hat edged in dirty brown fur. His yellow-brown hair and beard hung in strings from his head and long, shiny face. The sight of him made Elise shiver. He grinned a yellow-toothed smile at her, and his pale brown eyes lit up greedily beneath his prominent brow. As he walked toward her, he dropped his horse's reins so that the animal could go to water. A rigid, hinged Tartar's whip hung from his wrist.

"And this must be Mitka, your nephew, the boy they said rode into Kagalnik with you, Cossack," the Tartar said, staring at Elise. She wanted to run, but felt the ataman steady her with a firm hand against the small of her back.

The Tartar touched her chin with a dirty hand and his whip dangled before her.

"Don't think I have forgotten you, *boy*. Those green eyes are unforgettable."

Elise slapped his hand away from her face, and the Tartar laughed. "So you haven't been able to break her spirit either, Cossack. But I'll wager she's no virgin now. You Cossacks are too good to deal in slavery, but you're quick enough to relieve any woman of her virtue." He laughed again, as if he had just told a hilarious joke.

Outraged, Elise glanced at the ataman, but he appeared undisturbed by the Tartar's words.

"What do you want?" the ataman asked as he turned his back on the Tartar and began to loosen the girth on Sultan's saddle.

The bearded man took no offense at the sight of the ataman's back. He used the handle of his whip to scratch between his own shoulder blades before he went on. "Wouldn't Razin be interested to know that Mitka is a diplomat's wife? He'd want his share of the ransom, wouldn't he? And whatever else is to be had." The Tartar grinned lewdly at Elise. "But I could be persuaded to forget to tell Razin you have deceived him. A share of the little green-eyed slut could make me forget much."

"Perhaps something can be agreed upon. Let's talk about it," Elise heard the ataman say when he turned to face the Tartar. "Bring the horses, Mitka," he called back over his shoulder. The Tartar and the Cossack grinned at each other and laughed at that.

The Tartar slapped the ataman on the back. "That's the way to treat her."

The ataman glanced over his shoulder at her one last time, and Elise gave him one of the obscene gestures she had learned. He only laughed and turned back to the Tartar.

To think that only the night before she had been afraid he might really risk himself to kill the Tartar, Elise fumed. Now he was deep in friendly conversation with the monster.

For a fleeting moment she thought of mounting Sultan and plunging across the river, but she had just found Hawkins and learned something of where Anna might be. She had to take the chance that the ataman would keep their bargain—whatever it was.

Elise picked up the reins of the Tartar pony and led the horses after the men toward the stable. When she finished with the horses, she returned to the Lemkov cottage to get food for herself and for Hawkins. As she neared the cottage, she heard the men's voices and ducked back around the corner. They were absorbed in a dice game.

"I have it, Cossack. Bet the services of Mitka for your wager. I need help with my horse." The Tartar sat in the sun with his back to the Lemkovs' cottage wall, while Nikholai sat on a stool with his back to her. A little pile of coins and precious gems lay on the ground between the two men.

"Why not?" the ataman said with a shrug. "A day of Mitka's services in tending your horse."

Elise choked back an indignant gasp.

"No, no, Cossack," the Tartar protested. "More than a day. One day will hardly allow me to enjoy my ease. Three days. I demand three days at least to equal the value of my coin."

"It is but silver, Tartar," the ataman replied firmly. "I will give you two days. That is more than a fair exchange."

"All right. Two days," declared the Tartar. "And two nights. My roll first." He took the dice from the ataman and shook them. "Prepare yourself for a new master, Mitka," he said to no one in particular, and rolled the ivory cubes across the ground.

Elise could not see the dice, nor did she understand this particular game. But she did see the swinging, hinged whip, and a dull memory of sharp pain filled her. What was the ataman doing with her life? Did it mean so little? Elise began to back away as she watched the Cossack shake the dice slowly, deliberately. Why hadn't she had the good sense to take Sultan and run when she had the opportunity?

At the dolduna's cottage she requested food, linen towels,

and some of the aromatic herbs she had seen the woman use to ease Hawkins' breathing. Then she returned to the Kalmyks' camp. The old warrior once again greeted her respectfully and admitted her to his yurt. She found Hawkins' condition unchanged. The old servant drifted in and out of consciousness, and all Elise could do was make her as comfortable as possible.

Sickbed duty was not one of the things Elise liked. But for Hawkins she went to work brewing the herbs as directed and using the methods she had seen Natalia use. She placed the towels soaked in the aromatic brew across Hawkins' throat and chest. The vapors seemed to ease the woman's breathing.

As the afternoon passed, Hawkins talked to Elise of the past. Elise sat beside her, warmed the woman's hands between her own, and filled in the memories with her own words so that Hawkins would not weaken herself too much. They talked of Master James, of the bravery of Master William, and of the mischief of Master Thomas. Their conversation turned to Anna. They agreed that time was important—nine-year-old Anna was given to ailments of the lungs.

"You must find her soon, Miss Elise," Hawkins said. "I only ask that you do two things for me when I'm dead."

"Don't talk like that, Hawkins." Elise shifted uncomfortably on the floor of the yurt and rubbed Hawkins' hands with renewed vigor, as if that would keep death at bay.

"But I must," Hawkins said. "The two favors I ask are that you find Miss Anna and that you give me a Christian burial." Again Elise tried to protest, but Hawkins went on. "I know that won't be easy among these heathen people, but if I can't be buried on English soil, I must have at least a Christian burial. I'll rest easier." The old woman sighed. "You will promise me those two things, won't you, Miss Elise?" She searched Elise's face for agreement.

"Of course, Hawkins. If you die, I will do as you ask. Now, try to eat something to build your strength."

Hawkins refused to eat the food Elise had brought, but she gratefully drank the cherry-leaf tea.

The Kalmyks moved about the other side of the yurt as necessary, but respectfully. Elise realized only later that they had understood better than she that this was a death-bed.

The old servant was soon exhausted and fell into a light sleep. The yurt grew dark. Only the small fire in the center lit the interior. The Kalmyk family retired to their rugs, and Elise, too, wrapped herself in her burka. Before she drifted off to sleep, she thought of sending a message to the ataman, but decided against it. Why should she make herself easy to find for the ataman or the Tartar?

From time to time during the night, Elise roused herself to check on Hawkins. Each time, the woman seemed to be sleeping comfortably. And Elise slept again with a light, dreamless sleep that left her partly aware of time's passing and of the noises around her. Toward early morning, she heard a noise—a roar—then felt a jerk of her burka as she was dragged from her sleeping place.

## ❧ 13 ❧

# Death Ride

Elise felt herself suddenly hoisted into the cold air.

"So this is where you've been."

At first she didn't recognize the roar.

She struggled to free herself from the burka and from the powerful grip on the collar of her caftan. She struck out at her assailant, but he held her at arm's length. She felt like a helpless pup held by the scruff of the neck.

"Don't you ever do that again," Nikholai commanded in a voice that thundered. A storm flashed in his gray eyes.

Astonished, Elise stared at him. His pale cheeks were shadowed with a day's growth of beard, and his light eyes were underlined by dark circles.

"Let go of me," she said, struggling against his hold. Abruptly he released her. She dropped to the floor on all fours and scrambled away from him. He loomed over her, large and angry, his mustache set in a fierce line. The old Kalmyk warrior stood at the flap where he had just admitted the Cossack ataman. He grinned at Elise. Enjoyment of the scene sparkled in his eyes.

Aware of the audience, the ataman was forced to kneel before Elise to pursue their conversation in some privacy.

"You will not sleep away from me," he said in Polish so he could not be understood.

"I won't? Why?" she demanded, still too sleepy to remember why she was angry with him.

"You won't because it's part of the bargain," he declared.

"Ah, the bargain," she said with a bitterness in her voice that even she could hear. Now she remembered. "It's part of the bargain unless I'm gambled away to the Tartar."

Defiant and indignant, she put her hands on his chest and shoved him away from her. From the expression on his face, she thought for a moment that he was going to slap her.

Instead, as if he were trying to gain control of some emotion, he passed his hand over his face. She tried to edge away from him, but he leaned toward her.

"Leave the Tartar to me," was all he said finally. He looked away from her to the figure lying on the rug beside them.

"Is this Hawkins? Is she improved?" he asked before Elise could say anything else.

He leaned over Hawkins and gently placed a hand on her cheek. Elise watched and wondered how the ataman could shake her until her teeth rattled, then turn to a sick woman and be as caring and gentle as a new mother.

He turned to Elise with a questioning look.

"What is it?"

He put his hand against Hawkins' throat. Then he shook his head. "She's dead."

"No. I just checked her and she was sleeping peacefully," Elise said. "It's just that she's very weak." She placed her hand on Hawkins' throat. The old woman's skin was cool, dry, almost cold to her touch. She felt no pulse.

"No," Elise repeated, hysteria rising. She was unable to stop it. Hawkins couldn't be dead. She was just in a deep sleep. She couldn't be dead, Elise's heart screamed. "No!"

"Stop it." The ataman's tone was firm, almost a warning. "Mitka wouldn't cry over an old foreign woman's death." He took Elise by the elbows and drew her away from the dead woman.

Elise choked back a sob, but tears filled her eyes. "I know." She nodded, and the tears began to fall.

"She asked for a Christian burial. It's all she asked for."

"Perhaps the old Kalmyk will take care of it," the ataman said. He cast a glance around at the Kalmyk family. They sat quietly, respectfully, in the presence of grief. Gently he told Elise, "Say your farewells to your friend now. We can't stay here much longer without stirring suspicions among the Cossacks."

He rose from Elise's side and took the old Kalmyk warrior outside with him.

Tenderly Elise washed Hawkins' face with the now cool aromatic towels and tried to neaten her hair. With a comb offered by the Kalmyk woman, she arranged Hawkins' hair and wondered how many times Hawkins had performed this service for her and Anna. She sat alone for a few moments, saying the silent farewell she had not been allowed to say to her brother or to her husband. It gave her some grim consolation.

At last Elise whispered, "I promise you I will find Anna." She then returned the comb to the Kalmyk woman with a gesture of thanks, gathered her burka, and left.

When she emerged from the yurt, she took a deep breath and let the icy air clear her head. In the east the faded pink horizon marked dawn. The sky above glowed dove gray and the wind was steady. It was a fitting day for death, Elise thought.

The ataman joined her. "The Kalmyk will purchase a coffin, dig a grave, mark it with a cross, and ask the brother from the Medveditsa monastery who came to camp last night to tend to Hawkins' burial."

"Is there no priest near?" Elise asked. She was unable to keep the disappointment from her face and voice. "Can the old man be trusted?"

"The Kalmyks are independent but honest," the ataman replied. "When they deal with Cossacks anyway. And since the plague, there are few priests on the steppe, Countess. It is the best we can do even for our own."

She nodded. They walked away from the Kalmyk camp.

"There you are, Ataman," the Tartar called. He strode up to them and winked lewdly at the Cossack. "I looked for you at Danilo Lemkov's cottage, but he told me neither of you slept there last night. Find a nice love nest down by the river?" he asked in a low voice so the other Cossacks about couldn't overhear him.

Elise watched the cold breeze ruffle the fur trim of his hat.

"It must have been a rewarding night, Ataman," the Tartar added. "You both look like you tussled with the devil himself." The oily Tartar laughed at his own joke, baring his yellow teeth. "You don't look ready to meet my challenge today."

"I'll be ready, Tartar."

"Good. For I'm eager to regain my fortune and to enjoy Mitka's services," he said as he turned and strode off in the direction of the horses. He laughed again.

"What challenge?" Elise asked, stopping the ataman with a hand on his arm as he started toward the stable.

"The Tartar challenged me to a horse race to settle the final score between us."

"What score?"

"He accused me of cheating at dice," he said, refusing to look at her.

"Did you cheat?"

The ataman shrugged. "I always play to win."

A sense of doom crept over Elise's feelings. "Couldn't we just leave now?" she asked with a hand still on his arm. He looked down at her, disbelief plain in his face.

"There's no reason to stay now," she explained. "Hawkins is . . . gone. Let's just leave. Just ride out now. There's no reason for this race."

"Run from a Tartar who challenged me before Razin and other Cossacks of the Don? No. Never," the ataman declared. "We race at noon as agreed. You will stand among those who watch."

As noon neared, Nikholai groomed Sultan. The stallion switched his tail and stamped his hooves as if he scented a race on the wind. When the ataman finished his work, Elise began to gather the combs, brushes, rags, and hoof-cleaning tools into a wooden bucket.

As Elise worked, the ataman walked away with a Don Cossack in deep conversation about Sultan's fine qualities. She soon became aware of the Tartar's approach. With his saddle in his arms, he grinned at her. His tattered yellow khalat belled in the breeze, his wrinkled breeches were splattered with mud, and his boots were caked with dung. Bucket in hand, Elise backed away until she stood with her shoulders against the big blood bay's glistening neck.

The Tartar dropped his saddle to the ground and set his hands on his hips. He took a step back and judged Sultan's lines as if he were measuring his opponent. The wagering crowd was too far away to hear his words to her. "I'll ride you tonight, Mitka," he said, without looking at her. "I should have done it before, when I wanted, but I let that old merchant appeal to my greed. But I'll have you tonight, and you'll know your place beneath a man, and you'll like it." Only then did he turn to leer at her.

Elise felt her skin crawl. She turned as Sultan jostled her elbow—only it wasn't Sultan, it was the ataman. His expression was surprisingly calm.

"You must be a sweet ride, Mitka, and worth a good race, because the ataman doesn't want to give you up," the Tartar taunted in the face of the Cossack's stare. The ataman's eyes were unusually light and clear.

Elise looked from the ataman to the Tartar, then back at the ataman. Her hands and feet turned cold, and her eyes widened. She knew now why they called him Wolf. She saw death there in the light of his eyes, the cold gray of a stalking wolf.

Elise tried to release her breath, but a gasp came out instead of a sigh. The ataman's gaze fell on her briefly, but she was sure he didn't really see her. He turned and mounted Sultan in a smooth, sure motion.

With growing anxiety Elise watched him. She was responsible for this race, this challenge, this duel. As much as she wanted to believe this was merely Tartar against Cossack, it wasn't. It was the ataman against her enemy. For some reason, he had taken up her cause. She didn't know why, but she could not leave him alone with it.

Confidently the Tartar laughed and saddled his horse, with careful attention to a leopardskin blanket that didn't lie smooth, Elise noticed. When he reached for the saddle horn to mount, the ugly hinged whip dangled from his right wrist.

The Tartar turned his horse toward the starting line.

"I want to race too," Elise suddenly declared.

Both riders turned in disbelief to the woman dressed as a boy who stood between them.

"No," Nikholai said flatly in Polish. "This is between the Tartar and me."

The Tartar could only stare.

"No, it's not," Elise said, turning her back to the Tartar. "This monster killed my brother and sold my sister into slavery. I want to know what justice is meted out. If you refuse to let me race with you, then I'll follow you. You will not face him alone. You cannot deny me this."

Shouts from the Cossacks gathered at the starting line made the ataman, Elise, and the Tartar turn to see Stenka Razin stride up to the paddock. Danilo Lemkov, Filka, and Alena followed the flamboyant giant. The rebel's wide black pants flapped in the cold wind. As he twisted one side of his mustache between his forefinger and thumb, the gold rings on his fingers flashed even in the dull light of the cloudy noonday.

"Cossack. Tartar. Are you ready to race?" Razin boomed in a deep voice.

"We're ready, but the boy is a problem," the ataman explained with an indulgent smile. "Lemkov, would you hobble him? He seems to think he should be allowed to race because his services are at stake."

Amid shouts of laughter, Elise was seized and tied to the fence with a hobble rope. Straining against the horsehair rope, she turned to watch Razin walk to the starting line. He stood before the two racers, his legs apart, his arms raised, his red-and-gold caftan flapping in the cold December wind. High in his right hand he held a red leather purse heavy with coins and gems.

"The race is for five rounds of the course," Razin announced. "You both know it. No weapons allowed. Is either of you armed?" he demanded. The riders denied carrying weapons. Elise was certain they both lied.

"Good," Razin said. "So the first horse and rider across this line where I stand at the end of the fifth round wins this purse and the services of Mitka for two days. Agreed?" He shook the purse, and the coins jingled musically.

The riders agreed, gazes fixed on Razin and the purse.

Both horses pranced in anticipation as Cossacks cheered their approval. Without further discussion, Razin lowered his arms. The horses plunged across the starting line on either side of him.

Elise watched the ataman let the Tartar take the lead, and wondered at his planning. The racers dashed down the gentle slope of the hill, across the low end of the shallow valley, and disappeared up the draw at the base of the hill on the far side. Dust wafted back in the faces of the Cossack spectators, who already were placing new bets on the basis of who sprang away from the starting line first.

Elise tugged on her restraints again. Then she felt foolish when she realized that no one was watching her and that the knots weren't even drawn tight. She went to work on the rope with her teeth. By the time she had managed to pull one knot loose, she heard the horses come thundering over the far hill again. She turned to see the pair of racers hurtle past the starting line. The ataman had lost his cap, and she thought she saw a red welt across his face. The Tartar still raced ahead, making ample use of his whip. Elise worked frantically at the rope.

When she pulled free, she tucked the hobble rope into her sash and ran toward Sotnik. She still didn't know what she intended to do. But whatever the outcome, she would be there.

She yanked the hobble from Sotnik's forelegs and threw herself across the dun's back. She dug her heels into the surprised animal's sides and he struck out across the valley after the racers.

If Nikholai had had any doubts about killing the Tartar, they disappeared when the infidel lashed him across the face with the hinged whip. As soon as they were out of sight of the Cossacks on the first round of the course, the yellow-faced heathen had caught Nikholai full in the face with it. Nikholai had silently cursed himself for not being better prepared for the assault.

After they had completed one round of the course and were beyond the sight of the spectators again, Nikholai steadily eased the full-striding Sultan against the Tartar's horse. The sturdy but smaller horse could only yield. They plunged off course into the rocky, tree-lined creek. Sprays of water showered them.

The angry Tartar turned on Nikholai again with the whip. This time the ataman caught it with his right hand, jerked it from the infidel's grasp, and threw it aside. The Tartar shouted something, but Nikholai didn't trouble himself to understand. He urged Sultan against the Tartar's horse again, forcing horse and rider out of the creek and toward the steep hillside. He intended to put the course well behind them.

The horses crashed through thick underbrush and just beneath the low limbs of scrub trees. Nikholai and the Tartar had to lie close to their horses' necks to avoid being swept off their mounts by the limbs. Nikholai pressed the Tartar's horse relentlessly until they cleared the brush and started up the hillside.

The horses leapt powerfully from one rocky ledge, up to the next and the next, urged on by their determined riders. At the crest, the Tartar turned toward the river, as Nikholai had wanted. They raced the length of the ridge, neck and neck. The horses' heads bobbed with each reaching stride, their ears flattened against their heads and their nostrils flared. Horses and riders drank of the cold wind until their lungs ached.

Again Nikholai let the Tartar take a slight lead. Even in a race, he didn't trust that devil dog at his back.

Seeing a clear course ahead, the Tartar turned an evil grin on Nikholai and pulled a saber from beneath his saddle blanket. The Tartar brandished the short but lethal blade and slashed the air above him. Then he gave the shrill reverberating war cry of the Tartars. Chills prickled down Nikholai's back. He cursed. He had armed himself with only a knife.

As soon as Elise rounded the base of the hill and started into the draw, the crash of animals charging through underbrush told her where they were. Sotnik responded well to her leg commands. At her urging he leapt off the trail toward the creek.

The creek water was still muddy and lapped its banks. As she watched the sand and rock to see where the riders had left the creek, something caught her eye. She made Sotnik circle back and she jumped down to retrieve the Tartar's whip. She stuck it into her boot top and pulled the horsehair hobble rope from her sash to rig a sort of bridle—the rope over Sotnik's poll, across his nose, and looped through his mouth. Even that would give her greater maneuverability than leg control alone.

She vaulted aboard Sotnik's bare back again and urged him up ledge after ledge behind the Cossack and the Tartar. Then she heard the Tartar's battle cry rend the air. As Elise reached the crest, she saw something flash silver and disappear over the end of the ridge. She pressed Sotnik on, but when she reached the end of the ridge, she regretted her haste.

The ground fell away to a steep rocky embankment. Without a twitch of an ear, Sotnik leapt over the edge. Too late to do anything else, Elise leaned back to help Sotnik keep his balance as he plunged downward.

Vague memories nagged at her of Yergov's telling her and her brothers about strange things the Cossacks sometimes trained their horses to do. Plunging headlong down an embankment seemed to be one of them. Sotnik's hooves struck and shattered rocks, sending shards of stones flying through the air. Sotnik dodged a sapling, leapt a fallen log, but never broke his stride.

Ahead, at the bottom of the bank, Elise saw Sultan go down, then struggle to his feet. In a cloud of dust she saw the ataman leap upon the stallion's back as the blood bay regained his footing. Swinging his saber over his head, the Tartar whirled his little brown horse around to charge the ataman. Elise forgot to grasp Sotnik's mane as she recognized the menace. She pulled the whip from her boot and pressed Sotnik on.

She emerged on the tow road between the ataman and the charging Tartar. She heard the ataman curse. She ignored him. Sotnik needed only a nudge of her leg to turn him toward the Tartar. Elise rode down on the infidel, twirling the whip over her head as she had seen him do. She caught the Tartar across the side of the face. His fur-trimmed turban flew off, and his head snapped to the side.

Elise ducked the saber, but it sliced off the first section of the whip. She rode quickly beyond the Tartar's reach and turned to see the infidel continue his charge on the ataman. The Cossack pulled his knife from his boot. As the Tartar passed him, he ducked the saber and cut the Tartar's bridle reins. Elise heard the Tartar bellow with rage. She saw him bring his horse about and swing the saber again. The Cossack dodged it and pulled Sultan away.

Elise, now ahead of them on the tow road, turned Sotnik around and started back toward them. The Tartar, concerned about being caught between them, galloped his brown pony off down the tow road.

Angrily Nikholai turned on Elise. He did not want her to be part of this. "Go back. Now!" he ordered, with little hope that she would obey.

"No," was all she said as she pressed Sotnik after the Tartar.

Nikholai cursed her, the infidel, the river, the winter weather, and anything that came to mind as he spurred Sultan after them. Now, not only did he have to deal with a Tartar who was better armed than he, he had to worry about her too.

He wanted to be between the Tartar and Elise if the infidel decided to turn and charge again. Nikholai knew the absence of reins would divert the infidel for only a time. Like Cossacks, the Tartars could manage their horses well with only leg commands.

As Nikholai gained on Elise, he saw the Tartar ahead of her. In a quick move the infidel pulled the useless bridle off over the ears of his galloping horse and threw it back into Elise's face. She ducked and continued her pursuit. Nikholai urged Sultan to draw ahead of Sotnik.

The Tartar led the way from the tow road through another small valley and up onto another ridge. He was headed for high ground, and Nikholai knew what the heathen was up to.

"Stop, go back," he shouted at Elise as he pulled Sultan back even with her. "This is a death ride."

"I know," she shouted at him, never taking her gaze from the Tartar ahead.

"No, you don't," Nikholai shouted, and pressed Sultan's

shoulder against Sotnik's so that the dun slowed and drifted to the side.

"Stop it," Elise shouted, and brandished the now-shortened Tartar whip. There was no doubt about the determination in her eyes.

Before either of them could say more, they saw the Tartar ahead of them stop and turn. They halted. The heathen made an obscene gesture and shouted something Nikholai hoped Elise didn't understand.

"Just once, do as I ask and stay where you are," Nikholai ordered as he reined Sultan away from her. He wanted the Tartar to attack him, not Elise. But he moved away slowly, at an angle, toward the Tartar. If the heathen rode toward Elise, Nikholai could still intercept him. The Tartar's gaze followed him, as he had hoped.

Suddenly the Tartar shrieked his battle cry and lunged toward Nikholai, who whirled Sultan around toward the river as the Tartar charged after him.

Elise started at the sound of the battle cry. It was uncannily familiar yet alien. Fear bloomed in the pit of her stomach as she watched the ataman put his heels to Sultan. The blood bay reared back on his hind legs, then bounded straight for the Tartar. The Tartar swung his blade down, missed the ataman but caught the Cossack's shoulder on the upward swing.

Elise's heart stopped. She swallowed a scream. Sultan's next leap took Nikholai beyond the Tartar's reach again.

Still screeching his battle cry, the Tartar pursued the ataman along the ridge away from her. She prodded Sotnik to follow. She saw Nikholai ride over a small crest and disappear beyond. The Tartar followed.

Determined not to be left behind, and certain that nothing could be worse than plunging headfirst down the steep embankment, Elise pressed Sotnik into a headlong gallop. As she crested the small rise, she saw the ground disappear from beneath her.

The western horizon stretched out before them and the icy cold river spread itself below. Elise screamed and pulled back on the makeshift bridle. But it was too late. The rope offered too little control to stop the gelding from diving off the cliff.

## ❧ 14 ❧

# Vengeance Is Never Enough

In that eternal moment while Elise and Sotnik plummeted through the air toward the muddy gray river below, she recalled the thing that had nagged at her as she descended the embankment on the dun earlier. When Yergov had told of Cossacks who trained their horses to dive off cliffs, she and her brothers had laughed. How would you ever train a horse to do that or find anyone foolish enough to ride such a horse? they had asked. Yergov had shaken his head solemnly and replied that sometimes such feats were required.

Elise closed her eyes against the sight of the sheer drop. She clamped Sotnik beneath her and entwined the fingers of both hands in his mane. Then she prayed that they would clear the rocks and Nikholai and Sultan below.

The impact with the water nearly unseated her. Her feet stung through her boots. Her face burned. A sharp pain shot through her right side, and she wondered whether she had reinjured the mended rib. But her grasp on Sotnik's mane was good even though her hands were numb from the cold. The water closed over her head. She felt Sotnik do a gentle buck as his forefeet struck the river bottom and his back legs gave them a powerful push upward.

176

When they surfaced, the dun snorted once and swam confidently against the current toward the island ahead. She shook the water from her eyes and saw the ataman and Sultan disappear around the lower end of the island. Sotnik struck shore and sprang forward after his stablemate. Elise found her seat again and grabbed the hobble-rope reins as Sotnik charged up the bank.

The icy December wind struck her. Elise ignored the chill, threw off her heavy sheepskin vest, and urged Sotnik on. As she rounded the lower end of the island, she saw Nikholai ahead of the Tartar, moving upriver along the island's sandy bank. Elise and Sotnik followed, gaining rapidly.

Suddenly the ataman turned and charged the Tartar. The infidel raised his saber. The ataman threw himself against the stout man's chest and unseated him before the blade swept down. Together they fell, struggling to the sand, the ataman on top. They rolled into the water. The horses shied away. The Cossack grasped the Tartar's sword hand, but the Tartar's grip on the saber never loosened. With his free hand the Tartar landed a stunning blow to the ataman's temple. The Cossack disappeared underwater.

In the splash and spray, Elise couldn't see clearly what was happening. She understood that, wounded and with only a knife for a weapon, it was to Nikholai's advantage to force the fight at close quarters.

Elise approached slowly. The Tartar rose out of the knee-deep water and with a two-fisted grip swung the curved saber over his head. Once again he shrieked his battle cry.

Elise forgot that she was on the Don. She saw the flash of the blade against the bright blue sky of an October day. The Dnieper River shimmered in the late-afternoon sun, and the air was filled with battle cries and death screams. William was about to die at the hand of the Tartar, and this time she could stop it. She kicked Sotnik into a charge and dived at the Tartar. She grabbed his saber arm and threw all her weight against him. She didn't see Nikholai roll clear of the saber's reach.

Both Tartar and Elise tumbled into the deeper water. The current tugged at her clothes. Elise went under, but she didn't care. She clung to the Tartar like a dog at a bear's throat. The Tartar pulled at her grip, trying to peel away her fingers. Her grip was fast. Finally, with great effort the Tartar rose from the water and flung Elise away from him against the riverbank. Her own body weight loosened her grip. She thudded heavily against the sand. Pain shot through her ribs. She groaned.

Saber held to his side, the Tartar grabbed for her, but Elise managed to scramble upriver just out of his reach. She collapsed on the sand, her breath coming in ragged gasps, her hand on her side, trying to ease the pain. The renewed chill of the wind brought her back to the present. She glanced around to find Nikholai.

Relief flooded over her when she saw him on his feet. He stood knife in hand downriver from her, still in easy reach of the armed Tartar. Nikholai's curls were plastered against his forehead above the red welt from the Tartar's whip cut. Eyes still light and calm, he kept his gaze on the Tartar's saber. Elise watched in horror as a bloody stream coursed down his arm and dripped from his fist.

"She's mine now, Ataman," the Tartar boasted over his shoulder to the wounded Cossack. Elise stared up at the laughing Tartar. Beads of water glittered in his stringy beard, and his eyes gleamed maniacally. She had no doubt that he intended to kill them both. The weak one first—her. The Tartar took another step toward her, and she backed away an equal distance. Again she glanced past him at Nikholai.

This time the ataman's gaze was intent on her. He was telling her what to do, and she understood. She didn't like it, but she understood. She looked back at the Tartar and gave an imperceptible nod to Nikholai.

"I don't think you are man enough to make me yours," she taunted in Cossack. She rose unsteadily to her feet. Painfully she straightened herself to a full stance. Then without warning she slashed the remnant of the whip across the Tartar's face. Surprised, the dripping-wet heathen glowered. He turned away from her slightly to glance at the Cossack on his left. Nikholai remained motionless, clutching his arm.

"Don't you understand insults, you bloody damned heathen?" Elise shouted in English to his face. She made an obscene gesture. The Tartar laughed.

Elise stepped forward and slashed him across the face a second time. "If you want me, come and get me," she taunted again, and jabbed him in the belly with the whip end. The Tartar roared and grabbed the whip.

For a moment Elise's wrist was caught in the handle loop. She yanked once. She was still caught. The Tartar started to laugh. Panic rising, she yanked again and was free. She turned to dash across the island. The wet sand offered poor footing. She stumbled once and clutched her side to protect it, but she didn't fall. She managed to regain her pace and ran toward the higher part of the island.

She glanced back once to see the Tartar, saber held high, gaining on her. She jumped over a water-washed log but caught her foot on a limb. She fell to the far side. The saber blade thudded into the wet wood just above her head.

Elise forgot the pain in her side and jumped to her feet again as the Tartar worked the blade free of the sodden log.

She managed to run a few more feet. Her lungs ached. Cold air burned her throat, and pain shot through her side with every step. She fell again and heard his footsteps behind her.

As Elise turned to look up at the Tartar, she realized that to retreat farther was useless. Still on hands and knees, she stared up at the heathen. With surprisingly little emotion she watched him swing the blade over his head. She pressed her right side to ease the pain and sat back on her heels to face him.

She saw the fine-honed edge of the well-tempered blade gleam against the gray winter sky. A good day for death, she remembered thinking earlier. She studied the glittering bronze filigree on the hilt in the Tartar's dirty hands. The blade looked so sharp that the blow might be painless, she thought. She hoped for William's sake that it was. She caught the Tartar's gaze and held it. She forced herself to watch the lust for killing that shone in his narrow eyes. The sight made her sick, but to look away would betray everything.

The Tartar threw back his head to loose his horrible battle

cry. The air throbbed with the howl. Elise never took her gaze from his face. His cry rasped into a gurgle.

Only then did Elise close her eyes to shut out the sight. The Tartar's hot blood spurted across her. It sprayed on her hair, across her face, down the front of her shirt, even onto her hands as Nikholai's knife plunged deep into the infidel's throat. The saber thudded to the sand. The Tartar's body sagged in Nikholai's arms, and he threw it across the log away from Elise.

Immediately Elise turned to the river and was sick. She felt turned inside out and filthy. She wanted to wash everything away in the river—the sight, the smell, the feel. A strong arm grasped her collar and dunked her into the water.

"Did you have to let the devil get so close to you?" Nikholai shouted as he pulled her out of the water, then angrily dunked her again.

"No. Yes. I don't know," Elise sputtered as he pulled her out the second time. She pulled away from him and began to splash water on her blouse in a frenzied effort to get rid of the bloodstains.

He said no more but clasped her to him in a strong one-armed embrace. She leaned against him and could feel his heart beating rapidly, yet stronger and steadier than hers. Then she realized she was shaking.

"It's all right, Green Eyes. He's dead. He's gone," the ataman assured her. He still held her tightly.

"But it's too late," she cried. "William's dead. It's too late."

"I know," he said. "That's the flaw in vengeance. It comes too late."

She leaned against him, content to let him hold her, satisfied with the pressure of his chin against the top of her head.

The sound of horses made them look upriver. Cantering along the tow road as if out for a leisurely ride, she saw a party of three mounted Cossacks. Razin rode in the lead.

The ataman pushed her away. "Here, put this on," he said, taking off his vest. "It seems we've been missed."

"Nikholai, your arm—"

"That I can explain," the ataman said as he held out the

180

vest to her. She didn't understand the reason for the hint of a smile that he gave her. "But I don't want to explain the bindings that show through your wet blouse."

"What do we tell them? Is this murder?" Elise asked. She shrugged into the vest he gave her, then pulled off her wet sash and began to bind his arm.

"Let me do the talking. The Tartar wasn't in favor with Razin when the race started." He winced when she jerked a tight knot in the sash.

"Neither were you," she reminded him. They turned to face the rebel leader.

Elise's burka flapped about her knees as she stood with her head bowed beside Hawkins' grave. The winter sun hung low over the steppe, its feeble rays filtering through a thin blanket of clouds. Sunset was still two hours away, but the day had cooled. Behind her the horses lifted their noses to scent the cold west wind. Elise could smell the snow on it.

One grave before her was marked with a Tartar lance and the other with a Christian cross made of sticks lashed together.

How ironic, she thought as she pulled her burka closer about her, that Hawkins should be buried next to the very heathen who had wreaked this havoc on all their lives.

Elise's side ached dully despite the dry bindings the ataman had helped her to tie after Mistress Lemkova had seen to his arm. Elise felt tired, empty, sorry that she couldn't do better for Hawkins. Though exhausted, she was more determined than ever that her search for Anna must go on.

But nothing more would be learned here. Razin had banished them from Kagalnik for killing his ally, the Tartar. Elise suspected he was also annoyed because Nikholai refused to pledge Vazka to the rebel cause.

She said a short prayer, crossed herself, and walked to where the ataman and the horses patiently waited. With his help she mounted the dun gingerly. In silence he swung up on Sultan and led the way north toward Vazka.

They rode with only the jingle of the bridles and the hoofbeats of Sultan and Sotnik for company. The sting of the winter wind grew sharper. Twice, dry flurries of snow drifted across their path. The steppe was succumbing to winter.

Elise envisioned the warmth of Natalia's cottage. A fire would blaze in the oven, warming the rooms and cooking tasty food. It would not be home, but it would be a good place to be. If only she had Anna with her, but Vazka was in the wrong direction.

Elise looked over her shoulder toward the south. That's where she would learn what she needed to know. When she turned back, she saw the ataman watching her, his expression unreadable. She waited for him to take the reins from her, to tie her wrists to the saddle horn, but he didn't.

"I still want to go to Cherkassk, Ataman," she called to him as he rode ahead of her.

"I know," he replied over his shoulder. "I've decided there is an additional price for going to Cherkassk."

*"What?"* Elise shouted. She urged Sotnik forward to Sultan's side.

Nikholai smiled when he saw the irritation and disbelief flashing in her eyes. The terror of the death ride was clearly forgotten. He watched her cover her outrage. She sat back in the saddle and regarded him soberly.

"Do you jest, Ataman?"

"Oh, no, Countess. What is a trip to Cherkassk worth?"

He watched her casting about for an answer. She hesitated only a moment.

"Oh, Ataman, how can I hope to deal with you? You have years of experience in horse trading, in dealing with dishonest tax collectors and wily Gypsies. How could I ever hope to secure a fair trade from so shrewd and astute—"

"Spare me the flattery, Countess. What is it worth?"

"I don't know what you want of me," she said, almost wailing in her frustration. "Tell me. Whatever it is, I'll do it."

Satisfied that she was sincere, he told her, "When we return to Vazka, I want you to dress and behave like a Cossack maid."

"What? Dress like one of the village women?"

"I'm asking you to put as much effort into appearing to be a woman of Vazka as you put into being a boy of Kagalnik."

"Oh. And if I do this," she said, avoiding his gaze, "you will take me to Cherkassk?"

"Yes."

"When?"

"I can't say for certain when," he replied.

"But time is important. Anna may be ill, as Hawkins was."

"I realize that," Nikholai said, now watching the road before them, "but I have responsibilities I must see to first." He cast a quick glance in her direction before he went on. "Is it so much to ask, Green Eyes, for you to wear a woman's fine linens and embroidered blouses and skirts? Do you like boys' clothes so well?"

"I don't see how dressing as a Cossack woman will be of any advantage," she said. "Vazka's people don't welcome me as one of them. Why should I dress like them?"

He sighed and shook his head in exasperation. "If the Muscovites find you in Vazka, do you think you would be the only one to suffer? Put yourself at risk if you wish, Countess, but I won't let you endanger Vazka," he said, angered now. Her stubbornness was intolerable. "I can always have you tied and gagged and locked in the tack room."

He had not intended that as a serious threat, but he saw that she took it as one. She turned immediately still and pale. She looked so shaken that he had to resist the desire to tell her that he doubted Natalia or Kasyan would allow him to confine her if he tried. But he remained silent and watched her bravely lift her chin and take a deep breath.

"I will agree to this outrageous bargain only if you promise to take me to Cherkassk by Christmas," she said through bared teeth.

"Agreed," he said with a nod. "The earlier bargain still holds, of course. No escape attempts."

"Agreed," she said, staring at the road before them.

The snowflakes collected on her eyelashes. Nikholai watched her as she brushed them away. He hoped she had truly forgotten about the death ride. He wanted no more bad dreams for her.

"We'll have to find earrings for you, Green Eyes," he said, imagining her dressed as a maid. "Jade ones, I think. And fine linen for you to wear against your skin instead of these rough homespun towels." He reached across to tug at the bindings beneath her blouse.

"Will you be collecting payment on our other bargain tonight, Ataman?" she asked, eyeing him warily.

"Not tonight, Green Eyes," Nikholai said, still watching her. "There will be better nights for us to come together. Nights when you are not weary or sore. When your grief for your friend is not fresh."

They rode on in silence. Hoof-deep snow covered the steppe. The unshod Don ponies, their hooves grown long and curved, were frisky and surefooted despite the afternoon race.

Nikholai and Elise spent the night at the Vogol homestead and reached Vazka late the next afternoon.

# ❧ 15 ❧
# The Countess Is Dead

The frowning elders of Vazka's krug filed silently into the Fomin cottage and seated themselves on the benches.

When everyone was present, Ostap stood and read the letter from Leopold Polonsky addressed to the ataman and the krug.

The bleakness Elise saw in Nikholai's eyes made her heart ache for him, and she didn't understand why. Why should she take pity on this man who had tried to use her against her family? Momentarily he held her gaze across the roomful of men. Then he looked away.

"'I believe the Countess Elise Chatham Polonsky died with her husband, my uncle, and with her brother William in the Tartar massacre. Therefore, I refuse to pay ransom. You may present pretenders to me, as is your sly Cossack way, but I will never believe the countess could have survived the Tartars' vicious attack,'" Ostap read. "He signs it 'Count L. Polonsky.'"

Elise saw Nikholai glance at her with a new light of understanding in his eye.

Ostap put the letter down and looked around the room. The krug members sat erect, arms folded across their chests, faces stern. No one puffed on a pipe or drank from a cup or scuffled his feet.

Still dressed in her boys' clothes, Elise stood in the doorway with Natalia. There had not been time to comply with the ataman's request that she dress as a maid. Ostap had met them at the gate with the letter.

Elise was not surprised by its contents, but she was surprised to learn that the ataman had written to Oscar's nephew. She had assumed he had written only to her brothers. If she had known about the letter to Leopold, she could have warned Nikholai. Would that have changed anything? she wondered. The ataman had been a man bent on revenge when he sent out those dispatches.

"This means we have risked our safety to keep this Lyakh for ransom, and now we find that no one will pay for her," Vikola announced. The stocky Zaporozhie stood up and walked around the table. The krug watched him.

"We have still to hear from her brothers," Nikholai pointed out. He did not look at Elise.

"Do you believe her brothers care what happens to her?" Vikola asked. "Perhaps they agree with the new count. But that's not all. You go off to talk with the great Stenka Razin without consulting the krug. You admit that he welcomed you and invited Vazka to be an ally. Yet you refuse to let us join this great hero, who would throw off the yoke of the streltsy."

Mutters of agreement rumbled through the krug.

"Have you something to say to this, Nikholai?" Bogdan asked when the ataman did not respond to Vikola.

"I stand by my judgment of Stenka Razin," Nikholai said. "The war he wants may bring us defeat and a heavier yoke than the one we now bear."

"You may be content with your drove of horses, Ataman," Vikola said with a sneer. "The rest of us want more. We want our pay when it's due, and no tax on vodka. We want freedom from the threat of the streltsy."

Members of the krug nodded.

"The Don Host is working for all of those things for us," Nikholai explained. "These are not freedoms that can be acquired in a few hours, just as a war is not won in a day."

"That's not good enough," said Vikola. "The Host has said the same thing for years, and nothing has happened. Look at what Stenka Razin has done in two years. He has sailed the Caspian and brought Muscovite, Persian, and Turkish cities to their knees. This is a man who will make Tsar Alexis turn his ear toward the steppe and listen to the Cossacks when they speak."

More agreement from the krug members, noisily expressed this time. Then Ostap stood and spoke. "We want a new ataman, Nikholai Fomin. We want to follow Razin, and we need an ataman to lead us. One who is ready to fight. You have told us how you feel, and it is not what we want."

Elise followed Nikholai's slow survey of the room, from man to man. Some met his gaze. Some did not. Some coughed. Some shifted their weight on the bench. But none denied Ostap's request for a new leader. At last Nikholai nodded. "You are freemen. It is your right to elect the man you want to lead you."

Wearily he rose from his place at the table and walked to the corner where the ataman's staff stood, taller than he, decorated with the symbols of office and church. He set it before him. Elise watched Vikola's face brighten at the sight of it.

"This is the staff of Vazka's ataman," Nikholai said. "I surrender it to the krug, to be bestowed on the man who is elected by the free warriors of the village."

Bogdan, as the oldest, came forward to take the staff. He gave Nikholai an apologetic look.

Elise knew Vikola had plotted this, and she hated him for it. She was certain he had gone from krug member to krug member and had sowed the seeds of dissatisfaction or, at the very least, had provided the nourishment needed to make them grow. He had worked toward this end for some time—since well before she came to Vazka—but she could not dismiss a personal sense of guilt. Nikholai was losing his office as ataman because of her, because she had taken him away from Vazka when he should have been here to defend himself against this selfish man.

"Sound the drum for a meeting," Bogdan ordered.

In a noisy, almost festive commotion, krug members rose

from their seats and emptied the cottage. Nikholai stood alone in the corner of the room. He stared after them, his friends and allies. Only Kasyan lingered.

"Go on. You must choose too," Nikholai said with a gruff gesture of dismissal. Kasyan left.

Then he turned on Elise. "And you. Change your clothes and stay out of sight until we see how this is going to be settled." With that, he grabbed his own cap and left the cottage.

Elise followed him out the door as soon as she was certain he wouldn't look back. She ignored Natalia's protests.

The booming of the drum continued for some time, even though every Cossack warrior of Vazka was already gathered in the church square. The noisy men tramped about in the virgin snow and gradually formed a great circle several bodies deep. With little regard for the falling snow, they speculated on the reason for the meeting. As inconspicuously as she could, Elise walked along the edge of the circle, hoping to find a place where she could witness the election. Suddenly a firm hand seized her elbow.

"What are you doing here?" Kasyan demanded in a hushed undertone. "Women are barred from these meetings."

"I'm not a woman. I'm Mitka," Elise replied immediately. She pulled her cap on. "Besides, what about them?" She gestured to the clusters of village women who had gathered before their cottages to watch the meeting from afar. Snow had already covered their shawls in white. Daria was there. Her eyes grew wide as she recognized Elise in boys' clothes.

Kasyan looked at the women, then back at Elise. "Then stay by my side," he ordered. With his hand still on her elbow, he guided her around the edge of the circle to a position where they could see his father, Bogdan, with the staff of office, and the other krug members enter the circle.

The election seemed to be more an occasion to debate than a time to vote. Again and again, a Cossack warrior came forward to say how he wanted to ride against the Muscovites with Razin.

Finally Vikola Panko was nominated by Ostap. Vikola, who had remained standing at the back of the group of elders, came forward as if he had nothing to do with the proceedings. He took off his cap. Snow settled on his dark mustache and scalp lock, to contrast against his ruddy complexion and dark eyes.

"Is this not the man we need to lead us?" asked Ostap as the cheering of the Cossacks died. "Will we follow Vikola Panko?"

Shouts of accord echoed against the church wall and filled the snowy air.

Then a hush fell over the group as Bogdan offered the staff of office to Vikola. Vikola shook his head and refused it.

"Is this the tradition?" Elise asked. Kasyan nodded.

Again Bogdan offered the staff of office. Again Vikola refused. The third time the staff was offered, Vikola eagerly grasped it. War cries and shouts of triumph soared through the cold. Vikola held the staff aloft for all to see. Caps were thrown in the air, and men slapped each other on the back.

"What happens to Nikholai now?" Elise asked. "And to you?"

"We are warriors, freemen."

Barrels of vodka were rolled from the storeroom, and a celebration began.

"What is your first order as ataman?" Ostap asked. Members of the crowd grew quiet to hear their new ataman's first order.

"I set Nikholai Fomin to take night watchtower duty," Vikola said. "And I order him to surrender the Lyakh to me."

All voices died. Kasyan pulled Elise behind him before anyone could hear her strangled "No." She choked back her words and trembled all over.

Silently, respectfully, warriors on the other side of the circle parted for Nikholai. Elise had been unable to locate him earlier, but there he was, tall and proud as ever. Kasyan hushed her again.

Nikholai removed his cap and made a slight bow. Sparkling white snowflakes studded his dark curls, and he towered over the fierce Zaporozhie.

"I accept my duty as a warrior," Nikholai said. "I will watch from the tower as long as you order, Ataman Vikola Panko. But the countess is mine."

A deeper hush fell over the crowd.

"Do you defy your new ataman, Nikholai Fomin?" Vikola asked, stepping threateningly close to the taller man.

Nikholai stood his ground. "I appeal to you and the krug to reconsider your request for the countess," he said.

Snow drifted around them. Elise clutched at Kasyan's sleeve and realized she was biting her lip.

With authority, Bogdan stepped between the men. "The krug feels the captive should remain Nikholai Fomin's responsibility," the elder decreed. "She is worthless. Let her be sheltered under his roof."

Vikola opened his mouth to protest, but one look at the other krug members changed his mind. Reluctantly he said, "As you say. Let Nikholai Fomin feed and shelter her."

As relief flooded over Elise, she leaned against Kasyan. Over his shoulder, he gave her a small smile.

In the days that followed, Elise saw little of Nikholai. She had waited for him in his bed the first night. She did not want to be the one to break their agreement. But he never returned, even when she knew his watch was over. The next night she waited for him too, but again he stayed away. Natalia's only response to Elise's questions was, "He has to learn to live with this."

Upon Elise's request, Natalia helped her dress as a Cossack woman, accepting Elise's ability to speak Cossack without surprise, but she did give Elise a questioning look when she saw the St. Nikholas medal around her neck.

"Nikholai gave you this?"

"Yes," Elise said. "Before we rode into Kagalnik."

Natalia nodded her approval and said no more.

Completing her Cossack costume were an embroidered blouse, an apron, and a heavy three-piece skirt, bound together at the waist with a bright sash or girdle. Elise was satisfied that she looked as if she belonged in the village. But she could not bring herself to wear the head covering properly. Vanity won out over honor. She peered into Nikholai's shaving mirror, pushed the scarf back, and feathered curls across her brow.

Anna was often in her thoughts. Every time she buttoned a little girl's caftan or reminded a boy to wear his cap, she hoped that someone was doing the same for her little sister.

By the third day after the election, Elise wa
that Nikholai was avoiding her. Then, as she w
work with the horses, she realized that he avoided
He even had little to say to Kasyan. Did he feel s
ated or betrayed that he refused to speak to the villa    Or
was he angry? Men who had willingly followed him into
battle only a few weeks earlier had been quick enough to
elect themselves another ataman. She was the cause of much
of this, and he certainly had reason to be angry with her,
Elise thought. But she hated this coldness, this silence. She
would rather he shouted his anger.

The next morning, she went to the barn early, before she
fed the geese, before Natalia had food prepared. As Elise
had suspected, she found Nikholai asleep in an empty stall,
wrapped in his wolf-lined burka so that even his head was
covered.

"So this is where you've been sleeping," she said. "And I
was waiting for you in a warm, soft bed."

The hay rustled as the form under the burka moved.
"Ump," was the only response.

"You prefer to sleep with the horses?"

"Go away," came from the burka.

Elise walked into the stall and kicked a small, empty
vodka jug. "Is this why they call you Wolf?" she taunted,
determined to get some reaction. She kicked the booted
foot nearest her. "Because you slink away to lick your
wounds?"

He threw back the burka and glared up at her. His eyes
were bloodshot and a day's growth of beard shadowed his
jaw.

"Well?" she demanded.

She hardly had the word out of her mouth when he lunged
at her. He grabbed her ankle, pulled her down into the hay,
and pinned her there with his body.

"They call me Wolf because I eat maidens who wear their
head coverings improperly," he growled as he pulled the
scarf from her head and threaded his fingers through her
golden curls.

Startled, Elise didn't fight. She watched him, his gaze
intent on the curls caught in his fingers. She saw no anger in
his gray eyes, only pain, hunger, and need. She was unsure of

191

.. iat to say to him. His anger she could deal with. But faced with his pain, she was at a loss.

The warmth of his breath on her cheek and throat made her yearn to comfort him. When he kissed her, she put her arms around his neck and responded to his lips and tongue with demands of her own. Encouraged, Nikholai rolled over in the hay and pulled her atop him. She explored the firm warmth of his lips and the even feel of his teeth, and savored the erotic thrust of his tongue. He stroked her back, encouraging her to settle herself against him. He felt so warm and hard and needful, that with an instinctive feminine movement, she did.

"Wait," Nikholai said as he rolled her off him.

"What?" Elise watched him get up and leave the stall. Wasn't this what he wanted? She listened as Nikholai's footsteps stopped at the stable door. Maybe this was a mistake, she thought. She began to rise to follow him, when she heard the door bar drop into place, and she realized that he had every intention of accepting her unspoken offer.

When he came back, he spread the burka out on the hay. "Come," he said, and offered his hand. His expression was serious, intense. Faced with the consequences of her actions, Elise hesitated. Yet, there was the bargain and there was the hurt in his eyes.

She put her hand in his and brushed hay from her skirts before she joined him on the burka. Immediately he began to undress her. Off with her caftan, then her blouse and the red girdle of her skirt. He slipped her chemise off her shoulders, but he stopped when he saw the binding for her ribs.

"I don't really need this, but Natalia insisted," Elise assured him. She began to untie the bindings for him, but he brushed her hands away and finished the chore himself.

Then he removed his own shirt. Elise watched the play of his muscles across his ribs and chest as he pulled the shirt over his head. The wound the Tartar had given him was little more than an angry scar on his right arm. Fascinated with the beauty of him, she didn't think to cover herself against the cold. He laughed softly at her curious stare. Then he pulled her against him and began to rub her back soothingly.

Warm, tingling, life-giving blood flowed back into skin that had been tightly bound for several days. Elise sighed. With his hand on the back of her neck, he gently lowered her to the soft fur of the burka.

"A wolf starts with the throat," he whispered. And Elise gasped as he assaulted that vulnerable area with little searing kisses. His mustache tickled. He massaged her side, and each stroke of his hand shoved her chemise farther down over her hips. Softly he whispered soothing words to her, but they were unnecessary. She had little fear this time, and no desire to fight him or the new sensations he brought.

He pulled the burka over both of them, enveloping them in the soft warmth. Elise's world became Nikholai. She laced her fingers through his curly hair as he moved down her throat to her breasts. He massaged them, and they swelled beneath his hands until her nipples became sensitive to his lightest touch. Only then did he lower his mouth to one swollen bud, then the other. She felt his tongue on her breast and marveled at how the sensations seeped through her body.

His broad, warm hand caressed her belly, her thigh, then her mound, sending sweet warmth through her. She yielded willingly to his exploration. When he found her center, he used her own dew to caress her, drawing out each touch until Elise was aware of only the pleasurable burning and sweet ache of his lingering strokes. With his other hand on the small of her back, he kissed her belly—quick, hot, tickling kisses that made her conscious of her need for him.

She moved her hips against him and tugged on his hair to bring him back to her. His lips moved over her ribs, then her breasts. But he never stopped the stroking.

"I promise no pain this time," he whispered against her lips as he moved above her. Tenderly he filled her, making each thrust slow and pleasurable. She sighed with each sensation of sweet invasion. All the time, she was aware that he enjoyed a growing pleasure in this union too, yet she knew that his pleasure was different from hers. She heard him gasp and felt him shudder as he pressed himself into her. She held him firmly in her arms, but she felt oddly incomplete, sad. She was disappointed, and certain she had disappointed him somehow. He was still on her, his fingers tangled in her hair. Slowly his breath became steady and even.

When he moved on her again, he braced himself on his elbows so that he could peer into her face, but he did not withdraw.

"You keep yourself from me, Green Eyes," he whispered.

"How can you say that? I have given you everything."

"But you deny me the pleasure of your pleasure," he murmured as he leaned forward to nip her earlobe playfully.

"Perhaps I'm not the kind of woman who can share this," she offered. "What is that called, a cold woman? A woman without passion." Strangely, she didn't care what he said; she just wanted him to stay with her, in her. She closed her eyes and enjoyed the smell of him, of fine sweet tobacco and the scent that was Nikholai.

"You a cold, passionless woman, Green Eyes? I truly doubt that." He laughed against her neck, then kissed her lightly. "A woman without passion doesn't move her hips against her lover as you do, or know instinctively how to twine her legs about a man's. You only need more time, I think." He kissed her then, a long, penetrating kiss more intimate, demanding, and enticing than any before. Elise felt herself yield to the thrill. She felt his tongue—hard, challenging, and teasing—move over her lips and her own tongue. She met his challenge with her own exploration of his mouth. He groaned.

Without releasing her from the kiss, he pulled her hands from around his neck and stretched them out against the floor, her hands open in his. His weight pressed her into the clean hay, and she was powerless to resist him even if she had wanted to. Yet she was not uncomfortable under him. To her surprise, when he began to move inside her, his manhood was once again as hard and questing as before. She understood better now what he needed from her. She abandoned herself to the instinct to arch her body against his. To move her hips in rhythm with his.

Still he refused to release her from the kiss. His tongue thrust into her as rhythmically as his manhood. She felt totally consumed by him, locked in helpless pleasure, unable to please him or to find her own release.

When he took his mouth from hers, she gasped for air, for strength to stay with him, to reach heights he offered.

He kissed her brow and whispered, "Don't fight, Little Warrior. Let it come."

He slipped a hand beneath her buttocks and thrust deeper than before. Elise caught her breath and closed her eyes. She was beginning to understand. The pleasure he gave her with each movement was growing and building deep inside her. The sweet inner ache reached a hot needful glow. With one final thrust the glow burst and shattered into surging delight throughout her body. She did not hear her own soft cry of pleasure or see the satisfaction on Nikholai's face as he withdrew from her gently.

She let him pull her close. She laced her fingers through his chest hair and slept, but awoke moments later. Nikholai was trying to free himself from her grip.

"You hold so tight, Green Eyes," he assured her with a smile. "I'm not going anywhere." He pulled at her hand gently, and when he had freed it, he kissed her fingertips.

They lay quietly together, listening to the sounds of the village. A dog barked somewhere, and a child shouted laughter. A door slammed. A horse in the next stall snorted.

"You should have told me you were writing to Leopold," Elise said finally. "I would have warned you."

"I should have known myself," Nikholai replied. "How Leopold must have feared you. He saw you with the count and pictured a houseful of little heirs to deprive him of his uncle's title."

"Is that why he disliked me?" Elise asked. "I never thought of that. My brothers and I signed an agreement that we would lay no claim to the title or estates. And Oscar never came to my bed."

"But Leopold couldn't be sure of that," Nikholai concluded. "Now he makes his claim secure by declaring you dead."

"But I don't think James or Thomas would settle for that," Elise said. "I mean, they would honor our contract, but they would not ignore a ransom demand. You wrote to them?"

"Yes," Nikholai said, and shifted away from her a little.

He was relieved that she had not attacked him for trying to use her against the Polonsky family. What troubled him was whether to tell her the other news he had received—about her brother.

Along with the Host's dispatches had come a personal letter from his cousin in Cherkassk, Timofe Guska. Nikholai had chosen not to share its contents with the krug.

Timofe wrote, in response to Nikholai's request, that he had discovered, unofficially, that a James Chatham had sailed for the New World shortly after the count and Elise had departed from Warsaw. The Chathams were a respected diplomatic family, Timofe wrote, but he had uncovered nothing about Thomas Chatham.

Upon learning that news, Nikholai had brooded. How could her brother go off, leaving his sister in the protection of a frail old man with a nephew who wasn't to be trusted? He debated whether he should let her go on thinking her brother was about to appear at the gates of Vazka. Or should he tell her that it was unlikely anyone was coming for her?

He looked at her, and she gazed back, a soft smile on her lips, hay tangled in her hair, a womanly blush in her cheeks. No, he would not take her hope away. He kissed her lightly.

"You sleep in my bed every night," he said with a smile. "It is our agreement, remember?" He stroked a golden curl damp with perspiration away from her temple.

"I've been there every night," she reminded him. "You are the one missing." He kissed her again, lingering over her lips.

"We will still go to Cherkassk?" she asked.

His insides twisted painfully. Of course, that was what she had wanted, he realized. That's why she had come to him and offered herself. She wanted to find her sister.

"Soon," he said, and got up to dress.

The days fell into a pattern after that. Still assigned to the night watch, Nikholai came to his bed in the dark of early morn. He always found Elise there, sleeping soundly. Without disturbing her, he would kick off his boots, wrap himself up in his burka, and sleep beside her on top of the comforter. Often by dawn he would feel her curl up against him, her cheek against his back. He was certain he could feel the heat of her even through his fur-lined burka and the down comforter. He wanted her there, but he would not make love to her again. He began to hate the agreement they had made. He didn't like the bitter pain that coiled inside him when he remembered that she yielded to him because she expected him to take her to Cherkassk.

During the day, he often saw her helping Natalia with chores or playing in the snow with the children. Sometimes she followed him about the stable as he tended horses. She chattered all the village gossip and bragged about the children. He trusted her now. With the promise of a trip to Cherkassk, he knew she wouldn't do anything so foolish as to attempt escape again.

He also noticed that although he had been ousted and his warriors avoided him, the women of Vazka accepted her. It was no longer just the children who clustered around her. The women, too, joined her. They laughed with her, shared their concerns about the children with her, and poured tea for her. They seemed unsurprised that she suddenly spoke their language, and they did not resent that she wore her head covering her own way. With a familiar deference, they all addressed her as "countess."

During the long cold hours of watchtower duty, Nikholai realized that the countess had been right about his licking his wounds. He had carried a jug of vodka to the stable each night, feeling sorry for himself for several reasons—because he had lost his title of ataman, because his men had lost faith in him, and because he could not overcome the certainty that he would lose her. Her taunts had reminded him of the uselessness of self-pity. Her passion had made him forget it, for a while at least.

So what was done was done. Now he could only do his part as a warrior. He had watched Vikola declare Ostap his second in command. Then the ugly Zaporozhie had ridden off to Kagalnik with two warriors and gifts to seal Vazka's alliance with Stenka Razin. During the long winter months to come, the men would clean and sharpen weapons, tell tales of past battles, and dream of the glory to come.

197

# ✤ 16 ✤
# Our Lady of Tears

Brother Ivan arrived to wed Ganna and Filip. He was a short, round clergyman dressed in a long homespun caftan and wearing a brown beard that threatened to overwhelm him. Elise was certain that some pet must nest in those bushy whiskers. He was a jolly man, but he brought distressing news. Rostov was riding about the countryside, threatening anyone he thought might join in a rebellion.

In a small village to the north, the streltsy captain had allowed his men to beat to death a Cossack who was rumored to have ridden with Stenka Razin. In another village, a maiden had been raped by several of Rostov's streltsy soldiers. Vazka hummed with the rumor. The light of anticipation left the eyes of the warriors. The threat of battle was no longer months away.

Triumphant, Vikola returned and announced that Vazka was allied with Stenka Razin. The warriors cheered joyously, and the krug smiled satisfied smiles. Vikola grinned like a new father.

"And Stenka Razin asked me to sit with him amid all the riches he brought back from Persia," Vikola bragged. "We talked of defeating the streltsy. He is a great man, and with

198

him we will teach the boyars not to tell lies about us to the tsar."

Such foolishness was no less than Elise had expected, but she found it annoying. Nikholai came out of the stables long enough to listen to the news, then went back to his work. The rest of the village celebrated throughout the day and into the night.

Natalia never wavered in her work on the bridal crown of freshwater pearls and in making the wedding plans. She took Elise with her while plans were made and cooking done. Elise found it almost as festive as Christmas at home.

Seated on a bench near the fire in Mistress Tokina's cottage, Elise watched Ganna, Ganna's mother, and Natalia prepare food and make plans for the wedding and feast.

"Will Daria and Kasyan wed also?" asked Ganna.

"No," Natalia said. "Bogdan says she will not agree to wed. And when we asked her to join us in preparations, she refused."

"Kasyan is such a reasonable man. A good man," Elise said. "How can he love someone like Daria? I see such unhappiness in his eyes. Has the Gypsy cast a spell over him?"

The women laughed good-naturedly.

"No spell, Little One," answered the little dolduna. "Love and passion are all that is needed. And those two emotions are seldom reasonable."

Elise understood that. She smiled at their lusty tales of wedding celebrations. And she wondered once again why Nikholai had not made love to her since that day in the stable.

Memories of those secret moments with him drifted through her mind. It was such a wonderful thing for a man to use his strength to give a woman pleasure like that, Elise marveled. She watched Ganna smile and blush in response to a teasing remark from her mother. She wondered whether the young girl and Filip had already consummated their love. Had Ganna found pleasure in the act? Did Filip still want her?

The days since their return from Kagalnik and Nikholai's ouster had stretched into weeks. She was troubled that

Nikholai had not wanted her again and would not discuss the trip to Cherkassk. She was a little fearful of bringing it up because the mention of it had obviously annoyed him in the stable.

He joined her in bed each night after his watch and slept with his back to her. His presence kept the nightmares at bay. Elise was grateful for that, but she wanted to know his embrace again, his strong, warm touch, his breath on her cheek, his hand in her hair.

And she wanted to find Anna. When they had made the agreement, she had asked to go to Cherkassk by Christmas. They had already celebrated the feast day of St. Nikholas. Christmas Day was tomorrow, Ganna's wedding day.

"I will be the fifth generation to wear the bridal crown," Ganna said with pride. She put on the freshwater-pearl headdress and proudly named the others who had worn the crown before her. More women joined them to cook and talk and sing songs.

Between songs one woman asked Natalia to tell them the tale of Our Lady of Encampment. The little dolduna smiled proudly and began it as she worked over dumpling dough.

"Once, long ago, after a Cossack battle, the Virgin Mary, Our Lady of the Encampment, asked St. Nikholas to guide her on a walk through the Cossack land. She walked for a ways across the steppe and became thirsty. So she went to a cottage to ask for water. The cottage was silent except for the sound of women's weeping. She went to another cottage and another, but at each she found the same silence. It was the day after a battle, and the women mourned their men, who had not returned.

"It was very hot on the steppe, so St. Nikholas led Our Lady to a shaded wood near the river, where a clear, cool spring ran from the rocks. Our Lady knelt down over the spring to drink from it. She wore only a head covering and no ornament so she could do that. Then St. Nikholas returned her to the heavens, where she had no need of his guidance. Then he saw that she wore a headdress of many tiny pearls sewn in delicate designs. 'You found a beautiful kokoshynk in the Cossack land,' he said to her.

"'No,' said Our Lady. 'I found each pearl, one by one. See, they are the tears of Cossack mothers and wives shed for their dead.' And that is why to this day pearls are called tears in our Cossack land," Natalia said, finishing the story.

Suddenly the shiny, translucent beauty of the pearls made Elise shiver. Ever since her first days in Poland and in years that followed, when she lived near Kiev, she had known the Cossacks to be a courageous people. They accepted their place in the world as fighters on a frontier—the men died in battle and the women wept for them. How could one bear to be a bride, knowing such sorrow was the future? Elise glanced across the room at Ganna, who was happily showing her wedding dress to a friend.

Elise pushed away her dark thoughts and joined the two girls. She admired the gold-colored brocade.

"You will be lovely in this, Ganna," Elise said. "How wonderful to be a Christmas bride."

The two girls stared at her uncomprehendingly.

"You and Filip wed on Christmas Day," Elise said.

"Christmas is two weeks away," Ganna replied apologetically.

Then Elise realized her mistake. She had forgotten that Eastern Orthodox Christmas was the sixth day of January. Had Nikholai considered that when he made the agreement? Of course he had, she fumed. The bloody Cossack!

Embarrassed, Elise explained to Ganna how she had momentarily confused the dates of Christmas. The girls, who had known some Roman Catholic Poles, smiled understandingly. Then they returned to the wedding plans. Quietly Elise excused herself.

Once out of the cottage, she bolted to find Nikholai. After searching the stable and the watchtower, she found him in the long, low sod storehouse. He was inventorying bags of grain.

"You intended to mislead me, didn't you?" she accused immediately. He looked up at her with surprise on his face. Now he would play the innocent, she raged inside.

"Mislead you?" he asked. He pushed his cap back from his brow and unbuttoned his quilted caftan. He looked tired. After his night watch, he always slept well into the morning, but was about and working by midday. Elise disliked the dark circles under his eyes, but she refused to let that cloud her anger.

"I want to go to Cherkassk now."

"Now? It is late in the day to begin a journey, Countess," he said lightly as he turned back to the bags he was counting.

"You agreed to take me to Cherkassk by Christmas," she said. "That's tomorrow. We'll go by my Christmas. Tomorrow."

"Your Christmas? Polish Christmas? That was not the agreement." He sat down on a barrel and regarded her for a long moment. The set of his mouth was hard.

"Yes, we'll start tomorrow," Elise said. "I'll be ready to travel by dawn. The river isn't solid yet, so we'll go overland by sledge. You have a cousin there who will shelter us, don't you?"

"I'll decide when we'll leave, Countess," Nikholai said in a low, dangerous voice without looking at her. He turned away.

"I'm going tomorrow," Elise returned.

"Don't threaten me, Countess," he said with his back still to her. "Even you aren't foolish enough to try to cross the steppe alone in the winter."

"There's nothing I won't do to find my sister," Elise vowed angrily. "And I'd rather die in that effort than spend the rest of my life as a prisoner in Vazka." Nikholai faced her. The hard paleness of his expression startled her. In the cold silence that followed, she regretted her threat.

"There have been no messages from the Don Host," she said. "Perhaps my brothers are on some assignment and your letter never reached them. Whatever the reason, I'm worthless to you, Nikholai. I have done nothing but cause you problems. Why keep me here?" She stepped toward him, her hands open before her in appeal. "Set me free, Nikholai. Please."

"No," he said without hesitation, and turned away from her. "And don't ask again."

A sudden barking of dogs and whinnying of horses distracted them. Then the boom of the meeting drum echoed through the village. Nikholai turned to the door, dropped his quill on the paper, and brushed past Elise.

She wasn't about to let him get away from this discussion so easily. She stopped to blow out the lamp before she hurried out the door. In that time, he managed to disappear. Villagers emerged from their cottages and outbuildings to gather along Vazka's main street. Elise joined them. "Muscovites," she heard whispered. She knew Nikholai would be at the front of the crowd to greet the Muscovites, whether he was ataman or not.

Slowly, deliberately, the streltsy force rode through Vazka's gate. Each rider wore a long red caftan coat with a split skirt that warmed the legs of the soldier on horseback. A bandolier of musket powder and balls crossed each man's chest. Elise noted that each man had only a few rounds. Soft crimson caps covered their long hair. Most wore full beards, in the Muscovite fashion.

The villagers were silent. The riders said nothing. Hooves crunched on the snow, bridles jingling as the streltsy rode straight into the heart of Vazka. These elite members of the tsar's law-and-order force were well-armed with matchlock muskets—if not well-supplied with powder. Some carried a berdysh, a battleax also used as a musket rest.

Elise quickly estimated their force to be as large as Vazka's. Movement of a tall man across the way caught her eye. It was Nikholai, and she knew he was counting too.

At the head of the column rode the golova, or captain. His red-and-gold uniform was unharmonious with his red hair and white complexion. His caftan was of a richer fabric than his men's, and it was lined with fur. The emblem of the tsar, a double-headed gold eagle, flashed on his cap. At his side he carried the short staff of an officer. He was younger than Elise had expected, slender and small-eyed. Menace lurked there. A chill crawled down her spine. She was glad Nikholai was there. Finesse would be needed in dealing with this man.

Vikola, fists on hips, swaggered forward to greet the red-bearded officer. Nikholai and Ostap were there beside him.

From where Elise stood she heard the Muscovite congratulate Vikola on his new office, but his gaze rested on Nikholai. When the captain dismounted, the streltsy column remained guarded and on their horses. In theory, they were allies with the Cossacks, but the reality was different.

Arrogantly Vikola returned the greeting, addressing the captain as Alexander Rostov.

"When I was here last, you and your men were gone, Nikholai Fomin," Rostov said. "And you were still ataman then."

Nikholai said nothing.

"Then we heard about a pirate raid on the Volga," Rostov continued. "The burlaki said it was led by a tall Cossack on a red horse."

"Is that so?" was all the tall Cossack had to say.

"Bogdan Cherevik told me some story about all Vazka's warriors going south to help their brothers catch horses. Is there another big red horse like yours, Nikholai Fomin?"

"It is possible," Nikholai said with a shrug.

"Kagalnik is south of here, isn't it? You and your pirates wouldn't join this rebel fellow Stenka Razin, would you?"

"What if we did?" Vikola demanded.

Nikholai's big hand clamped Vikola's shoulder. "I don't know what you mean, Alexander Rostov," Nikholai said. "There are no pirates here. And Stenka Razin has told the Don Host he builds his city on the Don to live in peace."

"Yes," Rostov said. "I have heard that. I have heard, too, that a Polish countess now lives in Vazka. Is that true?"

Vazka's warriors rocked restlessly on their feet or moved to the side of a comrade to exchange muttered comments. Elise didn't expect them to protect her from the Muscovites, but she knew that if they admitted to her presence they admitted to pirating.

"Here she is," Daria called.

Suddenly Elise's wrist was seized by a small but firm hand, and she was pulled through the crowd toward the gate by the Gypsy. Elise resisted. Someone hissed, "No, Daria." Olga Umana plucked at the Gypsy girl's sleeve, but Daria shook free. Elise tried to plant her feet, but she was relentlessly dragged toward the men in the church square.

"Here is the countess, Captain," Daria called to the red-headed Muscovite. "Here is the proof you need. Nikholai Fomin captured her in the raid. He insisted on holding her for ransom, but none of us want her here."

She shoved Elise before Vikola and Rostov. The new

ataman looked uncertain, and the Muscovite stared in openmouthed surprise. Elise regained her balance and regretted not wearing her head covering properly. She put on her most innocent expression and prayed silently that she looked and sounded like a village woman—to this Muscovite, at least.

She bobbed a quick peasant curtsy and tried to remember to keep her gaze down, but she had already stared at him long enough to see the puzzlement in his face.

Elise fluttered her eyelashes and smiled shyly at the Muscovite. "Daria flatters me, brave Captain," she said softly in Cossack. "I am but a plain peasant girl." Then in halting Russian she said, "Welcome to our village."

The interest in Rostov's eyes grew.

Elise looked up briefly to see Nikholai standing there, his expression unreadable, his penetrating gaze on Daria. Daria winced as if struck when she turned to the tall Cossack. Instantly she released Elise and stepped away. Vikola looked uneasy but said nothing. Kasyan appeared at Daria's side. Rostov never took his gaze from Elise. He clicked his heels and inclined his head, just enough to appear courtly, but not quite enough to be truly respectful, Elise observed.

"Thank you for your hospitality," he said. "A plain maiden you are not. You are new to Vazka?"

"Well, yes . . ." Elise began.

"So, Alexander Rostov, once again you come to Vazka to partake of our hospitality," greeted Natalia. She pushed her way through the crowd to face the Muscovite. She carried a jug of vodka in one hand and a basket of bread in the other. "I knew you would hear of our wedding celebration and come to join in the merriment."

"Natalia Fomina, you know me too well," Rostov replied with what Elise recognized as evil pleasure. There was truth in his words and in Natalia's too. They appeared to be old enemies, well-acquainted and pleased to be called to face each other again. Elise remembered hearing that Rostov had somehow been involved in the deaths of Nikholai's father and uncle, Natalia's husband.

"I was just being introduced to . . . What is your name, my dear?"

Before Elise could reply, Natalia interrupted, "Oh, so you have met Nikholai's betrothed? They are to be wed tomorrow."

The little dolduna handed the vodka jug to Rostov. He took it gratefully and pulled out the stopper, sniffed the brew, then nodded his approval to Natalia. The villagers remained watchfully silent as he tipped the jug up to take a drink.

"Nikholai Fomin's betrothed, eh?" Rostov turned to Elise again when he had finished. Why had Natalia said that? Elise wondered. She glanced at Nikholai. His expressionless mask remained in place. She could change nothing, she realized. This was like a card game in which one played the cards as they were dealt.

"Tell me why the Gypsy calls you a countess," Rostov said.

"It is but a pet name," Elise answered coyly. "And I do come from the Polish side of the Dnieper." She smiled at Daria, whose expression played between frustration and chagrin.

"The pet name suits you," the captain said with one more admiring look. Then he turned to Nikholai, who still loomed near. "So, Nikholai Fomin, I find you are no longer ataman of Vazka but about to become a husband. Very domestic. Difficult to believe that there are those who think you a Volga pirate." The Muscovite captain took another long swig of vodka.

Elise saw the women watching uneasily, their small children gathered about their skirts.

The children. They had become so dear to her. Stepan, who loved the birds, and little Galya, whose rosy cheeks and musical laugh reminded her of Anna. Then there were Olga's twins, Vasili and Vasilisa.

Elise glanced anxiously at Nikholai. She wanted to shake that mask from his face. *Help me!* she wanted to scream at him. If he cared for nothing else, he should at least be concerned about the children. Instinct told her that Vikola feared Nikholai just enough to remain silent. But she needed Nikholai's assistance. She glanced at him, unaware of how the green of her eyes warned him.

"Please, Captain Rostov," Elise said boldly, "I don't

understand this talk of pirates. You can see there are no pirates here. Only merrymakers. Nikholai and I will be wed tomorrow. Ganna and Filip also. Brother Ivan has already arrived. We would be honored to have you and your men join us in the celebration."

She fastened her gaze on Nikholai's face and reached for his hand. He hesitated before he grasped her hand in his. His expression remained unreadable, but his grip was as powerful as the one he had used the night she pulled him up from the riverbank.

Daria squealed in protest. Her bracelets jangled and she stamped her feet in the snow. "Alexander Rostov, she lies. You can't believe her!"

Vikola straightened to his full height. "Ignore the Gypsy, Alexander Rostov. She is but a jealous woman."

Elise nodded and gave Rostov a beseeching look, one that asked for patience and understanding for the Gypsy girl. The streltsy captain glanced at Daria and laughed.

"A fair beauty to marry. A dark beauty who is jealous, and an aunt who makes the best vodka on the Don," the streltsy captain said. "Nikholai Fomin, I've always thought you had more than your share of good fortune with the women in your life."

"As you say, Alexander Rostov," Nikholai agreed with a small bow of his head. He and Kasyan exchanged sharp looks before Nikholai led Elise away.

Behind them, Elise heard Vikola issue orders to make the Muscovites welcome. The villagers swarmed around the streltsy with bread and vodka. Smiling now, the Muscovites dismounted and laid their weapons aside to partake of Cossack hospitality.

Elise glanced around quickly to see Kasyan nearly drag Daria off. Kasyan's face was lined with anger, and for once the Gypsy girl looked as if she regretted her actions.

Nikholai squeezed Elise's hand. Although her presence of mind no longer surprised him, her invitation to Rostov had lit a small light of hope in his heart. He knew it was a foolish hope, but the tiny flame persisted. He had to know why she had done what she did. "Have I been such a fine lover, Green Eyes?" he asked with a derisive smile.

She cast him a sharp look. "Don't flatter yourself," she

said. "I went along with Natalia's mad statement only for Vazka. For the children. Besides, you can't help me find my sister if you're hanging from a gibbet."

Nikholai frowned. He was indeed a fool.

"Smile, there's Brother Ivan," Elise said, and elbowed him. "Now we have to convince the good brother as well as Rostov that we are a loving couple. Anyway, Brother Ivan is a brother, not an ordained priest, so the vows won't be binding," she said. "The festivities will humor the streltsy, and we can send them on their way without their ever knowing that Vazka is Razin's ally."

"It's a good plan," Nikholai said, his frown disappearing as he realized that good fortune might be with him in this. "It's not as simple as you think. In Vazka, vows said before Brother Ivan are binding."

"What?"

"Brother Ivan weds everyone here and christens the children," Nikholai explained. "All is recorded in the church Bible. I can show you. Kasyan and Daria's betrothal is entered there. Brother or priest, the vows said in our church are binding."

"Who decided this? The bishop?"

"I decided it," Nikholai replied. He could no longer resist grinning. The countess looked up at him suspiciously.

"But you're no longer ataman," she reminded him.

"That doesn't matter," Nikholai said with certainty. "Vikola won't change this."

"But when . . ." Elise began.

Nikholai released her hand and stepped away to let the giggling village women surround her. He could see her speak, but didn't have to listen to her protest over the chatter of the women and laughter of the men around him. He smiled at her as they were carried off to be prepared for their wedding day.

# ❧ 17 ☙

# Vazka's Reluctant Bride

Elise was taken to Mistress Tokina's cottage to join Ganna. There the brides were treated to the traditional bridal bathing and hair washing, singing, and giggling.

Not long after Elise arrived, Teresa, Vikola's woman, brought Daria to the cottage and announced that Daria would be a bride the next day too. The dark-eyed Gypsy scowled so darkly that she momentarily daunted the happy women. Elise wondered what Kasyan had said or done to force Daria to wed him. Silence settled over the room as the women looked from countess to Gypsy. Elise decided that the reluctant bride would not spoil the festivities for Ganna. Calmly Elise smiled at the unhappy girl.

"Come join us, Daria," she invited. "Three is a lucky number. We will be three brides."

Daria nodded reluctantly and stepped forward.

Relieved laughter rippled through the women. Teresa gave Elise a grateful smile, then pushed Daria toward the baths. The women once more took up their conversations.

Little by little, Elise's anxieties melted away with the laughter. It was good to be part of a family again. To be warmly teased. To know one was accepted even with one's foibles—height, unruly hair, vanity. Had it been so long

209

since she had enjoyed banter with her family, with her brothers? Since she had time to play with Anna? She hadn't been able to enjoy those things after her marriage to the count, she realized. And she had missed them. There had been little time between social engagements and entertaining as befitted the count's position. After her marriage, life had been filled with protocol, social obligations, and appearances.

Her own wedding had been a day of little joy. Because the Chathams had officially been in mourning for their father, the ceremony had been quiet and discreet. She had worn a gown of somber gray and carried no flowers. Her brothers and Anna stood at her side, and the count was accompanied by his clerk and his nephew, Leopold. The church had been dark and cold on that rainy day. But here amid the laughing women of Vazka, that day seemed long ago and far away to Elise.

Now she gave herself up to all the sunny joy and excitement Ganna shared with them. Even Daria was unable to remain immune to it. Soon the Gypsy's frown softened, and Daria began to laugh with the women and joined in some of the more ribald songs.

During the preparations, Elise saw little of Natalia. When she did, she pulled the little woman aside to ask why she had said such a thing to Rostov. Natalia had a ready answer.

"How better to explain a strange woman in Vazka and to cast doubt on Daria's words?" Then she admonished, "Stand up straight, Little One. Yes, I have a gown for you. But I must lengthen it. About two rows of fur, I think," the dolduna said, and turned to leave the cottage, then stopped. "I think you should know, Countess. Nikholai has asked me to find his mother's wedding ring for the ceremony. It is a very old ring, long in the Fomin family, and of the ancient Roman handclasp design. Maria refused it and requested a new ring. Nikholai indulged her. There are other rings, but he has asked for his mother's ring." Then Natalia left.

A sharp, unpleasant thrill tingled through Elise. Knowing Nikholai had gone to such lengths frightened her, but she wasn't sure why. This was only a deception.

Elise learned from Teresa that the grooms were being

treated to a similar preparation: bathing and singing, with drinking and dancing besides.

Happy church bells awakened the brides at dawn. Vazka's women wasted no time in rousing and dressing their three brides. The dressing of Ganna and Daria was nearly complete when Natalia brought Elise's bridal gown to the cottage. She held it up against Elise to show it to the other women. Eagerly they admired the ivory brocade garment. The caftan gown was simply ornamented with a row of pearl buttons from throat to toe. Rich dark fur hemmed the skirt. The full, long sleeves were gathered tightly at the wrist with the same fur. The gown's simple lines allowed the textured pattern of the heavy fabric to shine and bloom in the daylight. Elise was unable to suppress a small gasp of appreciation as the others murmured hushed admiration.

"Where did it come from?" Elise asked, and lightly ran her fingers over the satiny texture.

"Mine, and my mother's before me, and her mother's before her," Natalia said. "And it pleases me to have Nikholai's bride wear this gown. You know he has been like a son to me."

Elise said nothing. How could she tell this woman who had been so generous and caring that this was not to be a real wedding? The little woman and Elise embraced. Then they began to dress Vazka's third bride.

According to tradition, a maiden's long single braid was to be fashioned into the double braids of a married woman. Ganna's shiny brown hair obeyed when they placed her family's bridal crown on her head. Then they attempted to smooth Elise's short, wild curls, but to no avail. The women soon gave up and fastened Natalia's crown of pearls in Elise's golden cloud of hair. Elise wondered if Natalia had foreseen that this wedding would happen, but she did not ask. Daria refused help and merely coiled her dark hair at the base of her neck and tied gold braid across her brow.

"Make ready," Teresa called from the window. "The grooms are about to call for their brides."

With cries of dismay, women scurried this way and that, putting the last touches on the maiden, the countess, and the Gypsy.

Curious, Elise pulled away from her dressers to peer over Teresa's shoulder. The crowd of men in Muscovite uniforms and Cossack celebration clothes gathered before the cottage. Their colorful caftans and jackets—purple, yellow, orange, and blue hues—glowed like freshly bloomed flowers against a snowbank. They sang and cheered for each groom.

First, Filip, dressed in a deep brown brocade caftan with black and gold embroidery, called for Ganna. She was radiant in her golden-colored finery. The women giggled and chided the bride for looking at her groom. Ganna smiled boldly at Filip. The groom blushed, but his embarrassment didn't prevent him from clasping Ganna's hand firmly and leading her toward the church.

Next, Kasyan appeared from the colorful throng. To Elise's surprise, he was dressed in the blue Don Host uniform. She knew he had been Nikholai's lieutenant, but she had not thought of him as a soldier. His fair hair was carefully brushed and his mustache neatly trimmed. His pride showed in his grooming, and his happiness shone in his eyes. Elise was unable to resist smiling for him.

The woman shoved Daria to the door to meet her groom. She was dressed in the bright reds of an Oriental bride. The light gleamed on her smoothed dark hair and the gold braid. As proudly and possessively as Filip, Kasyan took Daria's hand. Before she took the last step out the door, she cast a swift look of hatred over her shoulder at Elise. The unexpected intensity of the look took Elise's breath away. She forgot she was next.

Natalia fussed over Elise's dress and Teresa made one last effort to tame the curls, but it was too late. Nikholai stood at the door, awaiting his bride. She had always thought him a handsome man, but the proud Cossack officer at the door was new to her. He could not be the same unshaven pirate who had mauled her before his men and been her comrade in Kagalnik. The gold braid of his blue uniform enhanced his broad shoulders, and the red sash of a Don Host officer narrowed his waist. His full black trousers were neatly tucked into his shiny black boots. His black lambskin hat sat at a jaunty angle on his dark curls. Many hands pulled Elise to the door to stand before her groom. Still she stared. He looked so serious, almost grim, as he clicked his heels and gave her a little bow. Then a slow boyish grin spread across his face.

"You're not supposed to look at me, Green Eyes," he whispered as he took her hand.

"But you are a feast for the eyes," Elise stammered. Her glib tongue had deserted her.

"Ah, spare me the flattery," he said with a soft laugh, obviously pleased. "Green Eyes, you are the one who looks delicious enough for the Wolf to eat."

Elise felt the heat of a blush brand her cheeks. She avoided his amused gaze. The men behind him had not heard his words, but cheered her blushing embarrassment and began to sing another lusty song of marriage. Nikholai squeezed her hand and led her across the trampled snow toward the church.

The gay villagers and celebrating Muscovites followed, singing loud enough to drown the pealing church bells.

The church was bright with burning candles and fragrant with evergreen boughs. Snow-bleached sunlight poured through the narrow windows and glittered off the gold and silver halos of the saints.

The ceremony was a long one. Much of it was familiar to Elise, and some of it new. She tried to concentrate, but she couldn't. During the wedding preparations there had been little time to reflect. Now, as the ceremony wore on, she began to wonder whether Nikholai did indeed consider it binding. Then he would be as unwillingly bound to her as she to him. He would do that, she knew, if he saw their marriage as a way to protect Vazka from the Muscovites. With sudden understanding she raised her bowed head to stare at her handsome groom.

He glanced back at her briefly, his gray eyes clear and calm. He was giving her courage. She couldn't resist smiling back at him. He would do what he had to do to save Vazka, just as she would do what she had to do to find Anna. It was so simple. She didn't know why she had not seen it before. They both carried similar commitments that pulled them in different directions. Perhaps in another time and place they could have been true friends. Her brothers would respect a man such as Nikholai. Anna would like him too. In another time and place, they might have had a future together.

Nikholai bowed his head again and tried to concentrate on Brother Ivan's words, but he could not dismiss the golden vision of the countess at his side. His bride. In the ivory brocade and the pearl crown, green-eyed and golden, she was as beautiful and delicate as an apple blossom and as regal and self-possessed as a Persian princess. How could she be so many things at once? Sometimes he thought she was an angel sent to light his life. At other times, in the wee hours of the morning, he wondered whether she was a seductive demon come to tempt him into darkness.

Even if she were a demon, she had a weakness—the children. They had bound her to Vazka. Did she know that yet? he wondered.

Her hand was cold and trembled in his when he slipped the golden handclasp ring on her finger. He squeezed her fingers in a request that she look at him, but she refused.

The recording of the marriage in the Bible took only a few moments. Brother Ivan wrote Elise's name next to Nikholai's, and then three newly wedded couples paraded from the church amid songs and laughter from the villagers.

The Fomin cottage was full of benches and tables covered in white cloth and laden with stewed dried fruits, dumplings, honey-barley cakes, savory and sweet rice dishes, cheeses, and breads. With help from another warrior, Ostap carried in an entire roast lamb for the feast table. Saffron-spiced vodka was being served outside. Elise marveled at the variety of food and drink.

Inside, villagers were singing, eating, and drinking. Outside, in the snow, they found room to dance. Women danced with women, and women danced with men. Sometimes the men danced solo in the wild dashing and kicking of the Cossack tradition. And the Muscovites joined in it all.

After many toasts, the couples were seated, each at a different table. For some reason, Elise found that she and Nikholai were in the center of the room. Women bustled in every direction, carrying food and drink. The men shouted laughter across the room and from out-of-doors. Children squealed and dashed underfoot in play.

Nikholai and Elise were served, and the dining had only begun when the women around them began to shout, "Bitter. Bitter. Bitter."

Kasyan bestowed a solid kiss on Daria's unwilling lips.

Puzzled, Elise turned to Nikholai. "What do they mean, 'bitter'?"

"They mean the food is bitter and we must sweeten it for them," Nikholai explained. He put his arm across the back of her chair and leaned closer to her. Elise watched him closely as he tried unsuccessfully to control the mischievous grin that played at the corners of his mustache.

"How?" Elise felt suspicion growing inside her. She watched Filip and Ganna exchange a shy peck. "With a kiss?"

"Yes, but it must be done right to be successful," Nikholai said. He stood, pulled Elise to her feet, grasped her with one hand on the back of her head and the other on the small of her back so that she was almost bent over backward, and kissed her. The villagers—man, woman, maid, youth, and child alike—roared their delight, cheered, then returned to their meal.

Breathlessly Elise blinked at Nikholai. Her arms hung limply at her sides. If the wedding ceremony hadn't put a seal on their relationship, that display before the village had. And Elise knew it.

"Beware, Green Eyes," he warned with a smile. "They will demand that we sweeten their feast all day and into the night."

And so they did. Elise felt as if the horse had gotten the bit in its teeth. With each of Nikholai's warm, sweetening kisses, she could feel herself helplessly drawn into something she saw no escape from.

She had consented to this wedding to deceive Rostov and save the village. Now Rostov and his men were enjoying a fine feast and celebration. Vazka was safe and merry. She felt as if she had just become the bride of this Cossack and his entire village. Inside and out, so much good cheer and laughter jostled about the cottage, it was impossible for Elise to be angry. She danced with Nikholai and sang with the villagers. But in the pit of her stomach an icy ball of fear and despair began to grow.

The food on the tables was gone, the white cloths wrinkled and stained with spiced vodka and red wine. The fire burned low in the oven. Most of the wedding celebrants had wandered off yawning and in search of warm beds. Impatiently Nikholai watched Natalia climb down the loft ladder with blankets in her arms. He was eager to have Elise to himself. It had taken all the self-discipline he possessed to get through the last hours of festivities. Once Rostov had rudely claimed a kiss from the bride, and Nikholai had barely restrained himself from knocking the streltsy captain to the floor.

Natalia put on her caftan. "I'm going to stay with Olga tonight," she said. "One of the twins is fretful."

"You don't need to do that," Elise stammered. "I can go. The twins are always good for me."

"Little One, this is your wedding night," the dolduna said. She kissed Elise and Nikholai on the cheek and left.

In silence Nikholai watched Elise stroll among the benches and tables. She glanced at him over her shoulder as she drew her fingers along one of the crumb-covered tablecloths.

"It was a very festive wedding celebration," she said. "Everyone took great pleasure in it." She smiled quietly and sat down on a bench. "I think the deception went well, don't you?"

"How could you let Rostov kiss you like that?" Nikholai demanded. The insult had been rubbing for some time now, and his temper, his pride, was raw.

"Let him kiss me? I didn't *let* him do anything."

"Before the entire village, you simpered with Vikola and let Rostov insult me by kissing you," he said. "You didn't even protest." Nikholai paced the far side of the room, his hands clasped behind him. He kicked a chair from his path.

"I didn't protest because I wanted to prevent war in Vazka's streets," she said. "And I don't see how you can consider that kiss an insult to you. I was the one who had to suffer through his sour slobbering.

"Do not mistake me for a pawn in some game between you and Rostov. I repeated those vows today for Vazka's sake, just as you did. You and your aunt can dress me in Cossack clothes, you can feed me honey-barley cakes and put your mother's ring on my finger. But I will never be a

Cossack. I will not be bound to shed tears for the dead—for husbands and brothers. I will not."

She yanked the pearl crown from her head, threw it to the floor, and stamped her foot. Pearls crunched underfoot, spun across the wood, rolled under the table, and rattled into corners.

Was that what he was doing? Nikholai wondered. Was he trying to make her a Cossack? She would make a very good one, indeed. She had kept her wits about her with the Muscovites, when he had nearly lost his own.

He took a deep breath, wondering how much to tell her. How much to suggest. "Would that be such a terrible thing, Green Eyes? To be a Cossack? What if your brothers never come for you?"

Complete astonishment dropped over the anger on her face. Nikholai regretted his question. He realized that possibility had never occurred to her. That her sister might be dead was a fear she denied, yet lived with. But that her brothers would not come had never been considered.

She stepped back from him. "They will come," she stated. "I know it. And they know Anna will be with me." She kicked at the crown on the floor. Then, like a wounded animal, she sought the darkest corner. She huddled there, on a bench with her hands clasped between her knees.

Nikholai sighed and approached her quietly. He could feel his insides beginning to twist painfully. This pain was much worse than any Rostov or Vikola inspired. Nikholai sat down beside her and took her hands in his. She withdrew them. But in the moment he touched her, he felt the cold in her fingers and the trembling in her body. The fading firelight played across the satiny breast of her gown. Her breathing had become shallow and agitated.

"I'm sure your brothers will come, Green Eyes," he lied. "As soon as they know you need them." Mentally he cursed her brothers. "Come, sit by the fire where it's warm," he suggested. She allowed him to take her hand this time, and he led her to the bench near the oven. He urged her to sit down, and knelt before her.

"Let's forget about all the mean words, the threats," he whispered.

He held her gaze. Once, she had helped him forget. This time, maybe he could help her. She watched him warily, the jade green of her eyes dark and moody. "The food was good and the music merry. Today, because of you, Green Eyes, instead of fighting, Vazka danced. Tonight, let the pleasure of the day warm us. Let's be together without thoughts of tomorrow."

She remained thoughtfully silent. Her fingers were cold when she touched his temple. He knew that he had won, for the night at least. He led her to his bed, and they made love all through the night. In the firelit hours, he savored her petal softness and apple-blossom scent.

Loving the countess was unlike any passion he had known. Maria had been part of the life of responsibility he planned for himself. Perhaps she had had a right to resent what he asked of her.

Elise was life. For the first time in his existence something meant more to him than leadership and responsibility. Only two months ago he had not known life with her; now he could not think of life without her.

It made no sense. She mocked him. She had no interest in his plans. She defied the krug. She demanded only her freedom. And that was everything. He had little else to offer her except what he could give back to her. Pleasure. A few moments of happiness. Her sister.

By firelight he allowed Elise to explore him, and curiously finger his battle scars. When she asked about them, he silenced her with a kiss and made love to her again.

Elise awoke to the vision of pale morning light on the cottage wall. Contentment and warmth lingered deep inside her. She felt Nikholai's breath in her ear, warm and tingling. When she turned to him, she saw that he was dressed and sitting on the edge of the bed. He bent over her with a message.

"Rostov leaves later today, as soon as his men are recovered. Muscovites don't hold their drink well. Tomorrow we leave for Cherkassk. Vikola has given me dispatches to take to the Don Host. Make ready. Natalia will help." He kissed her ear and left.

## ❧ 18 ❧

# The Englishman at the Ball

They reached Cherkassk at dusk, when households light their lamps and build up their fires against the winter night.

Nikholai drove their sledge through the streets between the log homes as if he knew exactly where he was going. Elise could make no sense of the maze. At last they stopped before a two-story house that looked much like the others they had passed.

"Nikholai Fomin, what a wonderful surprise!" a tiny woman exclaimed. She peered around the ample figure of her serving woman, who had opened the door. "Martena, let them in. You must be frozen. Timofe will be so pleased." Over her shoulder she called, "Timofe, come greet our Christmas guests."

"Katia Guska, you are too kind," Nikholai said with a hand in the small of Elise's back. He urged her through the doorway. Charmed by Katia's smile and warm amber eyes, Elise followed the petite, waddling woman into the house. Impending motherhood overwhelmed Katia's tiny frame.

"Who is it, Katia?" Timofe asked as he strode into the room.

"Nikholai, what a surprise." The men embraced and

219

kissed in the traditional fashion of old comrades. To Elise's surprise, Timofe was smaller, but much like Nikholai.

"Please, Katia, Timofe, let me introduce you to my wife, Elise," Nikholai said as soon as he had removed his cap.

Elise smiled politely. She had learned not to dispute Nikholai's introduction. On the first evening of their four-day journey, she had been about to denounce the title of wife when a dark warning in his eyes silenced her. Of course, she realized, it was the perfect deception. Who would question Nikholai Fomin's taking his wife to visit cousins in Cherkassk? No one would dare treat her with less than courtesy.

"Welcome, Elise Fomina," Katia said, greeting her new cousin with a spontaneous embrace and a kiss on the cheek. "Nikholai, you should have told us you had wed. How long, my dear? Did he rush you into it? He's like Timofe, you know. Once they make a decision, they become impatient to see it through. Martena, make tea. Bring food. Timofe, put more wood on the fire. Our guests need warmth."

Katia led them into a spacious low-ceilinged sitting room. Persian rugs covered the floor, leather-bound books lined the walls, and brass lamps glowed in the growing darkness. The fire, in a handsome blue-and-white-tiled stove, was welcoming.

Katia never stopped talking. Pleasure beamed from her pretty heart-shaped face and bubbled out through her voice. Elise had little need to do more than nod. Katia was delighted to have a new cousin and guests for Christmas. She prattled on about the Christmas entertainments planned in Cherkassk and about how Elise and Nikholai would enjoy themselves.

Casually Nikholai settled himself in a rosewood chair near the stove. He exchanged the latest news with Timofe. And as his host related his own news, Nikholai began to fill his pipe with Timofe's tobacco. How like a married pair we are! Elise thought. And the Guskas made it so easy to play the part.

In the days that followed, Elise found Cherkassk more sophisticated than she had expected. The city was built upriver from the Turkish city of Azov, on the Black Sea, but just below the confluence of the Don and Donets rivers.

Despite the chain the Turks had stretched across the mouth of the Don, under cover of night and bribes, ships and caravans with exotic cargoes from Constantinople and the Mediterranean found their way to the Cossack city and on to Moscow's markets.

Nikholai told Elise that in the spring, when the streets of the low-lying city were often flooded, citizens traveled about by boat. That was how the city became known as the Cossack Venice.

But in the winter the city's muddy, frozen streets were filled with bright foreign costumes, flashy Cossack uniforms, seamen's shirts, and merchants' robes. Sleigh bells jingled, merchants chanted their wares, and sailors sang. Even in the cold, the streets rang with vitality and commerce.

Elise marveled at the daily sight of camels, street performers with dancing bears, and the winter carnival with trained monkeys, sword-swallowing Turks, and an ice slide.

Nikholai loved the ice slide with all the enthusiasm of a ten-year-old boy. Three times he picked Elise up and carried her down the mountainous slide, seated between his legs, his arms tight about her waist, his cheek against her ear. The wind bit their cheeks and tore at their hair. At the foot of the slide they tumbled into the snow.

"Please, no more, Nikholai Fomin," Elise begged breathlessly, skirts caked with ice, her cheeks stinging with the cold. She laughed from the pure exhilaration of the swift descent. But she wanted no more. "Spare me another trip down the ice slide."

With a full laugh, Nikholai agreed. When he laughed, his eyes were clear and dark, and his dimples softened the hard planes of his face. Elise liked him like this. He could be a most charming companion when there was no village to trouble him, she thought. He took her arm and drew her along to explore other entertainments at the carnival.

A puppet show caught her attention, and she was drawn along with the children to watch. Nikholai followed. The puppeteer folded his cloth and held it above his head so that he disappeared from view. Only the Gypsy, her husband Petrushka, and the Robber were visible. Like the children, Elise laughed and clapped her hands in delight at the ridiculous antics.

"Oh, how Anna would love this!" she whispered to Nikholai. "I wish she could be here." She sighed. Nikholai squeezed her hand and pulled her away from the giggling children.

They attended church and went caroling with other couples. Katia remained indoors, but she took great pleasure in introducing Elise to all the guests she and Timofe entertained in their home.

The coming baby fascinated Elise. She was delighted that Katia was willing to share the joy with her. At Katia's direction, Elise carried a small wooden chest into the sitting room, where they could go through the baby's things by the warm stove. Even as they talked and smiled over the tiny baby clothes—things finely embroidered and trimmed in lace—Katia could no longer hide her curiosity.

"Will there be a baby soon for you and Nikholai?"

"No, of course not," Elise replied too quickly. "It's too soon."

"Yes, of course," Katia said, and pinkened. "I didn't mean to offend. I only meant that sometimes it happens early, right away." She went on quickly, "That was not so for Timofe and me. But at last we start our family." She caressed her growing belly fondly. Then she changed the subject.

But the thought lingered in Elise's mind. For the first time since her marriage to the count, she thought about having her own child. Nikholai's baby—dark curls and gray eyes. A little fist with a powerful grip. Besides the pleasure Nikholai brought her in bed, he could give her a child.

Anxious and confused, Elise shoved the baby images away as quickly as she could fold and place the baby clothes back in the sandalwood chest. She would think only of Anna, she vowed.

Elise rested most of the day of the Christmas Eve ball because she wanted Katia to rest. Now she sat on the bed and watched Nikholai lather shaving soap for his face.

She wore only a clean chemise and a caftan loosely belted around her. She had attended too many balls in her young life to be particularly excited about this one. More important to her was Anna.

"So, what have you learned this week, Cossack?" Elise asked. "Is there no word about the Kalmyks with the eagle-wing standard?"

Every morning for the last week she had watched Nikholai and Timofe leave the house dressed in uniform to go to the Don Host. She did not delude herself that Nikholai spent his entire time asking about her sister. She knew that they met with other officers, shared reports and news, speculated on the turn of coming events—on the effect Stenka Razin would have on the future. While little was said among the women about the rebel, Elise was aware of the tension among the officers.

"Nothing definite yet," Nikholai replied. He stood shirtless before the shaving mirror. Elise stared at the fascinating cord of muscles in his back. "The scouts tell me that some Kalmyks are camped on the left bank north of here. The tribe has been in communication with Razin, but they do not carry the eagle-wing standard."

Elise was disappointed. At the same time, she was intrigued by his shaving ritual and by his broad shoulders.

Nikholai pulled on the end of his mustache to shave closer to it. Elise watched, suddenly captivated with the problems shaving around a mustache might pose. Satisfied with that side, Nikholai turned to the other, eyeing himself critically in the mirror.

"I think you left too much on that side," Elise offered. She chewed on the inside of her cheek to keep the grin from her face.

"What? You mean over here?" he asked, turning again to eye the side he had just completed. He swished the razor in the basin and went to work on that side again.

"Now it needs a little trimming on the other side," Elise pointed out. She sat up and hugged her knees and her newfound discovery: men had vanity too.

"Over here?" Nikholai looked closer in the mirror. "Where do you mean?" When he did not get an answer, he turned around. Elise hid her face against her knees, but she knew he would see her shoulders shaking with laughter.

"All right, Green Eyes," he said. "If you are to guide me in shaving and grooming my mustache, then I will dress your wild hair."

"I hear vengeance in your voice, Cossack."

"I have given up vengeance for more rewarding tactics," he said softly as he leaned over her upturned face. He kissed her lightly, then again, with a little more passion. Elise put her arms around his neck and returned his passion.

They were late in arriving at the holiday ball held in the Don Host kuren. If the Guskas knew why, and they probably did, they said nothing.

Although the surroundings offered less elegance than a European palace, the affair was as gay and colorful as any Elise had attended in the West. The kuren was decorated with festive, fragrant evergreen boughs and lit with many candles and oil lamps.

The guests were as cosmopolitan as the city streets. Elise saw bright European gowns and uniforms next to rich Turkish, Persian, and Cossack dress. The kuren hummed with a half-dozen languages.

Nikholai gave her an approving look when he removed her burka, as if he had not already seen her in her green gown. With encouragement from Katia and her dressmaker, Elise had selected a simple, traditional gown of green satin with an ivory brocade khalat lined with gold velvet.

At first he seemed eager to keep her at his side. He introduced her to the Don Host ataman, godfather of Stenka Razin, Kornil Iakovlev. The thin man bowed over Elise's hand. She was also introduced to the Muscovite envoy Gerasim Evdokimov and to the blond Swedish mercenary who had accompanied him from Moscow. They had brought word from the tsar regarding Stenka Razin's pardon. The Host had yet to make an official announcement on the outcome. Ill-at-ease, the Muscovites only offered polite remarks.

As they moved away from the emissaries, Elise turned to Nikholai, saying, "I know you know more than you tell me. Did the tsar accept the petition? Is Razin to be pardoned? Surely the tsar doesn't want a rebellion on his hands?"

"The tsar doesn't want to lose his Persian ally on the south either," Nikholai reminded her.

"Oh, tell me, Nikholai. Did the tsar pardon Stenka Razin?"

"I will not tell you, Green Eyes," he said, "because you would tell Katia, who would tell Martena, who would tell the servant in another household, and all of Cherkassk would know before Stenka Razin himself." Then with a grin he added, "Don't frown like that. Dance with me." And he led her onto the dance floor.

As the evening wore on, Nikholai grew more relaxed. He brought her spiced vodka and caviar on a biscuit.

"I've never liked it," she told him apologetically.

"But you've never had it the way it should be eaten," he replied. "It must be spread very delicately on a biscuit. See?"

He held the biscuit between them at mouth level and gazed into her eyes. They smiled at each other over the bit of food and shared delicious thoughts. "Try the caviar," Nikholai said at last, purposely breaking the spell. She tried it, to be polite; she finished it with pleasure.

He introduced her to his old friends and showed no concern about Elise's dancing with Timofe and other friends with whom he renewed acquaintances.

Eventually Nikholai wandered off, head-to-head in conversation with an old comrade. Elise was feeling a little deserted when Katia appeared without Timofe. "You know you are truly married when your husband deserts you at a celebration," she said with a laugh. "I hope you are enjoying our merrymaking."

"Yes, I am," Elise said.

The women talked for a few moments of the food, of their gowns and those of others, and of the guests—who was in attendance and who was absent.

"Tell me, Katia, please . . ." Elise began at last. For days she had listened carefully to the mention of names and to introductions. She wanted to know about one particular widow. "Is Aksinia Stockmana here?"

"Why?" Katia asked with a new alertness in her eyes. "You have heard what the gossips say? That Nikholai called on her. Don't believe it. Martena says Aksinia's serving woman told her Nikholai only stayed to drink tea."

Elise didn't spill a drop of her spiced vodka. Her hand remained steady. She was proud of her composure. Even if it was true, even if he did visit this widow, an old friend, why should it matter to her? After all, they were not truly married.

"Where is she?" Elise asked again.

"She is over there," Katia said with a vague gesture toward a slender ebony-haired woman dressed in yellow damask fashioned in the Dutch style. White point lace flattered the curve of her creamy shoulders and the line of her throat. Blue bows accented her narrow waist. The woman, with her shining black hair parted down the middle and curled over her ears, would be admired in any European court. Elise suddenly regretted her own Russian-style gown and her wild golden curls.

Aksinia Stockmana was talking with a clean-shaven man wearing a blond curly wig and a buff-colored military uniform trimmed in blue with gold braid. Elise recognized it as European but was unsure of the country. Cities of commerce were often visited by mercenaries who wore uniforms of no particular army.

Suddenly Elise realized that the pair was returning her rude stare. They began to walk across the crowded room toward her.

"Oh," Katia gasped, "I'm sorry. We can excuse ourselves."

"It's all right," Elise assured her, but she didn't feel all right. She wanted to leave. All the gaiety in the occasion had vanished. But she refused to retreat. Pride gave her courage.

Katia stammered for the first time since Elise had met her. She too quickly introduced Elise to Aksinia.

Aksinia turned to the small, blooming mother-to-be. "Katia, my dear, don't you think you should go rest?"

Katia looked uncertainly at Elise. "Yes, Katia. It's all right," Elise agreed.

As soon as Katia was out of hearing, Aksinia looked Elise over from head to toe. "Your gown is lovely. It must have cost Nikholai Fomin dearly."

"It was a gift from him," Elise replied. She was unable to think of anything clever.

"Nikholai has always been generous with his women," Aksinia acknowledged. "But I thought he favored the Western style. You know, he came to visit me just the other day. He was still recovering from the surprise of learning that

your brother is in Sweden on a secret mission for the Poles."
The almond-eyed woman stopped long enough to observe
the effect of her words on Elise. "But, of course you knew
that, Mistress Fomina. Nevertheless, Nikholai told me you
were English, and I thought you might enjoy meeting a
fellow Englishman. May I present John Sewell."

Elise turned to the man, who seemed bored and unable to
follow the Cossack conversation. She was numb inside, her
composure unruffled. So Nikholai had had word of Thomas,
and he had not told her.

"How do you do, Mr. Sewell?" Elise said in English. She
was pleased to be able to exclude the beautiful widow from
the conversation. John Sewell gratefully returned her English greeting and launched into a rapid speech that betrayed
his longing to speak his native language.

"I'm from around Canterbury," offered Sewell as they
talked. "Well, I was until Cromwell and his Parliament
usurped my family's estates. The same with your family, eh?
Now I'm a free man of the world. But I returned to London
not long ago."

"Oh, do tell me about it," Elise invited, trying to ignore
her own inner turmoil.

Sewell was a man of fair complexion with pale blue eyes
and faded brows. When he leaned closer to her, she noted
the purple spider veins across his nose. Soon Elise found she
was so glad to speak and hear English again that she never
noticed when Aksinia left them.

With no more urging than Elise's few words, John Sewell
described his visit to London only the year before. The city
was rebuilding rapidly after the fire and the plague only
three years earlier, he told her. Charles II's court was merry
as ever. His marriage to Portugal's Catherine of Braganza
and his fatherhood of Princess Anne had not kept the king
from his pleasures. Playwright John Dryden continued to be
a favorite of the court. His newest play then, *Sir Martin
Mar-All,* was well-attended. The English had signed the
Alliance of The Hague with the Dutch. Elise soaked up all
his English words like a steppe flower caught in a shower.

"But, fair lady, I think only of myself. Tell me, how do you
come to be in this obscure place?" Sewell asked at last.

Elise saw no reason to withhold from this man who she

was. He might be able to help her reach British or Polish officials. Briefly she explained how she had been captured by the Tartars, separated from her sister, and held for ransom by the Cossacks. She told him that she had had no word from her brothers. She omitted the details of her marriage.

"I know that name, James Chatham," Sewell said. "Your brother? Let me think. I saw the name on a list of company members who were to set sail for the New World. To South Carolina. My friend formed the company. He plans to establish a colony, Charles Town, in honor of the king. You did not know?"

"No." Elise shook her head. She could hardly believe John Sewell's words. James had always been fascinated by the New World. He had no reason to think she needed him. James was gone. He could not help her. Neither he nor Thomas was coming.

"Here, sit down." Sewell took her arm and led her to a bench. Once they were seated, he took her hand and leaned closer. "I know nothing of your other brother, Thomas. But if you need help, I will give it. I can get you out of here."

He leaned closer, and they discussed how an escape to Azov could be accomplished. She listened but debated within herself. John Sewell was a mercenary. Elise knew enough of the world to understand that that meant he fought for money. He had no real allegiance to any country. But what choice did she have? Her brothers could not help her. And Nikholai. He played a game she did not understand. She closed her eyes and pictured her Cossack pulling the petals from a daisy: "Aksinia . . . Elise . . . Aksinia . . . Elise . . . Aksinia. . . . " She shook the ridiculous vision from her mind.

"We can't leave tonight," Sewell confided. His eyes narrowed in an expression Elise didn't like. But he was a countryman, and he offered help. "I have to arrange for horses. I'll send you a message written in English as soon as I've made the arrangements. It may take two or three days."

"I'll wait for your message," she said at last. She could change her mind on the morrow.

"Good. I would never forgive myself for leaving you, a British lady, in the hands of these barbarians."

"What barbarians?"

Elise and John Sewell started and looked up into the kind blue eyes of a sea captain. His English was edged with a Dutch accent. His cheeks were a merry, weathered pink and his beard a gray-streaked white. Behind him stood Nikholai.

# ❧ 19 ❧

# Your Army and Mine

Oh." Elise jumped guiltily to her feet. "This is an Englishman, John Sewell." She spoke rapidly in Cossack. With a frown, Nikholai nodded curtly.

"This is Captain Johann Hals," Nikholai said in passable Dutch.

"Captain Hals," Elise replied, slipping easily into the language herself. She greeted the captain with a curtsy.

"It is a pleasure to meet you, Mistress Fomina," the sea captain said. "I spent three years at sea with your husband. He was an unhappy man then. I heard him vow never to marry again." The Dutchman laughed. Nikholai did not.

"You, a sailor?" Elise asked. She looked up at Nikholai, unable to picture him without his horses.

"One of the finest," supplied the Dutchman.

Nikholai and John Sewell remained silent, appraising each other in a manner just short of hostility.

"Mr. Sewell was just telling me the news of London," Elise said, trying to defuse the situation. Then she realized that remark could make things worse. "I mean, I asked about London after the fire, and . . . I mean . . ."

"You will dance with me now," Nikholai said. He grabbed her hand and pulled her away from the Englishman. She was

230

afraid the mercenary might be foolish enough to follow. But Captain Hals stepped in his way and began a conversation about the Alliance of The Hague.

They did not dance. Nikholai took her home immediately. They did not speak as they walked briskly through the streets of Cherkassk. Breathlessly she tried to keep up with Nikholai's long-legged stride. He held her elbow tightly, but she did not complain. Cheery light from other celebrating households fell from windows to light their way through the cold.

Elise broke the silence. "Surely you don't begrudge me a few words with a fellow countryman."

"Sewell is a mercenary. A man of bad reputation, Countess. Stay away from him." Nikholai's breath plumed into the night air.

"We only talked of home."

"Ump."

"Well, you didn't expect me to spend all evening talking with Aksinia Stockmana, did you?" she asked. "You are really the only thing we have to talk about."

Nikholai whirled her around to face him.

"We will not discuss Aksinia Stockmana," he said between his teeth. He shook her. "And you will never go near John Sewell again. He helped captives of the Turks once. He returned them home sick and injured and demanded a reward."

"Ow," Elise cried as she bit her tongue because of his shaking. "Stop it. Stop it." She pulled herself away and looked up into his face. She saw no dimples now, only hard, cold planes and frost on his mustache. "Reward or ransom. What difference does it make? And keep your Aksinia to yourself. I don't care. I don't."

But in her heart she knew that she did. The painful thought of his embracing the beautiful ebony-haired woman as he had embraced her just hours ago made her want to scream.

He knew where her brothers were, and he had told Aksinia, not her. Her brothers were gone. Anna was lost. What did he know that he had not told her? Elise suddenly wondered. She stared at him.

Was there no one she could trust? She was alone. She

clasped her hands over her mouth to capture her cry of pain, but to her shame, great tears of desolation streamed down her cheeks, stinging as they froze.

"Oh, don't do it, Countess," Nikholai warned. "You will not rule me with your tears." With his hand clamped on her elbow again, he led her to the Guskas' home. Elise lacked the strength to resist.

The next day, Christmas Day, Elise tried to have as little to do with Nikholai as possible. The day was celebrated with the traditional feast that ended with a pot of kutya, rice boiled with raisins and nuts. Timofe first threw a spoonful out the front door, saying, "Here is a spoonful for thee, Grandfather Frost. Please do not touch our crops."

Then, laughing, Katia threw a spoonful to the ceiling and implored Elise to help her count the grains that stuck. "That's the number of bees that will come in the summer to make our honey," she explained with a giggle. "Martena, you didn't make the rice sticky enough."

They all laughed, even Elise. Katia, busy with the festivities, hadn't noticed the silence between Elise and Nikholai until they sat down to exchange gifts.

"So solemn, you two," Katia prompted as they gathered by the tiled stove. "Open this box, Elise. I have been longing to know what it is since the boy delivered it yesterday. And, Nikholai, Elise dragged Martena from shop to shop and stall to stall to find this for you."

Elise was surprised to find herself blushing. More than once during their stay, she had found Nikholai reading Timofe's copy of the *Iliad*. As she should have guessed, he favored the passages about Hektor. So she had indeed searched Cherkassk to find a leather-bound copy of the *Iliad* in Greek. There was only one. And she had spent all her coins on it, coins Nikholai had given her for herself.

Proudly Nikholai stroked the leather cover of the gift and gave Elise a quiet smile of appreciation.

With another prompting from Katia, Elise pulled open the box sent by Nikholai. Katia gasped. Elise remained silent.

"Put it on," Katia chattered. "Put it on." She pulled the sable hat from the box and put it on Elise.

"It's beautiful on you," Katia went on. "And, see? There's a muff to match, with a satin lining."

Elise avoided Nikholai's gaze and smiled agreeably at Katia. The beautiful Aksinia's words echoed through her mind: "Nikholai has always been generous with his women."

Two days later Nikholai puffed idly on his pipe and watched a lump of ice melt on the floor of the Don Host kuren. He sat on the bench nearest the door with his long legs stretched comfortably before him. He was so absorbed in his thoughts, he hardly noticed the blasts of cold air from the door when a Cossack left or arrived.

Voices murmured and shouted about him in the smoke-filled room. But Nikholai paid no heed. His mind was on Elise. He still could not forget the image of her sitting with the Englishman at the ball. In the torchlight, the gold of her hair had shone brightly against the green velvet headdress and her ivory khalat. She had had eyes and ears only for the Englishman. Nikholai wished Katia had come to him sooner. He would have separated them before the conversation had gone too far.

Elise had been cool and distant since that night. Had the Englishman promised her anything? Did he know something about her brothers that Nikholai hadn't been able to learn? That he had not told her? With tales of London, had John Sewell fueled her desire to leave the steppe?

She had said nothing of that. To his surprise, when he warned her about Sewell, she had spoken only of Aksinia Stockmana.

The widow had made quite a scene when Nikholai had called to tell her personally of his marriage.

"I will not let you go so easily," she had threatened.

He should have been suspicious when she cajoled him into dancing with her at the ball. She did not know Elise was a captive. Yet he had little doubt that somehow Aksinia had made sure Elise met John Sewell. Did Aksinia hope to stir homesickness or jealousy? She wanted to cause trouble, of that he was certain.

But why? he wanted to ask her. Spite? They had been

lovers, but they had not loved. He would never live a city life, and Aksinia would never live life on the steppe. They both had known that from the beginning.

The morning session of the Host had been spent in settling a squabble between a landowner and a poor stanitsa. The stanitsa shepherds said the goats were theirs.

During the proceedings, the Muscovite envoy, Gerasim Evdokimov, sat next to Don Host Ataman Kornil Iakovlev at the head table. As an officer and a former ataman, Nikholai was a respected member of the Host's governing body.

A lecture against pirating was followed by an election of emissaries to accompany Evdokimov on his return to Moscow. As soon as the Swede returned from his mission to Kagalnik to inform Razin of the tsar's conditional pardon, they—Evdokimov, the Swede, and a Host representative—would depart for Moscow to assure the tsar of the Host's allegiance.

Nikholai rubbed his hand across his eyes and regretted drinking so much the night before. When he took his hand away to stare at the floor before him, a pair of well-worn red boots faced him.

He looked up into the lined face of a sinewy little Terek Cossack. The man wore a sheepskin coat covered in icy curls. A long mustache drooped over his thin mouth. Bushy brows marked the small brown eyes, which raked Nikholai from head to toe.

"You drank too much last night, Cossack," the Terek said. "Wouldn't be having woman trouble, would you? You are Nikholai Fomin? The Wolf?"

"Who are you?" Nikholai asked. He sat up straight and took the pipe from his mouth, but he did not stand. He tried to meet the older Cossack's gaze, but it was uncomfortably piercing. Nikholai already suspected who this was, and he decided he would rather have met all of Elise's brothers fully armed.

The little man squatted before Nikholai. "I'm Yergov, sometimes called the Terek. I heard you have a new wife. A blond girl with green eyes. She comes from the right bank of the Dnieper. Is that so?"

"Perhaps."

"I might know her," the Terek said, still appraising Nikholai. "Fine words and languages come easily to her tongue. She is a fighter."

Nikholai nodded. This man knew Elise.

"I want to speak with her. I want to know if this marriage is valid and if she agreed to it."

Nikholai rose to his full height and towered over the Terek. "She did and she is well."

The little man also rose. He tilted his head back and held his ground, as well as Nikholai's gaze. "I want to hear that from her."

Nikholai's first reaction was to say no. No good was going to come from Elise's meeting people from her former life. And he disliked being pressed by any man. Yet, part of him felt obligated to win the approval of someone in Elise's life. If not her brothers, then Yergov would do. His concern was that Yergov, a brother Cossack, might be more difficult to please. Nikholai flung his burka over his shoulder, picked up his cap, and said, "Come with me."

Just as Nikholai reached for the door handle, it was flung open. Off balance, Nikholai stepped back into Yergov. The two found themselves face-to-face with Stenka Razin. The huge man's presence filled the kuren.

The voices in the room died. A gust of icy wind whipped through the kuren. Torches flickered. Pipe smoke swirled and rolled to the rafters. No one moved.

Razin stared through Nikholai. Then the rebel shoved the two men aside and strode into the kuren.

"Where is this Muscovite envoy, Evdokimov?" Razin demanded. "I want no more news third-hand." He motioned to his men.

They shoved the Swedish envoy through the door. The man collapsed on the floor before Nikholai. He was so badly beaten that only his lank blond hair gave evidence of his identity.

Nikholai quickly counted the ten unshaven Cossacks who filed into the kuren and formed a half-circle behind Razin. They carried muskets across their chests, ready to fire.

Razin strode to the center of the room.

"Godfather, how dare you send a foreigner to tell me the tsar will pardon me for raids that brought riches and cannons to his city of Astrakhan only if I give up the streltsy who joined me?" He looked about the room, finally resting his glare on the men at the head table.

"Well, Ataman Kornil Iakovlev?" Sarcasm whined in Razin's voice. "Where is the tsar's real envoy?"

The thin, gray ataman rose slowly to his feet, straightened his shoulders, and spoke clearly. "Godson. This is Gerasim Evdokimov, envoy of Tsar Alexis." He indicated the other man seated at the table.

"Evdokimov." Razin acknowledged the broad man dressed in furs. "And who sent you, Gerasim Evdokimov? The tsar or the boyars?"

"I come from Tsar Alexis himself, Stenka Razin," the man said, almost too softly to hear. He did not rise from his seat.

"Speak up, man. By whom?"

Slowly the man rose to his feet. "The tsar. By Tsar Alexis himself," the envoy said, more loudly this time. He looked about the crowd of Cossacks for help, for support. All remained silent. Only the moaning of the beaten Swede could be heard.

"You lie!"

"Why should I lie?" Evdokimov asked. "Here is the document, the letter signed and sealed by the tsar himself. It says you offended the princes of Persia. Your raids broke the Muscovites' agreement with the Persians. That cannot be allowed. You must give up the rest of the cannon you took and the streltsy who turned against their own officers."

"So it's true," Razin said. "The tsar expects me to turn over my cannon and my men when we have already gifted half our booty to the Prince of Astrakhan. No." Razin shook his hands in the air and shouted, "I say no. No more. The boyars sent you. It is the boyars who are greedy. They steal from us to pay for the wars with Poland and Sweden. No more."

Some of the krug members cheered with Razin and his men. Iakovlev remained silent. The Muscovite began to tremble. Nikholai glanced down at the Swede, who now lay still, a smear of blood on the floor next to his purple cheek.

"Razin is mad," Yergov muttered matter-of-factly in Nikholai's ear.

Nikholai nodded.

The Don Host ataman spoke at last. "We have an alliance with Tsar Alexis. We have had it with the Romanovs for years, and we must respect it."

"My quarrel is not with the tsar," Razin said. "It is with the greedy boyars. They demand our remaining cannon, cannon we took from the Persians. They demand our fighting men. They would steal from us our only means for protecting ourselves against the Tartars. These are the same greedy boyars who treat poor runaway serfs as if they are no more than livestock. They would make us their serfs too. They will take our freedom!"

Those words struck a vein of fear in all of the Cossacks—landowner, stockman, merchant, fisherman, or shepherd.

"Would you support these boyars, Kornil Iakovlev?"

"I cannot disregard a document from the tsar, Godson."

"Then you are the tsar's fool," Razin said, shaking his fists again. "You take care of your people. I will take care of mine. I will not surrender mine to greedy boyars. Who would join me? All are welcome. Cossack. Tartar. Streltsy. Serf. Follow me. Follow me. We'll throw the boyars' envoys in the river. For God and Allah!"

Before the Swede was seized by one of Razin's men, Nikholai moved to block the way. He stood over the envoy. "No," he shouted. "Envoys are protected under a flag of truce, regardless of their message. Their lives are secure under the white flag."

"Bah," Razin returned. Unprepared for the rebel's powerful blow, Nikholai was flattened by the huge man's fist. He regained his stance as soon as possible, but the Swede had already been dragged away by Razin's men. Nikholai started after them, but Yergov pulled him back. "The odds are too poor, even for the Wolf," the little Terek said as he held Nikholai back.

Stenka Razin strode to the head table, where the Muscovite stood. Iakovlev stepped in front of the cowering envoy.

"Out of the way, Godfather," Razin warned. "Don't make me show the world how soft you have become."

"Stenka, this is foolish," Iakovlev said. "Don't add this offense to those Moscow is marking against us."

Razin's men began to chant. "Give Razin the boyar.

Boyar. Boyar. We want the boyar." Some of the Host members joined in. Thunder rose as men began to stamp their feet to the rhythm of the chant. More and more voices began to take up the words. Nikholai watched as Iakovlev looked around the room, trying to assess the situation. Whom could he count on? Nikholai sympathized with the old man. He knew well that desperate feeling.

Finally the gray old man stepped aside. With a crowing laugh, Razin grabbed the Muscovite by his fur collar and dragged him from the kuren.

"This smells bad, Nikholai Fomin," Yergov said. "I want no part of it."

"Nor I," said Nikholai as he rubbed his jaw. They left before they witnessed the fate of the tsar's envoys.

Red-eyed and swollen-faced, Martena met them at the door.

"I couldn't help it. I couldn't help it, Colonel Fomin," she sputtered. The hysterical servant bobbed bow after bow and sobbed into her apron. "She's so clever. I didn't know she wanted to go away."

Nikholai grabbed the serving woman's shoulders to halt her bowing and babbling. "Who wants to go away?" he demanded with more roughness than he intended.

Terrified, Martena wailed and covered her face with her apron.

"It's not her fault, Nikholai," Katia interrupted. Slowly the mother-to-be started down the stairs one at a time, leaning back to support the bulk that preceded her. Timofe rushed to steady her. When she reached the foot of the stairs, she continued. "Elise left a note. I found it in your bedchamber. It's addressed to you." She handed the folded paper to Nikholai. "Oh, Nikholai, I know this is my fault. I should never have told her what the gossips said or introduced her to Aksinia."

Nikholai stared numbly at the folded paper. From the feel of it, she had left him something. He was afraid to open it, to know what she had said before she left him.

"Please, don't blame yourself, Katia," he said earnestly, and tried to smile. He liked Katia. "There is more trouble between us than you can know."

"Read it in here, Nikholai," Katia said, motioning to the sitting room. "We will have tea in the kitchen."

He walked to the warm blue-tiled stove. He did not sit down. Nor did he notice the snow melting from his boots onto Katia's fine Persian rug. He just stared at the packet.

At last he unfolded the paper. The handclasp wedding band lay innocently atop delicately scrawled Polish words: "Nikholai, this ring belongs to you and your family. I am not your wife. I cannot take it with me. But I keep St. Nikholas. As you know, I must find Anna without the help of my brothers. I may need the saint's protection. E."

## ❧ 20 ❧

# The Cossack and the Coward

Nikholai jammed the tiny ring over the knuckle of his little finger. The pain of doing so distracted him from the ache in his throat. Ring or no ring, their marriage was recorded in Vazka's Bible. The whole village had witnessed their vows. She was his wife. She had no right to leave. Angrily he threw the wadded note into the stove's fire. He would find her, he promised himself. He promised her. Escaping him would not be that easy.

He paced the room, trying to restore order to his chaotic thoughts, to his chaotic emotions. So she knew about her brothers. The Englishman had told her something. She had gone with him, of course. And the mercenary probably intended to ransom her back to their government, just as he had done with others. Just as Nikholai had planned to do himself. He shook his head ruefully.

What had that foreign devil offered? he wondered. She wanted to find Anna. How could Sewell promise her that when Nikholai himself had been unable to uncover any information about the child? How was Sewell getting them away from Cherkassk? What would happen to them in the midst of Stenka Razin's mob? Nikholai was thankful she had kept St. Nikholas.

240

"Nikholai?" Katia appeared at the sitting-room door.

"Katia, are some of Timofe's clothes missing?"

"Yes, I just noticed his red jacket was gone from the hook by the door. Do you think Elise took it?"

"Yes. Now, tell me when she left and what direction she went in."

She described how a messenger had come with a note and how Elise had told her that it was only a polite greeting from the Englishman. Nikholai nodded and urged her to go on.

Katia had been tired after the holiday festivities, so they had planned no outings for the day, but Elise had asked to go to market with Martena. Then, while Mårtena haggled over the price of fish with a merchant, Elise disappeared. That was just before Razin's Cossacks began to race through the streets.

"I'm so sorry," said Katia, on the verge of tears. "You two are so perfect together. How could I be so thoughtless?"

"Do not blame yourself," Nikholai said. He noted with concern the dark circles below Katia's eyes. Her time would come soon, he suspected. He stood up and turned to find Timofe and Yergov standing in the doorway.

"She knows about her brothers," Nikholai said. "She must have learned it from the mercenary. She has gone with him."

"We can leave right now," Timofe offered.

"No," Yergov interrupted. "Let me go. She will come to me. I'll need a horse, Wolf. I left mine at the Don Host kuren."

Elise stopped again to work her foot down into Timofe's boot. She had been more fortunate in the clothes borrowed from Vazka's youths. Timofe's things, though smaller than Nikholai's, were too large to be comfortable or practical. The spiky frozen ruts of the muddy riverfront made it impossible for her to do more than hobble along behind Sewell.

"Come. What's the problem?" the Englishman snapped. "We've got to get through this riverfront area to reach the horses. I want to be beyond the city before dark." He retraced his steps to grab Elise's hand and drag her along behind him. "Where did all these insane bloody Cossacks come from?" he shouted over the battle cry of a pair of riders that galloped past.

"I don't know. They don't wear the Don Host uniform," Elise said, looking over her shoulder. She couldn't believe Sewell still wore a wig. She tried to stop again to work her toes into her other boot. Sewell yanked roughly on her arm, and she stumbled after him. When she regained her balance, she braced herself and yanked back. Sewell staggered to a stop and turned on her.

"If you want to get away from this place, you'll do as I say," he snapped. A pair of sailors passed them, and he lowered his voice so that they could not hear his words.

"I'll do as you say," Elise said. "Have patience."

He shot her an irritated look. He reached for her hand again, but she pulled away. "You lead. I'll follow," she suggested firmly. He looked vexed, but he led the way.

The high ground of the marketplace, church, and fine homes of Cherkassk were well behind them. They walked through narrow alleys of the lower part of the city. The kuren warehouses, built on stilts to avoid spring floods, blocked her view to the river, but Elise could hear the river on their left.

Then rhythmic voices raised in a chant reached them. She and Sewell turned another corner and emerged on a broader thoroughfare. A pack of ragged Cossacks chanting, "Boyar, boyar!" brushed past them toward the skull-and-tails standard.

Near the standard rode Stenka Razin. Over the churning sea of heads around the rebel she saw two men being carried. With horror she recognized the Muscovite envoy and his Swedish assistant. The blond man seemed lifeless, but the fat man, once dressed in furs and burgundy wool, screamed and struggled against his captors. The mob tore at his clothes and mimicked his screams. His eyes were wild. His face was battered and his boots gone.

"What are they going to do with them?" Elise gasped.

"Throw them into the river," Sewell told her. Neither of them could stop staring at the seething mob and its victims. The faces Elise saw around them were knotted and warped with hate.

The winter cold of the day sliced through her. She turned

away, but found her way blocked by more Cossacks crowding toward the river. They were not all Razin's Cossacks. Elise saw the blue of the Don Host uniform in the crowd. She wondered where Nikholai was.

She turned back to Sewell. He gripped her arm tightly just to keep them from getting separated among the shoving, smelly bodies. The mob swept them closer to the river.

Elise was helpless. She watched as the mob carried the unfortunate envoys—the Swede, who was either unconscious or dead, and the screaming Muscovite—out onto the stone landing that extended into the Don.

Two Cossacks took the Muscovite's arms and legs and began to swing him. Back and forth. Back and forth. The man howled. His cry rose through the air, then was cut off by the ice-filled water of the Don. He bobbed up only once amid the chunks of ice, then disappeared. The Swede was tossed in unceremoniously and disappeared.

The mob cheered, then began to sing and dance with one another.

Elise was jostled against Sewell. He steadied her. She felt sick, as she had at her morning meal. She just needed some fresh air and a little warm soup. The thought made her cover her mouth.

"This way. The mob is thinning," Sewell said. Elise did not fight his grip this time.

"Hey, where are you going, foreigner?" demanded an ugly Cossack with a scarred face. He grabbed the cuff of Sewell's uniform and swung the mercenary around.

Sewell released Elise and struck the Cossack in the face. Blood spurted from the man's nose. He paid no heed to his injury. He rounded on Sewell with a blow that would have sent the Englishman to the ground if he had not stumbled back into Elise. She fell. On hands and knees, she struggled to rise before she was stepped on.

The Cossack mob tore off Sewell's curly wig and ripped the cuffs from his coat. The mercenary struck at one bearded Cossack, but two more grabbed him and started to drag him toward the river. He resisted.

Elise blinked when she saw the Englishman wigless. He was balding, with only a fringe of pale hair from ear to ear.

"Boyar, boyar!" the enraged warriors shouted. The mob

shoved Elise to the ground again when she had just managed to get one foot under her. She struggled to her feet again after the scar-faced Cossack stepped on her gloved hand.

"He's not one of the tsar's boyars!" Elise shouted to be heard over the chanting. She struck at the grasping hands. "Stop. Stop. What would a boyar be doing here? Watching his fellow boyars be drowned? He's an Englishman. A soldier who has fought against the Turks and Tartars as you have."

"Boyar or foreigner, we don't need either in Cherkassk," shouted a Cossack who wore a black horsehide for a burka. "They carry tales." He grabbed Sewell's buff-colored coat collar.

"Ah, brother," a familiar voice interrupted with a friendly blow on the burly Cossack's arm. "What have you got there?"

Elise whirled to see Sultan beside her.

"No," she wailed. "Damn you. No!" She turned to run, but the tail of her—Timofe's—jacket was caught. She turned to pull free and looked up belligerently. Then, "Yergov!" she gasped, staring into the face of a true friend. He released her jacket. She took a step toward him, but Sewell renewed his grip on her arm.

"Free the boy, Englishman," came an authoritative demand from the rider behind Yergov. Elise looked over Sultan's rump to see Nikholai on Sotnik. He watched her with dark, angry eyes. But he said no more when Yergov silenced him with a gesture.

She was relieved to have the mob's actions interrupted, but she would not go back with Nikholai. Never. Aksinia. Her brothers. The ransom. He had betrayed her. Never.

"We're going to throw this foreigner into the river," the burly Cossack said. His scar-faced friend was trying to stanch a bleeding nose. "We have no quarrel with the boy. But this foreigner, once drowned, will carry no tales."

"True," Yergov agreed. He eyed Elise disapprovingly. "What are you doing here with this foreigner, Mitka?"

"You know the boy?"

"Yes, my nephew," Yergov said with a wave of his arm. "We got separated when this party started."

"So you would corrupt our youth," accused the burly

Cossack. He gave Sewell another shake. Sewell's eyes narrowed.

His grip tightened on Elise's arm. In English he spoke to her. "Tell your Terek friend that if he doesn't want to see you thrown into the river with me, he will get me out of this too."

"What?" Elise asked, certain she had heard incorrectly.

"Do it," Sewell hissed. He twisted Elise's arm so that she winced, but she did not cry out.

"What says he?" asked Yergov quietly in Polish.

"He asks to be saved from the Cossacks."

"Or what, Mitka? Tell me all," Yergov said, seemingly concerned with a strand of Sultan's mane. Nikholai remained silent, but Sotnik pranced.

"Or he will drag me to the river with him."

"What's going on?" demanded the burly Cossack. "Speak so that I can understand."

"Leave the boy and the foreigner to me, brother," Yergov suggested. "I'd like to teach the foreigner a lesson of my own."

"We'll help," the Cossack offered with a laugh. "Then we'll drink to his fate together."

"I must return the boy to his family," the little Cossack said with a shrug. "Have it your way. The foreigner is yours. Come up behind me, Mitka."

Sewell twisted her arm more.

"Release the boy," Nikholai demanded.

"Aren't you Nikholai Fomin?" asked the scar-faced Cossack. "The one called Wolf? You killed more Turks than any Cossack in 'fifty-four."

All the Cossacks in the group around Sewell turned to stare at the tall man on the dun horse.

Nikholai shrugged. "Will you not trust me to deal justly with this Englishman?"

"No," Elise shouted. "No, Nikholai Fomin. You will not cheat me out of this." Sewell stared at her. Her rage was so great he released her and stepped away.

Yergov shook his head. "The boy is misguided. You know how youth is," he explained to the other Cossacks.

"Oh, take the foreigner and the boy with you, Terek," the scarred Cossack said. "We will find other fish to throw back to the river, eh?" He looked around to his friends for agreement. His friends cheered the idea, and they struck off toward the section of the city where foreigners lived.

Sewell straightened his lapels and picked up the shreds of his wig from the frozen, muddy street.

Yergov extended his hand to Elise. At first she refused it.

"Go with them," Sewell said, placing his wig on his bald head. "If they want you so badly, they can have you. No reward is worth this kind of risk."

Dismayed, Elise stared at the Englishman. Then she glared at Nikholai. "I will not return to him."

"Come with me," Yergov said quietly.

Elise took his hand and vaulted onto the horse. Once astride Sultan, behind Yergov with woolly curls of his coat in her grasp, she felt safer than she had since that day in October on the Dnieper. Yergov could be gruff, tight-lipped, and demanding. But she could trust him. He would tell her no lies. Elise gave a small sigh of relief.

Shouting erupted from down the street. The four turned to watch a band of Razin Cossacks drag a pair of Dutch sailors from a vodka shop and chase them down the street.

"I'm getting out of here," said Sewell. "Russians are crazy when they get suspicious of strangers." He ran toward the stable he had pointed to earlier.

"Stay with him?" Elise cried as she bounced along behind Yergov on Sultan. "But he lied to me."

"You'd rather trust the Englishman?"

"I'd rather go with you," Elise said. "You wouldn't lie to me." When she received no answer, she asked, "Would you?"

"I might, if I thought the truth would cause you to lose your courage."

Elise said no more as Nikholai rode ahead of them, leading the way from the riverfront to the Guskas' home. The same streets that had rung with Christmas carols and sparkled with gay lanterns only days ago were now dark. Smoke drifted down from chimneys, and fog crept in from the river. Screaming laughter and senseless shouts echoed through the narrow ways. Only drunken Razin Cossacks were abroad in the murk, staggering from one vodka shop to another. Elise renewed her grip on Yergov's coat.

"You saw what almost happened to the Englishman," Yergov reminded her. "Thomas can't be reached now. Stay with Nikholai Fomin in Vazka. It is the best way. I will search for Anna."

They rounded the corner of the Guskas' street. Elise saw the tall caped figure of Nikholai dismount. Orange torchlight glittered on the rutted snow and hardened the planes of his face.

How great was his anger? she wondered. He could be no angrier than she was. Yergov halted Sultan before the Guskas' door.

"You lied to me," Elise accused immediately upon sliding down from the stallion's back.

"You broke your word," Nikholai countered without a flicker of guilt in his expression. He made no move.

"My obligation to my word dissolved when you lied," she said.

"I told you no lies. And I think you knew where Thomas was all along," he charged.

She had suspected where Thomas was, but she would give the ataman no credit for the insight.

Yergov dismounted and stood behind Elise.

"She will stay with you this time," the little Terek said.

"I did not agree to that," Elise said.

Nikholai stepped toward her, his scowl harsher, if that was possible.

Elise felt panic rise. She grabbed at Yergov's arm. "Don't you see this is what he wants?" she whispered to the Terek. "I think he intends to avenge the loss of his family estates by keeping me forever."

"Nikholai Fomin will know when it's time to release you." Yergov gave the tall Cossack a meaningful look. "I'll care for the horses, then be on my way."

Still grim-faced, Nikholai reached for Elise's wrist.

"Don't you start that too," she snapped, and pulled away.

Nikholai stopped and glanced at Yergov for an explanation. Yergov shrugged and led Sultan and Sotnik toward the stable.

Nikholai turned back to her. "Countess, this way, please." He indicated the way into the house with a mocking bow.

Head held high, she marched inside, hoping to find Katia. The little mother-to-be could allay Nikholai's anger. But no one greeted them.

The kitchen glowed with the feeling of warmth and security. Elise pulled off Timofe's gloves and sniffed the air. The heat made her cold cheeks tingle, and the aroma of food made her stomach growl.

"Mistress Fomina?" Martena said when she looked up from the kettle of fish-and-rice soup she stirred. The servant had never seen "Mitka." She blinked before adding, "You are all right? We were so worried about you with the terrible things going on in the streets. Let me take your coat." Martena wiped her hands on her apron and helped Elise off with the red jacket.

"I'm sorry if I upset you," Elise apologized.

"Food for Mistress Fomina," Nikholai ordered as he brushed past them. Martena scurried back to the soup kettle.

"Sit," he ordered, pointing to the kitchen bench.

"Be angry with me if you like, but spare the servants," Elise hissed. He glared back. She met his glare. With intentional, maddening sloth, Elise strolled to the table, brushed off the bench, and finally sat. Nikholai pulled off his gloves and slapped them on the table. He sat down.

Hurriedly Martena put a plate of goat cheese and barley bread on the table next to the honey pot. She drew a cup of hot cider and, with a wary look at Nikholai, set it before Elise.

"Where's Katia?" Elise asked as she pulled off her cap and laid it aside with the gloves.

"In bed. Master Timofe is reading to her," Martena said. "She had pains after you left. The midwife said it was false labor."

"False labor?" Elise looked down at the plate, afraid to ask what had happened in her absence. She hoped her escape attempt had not affected Katia's condition. "Is she all right? And the baby?"

"Yes. Yes," Martena said, setting a bowl of soup before

Elise. "She will be better now, knowing you are back. I'll tell her."

"Eat," Nikholai ordered, and handed her the honey-covered bread he had just prepared. "You ate nothing this morning."

Dispiritedly Elise began to eat the bread.

Martena returned to the kitchen and found work as far from the table as possible.

"You planned to go to Azov with him, didn't you?" Nikholai accused softly so that the serving woman could not overhear. "You went off with a stranger. A man you have met only once. You thought nothing of how people here would worry." He shoved the bowl of steaming fish soup closer to her.

She took it. The aroma whetted her appetite. She knew he was trying to make her feel guilty. And she did feel terrible about upsetting Katia. She spooned the hot soup down and covertly eyed the wedding ring on Nikholai's little finger. She prayed he would not ask her to wear it again. She would rather he bound her hands.

"Why did you go with him? What did the Englishman offer you?"

"What do you think he offered me?" she asked. "Freedom. And he offered to help me find my sister. He did not lie to me about my brothers." In her renewed anger, Elise unintentionally banged the spoon on the table. On the other side of the kitchen, Martena jumped.

Nikholai leaned across the table. "I have promised to give you all of those things, but you turn to the Englishman. Why?"

Elise leaned across the table to meet his anger. "Because he is my countryman. He has no village to trouble him. No rebellion to fight. No woman to throw in my face. He has no grudge to settle."

Their gazes held across the narrow space for a long moment. To Elise's relief, Nikholai's gray eyes were clear and dark. At last he turned and rose from the bench. He paced across the kitchen and back, pulled off his burka and dropped it to the bench.

Elise returned to her soup and wondered what she was

going to do now. Her brothers were off on their own adventures. Even Yergov had refused to take her. The Englishman was a coward and a traitor. Only this mad Cossack would have her.

Nikholai took his seat across from her. He sliced more cheese and bread and gave it to her before he took some for himself.

"You know how my plans for vengeance turned on me," he said quietly as he finished the cheese. "Aksinia Stockmana is of no importance. I will not discuss her. But do you truly fear I intend to make you pay for your husband's offenses?"

"If you don't, then why do you refuse to release me?" Elise asked. "Azov would be easy to reach from here. You wouldn't even have to accompany me."

"But if I released you to go to Azov, you would learn no more about your sister," Nikholai pointed out. "Besides, the state of affairs right now makes it too dangerous for you to travel alone, and the weather can turn bad at any moment. As Yergov said, I will know when the time is right to release you. We will discuss it no more."

Elise watched him rise from the table again. She had not expected him to agree to her release. She sighed and hoped he was going to leave her to eat in peace. He unnerved her, watching every bite she put into her mouth, as if life depended on it.

Now that his anger had subsided, she relaxed. She was suddenly aware of being full of food and warmed to the bone. She knew she could trust Yergov to find Anna.

"Martena, prepare a bath for Mistress Fomina and help her to bed," Nikholai ordered over his shoulder with an edge in his voice that jolted Elise from her lethargy. He leaned toward her across the table. "We leave Cherkassk tomorrow," he said. "We learned while we were out searching for you that Ataman Iakovlev has refused to call the Host to a vote. Vikola Panko must know that the Host does not officially support or deny Razin."

## ❧ 21 ☙
# The Lookout

Elise went to say farewell to Katia the next morning. Pale and still abed, Katia smiled at her when she entered the room. Elise apologized for upsetting her. Katia waved the apology aside.

"It was the excitement of the Christmas holiday," Katia said with a sigh. "All is well now. I'm sorry you must leave. You are welcome here anytime, you know."

Elise swallowed tears of sorrow at parting, for she truly liked Katia. They kissed cheeks and embraced.

Wearing the sable hat and carrying the muff Nikholai had given her as a Christmas gift, Elise allowed him to tuck her into the sledge. Their sledge was too small to be pulled by a troika, a three-horse hitch. But Nikholai had packed it full of things for the village. When one of Razin's Cossacks halted them at the gate watchtower, Nikholai simply said he carried news of Stenka Razin's takeover of the Don Host to allies in Vazka. Without further delay, they were allowed to leave the chaotic streets of Cherkassk behind.

They traveled side by side in thoughtful silence. Besides her guilty feelings about Katia, Elise was aware of a sense of remorse where Nikholai was concerned. Katia had let slip as they exchanged farewells that he had spent the night in a chair next to the sitting-room stove with a jug of vodka. He had terrified Martena by prowling about the house and issuing gruff orders.

"I don't know what troubles the two of you," Katia began. "Pay no heed to Aksinia's words. Be patient with Nikholai. You are very important to him."

Elise knew the Cossack hadn't spent the entire night with the vodka jug, for she remembered the gentle sinking of the bed with his weight and the warm tickle of his mustache on her brow. She was certain he had stayed with her for a while. But at dawn she had awakened alone.

The return trip to Vazka seemed shorter than the journey to Cherkassk. The unspoken truce between her and Nikholai allowed her to snuggle against him under the blankets and furs. She slept most of the way. Often she awoke with her head against his shoulder and his arm around her.

He had promised her freedom in time. Yergov had promised to find Anna. She was content to leave it at that for now.

Vazka appeared quiet as they drove through the gate. Elise and Nikholai had hardly alighted from the sleigh and entered the cottage when Vikola crunched through the snow to demand the news.

Before Nikholai could convey all that had happened, Bogdan, Ostap, Kasyan, and Daria arrived. Then, seated at his table, Nikholai told the story of Razin and the Don Host once more. Elise helped Natalia with serving tea and listened from the next room. She felt a little flutter of pride when he told of confronting Razin about the treatment of the tsar's emissaries.

"You challenged Stenka Razin?" Bogdan asked, awe in his voice.

"Iakovlev deplored the emissaries' treatment too," Nikholai said.

"And Kornil Iakovlev had to back down from his godson," Vikola said. "Vazka's krug will be pleased to hear this." Ostap agreed. The new ataman and his lieutenant left to call a krug.

Bogdan and Kasyan looked across the table at each other, then down at their cider cups.

"Go," Nikholai ordered. "You are his men now. Vazka must stand together," he added impatiently. The two men left.

In the silence that followed, Elise stifled a yawn and saw a look of concern pass between Natalia and Nikholai.

"She ate nothing this morning, Aunt," Nikholai said gruffly. He stared down at the inventory Bogdan had given him to look over. "Feed her and put her to bed."

The little woman turned to Elise and searched her face. "Was this the first morning you have not eaten?" she asked.

"No," Elise said. She shrugged. "I'm just tired from the trip. Katia and Timofe entertained us so gaily."

"Nushka, this is not the best way to get what you want," Natalia said. Guilt appeared on Nikholai's face. Then, despite Natalia's grave expression, he smiled, a small smug smile Elise recognized as male vanity.

"Out, Nikholai," Natalia ordered. "I must talk with the countess alone. Out."

Without saying a word, Nikholai picked up his pipe, put on his caftan, and went out into the cold. Elise looked back at Natalia, still confused by the woman's frown.

Natalia took her hand. "When was your last monthly flow?" she asked. "You had one shortly after you arrived. I was relieved there would be no Tartar child. Have you flowed since then?"

"No," Elise said. She was beginning to understand. The little dolduna described other symptoms to her. Elise recognized most of them. She tried to remember the times she had been with Nikholai—had a child been conceived the night she had tried to escape across the river?

Elise clasped her hands in her lap. When she had married the count, she had wanted a baby, longed for a baby, dreamed of a baby. Then she had had to put the dream aside. She could hardly allow herself to believe it now. Dark confusion clouded her dawning joy. This was what Nikholai had wanted all along, she realized. And somehow, he had known about the child before she did—pushing food at her, wrapping her in furs and blankets. Why? Retribution? Was this part of his plan? To shame her? Elise jumped up, grabbed her caftan, and ran out of the cottage.

Nikholai counted the barrels again and looked back at Bogdan. "It counts the same every time, old friend," he said. "We are going to have little enough to eat until spring." He was glad that Bogdan had been given Ostap's responsibilities as village clerk. The elder could be trusted to be even-handed in keeping the inventories and doling out the rations. Ostap had always been reliable, but Nikholai doubted the new lieutenant's strength against the sway of Vikola's influence.

Bogdan nodded. "There was no more to be had in Cherkassk?"

"I brought with me what the merchants would sell," Nikholai said. "I left money with Timofe to purchase more flour or grain for us if he could find it. Its price was dear."

"Well, praise to St. Nikholas, the fishing has been good," Bogdan said. "And we have enough hay to get the horses through until the snow melts."

Both men looked up as the storehouse door opened and closed. Elise stood there, serious and subdued, her hands tucked into the long sleeves of her caftan, her lips pale with cold.

"I have things to attend to, Nikholai Fomin," Bogdan said, hastily gathering up the lists of stores.

"Yes, show these inventories to Vikola," Nikholai said. "Remind him we must be careful with what we have. No fattening the horses on grain or giving supplies to Razin."

"I will, Nikholai," Bogdan said, "but he is a headstrong man."

Bogdan greeted Elise politely as he left, closing the door behind him. Nikholai rose from the barrel where he sat. An oil lamp on the crate next to him was the only light.

He watched Elise enter its golden glow. He had expected her to follow him immediately when Natalia told her what she had not realized herself. An hour had passed since he left the cottage.

He was certain she would see the child she carried for the trap he had planned it to be. She would be angry. But he hoped in time she would come to accept their child. Suddenly he felt foolish. A child had not bound Maria to him. Why did he think a baby would hold this woman?

"Where have you been?" he asked.

"In the church," she replied softly. "Thinking. Praying." Her expression was pensive as she wound her way among the barrels of dried, salted fish, bags of grain, and crates of tools, her gaze lowered. Her lashes were dark against her creamy cheek.

When she stood before him, she looked up into his face and asked, "Why?"

"Why what, Countess?" He busied himself with the papers.

"Don't play the innocent with me, Cossack," she said. "Why did you want this?" She held his gaze steadily. He saw no real anger in her eyes. She wanted to understand. "Now that I'm with child, will you send me back to Warsaw in shame?"

"Send you and my child away?" Nikholai stammered, surprised that she would think that of him. "Even I would not pay that price to insult the Polonsky family," he said. "If you leave, the child will stay with me."

"But you know I won't leave my baby," Elise said, her tone more anxious. She looked around her as if casting into the shadows for an answer. "What is it you are doing? You promised me freedom. Yet you bind me to Vazka. Why?"

Her growing anxiety troubled him, but his response was firm. "The child will stay with me. You will be free to stay or go as you please."

"You put an impossible choice before me. Why?"

Nikholai shrugged and turned away. "What would you do if you returned to Warsaw tomorrow?" he asked. "Would you return to your beloved family, to Leopold Polonsky?"

"Of course not." She blinked at him. "I have to find Anna first. Now I have to think of a baby."

Nikholai stared at her with growing understanding. Freedom for her meant finding Anna.

"Yergov will find Anna," he promised. "I will take care of you and the baby."

Elise looked away from him and chewed on her lip.

Nikholai ached to reassure her with a touch, with a kiss. He wanted to bridge the chasm that threatened to open between them again.

"Yes, Yergov will find Anna," she replied, still chewing her lip. Then she turned away and touched one of the barrels thoughtfully. "Did I hear Bogdan say supplies are short?"

Nikholai resisted the urge to demand a promise to stay. He was taking a terrible risk with her life because of his own selfishness. He ran his fingers through his hair. "There will be enough, but just enough," he said, observing how easily she led him from one topic to another.

She asked about the problems, and he told her a little. He left out his suspicions that Vikola had given supplies to Razin.

Nikholai suspected Razin had his hands full with that wild, undisciplined rabble he had amassed on the island. They would want food. Let them hunt game instead of threatening hardworking Cossacks and taking food out of the mouths of women and children. Nikholai vowed silently to take care of his own.

The dark weeks of winter slipped by in a routine that grew comfortable for Elise. The sickness in the morning disappeared. She found she had more energy, but sometimes the exhaustion still overwhelmed her.

In February, a break in the weather brought Fydor, the minstrel. He sang of Razin's return to his island and of the rebels' planned offensive in March. Elise noticed that Nikholai did not seem particularly surprised.

The minstrel also brought news from Cherkassk. Katia and Timofe were the proud parents of a baby girl, Sophia. They asked Elise and Nikholai to be godparents. Nikholai tried to hide his pleasure, but Elise saw it. She would never understand this man, she sighed to herself.

He slept beside her, wrapped in his own burka. Sometimes he touched her affectionately, and once he kissed her. She saw desire flash in his eyes, but he left her to sleep alone. Why? she wondered. To her surprise, even with the babe growing inside her, she longed for his touch.

She saw little of him during the day, when he was about the village or in the stable. She knew that with Bogdan's help he managed to be at all the krug meetings, whether Vikola wanted him there or not. Messengers rode in and out of the gate every week. Sometimes they stopped to talk to Nikholai privately.

Vikola's resentment of all this was plain whenever the two men passed each other. Vikola glared at the tall gray-eyed Cossack. Nikholai cast the Zaporozhie cool, condescending looks. Elise avoided Vikola. She didn't want to become the reason for open conflict between the two men. But she could see that the whole village knew the uneasy coexistence could not last.

One mild, cloudy day, Elise helped Natalia and Bogdan divide a barrel of flour and dried fish among the villagers. They worked in the snow just outside the storehouse. The women lined up patiently to receive their portions.

Elise, who had been bending over an open barrel, straightened and rubbed the straining muscles in her back. She helped Bogdan make a quick count of what remained. Two barrels were unaccounted for on Bogdan's lists. Elise read over his shoulder and counted again. Two barrels were missing.

Just then Vikola, grinning broadly with his own beneficence, strolled by. Ostap followed him. The new ataman greeted the village women and children, who responded with nods of deference.

"Two barrels are missing, Ataman Vikola Panko," Bogdan spoke up immediately. "See my accounts."

Vikola frowned and shook his head. Instinctively Elise perceived that the Zaporozhie knew something about the missing supplies.

"Why would two barrels be missing, Ataman Vikola Panko?" she asked innocently but without lowering her gaze. "How could that happen? Only you and Bogdan have keys to the storehouse."

Vikola stared at her. "I don't know, Mistress Fomina," he said, meeting her gaze. "Perhaps the devil took them for himself." He uttered a mirthless laugh.

"Bah," Elise said with a wave of her hand. "The devil could find more and better food elsewhere."

Silently the village women and children watched this exchange. A few warriors joined the group.

"I am ataman here now, Mistress Fomina," Vikola declared. "Vazka's supplies are my concern." He turned to order Bogdan to go on with dividing the food, but the elder was gone.

"Finish this, Ostap," Vikola directed.

"As Vazka's new ataman, and as a man of great foresight, surely two barrels of flour can't disappear without your knowing something about it," Elise persisted. Natalia tugged warningly on her sleeve.

"Vikola Panko is ataman now," Daria interrupted. "He can do with the supplies as he sees fit."

Scowling at each other, Vikola and Elise ignored her. Hatred hardened in Vikola's eyes. Elise summoned her courage to ignore it. She would not let this go. People's lives were at stake.

Beside her, Ostap began to dole out grain. None of the village women made a move to accept it.

"Go away, woman," Vikola growled. "None of this is any of your concern."

Elise didn't miss the involuntary movement of his right arm. He wanted to strike her. She realized she had heedlessly insulted him once more. Only fear for her babe made her back away.

"Touch her and I'll spill your guts onto the snow," threatened a low, lethal voice at her side.

Elise turned in surprise to see Kasyan standing there, his hand on the hilt of his knife, his gaze fastened on Vikola.

"No," she protested, and raised a hand to stay Kasyan.

Without a look in Elise's direction, he dragged her from between them. Vikola reached for his knife.

"What's going on?" Nikholai demanded, striding into their midst. Bogdan followed him.

"Your foreign woman causes trouble," accused Vikola.

"I asked about the two missing barrels of flour," Elise said.

"She was sent to divide us against each other," Vikola warned.

"Tell me about the barrels," Nikholai said, looking from Vikola to Elise and Kasyan. He moved between the two men.

"Our ally Stenka Razin requested help from us," Vikola

258

said. He took his hand away from his knife and shrugged. "He needed food, so I sent two barrels of flour."

"We don't have two barrels to spare," Nikholai snapped.

"The krug approved it," Vikola said.

"Is that true, Bogdan?" Nikholai asked, without taking his gaze from Vikola's face.

"I attended no krug where such a vote was taken," Bogdan replied.

"It was an emergency meeting," Vikola said. "You could not be found, Elder."

"And what will Stenka Razin give us in return?" Nikholai demanded. Elise saw the light of the Wolf begin to surface in Nikholai's gray eyes. Urgently she tried to move between Nikholai and Vikola. Kasyan drew her away again.

"He will give us victory over the Muscovites," Vikola answered proudly.

"That will mean little to the starving people we bury," Nikholai said with a gesture to the cemetery beside Vazka's church.

"There will be no deaths in Vazka because of Stenka Razin," Vikola announced, looking around at the villagers. "We will hunt and fish. Cossacks feed Cossacks. No one will starve. Who rides with me to chase the antelope?"

The warriors cheered, "To the hunt."

Elise sighed in relief as she saw the killing light fade from Nikholai's eyes. He watched in silence as the warriors led horses from stables and brought out loaded weapons.

Soon the hunting party rode through the gate, with Vikola in the lead. Kasyan and Nikholai did not ride with them. Bogdan and Elise finished doling out the flour.

"Why don't the Don Cossacks grow their own grain?" Elise asked Bogdan as they emptied the last barrel. "I remember seeing the Cossack fields along the Dnieper golden with wheat and rye. Isn't the steppe soil rich enough?"

"The soil is rich, especially along the river, but the Don Host decided that to till the soil would make the Muscovites think of Cossacks as serfs," Bogdan explained. "We will not be bought and sold with the land. So we remain raisers of stock, fishermen, and river people. Freemen."

Two days later, the hunting party returned exhausted and

with only enough antelope to add a little meat to each of Vazka's soup kettles, but the restlessness was gone and tempers had cooled.

Elise and Nikholai watched spring come to the steppe from Vazka's lookout, high above the river. As soon as the snow began to melt, Nikholai led her down the steep path through the gray undergrowth to the rocky ledge. From there they could see for many versts up and down the river. In times when the Tartars raided villages, a Cossack was constantly on watch there. But now it was seldom visited. Except by lovers, Nikholai told her. Elise smiled but made no comment.

She had no difficulty knowing how she felt about the baby, but Nikholai was another matter. The stalking light she had seen in his eyes was disquieting. The knowledge that he had once planned to use her in vengeance still lingered in the back of her mind. Yet there were many things she admired in him. His patience, his gentleness and understanding. She had not forgotten the night he had held her while she cried out in her grief.

Nikholai pointed out the direction of Voronezh to the northwest and Kagalnik to the southwest. The sun shone brightly on the Don as it threaded its way through the islands like a silvery ribbon in a maid's braid.

"When Yergov brings Anna to you, he will cross at that ford," Nikholai told her.

The cold March wind swirled about the bluff. Nikholai wrapped his burka around them.

Elise leaned back against him, enjoying his solid warmth and the soothing timbre of his deep voice.

He told her how the steppe hills beyond the river would soon bloom green and yellow with crocuses. In the evenings the grasses would flicker with glowworms.

A sudden intense fluttering in Elise's middle startled her. "Oh, there it is again," she whispered, as if her voice might still the first tentative movements of her child. She put her hand on her roundnesss.

"What is it?" Nikholai asked, suddenly alert.

"It's the babe," Elise whispered. "Do you want to feel?"

Before he could answer her, she took his hand and placed

it where she had felt the movement. As if sensing another presence, the babe became shy and still. But Nikholai waited until the babe moved again.

The light of his smile dazzled Elise, and she was glad she had shared the joy with him. He spread both of his large hands over the baby, eager to feel life again, but the babe had gone back to sleep. Nikholai laughed softly.

"A son or a daughter?" he asked. "What does Natalia say?"

"She won't tell me," Elise said. A slight chill passed over her. She snuggled closer to Nikholai for warmth and reassurance.

"Perhaps it is still too early," he said.

"Yes," Elise replied, but she thought differently. She was certain Natalia was withholding something.

Nikholai turned her to face him and kissed her soundly. "It grows cold," he said. "Let's go home."

Natalia was gone that evening to help Polya Zykova with a sick child. Nikholai was in a contented mood. His teeth gleamed when he smiled and laughed. He took his bandura down from its peg and sang to Elise. She was not surprised when he sat down beside her on the bench and pulled her close. He teased Elise's ear and the back of her neck with his lips and mustache. He spread his hands across her belly as he had at the lookout.

That first night of captivity, when he had touched her bare shoulder as she stood before him in her chemise, she had known she was vulnerable to him. She had been frightened then because she didn't know what that meant.

Now she knew, and she welcomed the touch of his hands, the warmth of his breath, and the pressure of his body against hers. The taste of him and the vodka he had drunk lingered on her lips and made her want more. She turned to him, put her arms around his neck, closed her eyes, and raised her face for another kiss.

Nikholai laughed, a laugh of discovery and delight. He picked her up from the bench and carried her into the bedroom, where a single candle flickered on the table.

# ❧ 22 ❧

# Spring Dies

Kneeling on the floor before her, he pulled her embroidered blouse over her head and began to untie her chemise.

Elise sighed, closed her eyes, and savored the feel of his dark curls between her fingers. She could hear his breathing, as shallow and uncertain as hers. Each encounter with him was still new to her, but she was willing to let him be her guide.

He slipped her chemise from her shoulders and cupped his hand over her bare breast. Tenderly he drew the nipple to a peak with his lips. She shuddered, unaware until now that her breasts had become so swollen, so sensitive.

She felt the pressure of his broad hand against the small of her back as his mouth sought her other breast. He unfastened her skirt with his free hand. She helped. She wanted to be free of garments so that she could accept his touch.

Gently he pushed her back on the bed and pulled the skirt and underthings down over her legs. He tossed the clothing aside. With his hands resting on her thighs, he regarded her with a lazy smile. In one smooth movement he swung her feet onto the bed.

He stood. Elise stretched, arms over her head, allowing his eyes to caress the full length of her bare body. She watched curiously as he threw aside his shirt and caftan, pulled off his red leather boots, and untied the sash to his wide black pants. He kicked his clothing aside and stood at the edge of the bed, his full erection silhouetted against the halo of the candle.

Suddenly Elise was daunted. She had never really seen a man fully ready for a woman.

"Don't be afraid, Green Eyes," Nikholai whispered as he lowered himself next to her. "It's very easily gentled. We'll be very careful of the babe. Let me show you."

He took her hand and placed it against him. His gaze held hers so that she could not hide from him the surprise, then shy delight that played across her features. For all its rigid hardness, his full manhood was smooth and velvety to her touch.

He closed his eyes and sighed as her light, curious strokes became bolder. Then with a low moan, he pulled her hand away.

"No more now," he whispered. Then he leaned over her and covered her face with kisses. He kissed her neck and shoulders. His fingers feathered across her nipples first. Then, with his tongue he sent fiery shocks of pleasure through her. One breast, then the other. Lovingly he stroked her round, full belly. She closed her eyes and lost herself to the warmth of his hands. He continued to stroke her and smile into her eyes. Then he dropped light kisses on the roundness where their babe slept.

Elise realized he was greeting their babe. She sighed and admitted to herself that she could love this man.

With a devilish look Nikholai settled himself on his knees between her legs. At first Elise was embarrassed to be exposed to him so, but he took no interest in that. Or that he was also gloriously exposed to her. His hands rested quietly around her ankles. Gently he drew his finger down her left instep. He lifted her foot to his lips, kissed it, then drew his warm, firm tongue down her instep. Elise gasped with delight at the sheer thrill his touch sent through her whole being.

She opened her eyes to see Nikholai's expression, but he was bent over her foot, concentrating on every touch. He caressed her calf and kissed the inside of her knee, then the inside of her thigh—each kiss closer to the hot, moist center where she longed to hold him. His fingers stroked her tantalizingly as his kisses trailed across the inside of her thighs with maddening pleasure toward that blissful lovers' destination.

He lowered himself beside her again, pulled her left leg over his hip, slipped his hands around her buttocks, and eased himself into her. She accepted him gratefully, wanting and needing him as much as he wanted and needed her. Instinctively she massaged the hard muscles of his back as he set the rhythm of their sensuous journey.

He rocked her slowly at first, so each enticing thrust promised more pleasure. Elise clung to Nikholai and urged him on. She felt the smile on his lips against her face as he whispered to her to have patience. Their pace quickened and built. The pleasure flourished. Elise matched his movements until the yearning to arch against him came. Shimmering ecstasy blossomed into her and thrilled throughout her. She gasped and held him to her until she felt his answering shudder of pleasure.

Slowly, his lips still against her neck, he released her. She had nearly sunk into an exhausted sleep when she felt his lips brush against her ear.

"Green Eyes," he whispered. "All I have is yours. I'll take care of you and our babe. Stay. Share life with me."

Elise was blissfully unable to reply. But she heard him. She fell asleep. No nightmares . . . no fear . . . no panic— she was safe, wanted, and loved.

After Elise had so willingly accepted him, Nikholai was disappointed that she had made no reply to his request. Instead, she began to spend part of each day at the lookout, watching the river ford. Whenever he joined her there, she would smile at him brightly, share the recent village gossip, then resume her vigil.

Nikholai worried about her walking along the steep path without him. Patches of snow still lingered in the shade. He could not be at her side all the time; he was helping the warriors prepare to join Razin. She seemed surefooted enough, and the babe had not grown to such a size as to make movement difficult for her.

When he could, he sought her out to share her company, to share spring's arrival on the steppe. Together they watched the poplar trees become fuzzy with buds and the grasses grow green. The sky was filled with birds, and the riverbanks were alive with animals. The river level rose with the melting of the snow.

With a smile on her face and eagerness in her eyes, she watched the ford as if her will would make Yergov appear. She looked well and happy. Nikholai was relieved. It was March: the worst of winter had passed. Food would be found.

Razin sent word to the towns and villages of the Volga provinces—Tambov, Penza, Simbirsk, and Nizhny-Novgorod—that he had rebelled against the boyars who held the tsar captive. He claimed he would defeat them and set free the tsar and patriarch.

To the krug, Vikola Panko read a separate letter addressed to him from Razin. In it the rebel stated plans to seize first Tsaritsyn, the Volga River city on the portage road from the Don. He hoped to cut off the tsar's communications to Astrakhan. Then he planned to take Astrakhan and retake the ships and cannon he had given to Prince Prozorovsky. He would begin his campaign in April.

"For God and Allah," some of the krug members cheered. Vikola gave orders for the first group of Vazka's warriors to join Razin's forces immediately. They would ride out in two days under Ostap's command. Vikola would bring the rest with him later. Nikholai Fomin was ordered to remain in the village to aid the elders.

Nikholai was not particularly surprised by this exclusion. He had infringed on Vikola's authority too many times. Nikholai missed the excitement of preparing for battle, but he found he was more interested in what happened to the village—to his wife and child.

The day Vikola was scheduled to leave Vazka was no different to Elise from any other. She fed the geese, the few that had been allowed to survive the winter for their down. She followed Nikholai around the stable for a while, then went to the lookout. She tried not to trouble him too much these days.

She sensed his pain in being forbidden to ride with his men into battle, but she was relieved. She didn't want to see him ride into danger. She shared his feeling that the Muscovites could muster great forces against the Cossacks if they chose to.

She leaned against the rocky bluff, listened to the call of the hunting falcons, and delighted in the delicate perfume of the steppe wildflowers that drifted to her on the wind.

She didn't see the lone rider at the ford until a flock of cranes took startled flight from the marsh. She stepped forward to get a better view of him as he began his crossing. The rider was a small man, a Cossack from his dress, on a little bay horse. She could not distinguish features, but from the way he sat his horse, Elise was certain it was Yergov.

At last. He was alone, but he would have news, she thought. She negotiated the steep rocky way with little difficulty and hurried toward the gate.

"Why such haste, Countess?" Daria called.

Elise did not see or hear the Gypsy. Her thoughts were fastened on Yergov. When she did not reply, Daria turned to wave at Vikola, then followed her.

Elise never noticed the riders. Still light-footed, she ran toward the gate. So determined was she to know Yergov's news as soon as possible that she didn't hear the hoofbeats of Vikola's horse behind her. The blow on the back of the head caught her just as she reached the gate. She fell against the horse's shoulder, then struck the hard earth as a pain shot through her side.

As she tried to crawl to her feet again, she wondered if the horse had stepped on her. A sharp, then piercing pain spread through her, and darkness swallowed her.

Kasyan burst into the stall with a blast of cold air. "Nikholai?"

Startled, the chestnut colt broke away from Nikholai's gentle hold. "Yes, what is it, my friend?" Nikholai asked, still intent on haltering the colt.

"Natalia sent me for you," Kasyan said breathlessly.

"Now?"

"Now, Nikholai," Kasyan said quietly. "The countess is hurt."

The path. He should never have shown her the lookout, he cursed to himself. But Kasyan led him toward the gate. There Vikola sat on his horse, and beside him stood Daria. Before them on the ground, Natalia bent over the countess. Nikholai went to her.

"Elise?" He knelt beside her.

"She was trying to escape, Nikholai Fomin," Vikola said. "She knows too much. We cannot allow her to escape now."

Nikholai stared up at the ugly Zaporozhie in disbelief.

Elise moaned, and he forgot Vikola.

"She breathes," Natalia said. Nikholai noted the rapid rise and fall of Elise's chest. Her head covering had been knocked off. She moaned again, her head rolling from side to side. Her eyes fluttered open.

"Oh, Nikholai," she whispered, and tried to sit up. "Yergov is coming. I saw him."

"Be still, Green Eyes." Nikholai spoke softly and took her hand. "Where do you hurt?"

"My head," she said, and closed her eyes. "And I think the horse stepped on me." Then she sobbed. "Oh, something is wrong."

"We must get her back to the cottage," Natalia said.

Nikholai wasn't listening. He stood up and faced Vikola, who had finally dismounted. Vazka's warriors gathered behind their new ataman. Prepared for their departure to join the rebellion, they were fully armed. Kasyan rose too.

"You rode her down?" Nikholai accused.

"I tell you, she was trying to escape again," Vikola said.

"It's true," Daria agreed. "I saw her running for the gate."

"If she should fall into the Muscovites' hands, she would reveal what she knows about Stenka Razin's plans and our cave."

"You think she was trying to escape?" Nikholai shouted. "On foot? In the middle of the day?" He stepped over Elise and reached for Vikola, who braced himself. Before Nikholai could strike, Kasyan interfered. The warriors pulled Vikola back. Struggling against restraining arms, the two men glared at each other.

"I ought to kill you," Nikholai threatened. He truly wanted to feel the crunch of Vikola's jaw beneath his fist. He fought against Kasyan's hold.

"You're a fool for a pretty face, Nikholai Fomin," Vikola shouted back. "You'll regret it one day. You'll see. She'll betray you one way or another. Just as your first wife did."

Maddened, Nikholai pulled free of Kasyan and charged Vikola.

Elise's moan froze him. No one moved.

"We must get her to the cottage, Nikholai," Natalia insisted.

Anger pushed aside, Nikholai returned to Elise and picked her up. He didn't notice her weight, only the sticky, warm blood that had already soaked through her skirt. He started for the cottage.

Nikholai carefully placed Elise on their bed and began to make her comfortable by removing her boots and loosening her blouse at the neck. She was partially conscious, so he talked soothingly to her.

"You must rest, Green Eyes."

"I don't want anything to happen to the baby," she cried.

"I know," he said, removing her embroidered apron.

"I wasn't trying to escape," she said. "I saw Yergov. Where is he? He'll need help to find Anna. Will you help him?"

"I'll help him," Nikholai promised. "Now, rest."

Satisfied with his promise, Elise lay back on the bed. Nikholai brushed stray curls away from her clammy forehead.

Abruptly Natalia pulled him away and pushed him into the other room. He glimpsed a village woman sitting down on the bed next to Elise.

As soon as they were out of Elise's hearing, Nikholai turned to his aunt. He didn't know how white his face was, how drawn the lines around his mouth. He shook his head.

"I can't lose her. I can't lose her," he pleaded. "Do something to save her and the babe. Make some potion. Chant some spell. I'll find a priest. Do something!"

"You won't lose her, Nikholai," Natalia said. "I promise. The baby I can do nothing for. But the countess is strong. She will live."

Nikholai turned away from his aunt and sat down on the bench, covering his face with his hands.

"Nikholai, listen to me," Natalia went on. He felt her

reassuring hand on his shoulder. "I know this is hard for you. But I swear I have seen many children for you and the countess. Beautiful dark-haired sons and daughters with green eyes. They will make you proud, Nikholai. But this one you will lose. I'm sorry, Nushka."

Natalia left him. Silently Nikholai fought all the dark anger. He wanted Vikola dead. He cursed the day he had shown Elise the lookout. He wanted to strangle Daria. He longed to roar in rage, to bay his grief, to howl his pain to the moon as the wolf does.

Natalia returned. "Go, Nikholai. You have things to do." Her strong little hands tugged at his larger ones, still covering his face. "Here, take this." She forced him to take the white ermine muff with the doll. "You will need this. Yergov is outside with Kasyan. He says he knows where to find the Kalmyks with the eagle-wing standard."

Vikola rode away with Vazka's warriors. Nikholai ignored the event. He finished saddling and packing Sultan and tried once more to see Elise. Natalia stopped him at the cottage door. Elise's cries chilled his blood and left him trembling. Yergov led him to the horses and out of Vazka.

When Elise had recovered her strength enough to visit the small grave, she went alone. She had lost much blood and her memories of the hours after the fall were hazy and best forgotten. Though her strength returned, the pain remained. Despite the hurt, Elise lingered over the tiny grave Bogdan had dug in the churchyard.

She did not weep. She was too empty. How could it be? she wondered. Each day still dawned bright and blue. Birds still sang and the flowers still bloomed. Her baby was dead. For Elise life had no color, no song.

The days passed slowly. No word came from Yergov or Nikholai. Then one afternoon as Elise stood over the fresh grave, Yergov rode through the village gate with a child in the saddle before him. Elise gasped. Anna wiggled free, jumped from the horse to the muddy village street, and ran, her arms held wide, toward Elise.

The sisters threw their arms about each other. "Let me look at you," Elise demanded. "Are you all right?" She knelt in the mud and touched Anna, her arms, her shoulders, her hands. She turned her sister around to make certain all was well. The child giggled and threw her arms around Elise again.

"I am well," Anna cried. "Yergov and Nikholai saved me."

With Natalia's help, they bathed Anna and found clothes for her. Anna was thin, but otherwise seemed to have fared well. She chattered about the Kalmyks. She had been afraid when she was separated from Hawkins, but the Kalmyks had treated her with the same kind indulgence they bestowed on their own children.

Later, while Natalia fed Anna a big meal, Elise found Yergov to thank him. The Terek dismissed her gratitude with a wave of his hand.

"I'm glad you are happy, Little Warrior," he said. "But you must thank the Wolf. He was a tireless searcher."

Elise sought out Nikholai. When she was unable to find him in his usual places, she returned to the cottage. He was there with Natalia, who was tucking Anna into the bed Nikholai and Elise had shared. He sang a lullaby to the child, but disappeared as Elise finished tucking Anna in.

After that, Elise could never find him alone.

He never attempted to return to the bed he had shared with her, so Anna continued to sleep with her. Though sunny-natured as ever, Anna refused to be parted from Elise.

The child did not learn languages so easily as Elise, but she quickly picked up a few words and joined the children in London Bridge and other games they taught each other. She played happily with them as long as Elise was in sight. She often approached Nikholai, who gave her a pink-tongued puppy for Branch Sunday. He always took time to listen to her. It was only when Elise appeared that he suddenly became too busy for conversation.

As Easter approached, Elise still did not have the heart for festivities. She was pleased to have Anna with her again, but the aching loss of the baby was still with her. Besides that, she sensed she had lost Nikholai.

Natalia and Anna happily set about gathering eggs for the traditional pysanka. The cottage was redolent with the cooking of dyes. Natalia even shared her recipes for dyes with the child: Yellow from onion skins. Red from sandalwood. Green from sunflower seeds. Black from sunflower-seed husks. Then they spent quiet evenings decorating eggs with traditional symbols. Beeswax was used to help create the designs. Natalia brought out her fine writing tool, the kystka. Elise listened to Natalia explain to Anna that the pysanka was an ancient symbol of hope, rebirth, and the Resurrection.

Natalia took Anna along when she exchanged eggs with friends and acquaintances as a gesture of goodwill. To Elise's surprise, Ganna, who had been a bride with Elise, presented her with a beautifully decorated egg.

"For a great love, and in token of the Resurrection, whereof we rejoice," Ganna said, delivering the traditional phrase as she handed the ornate red egg to Elise.

As Elise turned the simple, elegant gift over in her hands, comfort settled over her raw grief. She knew that somewhere, her child was safe with William and Hawkins, with her mother and father. Our Lady of Tears would see to that.

Near the end of April, a Cossack messenger from Stenka Razin appeared at Vazka's gate.

"Stenka Razin has taken Tsaritsyn," he shouted to the villagers who gathered around to hear the news. All cheered.

With a big grin, the graying Cossack messenger went on to tell the whole story of how the monk Chevdor had gone into the city to warn the citizens of Stenka Razin's coming. The frightened voevoda and his streltsy troops had prepared to defend the garrison at the heart of the city. Tsaritsyn's people flung open the city gates and greeted Razin, carrying icons and singing songs of victory.

"Then our brave Cossacks rode under the garrison wall," the messenger said. "They braced their lances against the wall and climbed up them and across the wall while the rest of us threw torches over their heads at the streltsy."

The captured voevoda was tied to a rope by his own townspeople and thrown into the river. They dragged him upstream, then downstream, until he drowned.

Vazka's villagers cheered again. Standing near the gate to the churchyard, Elise listened and watched Nikholai. She wondered what he was really thinking. One evening she had seen him in the churchyard near their baby's grave, his head bowed. Then he looked across the river. Did he grieve as she did? She had almost gone to him then, but Anna had come to her with a cut on her finger. Now Elise thought she saw a wistful look on his face as he listened to this battle story.

The messenger had more to tell. Only two days after the victory, scouts had spotted a fleet of Muscovite longboats coming upriver from Astrakhan. Prince Prozorovsky had received word from a spy that Stenka Razin planned to march against him. So the prince had sent a force of eight hundred Muscovites and Tartars to meet the rebel. Unaware that Tsaritsyn had already fallen, the Muscovite forces rowed up to the city's landing, only to be attacked by Cossacks, who were on the city walls and in boats on the river behind them.

"All but three hundred were killed," the messenger said. "They were given the choice of death or work as oarsmen. Only a small force under Prince Lvov near the city of Cherney Iar now stands between Stenka Razin's victorious army and Astrakhan."

Villagers pressed in around the messenger to learn news of sons, husbands, and fathers. Elise watched Nikholai stride away purposefully. He sent the messenger away the next day.

A week later he began the morning with a march in and out of the cottage. In his arms he carried supplies, and he threw directions over his shoulder to Natalia. He wanted food packed. Then he disappeared into the tack room, only to reappear carrying tack and weapons.

"What is it?" Elise asked the little woman, who wrapped dried fish in clean cloths and stashed them into a bag.

"Nikholai will tell you," she said with a frown.

Daria suddenly swished into the room. "Here, old woman, add this to the bag," the Gypsy girl said. She threw a loaf of bread and some goat cheese onto the table. She pointed a finger at Elise. "And you, Countess. Nikholai sent me to tell you he wants to speak with you. You'll find him in the stable."

## ✢ 23 ✢

# Spoken in a Moment of Passion

A single shaft of spring sunshine spilled through the stable window and puddled in a square on the hay-strewn floor.

Elise approached Nikholai quietly, crushed hay whispering under her feet. The bright puddle separated them in the darkness. He stood with his back to her, working with the saddle he had set on Sultan's back. She knew he had heard her footsteps, but he did not turn or speak. She clasped her hands behind her and waited.

The stallion greeted her with a snort and a bob of his head. Outside, she heard the shouts and laughter of the children at play. She wanted to join them and not be here where she must listen to words she knew she didn't want to hear.

When Nikholai turned to her at last, his face was somber. She met his gaze and thought she saw his gray eyes soften. He turned away again, too quickly for her to be sure.

"Your return to Warsaw has been arranged," he said, snapping a stirrup leather into place.

Elise gasped, unprepared for this. "You heard from Thomas?"

"No," Nikholai said. He continued to speak over his

shoulder. "Yergov and I have arranged it. He will take you and Anna to Azov. There you will meet Captain Johann Hals. You remember the Dutch sea captain you met in Cherkassk? He is a good man. There is some unrest on the right bank of the Dnieper now, but Hals will be able to get you and Anna safely through to Warsaw."

"But why now?" Elise stammered. "You could have sent me away before this, couldn't you?"

In silence he turned to her. The light pouring into the stable cast hard shadows on his face. "I'm going to join Razin. You are going home."

His gaze was level and steady, but Elise sensed he withheld something. "What does Daria have to do with this?" she asked.

"She is going with me. She wants to be with Kasyan."

"You are taking Daria?" Elise asked in surprise. She stepped into the square of light, unaware of how it lit her hair and cleared the green of her eyes. Her anger swelled and erupted. "Just like that? After all we've been through? You bloody Cossack! You are going to send me away and go off with Daria to fight this bloody rebellion you don't believe in."

His eyes were dark and quiet, but she saw the anger in his stance. "You have pleaded for your freedom from the first, Countess," he said. "Now I give it to you, and you rant at me like a jealous woman."

"I do not," she snapped, and shook her head. "I have not asked to leave since you found Anna. Why do you do this now?"

"Because it suits me." He turned away from her and bent over to check the saddle girth.

Elise fought the hollow desperation growing in her chest. "The war I understand, but why send me away? You asked me to stay with you."

His head came up quickly, but he did not face her. "I never asked that. Never."

The edge in Nikholai's voice cut her. He had declared his feelings the night he had made love to her and their baby. She didn't understand why he denied it now. Her heart pounded, and she tried to catch her breath. She was drowning. She stepped closer to him.

"You told me with your touch, Nikholai. With the way you loved our baby. You asked me to share life with you."

He began to tug viciously on the saddle girth. Sultan nickered a protest and nipped at his master's elbow. Nikholai ignored the stallion. "You misunderstood, Countess."

"I did not misunderstand," Elise persisted. "You asked me to stay with you. I have yet to give you my answer."

He stopped working with the saddle and turned to her, his face cold and still. "No answer is required. You read too much into a few words spoken in passion."

Stung, Elise stepped back from him, into the shadows. She hoped the darkness would hide the pain in her face, but it didn't.

He turned away and led the stallion and Sotnik through the shaft of light and from the stable. Elise stood alone, trying to catch her breath, trying not to cry.

He was right, of course. She had demanded, begged, and bargained for her freedom from the first. Now there was no need to leave. Anna was with her. No one awaited her in Warsaw. She could return to claim the settlement and dower house given in the marriage contract. Leopold would have to surrender those to her once she made herself known. Even without her brothers, she had enough friends to assure that.

But Elise didn't want Nikholai to go away to fight with men who no longer wanted him as their leader. She closed her eyes tightly against tears of pain and fear. She wanted to understand. She had seen his gaze stray across the river, and she knew that in his heart he followed his men. And yet she was certain he had told her in his own way that he loved her and wanted her to stay.

Head held high, tears held at bay, Elise joined the villagers before the cottage as they watched Nikholai make his final preparations. Daria's mother gave her daughter a farewell kiss. Nikholai tied the food bags to his saddle and packed Sotnik with tokens mothers and wives had asked him to give to sons and husbands when he found them along the Volga. And all had given him greetings to convey to their loved ones. The mood of the group was happy and excited.

Elise hung back. If his feelings had changed, hers hadn't.

She loved him. The ache in her throat spread to her heart. She bit her lip and wished she had realized it sooner.

His packing finished, Nikholai named Bogdan village leader. Then he accepted from Natalia the traditional vodka and bread served to a warrior on his departure for battle.

He was about to mount Sultan when Elise called, "There is one last thing you must take with you, Cossack."

The village women fell silent and made way for her.

The wary look that passed over Nikholai's face almost discouraged Elise. But she summoned her courage and took the St. Nikholas medal from around her neck.

She held it out to him as though she would put it over his head. "You must take St. Nikholas with you," she said.

Nikholai hesitated. Elise thought for a moment that he was going to merely reach out and take it from her. His eyes turned dark and unreadable as he watched the shiny medal swing on its chain. He took off his cap, stepped before her, and bowed his head. A sob caught in Elise's throat.

On tiptoe she stretched to pass the chain over his head and around his neck. Her hands trembled and she was afraid to touch him. Without raising his head, he seized her by the elbows. Nearly lifting her off the ground, he kissed her so hard and with so much longing that tears streamed down Elise's cheeks.

"Good-bye, Green Eyes," he whispered against her lips. Abruptly he let her go and mounted Sultan. Leading Sotnik, he rode out the gate and never looked back.

Before Daria mounted, she laughed at Elise and said, "See, now it is I who ride with him, Countess. Good-bye." Awkwardly the Gypsy girl scrambled onto her horse.

With the heat of Nikholai's kiss still on her lips, Elise was unsure whether victory was Daria's or hers. She did know that it was Daria who followed him out the gate.

"How soon will you be ready to leave?" Yergov asked when Elise had tucked Anna into bed. After Nikholai left, the day had been a long one. Elise had been unable to keep her thoughts on her chores or on her prayers when she visited the tiny grave. She had sung the lullaby Nikholai had taught her to Anna as she tucked the down covers around her little sister.

Now Yergov sat at the table before the oven and filled his pipe. "We should go soon, Little Warrior."

Elise sat down across from him.

"We're not going," she said.

"Oh?" There was no surprise in the Terek's voice.

"We'll stay until the warriors return."

"Nikholai Fomin told you of the danger?" Yergov asked. "You know Captain Hals awaits us. Arrangements have been made."

"Yes, I know," Elise replied. "Like Nikholai, I think bad times are ahead. Bogdan is going to need help." The little Terek remained silent. She studied her hands spread on the table before her. "I can't leave, Yergov. Too much of me is here now. My baby."

"Your heart?"

Elise nodded.

"I thought so. You have grown into a woman, Little Warrior. The decision is yours. You know both of us will have to explain our disobedience to the Wolf."

Elise smiled a painful smile. "I know," she said. "So, you must go to Captain Hals. Thank him and tell him we are not coming."

Yergov stayed a few more days. Elise sensed he was satisfying himself that she would be all right. He assured her on the day he left that he would continue to try to get word to Thomas.

At first Bogdan conferred with her on problems that had to do with the women. Then he and the elders discussed other matters with her. Soon her attendance at krug became a regular event.

Without the men, the villagers had less roasted game meat. The women planted gardens full of sunflowers, cabbages, melons, and cucumber vines. Natalia fussed over her young apple trees and talked to the bees. The children often minded the goats and sheep. Anna learned to feed the geese, and Elise began to spend time with Nikholai's horses. She was pleased with Commander's progress. The summer wore on, warm and breezy. Anna became sun-browned, and her ease with the language grew. Vazka's children took her by the hand and made her one of their own.

Messengers and merchants brought news of Razin's successes. At Cherney Iar, Razin's forces—now more than seven thousand—met the deputy voevoda's force of streltsy and Polish soldiers. Fighting was brief and light. Prince Lvov surrendered, and his life was spared. The streltsy joined the rebellion.

In late June, Razin took Astrakhan easily, with most of the city's streltsy going over to his side before a real battle could be fought. Vazka's warriors suffered no losses.

With great delight the Cossack messenger told of the carnage. Prince Prozorovsky, his nobles, city officials, and their families had been found in a church where they had taken refuge. Without ceremony, almost four hundred of them were thrown from the church's bell tower.

"And there sat our little father, Stenka Razin, drinking vodka with his comrades and watching as enemy after enemy fell screaming to his death," the messenger said. "He spared a few Europeans. And in all the fighting, he was never injured. It must be true. The dolduna's spell protects him."

Elise turned away sickened. She did not like to think of Nikholai there, among such barbaric men.

A few days later, another north-bound messenger brought news of Astrakhan. Razin retook the brass cannon he had originally taken from the Persians, and he set fire and sank the *Orel*, Tsar Alexis' European-built sailing ship. It was the first of a great fleet the tsar planned for bringing the Muscovites out of their isolation. Elise knew then there would be no going back for the rebels. If Razin lost, the tsar would show little mercy.

In the fields, women cut steppe hay and stacked it to dry. Wild asparagus was harvested. Pickles were made. The children collected mushrooms from the woods along the river. The old fishermen who had stayed behind cut and dried their catch.

In July news came that Razin had organized a Cossack-style government in Astrakhan. Divided into units of one thousand, one hundred, and ten, the citizens elected their own officers. The officers attended a krug and elected major officials.

One of Razin's trusted comrades, Vasili Us, was left in charge, and Razin had sailed back up the Volga with a flotilla of two hundred boats and two thousand Cossack horsemen riding along the shore. He would be at the annual harvest fair at Tsaritsyn for a few days.

This fair was not so large or well-known as the fair at Nizhny Novgorod, but for almost a month peasants and merchants would congregate there to exchange goods and celebrate the harvest.

Elise told the elders that some of the women wanted to attend. The event was only a two-day ride from Vazka. A three-day ride with women, the elders reminded Elise. But she was not discouraged by their attitude. Ganna wanted to see Filip, and there were others who wanted to see husbands and enjoy the fair.

Elise thought of seeing Nikholai. Did he know yet that she had remained in Vazka? For the first time in the months of hard work, she considered how he would feel about her refusal to leave. Had her decision to stay been the right one? she wondered.

The krug was concerned about a lack of armed warriors to ride with the women.

"I'll dress as a boy and carry weapons," Elise volunteered.

The elders stared at her. Although they were learning to accept Elise in a way they had not accepted other women, she knew her ideas and actions still startled them. Only Bogdan knew much about her trip to Kagalnik. With the memory of Ganna's eagerness to see Filip still fresh in her mind, Elise determinedly played her last card.

"Whatever happens in this rebellion, Vazka's warriors will need gunpowder," she reminded them. "We need salt and grain. In the cave, down near the river, are goods— fabrics, brass bowls, and pitchers. Fairgoers will buy and ask no questions."

The glow of greed and the need to feed, clothe, and protect their families warmed the eyes of krug members. After a little more discussion and some urging from Bogdan, the elders agreed to allow a small group of women to sell stolen goods, dried fish, and wool at the fair. Bogdan and two other elders and Elise would serve as escorts. Natalia gladly offered to care for Anna.

Nikholai stared at the jade earrings lying in the dust. They hadn't been polished for some time, but that didn't obscure their vital luster. A camel brayed a few stalls away. A food vendor chanted the sweetness of his wares to passing fairgoers. The late-afternoon air smelled of cooking fires, dust, and dung.

"I fancy those earrings, Nikholai," Daria whispered into his ear. Her breath was sour and her company dull. He didn't care whether she liked the earrings or not. They reminded him of a pair of lustrous green eyes, a pointed smile, and glowing creamy skin that smelled of apple blossoms. Unexpectedly, his loins ached. He had promised Elise jade earrings once. He would give her these, if she were still there when he returned.

No, she wouldn't be, he chided himself. When the first defeat came—and it would come—she would have the good sense to take Anna and leave. But for now, he liked the thought of her in Vazka, confounding the elders, spoiling his horses, and teaching the children games about bridges that delighted and mystified them. They had never seen such structures. Nikholai smiled to himself.

"Look at the gold workmanship, Nikholai," Daria pointed out. She pressed her breast against his arm and whispered into his ear, "Win them for me. I will be grateful."

The Gypsy had been offering her gratitude since the first day of their journey. Nikholai had little interest in it.

"I'll win the earrings," he told her without taking his eyes from the jewels in the dust, "but not for you, Daria."

She snorted and pursed her full lips into a pout. "You've been impossible ever since you learned the countess waits for you," she accused. "Vikola wants to banish you."

"So he is fond of saying," Nikholai muttered as he mentally calculated what it was going to take to win the earrings. "There are other kurens I can ride with."

The Tartar who had thrown the gems down for a wager noticed the Cossack's interest. The stakes went up. Nikholai played coolly, rolling the dice with skill. Daria tried to speak to him again, but he shrugged her off. His concentration was on winning what he wanted.

With the same methodical patience, Nikholai had found Vazka's warriors near Cherney Iar. Cap in hand, he had humbly asked the man who had ridden down his wife and killed his child for permission to join the ranks of Vazka's kuren. Vikola Panko had not been gracious. Before the warriors, he had insisted that Nikholai vow not to cause a rift in the kuren. Nikholai so vowed.

All the time, the tall Cossack was aware of the pleasure it would give him to ram a dagger underneath Vikola's ribs and into his heart. No, that would be too quick a death for a man who had given Elise such pain.

He decided the Zaporozhie's death would have to be something more excruciating. He would be patient. An opportunity would come.

As they had been laying siege to Astrakhan, a message came from Bogdan—written at Natalia's direction—to say that Elise had remained in the village.

"Only a spy would stay, Nikholai Fomin," Vikola said when he learned the news. "She will betray you."

"Why are you so fearful of spies?" Nikholai threw back. "Only a fearful spy would be so quick to accuse another."

Silence fell on Vazka's warriors.

Vikola lunged and Nikholai stepped aside. Razin's order to immediately advance on the city quelled the conflict.

Despite his defense of Elise to Vikola, Nikholai was angry that she had disobeyed orders. Then he laughed to himself at the realization of his folly. He should have known the countess would reject a direct order. Had he turned his back and let Yergov offer her escape, she would have pulled Anna onto a horse and been gone.

That day in the stable he had known his cruel words struck the intended target. The pain on her face knifed through him. He almost confessed he meant none of it. That he wanted her at his side forever. But he had remained silent. He couldn't let his selfishness bring her pain again. Loving sometimes meant letting go.

Her words, "I have yet to give you my answer," had echoed through his memory as he rode across the steppe to Cherney Iar. But he had not allowed himself to believe she would stay.

Then he had learned she was still in Vazka, and Vikola had called her a spy.

"You won the earrings, Nikholai," Daria said, clapping her hands in delight. He picked them out of the dust and slipped them into his pocket. Daria frowned.

"Go see what your husband has found for you," Nikholai said. He waved to Kasyan, who was running toward them between the rows of fair stalls. Behind his comrade, Nikholai saw the riders, Bogdan and Vazka's women, slowly guiding their horses through the crowd. Eagerly Nikholai glanced from rider to rider, unsure of whom he sought until he saw the red cap that belonged to "Mitka."

## ❧ 24 ❧

# The Fair Before the Storm

When a hand grabbed Elise's sash and dragged her from her horse, she was more indignant than frightened. She thought Nikholai was her angry assailant. She had disobeyed his orders by staying in Vazka, and she expected him to rail at her.

She jolted painfully to the dust on her buttocks. Without hesitation she jumped up and whirled to confront her attacker. She had her defense prepared. But she faced Vikola, not Nikholai. Her reaction was immediate. She aimed viciously for the Zaporozhie's face. The impact of her fist against his jaw stung her knuckles.

The astounded ataman staggered backward into Ostap's arms. Elise prepared to strike again. Kasyan blocked her.

As the fair Cossack pulled her back, she saw Nikholai appear out of nowhere with Daria at his side. He grabbed Vikola's collar with one hand and struck him across the face with the other. The Zaporozhie struck Nikholai with a blow against the side of the head that caught the tall Cossack off balance. They both fell to the ground amid the sound of cracking knuckles and grunts of pain. Nikholai's cap rolled across the ground as a cloud of dust billowed up around the battling men.

Elise tried to pull free of Kasyan. This fight was hers too. But Kasyan held her fast.

"Ho, warriors," shouted Stenka Razin. He ambled up to the circle that had formed around the fighting men. Filka, Zamurza, the standard-bearer, some other officers, and Alena, his woman, followed him. "What is the cause of this conflict?" he demanded.

"It is Vikola Panko and Nikholai Fomin, Little Father," Kasyan replied respectfully as he restrained the struggling Elise.

"Ah, I have seen this coming for some time," Razin said with a nod. "Nikholai Fomin does not accept his loss of leadership well. They are going to kill each other. Break them up, Filka. I have no desire to lose good men to a brawl."

The first attempt by two of Razin's officers to separate the Cossacks was unsuccessful. Two more officers waded into the fray to drag the men apart.

Finally they stood apart. Vikola's right eye was already turning purple. Blood trickled from Nikholai's lower lip.

"You two set a fine example for your men," Razin scolded.

"Spy," Vikola accused, pointing at Elise. "Nikholai Fomin brings a spy to our camp."

"Spy?" Razin turned to Elise. A grin spread across his scarred face when he recognized her. "Mitka, a spy? The boy who chased a Tartar off a cliff and into the river? You must be mistaken, Vikola Panko. Mitka Stetskov is welcome in my camp anytime. Just remember, boy, the Tartars here are sworn allies. No more death rides, eh? And no more fights, you two."

The giant Cossack laughed and gave Elise a hearty pounding on the back before he turned to Daria. "Ah, beautiful Gypsy. Join us. We go to the river for a swim."

Daria smiled and with a toss of her head joined the group. As they walked away, Elise saw Alena cast the Gypsy a resentful look. Kasyan stared at the ground and said nothing.

"Mitka?" Vikola glared at Elise in disbelief. Without another word, the Zaporozhie followed Razin's entourage toward the river. So did Kasyan. Nikholai bent to pick up his cap.

"We have horses to care for," was all he said.

Elise tried to clean the cut on his lip, but he brushed her away and turned to help the warriors with the packhorses. Elise caught the sympathetic glance Ganna cast her way. Was Nikholai's indifference so obvious? she wondered.

When the unloading was complete and Elise had helped hobble the horses, Vazka's warriors and their women strolled away. Elise waved to Ganna and Filip.

She loitered as Nikholai and Bogdan talked. She was determined not to let Nikholai's neglect disappoint her. Coming was no mistake. Vazka would have gunpowder and supplies. Ganna and Filip were reunited. Elise looked over her shoulder toward the dusty fairground.

If Nikholai did not want to talk to her, she would explore the fair. She could smell food cooking and she was hungry. She rubbed her sore hand, then her stomach, and tried to sort out the source of the delicious aroma. The gesture attracted Nikholai's attention. With a frown, he dismissed Bogdan. He took her uninjured hand and pulled her along behind him toward the music, chants, and laughter.

"You shouldn't have come."

"I'm glad I came," she replied defiantly. "Did you see how happy Ganna and Filip were?"

They passed a group crowded around a dancing bear, and another ring of onlookers who cheered Oriental acrobats. Elise strained to see as much as she could as Nikholai pulled her along. She only glimpsed a snake charmer.

At a crowded stall, he stopped. The keeper, a fat, merry old woman with a toothless smile, greeted him immediately. Without delay she shooed some lingering patrons from a bench and prepared a plate of meat pies and barley cakes for them.

Nikholai shoved a pie into Elise's hands and motioned for her to eat. She did.

"I couldn't trust you to do as you were told, could I?" he asked. "Did Yergov make no attempt to force you to go?"

"No," Elise muttered as she licked spicy sauce from her fingers. She relaxed, relieved that at last he had accused her of something. She was so hungry she had forgotten her table manners. Sometimes it was easy to be a boy. She swallowed the food. "He knew better."

She glanced at Nikholai to see his reaction. He merely nodded, unsurprised. He offered her a honey-barley cake.

"You know, feeding me isn't as important as it once was," she reminded him solemnly. She took a bite from the cake.

He looked away quickly. "I know."

Elise stared at him, waiting. Wasn't he going to rant at her, blame her for everything?

He looked back to her. "You are well?" he asked. She knew he meant from the loss of the baby. Her bleeding had stopped, as it should, and Natalia had long ago declared her healthy. But his obvious concern surprised her. Elise blushed and nodded. But the thought of the baby made the food lose its flavor. She put the unfinished cake back on the plate.

The hour was late. The summer light turned purple, lingered, then faded to smoky blue. Torches flickered. Singing grew louder, laughter heartier, the dancing merrier.

"I should have stopped Vikola," Nikholai said, watching the passersby.

Elise could hardly hear him, his voice was so husky, filled with anguish. "It's one thing to let him become ataman because the warriors want to follow a man I don't believe in," he said. "But I should have stopped him from laying a hand on you."

Elise stared at him and blinked hard to keep the tears from forming. She had been so certain he blamed her. The silence, the brooding, the distance he had kept from her. How could she have not seen that he, too, suffered?

Around them, Cossacks from the Don, Yaik, and Terek brotherhoods ate and talked. Tribesmen drank and laughed together. Elise and Nikholai sat on a bench with a plate of food between them, to all appearances a Cossack warrior and his nephew. She could not share what was in her heart, could not take his hand. She could not tell him that she, too, had gone over and over what she should have done to prevent what had happened. The world pressed too close and kept them apart.

The chanting of church songs and the tinkling of brass

bells reached her ears. Elise followed Nikholai's gaze to a torchlit procession making its way among the fair stalls.

Above the chanting group, like a standard before an army, bobbed the three-rung cross of the Orthodox Church. A short, chubby man walked slowly alongside with regal bearing and a hand raised in blessing. His rich church robes shone in the light of the torch flames. He wore the tall hat of the Muscovite patriarch. Beside him marched a boy of about thirteen also dressed in rich clothes.

"Who is that?" Elise asked.

Nikholai gave a cynical laugh. "It is the Patriarch Nikon and the Tsarevich Alexis. Razin has outfitted boats for them."

"What?" Elise exclaimed. "We heard that the tsar's son died last January. And everyone knows Nikon was locked away in the north four years ago."

"Not according to Stenka Razin," Nikholai said. "They are here with him. The boyars only faked the tsarevich's death. And Stenka Razin has freed Nikon."

"That's cruel," Elise said. "Do the people believe it?"

"People believe what they want to believe," Nikholai said. "The story brings the Old Believers out to support Razin's cause. And Brother Chevdor enjoys playing the part of the patriarch. But come, enough of this sham. Come see the flotilla." Nikholai wrapped the remaining honey cakes in a cloth and pocketed them. He paid the stall keeper and led Elise to the river.

Even as he rowed the small boat toward one of the sixteen-foot barkas the Cossacks sailed on the rivers and seas, Elise truly believed he intended to show her a boat.

Anchored just off one of the islands, the craft made a perfect love nest with the folded sails as a bed. From the riverbank, no one could see them. Nikholai began with a kiss that surprised Elise, but she yielded to it willingly. He undressed her quickly, lingering only to stroke and kiss her bare skin as it was exposed. Then he put the jade earrings in her ears. They were all she wore that night.

The boat rocked gently beneath them. Overhead the stars glittered brightly. On the horizon a thunderstorm played— pink and white lightning glimmered up through the domes and towers of a fanciful city of clouds.

"Better than even the king's fireworks," Elise whispered. She and Nikholai lay side by side, her head on his arm, her hand spread across his hard, flat belly. "And put on all for us."

"Fireworks for lovers?" There was a hint of amusement in Nikholai's voice. Elise was not offended. He went on, "There are no finer storms in the world than those on the steppe."

Elise closed her eyes to better listen to the distant rumble of the thunder, the even beating of Nikholai's heart, and the rhythmic lapping of the water. Nikholai's ardent but tender lovemaking had made her feel whole again. Their sailcloth bed smelled of sunshine and fresh air. The air was so warm, the breeze so caressing, she had no desire to cover herself.

"You don't believe him, do you?" she asked Nikholai at last. She was certain it was on his mind.

"Believe whom about what?" His eyes were closed.

"Vikola," Elise said. "You don't believe I'm a spy, do you?"

"I believe my reputation is ruined," he said. "At this very moment Stenka Razin's warriors are laughing among themselves and saying Nikholai Fomin prefers blond boys."

Elise didn't think he sounded concerned about his reputation. Rolling to his side, he propped his head on his hand and leaned near her.

"Are you a spy, Green Eyes?" he asked. "Our movements have been anticipated," he said, looking down into her face. "When we started to move north again from Astrakhan, there was an attempt on Razin's life one night. A spy is among us."

"I have known nothing of the army's movement except what has come to Vazka by messenger."

"How many languages do you speak and write, Green Eyes? Polish, Russian, Cossack? You've learned Tartar. You must know German. I've heard you speak Dutch. French?"

"Latin, Greek, and I learned a little Italian from a court musician," she added. "But you speak more than one language. That is hardly a crime."

"Perfect for a spy," Nikholai said. "And it is interesting that you have a brother on a secret mission in Sweden."

"I have nothing to do with that," she said. "Besides, if

Thomas is involved, there can't be a lot of subterfuge. He's probably just agreed to some unofficial meetings or he's a courier. He's an Englishman. He would be obvious. Just as a woman from the outside is obvious. A spy wants to go unnoticed."

"Yes, but a woman can gain access—a kind of intimacy to leaders that no man could," Nikholai pointed out. "We all knew that Bogdan Khmelnitsky sent women spies deep behind Turkish lines to gain information in the fifties. They were very successful."

"This way?" Elise asked, trailing her fingers down the middle of his chest, through the dark curls. "If I were a spy for the Muscovites against Razin, would I seek you out?"

Nikholai hesitated. Elise saw the pain in his face and regretted her words. "You would seek out the leaders," he said.

Elise touched his face. "Yes. Not a crazy Cossack in disfavor with Stenka Razin."

He smiled a wry smile. "There is truth in your words." He leaned over to kiss her.

They whispered endearments to each other while making love again. Elise asked him not to blame himself for what had happened to their child. Nikholai did not respond, but he kissed her fingertips and clung to her hand as they slept.

When the deepest part of the night came, when the frogs had ceased to sing and the thunderstorm had moved on east, when no more laughter drifted across the water from the fairgrounds, Elise awoke. Premonition lay heavy on her. She sensed Nikholai was already awake.

"Where do you go from here?" she asked.

"I'm not invited to Razin's krug," he answered with bitterness in his voice. "But rumors say we move north upriver toward Saratov. Then on to Samara and Simbirsk."

"Why not to Moscow before the tsar can muster his forces?"

"I asked the same question and received no satisfactory answer," Nikholai said. "I think Razin may be counting on Ukrainian forces from the west to move on Moscow. But we've had little communication with them. I can't be certain of that."

"Take me with you," she whispered. She turned on her

side and looked into his face. "You know I can keep up. I'll play groom to your horses if you wish, or I will escort the women."

"Green Eyes," he began with a shake of his head and a chuckle, "when I want to keep you, you run away, and when I set you free, you search me out."

"Anna is safe now," she replied. "She and Natalia adore each other. I have no need to leave you. Think how I might be useful. I can translate dispatches, and help write them if need be."

"I will not consider it."

"Why?" she asked. "Daria is here."

"Daria is Kasyan's affair."

"Kasyan considers Daria's desires."

"Perhaps he is afraid to leave her behind," Nikholai retorted.

Elise recalled the desolate look on the fair Cossack's face as Daria walked off with Razin. "Is Kasyan happy with her?"

"I don't know," Nikholai said, staring at the sky. "Daria is not a woman who brings happiness to a man."

"I could bring you happiness if you let me go with you," Elise whispered. She kissed his collarbone.

"I will not be swayed, Green Eyes," Nikholai said with another chuckle. "If you will not return to Warsaw and safety, you will stay in Vazka."

They made their bed on the sails for two more nights. Vazka's goods sold quickly. Elise's disguise amused Vazka's warriors. Despite Vikola's dark looks, it pleased them to call her Mitka and to invite her to drink with them. She accepted sometimes. Then they teased the boy about not draining his cup in one draft. But they would not invite her to gamble.

Word had reached them that a Cossack force from the west had taken Voronezh and that the peasants in Penza, Tambov, and Ryazan had burned buildings within twenty-four versts of Moscow. Razin was eager to move north. Daily, more men and boys arrived to join his force, many of them carrying only pitchforks and scythes as weapons. What they lacked in armaments they carried in enthusiasm.

Nikholai and Elise said farewell to each other in the boat

under the stars. There could be no display of emotion between them when "Mitka" rode away.

At first, the news from Stenka Razin's army was good. Village after village fell to the Cossacks as unhappy peasants betrayed officials and landowners. When Samara threw open its gates for Razin, messengers said, nearly a million men followed the great rebel. Elise recalled the diversity of the rebels at the Tsaritsyn fair—different languages, cultures, and religions—and wondered how Razin could control such an army with the few officers he trusted. Their only common interest was their foe.

In September, Fydor, the minstrel, sang of the rebels' approach to Simbirsk with battle drums booming. The Muscovite force commanded by German officers assembled near Kazan but was still too small to dare an attack on the enormous rebel force.

# ❦ 25 ❦

# The Citadel of Simbirsk

Prince Miloslavsky may be a Muscovite dog, but he's no fool," Razin said as he eyed the fortified citadel of Simbirsk. The castle sat high atop two barren terraces, each side exposed to open view from the ramparts above.

Before the citizens had thrown open the city gate, Prince Miloslavsky, voevoda of Simbirsk, and four regiments of streltsy had retired to the fortress. They had been there under siege for almost a week.

The unusual September sky still wore the flat blue of summer. The fortress walls wobbled in the summerlike heat waves. From the main tower the double-headed golden eagle of the red Muscovite flag fluttered in the breeze.

The gleaming white skull-and-horsetails standard loomed above the mounted Cossack officers. Razin, Filka, Zamurza, the standard-bearer, Vikola, Nikholai, Kasyan, and a few other officers observed Simbirsk's stone walls from the command pavilion just beyond cannon range.

Nikholai and Kasyan exchanged looks of agreement. They saw no indication that Simbirsk was about to fall.

They were among the officers now because each had been promoted to command a group of ragtag peasants. With the numbers that had joined the rebel army, even Razin could not afford to overlook officers so qualified as Nikholai and Kasyan.

The appointment had set ill with Vikola. While the Zaporozhie said nothing of it in Razin's presence, he complained to the warriors of Vazka, who listened silently.

The mounted Cossacks and their Tartar allies carried firearms, lances, and sabers. The woodland tribesmen, the Cheremiss and Mordvas, were unfailingly lethal with either spear or bow and arrow. The only advantage the unarmed peasants had was their number.

Soon after the siege began, Nikholai and Kasyan's peasants had built earthen ramparts and moved the Cossack cannon into place. The terraced hillside shook by day with cannon blasts—Cossack and Muscovite.

Breastworks of green logs were raised. By night, powder kegs were hurled over the walls from those breastworks. Several night attempts were made to breach the fortress walls, but all failed. Simbirsk smoked and burned and stood undefeated.

Just that day messengers from Miloslavsky bearing desperate pleas for aid had been intercepted and tortured.

"Look at this," Razin said, shaking the intercepted message at his officers. "See? Miloslavsky writes of eating dogs and horses. Their water is severely rationed. Simbirsk will fall soon. Anytime."

Again Nikholai and Kasyan exchanged weary looks. They were stripped to the waist and covered in soot, dirt, sweat, and blood. They and their men had worked diligently around the clock for almost a week.

Razin turned to another officer. "What did the scout say, Vikola Panko?"

"Little Father, the Boriatinsky's Muscovite force advance from Kazan. They wear armor and carry firearms," Vikola said. "The Cheremiss and the Mordvas are unable to get close enough to get off fatal arrows. The Boriatinsky will be here in two days."

Nikholai noted grudgingly that Vikola still looked as fresh as a spring-blooming crocus. Without thought he rubbed his aching shoulder. The Zaporozhie had been left in charge of

Vazka's mounted force, which Razin was keeping in reserve. Vazka had suffered no losses so far. Nikholai was glad of that, but had little hope the good fortune would hold.

Stenka Razin paced the length of the pavilion and back. Dusty footprints marked the red silk carpet. The hemp-cloth tent snapped in a cool west breeze. Although the days were still bright and warm, the nights had turned frosty. Winter was their other enemy.

"We must defeat Boriatinsky's Muscovites before they reach Simbirsk," Razin said, pounding on a small table he used as a desk. "We will do it."

He ordered the mounted Cossacks and Cossack boatmen to march overland to meet the Muscovite forces to the north. Vazka's warriors and Kasyan's peasants would accompany him.

The siege forces were left under Filka's command. The skin on the back of Nikholai's neck prickled as he watched Razin and the Cossack mounted forces ride out the city gate. He knew the Muscovites in the fortress towers watched too.

The first reports from the battle to the north were good. Cossack forces held their ground. Little Father was everywhere, urging the peasants, tribes, and brotherhoods to fight on against the Muscovite dogs.

Nikholai couldn't bring himself to cheer with the others when they learned the news from the messengers. They had no word of Vazka's warriors. Miloslavsky's cannon had finally hit the earthworks, and several of Nikholai's peasants had been lost. He disliked losing men.

The next message from the north was in much the same vein. Then, for a day there was no news. Filka pretended it was of no concern. A messenger had been waylaid, he said.

About midday on the third day, the booming of the battle drum called Nikholai to the pavilion. He was reluctant to leave his peasants. Muscovites in the fortress had suddenly begun to press their defense.

Inside the command pavilion Nikholai encountered Cossack officers milling around someone lying on the carpet. The skull-and-horsetails standard leaned in the corner. Zamurza, the standard-bearer, was missing.

The officers shouted and cursed one another. Nikholai pushed his way through the group to find Stenka Razin lying semiconscious on the rug. Daria and Alena knelt beside him, trying to stanch a flow of blood from his head. His right leg was bound.

"It's gone. It's gone," Filka chanted as he threw charts and written dispatches from one side of the desk to the other. "The magic is gone."

Nikholai saw Ostap and grabbed him.

"Oh, Nikholai Fomin," Ostap cried with relief on his face. "Zamurza died trying to protect Stenka Razin. And Little Father has lost his magic. The tribesmen saw. They ran. Boriatinsky's forces approach the north gate."

"What of Kasyan and Vazka's warriors?" Nikholai demanded.

"Filip is dead," Ostap said. "Kasyan is wounded. The Muscovites were well-armed. We stood as long as we dared. Then we brought Little Father out with us."

"Where are they, Ostap?" Nikholai could barely make himself heard over the curses and shouts of the others. Renewed cannon volleys from the fortress added to the confusion.

"Vikola ordered us to remain at the north gate," Ostap said. "Then he left with Razin. It will be a massacre when the Muscovites arrive. I hoped to find some relief forces here."

Nikholai turned to see Vikola and Filka leaning over Stenka Razin.

"Little Father does not want to go to the boats," Filka said.

Vikola argued, "It is the only way to safety. Most of the peasants at the front have already run. We must save ourselves."

Alena dabbed the blood oozing from Razin's head wound. Daria brushed the flies away from the leg wound and agreed with Vikola.

Razin waved a hand at Alena. "Send her away with the women," he rasped. His face was white and his voice little more than a whisper. Alena's icy gaze halted the officer who reached for her.

Without hesitation Nikholai seized Daria's arm and

pushed her out of the pavilion. "Go to your husband," he ordered. He cared little for her safety. "Bind Kasyan's wounds. Comfort him. Behave as a wife."

"No," Daria cried, and shrugged off Nikholai's hold. "I go with Little Father. I can't help Kasyan."

"Take her, Ostap," Nikholai said. "I will meet you at the north gate shortly. Prepare the men to move out quickly." The Gypsy screamed as Ostap dragged her away.

Nikholai returned to the pavilion to find Vikola. Two officers passed him carrying Stenka Razin on a board to a waiting wagon. Inside, other Cossacks piled chairs, rugs, and papers onto a fire. Black smoke boiled into the perfect blue sky.

Vikola, like the others, rushed about the pavilion, sifting through the chests and boxes, pocketing valuables and throwing useless things into the fire.

Nikholai caught the Zaporozhie by the shoulder and whirled him around.

"Coward," he accused through his teeth. "You would leave your men without leadership, without support and encouragement."

Vikola struck at Nikholai, but the tall Cossack ducked. In doing so, he released his hold on the Zaporozhie. Vikola ran from the pavilion and mounted his horse.

Nikholai flung himself across the rump of the horse. His hold was precarious. Each stride jolted him. He swung one leg over the rump and reached around Vikola for the reins. They fought for control of the horse, Nikholai pulling away from the city gate and Vikola seeking escape.

Vikola elbowed Nikholai in the ribs and kicked the horse. Confused, the animal lunged forward, jumped the earthworks, and bolted across the terraced battleground. Cannon volleys thundered around them. Musket balls whizzed between them. Nikholai tried to drag Vikola from the horse. He wanted to clamp his hands around the coward's throat and strangle him. But the Zaporozhie was not easily unseated.

A Muscovite cannon volley struck immediately before them. Dirt and rock pelted them. The frightened horse reared, forelegs flailing in the air, then fell backward.

Nikholai jumped clear. Vikola was penned beneath the horse. All struggled to regain their feet. Nikholai started toward the Zaporozhie. Screaming of a second volley stopped Nikholai. He had no death wish for himself. The force of the impact slammed him against the scorched earth. The horse screamed. Then was silent. Dirt rained on him.

Nikholai scrambled toward a trench, and peasant hands welcomed him to safety. Over his shoulder he glimpsed only a flesh-littered crater where the Zaporozhie and his horse had fallen.

In the church Vazka's women prayed. Elise kept her vigil at the lookout with one eye on the ford and the other on the northern horizon. She murmured a prayer. It could do no harm, she thought, but she wanted to do more.

Since the end of September, no word had arrived from Razin's army. The last message had told of Muscovite forces advancing on Simbirsk.

The refugee families who had passed through the village were confused about events in the north. They accepted Vazka's hospitality gratefully and hurried south.

Elise pulled her caftan closer. The October breeze was cool and the sky cloudy. Dry leaves rattled in the brush around her. Across the river, the steppe grass was taking on its autumn-red hue.

This time last year she had still been the young mistress of an elegant household, a hostess, and a countess. She wore fine gowns and selected rich menus. Only a year ago, but it was a world ago. So much had happened. When she thought of Nikholai, of his smile, of his lovemaking, she did not miss the old life.

Now she sat on a krug, among elders of the village, battle-hardened men, and helped plan for winter. She wore a head covering and felt boots. She favored honey-barley cakes when she could get them and rode the horses and played with Anna whenever she desired.

To her surprise, the simple outdoor life agreed with the child. Anna played among the Cossack children as if she were one of them.

So when Yergov sent word that Thomas was on his way to

Cherkassk, Elise received the news with mixed feelings. As much as she longed to see her brother, all she really wanted was for Nikholai to return safely to hold her again.

She heard footsteps on the rocky path above.

"Elise. Elise," called Anna. The child came running down the path toward the lookout ledge. "Bogdan bade me to find you," she said breathlessly, her cheeks aglow with excitement. "Daria has returned."

Elise found the Gypsy girl seated at her mother's table, gobbling down fish soup as though she hadn't eaten in days. Her hair was tangled and dirty, her face thin and haggard, her clothes covered in soot, dust, and blood. Dread filled Elise, but she tried not to show it.

Bogdan stood beside Daria's mother. He shrugged when Elise cast him a questioning look.

"Daria," Elise began, "we are glad you have returned safely."

Daria looked up. "Are you? Don't you wonder where the others are? Well, they won't be coming back. You'll see. They'll all be dead soon, if they aren't already."

"Did you travel together?" Elise asked, slowly taking a seat across the table.

"No." Daria stuffed a piece of black bread into her mouth. "I would have gone with Vikola, with Razin and his officers. Nikholai held me back. Razin's probably in a city now, enjoying good food and music. He will heal fast. He's a strong man."

"So, Stenka Razin was wounded?" Elise asked patiently. She glanced over her shoulder to see Bogdan clench his fists at his sides.

"And what of your husband?" the elder demanded.

"Yes, Little Father was wounded," Daria said with a wave of her hand. "And Kasyan's dead. Vikola too. The Muscovites defeated Razin. Peasants massacred. Hack, hack. Cannon balls, boom, boom, everywhere. The screaming. The stink." Daria pointed to her soup bowl. Her mother refilled it.

"Razin's officers took him away," she continued. "The burlaki sailed away in their boats. The mounted Cossacks escaped. Nikholai made me go with Kasyan. Now Kasyan is dead, and what do I have?"

Elise held up her hand to silence Bogdan, who was about to grab the Gypsy girl about the throat.

"And what of Nikholai?" Elise asked. With a steady hand she passed Daria another piece of bread.

"Oh, the cursed Wolf lives," Daria said.

Elise's heart fluttered. He lived. With effort she remained calm. "Where did he go?"

"He said something about a pirates' camp," Daria said. "The streltsy is everywhere, stronger than ever. Cossacks swing from the gibbet already. Soon the roads of the Don and the Volga will stink with rotting Cossack carcasses." Daria gave a joyless laugh. Bogdan and Elise stared at her, speechless.

"You are a fool, Countess," Daria said with a laugh. "I promise: you will regret staying in Vazka."

Outside the cottage, Elise turned to Bogdan and touched his arm. "I'm sorry."

Bogdan nodded.

"Is there nothing we can do to help Nikholai and the others?" she asked. "What happens in a Cossack retreat?"

"Cossacks scatter, hide, take refuge where they can," he explained. "So there is nothing for the enemy to attack. But Nikholai Fomin will keep the warriors of Vazka together."

"Where would they go?"

"They would not return to Vazka," Bogdan said. "Nikholai would not lead the Muscovites here." Suddenly the lines in the elder's face lengthened and deepened. "When your brother comes," he said, "you must go with him, Countess, before the Muscovites make us all suffer."

In the days that followed Daria's return, Thomas did not arrive. More refugees passed through the village, telling tales of Muscovite streltsy searching the countryside and of grisly gibbetings. Samara and Saratov had closed their gates to the wounded Razin. The same people who had welcomed the rebel as a liberator now refused him aid.

Elise feared for Nikholai and Vazka's warriors. Did they have shelter, food, ammunition? Winter was only weeks away.

A small jewel of hope came in a letter from Timofe, sent with a pack train of flour and salt. He wrote that Don Host Ataman Kornil Iakovlev thought he could get a pardon for

Nikholai Fomin and his warriors for his support against Razin during the Christmas krug.

Elise wanted to go to Nikholai immediately. She pored over the maps, certain she could find the pirate camp. The krug said no. The pardon was not a reality; the risk of leading the streltsy to Vazka's warriors was.

## ❧ 26 ❧

# Come Ransom a Traitor

Open the gates in the name of Alexis Romanov, Tsar of All the Russias," shouted Rostov for the third time.

Elise nodded to the boys to pull Vazka's gates slightly ajar so that she, the krug, and Bogdan, carrying the ataman's staff, could emerge to greet the Muscovites. The sky was gray, the wind cold, and the ground muddy after three days of fall rains.

What little optimism Elise had deserted her when she and the krug stood before Rostov and saw the battle-weary streltsy behind him. These were no fresh-faced boys who could be easily diverted with a wedding feast.

"Ah," Rostov said with a laugh. He made no move to dismount. The legs, belly, and chest of his golden-brown gelding were splattered with mud and sweat. "So Vazka now allows a woman among the krug. I remember you. Nikholai Fomin's bride. I've come for your husband, my dear."

Elise felt Bogdan bristle at Rostov's familiarity. She touched the elder's arm to assure him it wasn't important.

"Nikholai Fomin is not here." Elise spoke clearly to the red-bearded streltsy officer. She stepped forward and presented him with a poised, regal countenance. The krug

301

members closed ranks behind her. She hoped she appeared more confident than she felt.

She noted that bags of fresh gunpowder dangled from the bandoliers across soldiers' chests. Their lances gleamed in the dull daylight. In a quick movement—one they had learned from Cossacks—they could level their lances and charge.

"Are you going to tell me some ridiculous story that he is chasing wild horses?" Rostov asked with a wave of his hand. Then he leaned forward in the saddle. "I cannot prove he is the pirate on the Volga, but we know he was one of Razin's officers at Simbirsk. In fact, several of Vazka's warriors are wanted. Kasyan Cherevik. Vikola Panko. Bring them out."

"They are not here," Elise replied. She held his blue-eyed gaze and never wavered, never blinked.

"Allow us to see for ourselves," Rostov demanded.

She and the krug had already decided it was vital to keep the Muscovites from riding into the village. From behind their wooden palisades the Cossacks could defend themselves. To admit the Muscovite forces inside the walls would be suicide.

"You will forgive us, Captain," Elise said. "We mourn the loss of family members and are not entertaining visitors at this time. You are a clever man, Captain Rostov. You know Nikholai Fomin would not lead Muscovite troops to his home."

Rostov eyed her resentfully. His gaze shifted to the stanitsa walls behind her. "Then where is he? Do you know?"

Before Elise could reply, Daria crowded in front of her.

"She tells the truth," Daria said. "They are not here. But she knows where they are. I saw her looking at the maps." Daria poked her finger at Elise. "You know where they are."

Elise shoved Daria's hand away. Daria slapped her. Taken by surprise, Elise staggered back against Bogdan. The Gypsy went after Elise again, reaching for her hair this time. Bogdan warded off the Gypsy's attack and pushed Elise behind him. Elise strained against the desire to go after the Gypsy, but the smirk she glimpsed on Rostov's face stopped her. She would not provide the Muscovite with entertainment.

Frustrated, Daria backed away.

"Bogdan?" Elise whispered to the elder as she stood at his shoulder. "I owe you much. Can I depend on you still?"

"Of course, Countess," he replied without looking at her.

"Then trust me, friend," Elise whispered again. "I will need your help to make this work."

The elder gave her an imperceptible nod of assent.

Elise stood up straight and tried to regain her composure. Rostov dismounted and strode through the mud to stand before her.

"So, you know where he is," Rostov gloated. He chucked her under the chin like one patronizing a child. "You can tell me now or . . . we have ways of learning what we want to know."

He signaled his men. They immediately spread into a single line, lances lowered and ready to charge. "Tell me now."

Unexpectedly, Rostov twisted his hand in her hair until she was certain he would pull it out. A small cry of pain escaped her. With the same suddenness, he released her.

Elise staggered away from him and turned to see a lance pressed against Bogdan's chest. The elder was helpless.

"You know where your husband is? Tell me."

"Yes, I know where he is," Elise admitted reluctantly. She tried to control her ragged breathing. Her scalp stung. She feared for the elders, for Anna, for Natalia—for them all.

A victorious grin broke across Rostov's face.

"What do I get if I lead you to him?" Elise demanded.

Rostov's mouth dropped open. "Why do you think you should get anything but your life?"

"You want something," Elise said. "I want something."

"What is it you want?"

"You will leave Vazka untouched and Daria goes with us," Elise said, unsure why she asked for Daria beyond the fact that she didn't think the Gypsy should be trusted in Vazka.

"Daria?" He looked at the Gypsy, who smiled at him coyly. He shrugged. "I want Nikholai Fomin. I agree."

Elise was allowed only to change her clothes. Mounted on an old black mare, she rode away with Rostov, the streltsy, and Daria. She left the last good horse, the sorrel mare, for Bogdan.

303

The portage road between the Don and Volga was crowded with cartloads of refugees fleeing from the rebellion and the Muscovite retributions. Still, Elise found it difficult to delay travel. Travelers were quick to move aside for the tsar's streltsy.

Outside Tsaritsyn they passed a gibbet heavy with Cossacks. The rebels had been stripped naked, their hands chained behind their backs, and their legs roped together. Stark pain twisted their faces. From the iron hooks in their ribs, tiny rivulets of dried blood trailed down their bare bellies. The ravens circled overhead and settled possessively on the gibbet crossbeam. Elise knew their feast would start with the glassy, staring eyes.

Sickened, she wanted to look away, but dark fascination held her. Her stomach churned, but she did not vomit. She just knew *that* must not happen to Vazka's warriors.

In two days they were on the west bank of the Volga. Elise led them north as slowly as possible. Daria was more help than she knew. The dark-eyed girl complained of the long hours in the saddle and amused the soldiers with her swishing skirts, jangling bracelets, and teasing smile. With a woman like that around, they had little interest in Elise's tall, slender form, dressed as a boy.

At the end of the third day Elise found the Volga crossing the Cossacks had used after the pirate raid. She was disappointed to have come upon it so soon. Briefly she considered trying to take them on north, but decided against it. She felt it was best to keep Rostov satisfied that she was truly leading him to his quarry.

That night Daria disappeared with Rostov into the thick undergrowth along the river. Elise heard the Gypsy giggle as they crept away, but she said nothing. She pulled her caftan closer about her and wondered whether Bogdan had found Nikholai, and whether Nikholai had agreed with the plan.

She curled up on the sand to sleep, her last thought that she would rise before daybreak to spot the North Star and the sun on the horizon. She must keep their trail angled north.

"You are sure? A boy in a red cap? It is the countess?" Nikholai asked from where he sat on a tree stump. He looked up at his scouts. "She led the Muscovites right to us?"

Pain and disbelief played across his face. She had resented him as her captor. He understood that. But to do this . . . So spiteful. So like a woman. Like Daria or Aksinia, but unlike Elise. He couldn't shake the disappointment that settled over him, or the pain in his gut.

His scouts watched him, then looked at one another and shrugged.

"She must have remembered this encampment location from her journey with us and guessed that we would come here," Kasyan said. He had limped up to the circle of men just in time to hear the last of the scouts' report. His leg wound was well-healed, but permanently twisted.

"She has betrayed us to the Muscovites," Nikholai said, his voice hard. "How do you explain that? She is the spy."

Kasyan sat down on a fat log. Almost as if he were ashamed of something, he refused to look at anyone. "Daria is with them," he said flatly.

"We have to ambush them," Nikholai said. "We need their guns and powder. I don't know if we can save Daria."

Nikholai turned to the scout, a new warrior who had joined them during the retreat. He was an experienced, reliable man. The other was a man from Vazka. He had recognized Elise and Daria immediately. "Where do the women ride in the column? Was she bound?" Nikholai asked.

"He . . . she wears a red cap and rides like a boy next to the Muscovite streltsy captain," the scout repeated. "Sometimes they talk to each other, and she points the way, mostly east and a little to the north. She is not bound. The Gypsy rides at the captain's other side."

"She has missed the exact place," Kasyan pointed out. "Nikholai, maybe this is not what it seems."

"I think she has come amazingly close," Nikholai said, "for a woman. How many streltsy did you count?"

"About seventy-five," the scout said. "And two outriders serving as scouts. They didn't see us."

"An even match," Nikholai thought out loud. About forty of Vazka's warriors had been lost at Simbirsk. And Vazka had been fortunate compared to other kurens. As they fled, others had joined them—Cossacks and peasants. Good fighters, ready to follow orders without question. After Vikola was killed, no election was held. Vazka's warriors had simply turned to Nikholai for orders, and he had given them. He was ataman again.

They had fought their way clear of the Muscovite forces, commandeered a deserted wagon, and moved south and east. Nikholai had anticipated that the cities that once welcomed Stenka Razin would turn on him. And he had been right.

They had stayed clear of Samara and Saratov. Before they turned east away from Saratov, Daria had bolted. She had nursed Kasyan's painful leg wound, but her presence seemed to give him little ease. She had sat beside her husband and rocked to and fro, sometimes singing tuneless little songs to herself. For the most part, Nikholai ignored her. But when Kasyan's wound became infected and he burned with fever, Daria became hysterical.

"He's dying," she screamed. She climbed out of the wagon. "We're all going to die. Because one man thought he could fight the tsar of Muscovy, we are all going to die. I hope Stenka Razin is dead and burning in hell."

The Cossacks, dust layered across their faces and on their backs, had stared at her. Nikholai dismounted. Concerned that her hysteria was contagious, he slapped her. She screamed more, and he slapped her again to silence her.

"Go," he ordered, and pointed toward the west, toward Saratov. "If you don't care about your husband enough to make the best of this, then leave. We don't need your cowardice here."

Crying and cursing, Daria had gone, on foot. Nikholai never doubted that she made it as far as Saratov. Women like Daria would always survive.

Her defection was no more than he had expected. Women lacked the stamina for this kind of thing. He even doubted they had the loyalty. Daria had left Kasyan. No doubt Elise had left Vazka. The novelty of Cossack life would have disappeared. She would have heard about Simbirsk, and would have packed up Anna and left for Cherkassk, for safety and Poland.

Nikholai took over driving the wagon and caring for

Kasyan. Kasyan was conscious, and Nikholai was certain his comrade had heard the scene outside the wagon, but the two men never discussed Daria's defection. Nikholai cleaned the wound, he fed his friend, and bathed his body when the fever burned.

For two more days they had traveled south and east. They circled the campsite where Elise spent her first night in Cossack captivity. They encountered a Kalmyk tribe, but no others. The Kalmyk healer was helpful in treating Kasyan's wound. So Nikholai ordered his warriors to settle in.

For meetings, they built one roomy sod building with an oven and threw up wood-and-hemp-cloth cottages for sleeping. They could pass the winter here. Antelope and small game were plentiful. The spring water was sweet. Nikholai hoped that at the turn of the year they could begin to return to Vazka, a few men at a time, never enough for the Muscovites to understand what was happening.

But the countess wasn't going to let it happen that way. Once again, he had underestimated her.

"Continue to watch them," Nikholai ordered. "When they camp for the night, we will prepare to attack. Kasyan, tell the men to prepare to ride north to ambush Rostov and his streltsy."

"And the countess and Daria?" Kasyan asked before he rose from his seat. He stared at the ground.

"They will take their chances along with the rest of the fighting men," Nikholai said. He thought a moment. "No, perhaps not. I want her to know that we understand her game and that she has lost." Then he turned his back on his friend and disappeared into the sod building.

"You know, Alexander Rostov," Daria said as she stared over the campfire at Elise, "I think she is tricking us."

"How?" Rostov asked. With his uneven yellow teeth he tore a hunk of meat from a roasted game bird. Earlier Elise had watched one of the streltsy shoot the bird. The captain had confiscated it for himself and Daria. The streltsy soldier had grumbled, but another flock of birds took to the air, so they all dined well that evening. Except Elise. She stared with little interest at the piece of meat her guard had given her. And she listened.

307

"I don't think she is taking us to the pirates," Daria said.

"Of course she's not," Rostov said. He took another bite. "She's trying to set us up for an ambush. But don't worry, my sweet Gypsy." He grinned at Daria, then across the fire at Elise. "The Wolf won't attack us so long as his wife is along. We don't need her to take us to him. He will find us."

Elise forced herself to be silent and her face to remain expressionless. What a fool she was! She should have known Rostov would see through her ploy. She had drawn him away from Vazka. But if Bogdan failed to reach Nikholai, she had put him and his warriors at great risk.

Her original plan had been to slip away, disappear into the night, as soon as they neared the old pirate campsite. And leave Rostov and his streltsy to be ambushed by the Cossacks.

Rostov must have anticipated that. As soon as they had crossed the Volga, he appointed her a personal guard—one that even stood over her as she slept. When she needed to relieve herself, she was accompanied by Daria, with either Rostov or the guard within hearing distance.

They had been riding several days now across the steppe toward the Urals. She had seen no smoke signals, no unidentified scouts on the horizon. She knew the plan had gone awry.

So many things could happen to even a veteran rider like Bogdan. Trouble in fording a river. The mare could come up lame. He could be waylaid by another detachment of streltsy.

Elise regretted that she had not armed herself at least with a knife. It would have been easy to hide. Rostov was so sure of himself that he never had her searched.

At dawn Elise awoke with the realization so true and solid before her that she wondered why she had been unable to see it before. Daria was the spy. She had sensed it the day Daria betrayed her at Vazka's gate, but not realized it until now.

Daria had used Vikola, and now she used Elise to help Rostov take Nikholai. Elise sat up and watched the pink brighten on the horizon. She shivered from the cold. Her body ached from the long hours in the saddle and the short nights on the hard ground. She was exhausted. Events were out of her hands, and she didn't know how to change that. She prayed Thomas would be in Vazka soon to take care of Anna.

"You will take me to Tula when this is over," Daria said, clinging to Rostov near the morning campfire. "You will free my brother and buy me a house there." She nuzzled Rostov's ear.

"Sure, sure," Rostov said, holding his cup out for tea.

"You will have the Wolf of the Volga at last," Daria chattered as she poured tea. "You will be back in the army's good graces, and my brother will be free."

"Yes," Rostov said. He looked off over the steppe with a small smile of satisfaction. "And I will make Nikholai Fomin pay for my loss of good reputation."

Around noon, Elise sensed someone watching her. She scanned the horizon for signs of smoke or scouts but saw none. Rostov's scouts seemed unaware of any threat.

The travelers rested in a rocky gully. A small spring furnished water for the horses. The October day had begun bright and crisp, but now clouds gathered. The wind turned cold and whipped down from the north. They built no fire. The Muscovites rested casually on the ground, talking among themselves.

Elise felt exposed. They were in an ideal position to be ambushed. Was this some trick of Rostov's to lure Nikholai into the open? Every time she looked up, she expected to see Nikholai and his warriors on the crest of the next hill, ready to ride down on them.

At twilight, Rostov ordered camp made on a wide ridge. Elise felt better about this site. Enemy approach would be easily spotted. She sat next to the small campfire and waited. A misty gray canopy of clouds hung over them. The sun disappeared below the horizon in a dull yellow glow.

She was the first to see the Cossack with the truce flag. He rode up the draw in the gray half-light of dusk. She did not recognize the warrior, but she knew the horse—Sotnik. First her guard, then Rostov turned to see what claimed her attention.

Belatedly Rostov's sentry cried an alert. Anger flashed across Rostov's face. He struck Elise with the back of his hand.

The blow sent her rolling through the tall steppe grass.

"You knew," he shouted. "You knew they were out there."

Daria laughed.

Elise clutched her aching chin. She tasted blood, but her jaw still moved.

The Cossack remained motionless, one hand on Sotnik's reins and the other holding the lance with the white flag tied to it. Rostov strode toward him and motioned the streltsy soldiers away. Warily Elise followed, her hand still on her jaw. Daria joined her. They stood behind Rostov just close enough to hear the messenger's words. The truce flag snapped in the northern wind.

"What is your message?" Rostov demanded.

"Nikholai Fomin wishes to meet with you, Daria, and the one called Mitka," the hard-faced warrior said in a sharp voice. Despite her throbbing jaw, Elise felt a chill run down her back.

"Where?" Rostov demanded. "When?"

"Where the creek forks," the Cossack said, and gestured with his lance to the west, where the creek below joined another small tributary. It was an open, grassy area easily visible from the hills around it. "Now."

"I will not go down there alone and unarmed," Rostov said.

"Bring two armed men if you wish," the Cossack replied. "Nikholai Fomin will also bring his lieutenant and two armed warriors. But Mitka and Daria must be present."

"As he wishes," Rostov said with a smile.

The Cossack galloped down the draw. Rostov turned to Elise. "So Nikholai Fomin is going to fall for the bait."

Elise ignored him as she watched the Cossack join the men awaiting him at the foot of the ridge. She knew Rostov was mistaken.

The streltsy captain wasted no time. They rode to the fork. No one met them there, but Elise knew they were being watched. Momentarily she forgot about her throbbing jaw. She wanted to see Nikholai again, to know he was well, to touch him. She hoped she could communicate with him somehow.

Rostov, Daria, and Elise dismounted. Guards with a truce

flag remained on horseback, casting uneasy glances about them.

At the sound of hoofbeats, they all turned. Elise's heart gave a little leap at the sight of Nikholai, tall and proud in the saddle. Beside him rode Kasyan. *Kasyan!* He was alive! She almost laughed with the pleasure and gave him a little wave. He did not return her greeting. Nikholai dismounted and gave Sultan's reins to his lieutenant.

As he approached, Elise thought him a little thinner than she remembered. His clothes were tattered, but he was clean-shaven. Then she saw his face, hard and lean. He held her gaze with the light, stalking eyes of the Wolf.

Elise turned cold and shrank inside. She looked at Kasyan, who remained mounted. His gaze followed Daria and Rostov. Daria showed no pleasure in seeing her husband.

Nikholai stood before Rostov with his legs apart and his fists braced against his hips. Elise knew he had already decided what would happen. Rostov's words were only sounds on the wind.

"I have something you want . . ." Rostov began. He nodded in Elise's direction. "Your wife."

## ❧ 27 ❧

## Stranger in the Mist

Your wife led us right to you," Rostov said. "So, knowing how you Cossacks like to deal with your own traitors, I'm willing to make an exchange."

"For what?" Nikholai asked.

"You," Rostov said. "You return to Moscow with me, in exchange for the lives of your men and your betrayer."

"My betrayer," Nikholai repeated. Again Elise felt the gaze of the Wolf fall upon her, and she heard the irony in his voice. She stepped away from Rostov.

"Nikholai?" she appealed softly so that Rostov could not overhear. "Did Bogdan—"

"You know, Alexander Rostov," Nikholai interrupted, "I find no value in bargaining for a traitor."

Elise felt the stares of Rostov and Daria then. She looked up into Nikholai's passionless face. None of this was real, she thought. This could not be the same man who sang lullabies to her and fed her honey-barley cakes. She closed her eyes to shut out the memories, to shut out the sight of his penetrating gray eyes.

"But she is your wife, Nikholai Fomin," Rostov stammered.

She heard the whisper of wood and metal against fabric.

312

Nikholai pulled his pistol from his sash. Then she felt the cold metal against her brow. The hammer clicked as he cocked it. She stood silent and still, anger slowly replacing her fear and exhaustion.

"She has always denied that she was my wife," Nikholai said. "See, I wear the wedding ring, not she. I will offer you another trade, Rostov."

"Nikholai . . ." Elise whispered, partly because her voice had deserted her. She opened her eyes to meet his gaze, and spoke rapidly. "Timofe sent food and gunpowder. Vazka is well-provisioned for the winter. He also sent word that Iakovlev thinks he can get a pardon for you and the warriors of Vazka. Nikholai, please hear me. You must go to Cherkassk."

Nikholai pressed on, his words directed toward Rostov, his gaze still on Elise. "I will spare the lives of you and your men in return for your weapons and powder. I don't want this woman."

Elise closed her eyes again. He would not listen to her. The wind was cold on the back of her neck. Her jaw ached. What would Rostov do with a worthless captive?

She felt the cold metal of the gun barrel trail along the side of her face to her jaw and press against the tender bruise Rostov's blow had left. She tried not to wince.

"Don't leave me here with him, Ataman," she said. Her voice had returned with her anger. She opened her eyes and fixed him with a green glitter. "I'll make it easy for you, Nikholai. This is a love mark from Rostov."

The streltsy captain heard and laughed.

Elise didn't even think to breathe. She meant what she had said: better to die cleanly now than at Rostov's hands. Yet she was fascinated with the way the light went out of Nikholai's eyes and they flashed dark.

A horse snorted and stamped his hoof. A bridle jingled, and saddle leather creaked. Elise still held her breath as Nikholai glanced over his shoulder at Kasyan, who dismounted. When the ataman turned back to her, his expression was troubled. He took the gun away and released the hammer.

"The countess is yours," Nikholai said to Rostov. "Her treachery has earned a slow death. I leave that to you and your men. At daylight, if your weapons aren't stacked with your bandoliers, and your men ready to ride out, we will massacre you all."

"Ataman," Elise said softly, "don't attack the Muscovites. You risk the pardon."

He turned his back on her. He had heard nothing she said, she thought in despair. Was this how it was to end?

"Kasyan?" Elise appealed.

"No," Daria screeched. She started toward Elise.

Rostov held her back. "Be quiet," he commanded.

Without a word, Kasyan dropped the reins of the horses and limped toward Elise. Nikholai blocked his lieutenant's way, but Kasyan shoved his ataman aside. Startled, Nikholai stared at his lieutenant's back.

Pale and shaken, Elise turned a look of relief on Vazka's lieutenant. Nikholai watched, his anger smoldering. She spoke rapidly, earnestly, and Kasyan listened, nodding agreement from time to time. What story did she tell him? What tale of woe to excuse her becoming a traitor? Nikholai wondered. Kasyan had always been too easily swayed by her.

Nikholai turned to stare at Daria. He realized that Kasyan had ignored his own wife to go to Elise. He watched Kasyan take both of Elise's hands. They kissed as comrades would. Nikholai's fury nearly exploded. He turned away and grabbed the horses' reins with such fierceness that the animals tossed their heads and shied away.

Kasyan limped back to his horse and mounted.

As soon as they were out of sight of the flat creek area, the four Cossacks rode into a draw. Without dismounting, they waited to see whether they had been followed.

For a few moments, only the rapid breathing of the horses and the rustle of the wind through the dry steppe grass could be heard.

Nikholai could bear it no longer. "What did she say to you?"

Kasyan eyed his ataman coldly, a look that Nikholai had never received from his friend. Defensively Nikholai sat up straighter in the saddle and squared his shoulders.

"She told me of the pardon," Kasyan said with little emotion. "She said she is afraid something has happened to my father. And she asked me to do what I can to be sure that Anna returns to Poland with Thomas. He is on his way to Cherkassk."

"And what else?" Nikholai demanded, suddenly aware of a burning spot in his gut. "You gave her something. I saw. She slipped it up her sleeve."

"I gave her my knife, Nikholai Fomin," Kasyan said, looking straight ahead at the empty steppe. "She asked not to be left defenseless with the Muscovites."

"You fool," Nikholai said. "She can't defend herself against them with a small knife." The burning spot grew larger.

"She knows that," Kasyan replied.

The coal became red-hot and glowed. Nikholai closed his eyes and felt the bile rise in his throat. He had known when he put the gun to her head that he could not kill her. No matter how great her betrayal, he could not end her life. Nor could he let her destroy herself. To do so would damn her soul—and his—for all eternity.

"She is a traitor," Nikholai repeated. "She didn't deny it."

"You believe the Muscovite?" Kasyan asked, his voice hard and mocking. "The man who deserted his men in battle. The man responsible for your father's death. You're a camel-headed jackass."

"What?" Nikholai stared at his lieutenant in disbelief. The anger and pain in his friend's face mystified him.

The two Cossacks that had ridden with them as guards and flag-bearer glanced at each other. Then they began to move their horses clear of the ataman and his lieutenant.

"You're a son of a camel-headed jackass," Kasyan taunted. He leaned toward Nikholai and added, "I'd like to rub your face in dung."

Nikholai hesitated, but the pain in his gut and the urge to strike exploded. He hit Kasyan. He expected to unseat his lieutenant, but the fair Cossack merely sat up straight and gave a satisfied grunt.

Then the younger man landed a blow on Nikholai's jaw. The ataman found the pain gratifying, much more satisfying than the burning glow inside him. If Kasyan wanted to fight, so be it. Nikholai threw himself at his friend, butting his head into Kasyan's belly. They both fell backward to the ground. The horses danced away.

Nikholai struck blindly at his lieutenant. Kasyan struck back with more precision and just as much anger and frustration.

The other two Cossacks calmly led the horses from the fighting area and watched. One suggested a wager. The other shook his head. "It's impossible to guess the outcome of this fight," he told his friend.

Nikholai and Kasyan pulled each other to their feet. Kasyan swung at Nikholai's head. The ataman ducked and punched Kasyan in the belly again. The tall Cossack didn't remember what this fight was about. It just felt good. Kasyan staggered back a step, straightened, and kicked Nikholai in the knee. The ataman went down, and Kasyan threw himself on his comrade.

Kasyan rolled the ataman and pinned him facedown against the ground. Arms twisted behind him, face in the dust, Nikholai was forced to listen to Kasyan.

"The real traitor could have blown your head off, and you would never have known what happened," Kasyan rasped. "You're afraid to believe in the countess. You wanted her to betray you."

Nikholai struggled and twisted against Kasyan's hold. The pain in his gut began to burn and glow again. He rolled to his side and threw his legs against Kasyan and brought him to earth. He straddled Kasyan and pinned him to the ground by the shoulders. The two men faced each other. Astonished, Nikholai saw that his lieutenant, his friend, the man who was like his brother, wept.

"Don't you see she has tried to save Vazka?" Kasyan said in a tight voice. "Can't you see? She has been betrayed too."

"Who is it?" Nikholai demanded, shaking Kasyan. But the younger man did not answer. He didn't need to.

The burning in Nikholai's gut thrived. He saw Daria's face as she stood next to Rostov. The Gypsy's face bore no marks. Rostov called Elise a traitor, not the dark-haired girl who stood at his side like a partner. Nikholai released Kasyan and sat down on the ground next to his friend. He felt as if he had been kicked in the stomach by a horse. He took a deep, painful breath and began to think.

What had Natalia said? he tried to recall. "Be wise enough to trust her."

Elise was so cold, achingly cold. The soft weight of the wolf-lined burka enveloped her. Nikholai's warmth and scent lingered on the fur and comforted her. She snuggled against it, pulled it closer. Coarse fabric scratched her cheek. Instantly she awoke.

She sat up, clutching a rough blanket, her only cover against the night. She looked across the dying fire at Rostov and Daria, who also slept under the hemp-cloth shelter. With darkness, a cold mist had begun to fall. The shelter had been rigged for the captain and his "captives." A short distance away Elise could see a low fire where the streltsy huddled under their own canopy.

After their meeting with Nikholai at the forked creeks, Elise was numb. Her mind did not work. She simply did as she was ordered. Rostov rallied his forces. He told Daria he had no intention of giving up his arms and riding away.

"I didn't think he'd shoot her," Rostov hissed. "And I never thought he would turn his back on her like that. Then he has the insolence to threaten me."

"I'm not surprised," Daria said. "He does not fall for the obvious. But it was easy to make him believe that his wife is the spy."

Yes, Elise thought, if he believed his wife a traitor, he did not have to think of the future with her. He could shed his regrets about the baby. He was free to go about the business of being responsible for his men, for Vazka.

Rostov refused to give Elise food and allowed her only one blanket. "You are worthless," he hissed. "I would put a gun to your head myself if I could spare the powder."

She didn't care. The numbness that had settled over her allowed her to drift off asleep again. Then for some reason she awoke later. The two campfires glowed faintly red. In the quiet she heard the horses snort and nicker, nothing out of the ordinary. Yet Elise sensed movement in the mist beyond the two canopies.

The hair on the back of her neck tingled. She knew instantly this was how Nikholai would come. He would not wait for a morning confrontation. His attack would be unexpected, swift, and fatal. She sat up and slipped the knife from her sleeve.

She heard something near Daria. Elise got to her knees, freeing herself of the blanket. She saw the form of a Cossack slip in under the shelter. Before she could gasp or move, a hand from behind clamped over her mouth, and another knocked the knife from her hand and grasped her about the waist.

The dark figure leaned over Daria. The Gypsy muttered something, then sat up to gaze without fear at the Cossack.

Elise's assailant tried to pull her away from the scene. His hold was powerful. With her back against his hard belly, she couldn't knee him in the groin. She feared being dragged out into the darkness.

"Kasyan," Daria whispered before he silenced her with his hand over her mouth. Elise watched the wild-eyed Gypsy struggle as Kasyan pulled a dagger and plunged it up under her ribs and into her heart.

The night whirled black and red around Elise. She wasn't aware of struggling against her captor, but the growing pain of his grip made her realize she was still attempting to free herself. The cruel hand over her mouth silenced her scream. She knew she would be next to receive the dagger. She fought for her life, but she couldn't take her gaze from Kasyan and Daria.

She cared nothing for Daria, but she ached for Kasyan. He loved Daria, for whatever reason, but the Gypsy had always betrayed him.

Daria's body sagged against Kasyan. He stared into her face, her dead eyes. With a bloody hand he stroked her cheek. Slowly he lowered her to her sleeping pallet. Then he turned to Elise. Even in the darkness she could see the anguish in his eyes.

Rostov snored and rolled over. The three of them—Kasyan, Elise, and her assailant—tensed until the streltsy captain was still again.

Then Elise's assailant dragged her to her feet. She viciously kicked him in the knee. He groaned and stumbled. For an instant she thought she might gain her freedom.

"Stop it," he commanded in a whisper in her ear. He

cursed. She knew it was Nikholai. She kicked again. He cursed again and shook her.

"Stop, both of you."

Elise opened her eyes to see Kasyan standing before her. He glanced at Nikholai over her shoulder, but when he spoke, he spoke directly to her. Nikholai slowly took his hand from her mouth.

"Can you see the men down the slope?"

She looked in the direction he pointed. She saw movement, but she could not make out who was there. She felt Nikholai's rapid breath against her hair just above her ear.

"Go to them," Kasyan ordered.

"They will take you safely away," Nikholai whispered. Gently, reluctantly, he released her and turned her to face him.

"Go," was all he said as he gazed at her with regret. Elise knew he no longer believed her a traitor, but she sensed farewell in his voice, in his face. There were things she wanted to say; she turned back to him.

"Go," Nikholai said roughly, and pushed her away.

Gunfire flashed. The three turned in the direction of a cry from the streltsy's shelter.

"Go," Nikholai ordered again. Pulling his saber from his sash, he waved her away. Both he and Kasyan started toward the campsite.

Elise turned back to the figures she had seen in the mist. She stumbled a few steps into the darkness.

"Elise?" said a voice long familiar and too long absent from her world. "Here."

Elise saw his face and began to laugh and to cry. "Thomas!"

## ❧ 28 ❧

# The Homecoming

Kasyan ran straight toward the fighting under the streltsy canopy. Nikholai went back for Rostov—the man who had struck Elise.

Under the hemp-cloth shelter, Rostov was already on his feet and reaching for his musket. When he saw Nikholai, he took aim. Nikholai knocked the gun barrel aside. With both fists he rammed the Muscovite in the middle. Musket balls exploded through the hemp cloth above.

They both fell. Rostov flung the musket aside and reached for his saber. They rolled clear of each other and jumped to their feet. They sized each other up across the glowing fire.

Nikholai faced the Muscovite with no fear. Elise was safe. Gone. He had lost all that was worth fighting for. The pardon held no value. Rostov's men were battling for their own lives. Nikholai faced Rostov alone, on equal terms.

Each wielded a curved saber blade.

"At last, Wolf, you will pay for dishonoring me with your accusations," Rostov said with a cruel smile. When he stepped back, his foot struck Daria'a body, and he kicked it aside without looking.

"You dishonored yourself," Nikholai replied. "You deserted your men in the field against the Poles. My father

320

died, and my uncle and many others. Even Muscovite dogs don't reward that kind of cowardice."

Rostov snarled and struck at Nikholai. The Cossack parried, then took up the offense. He drove Rostov back with each swing of his saber. He ignored the pain in his knee. Rostov defended himself, furiously circling beneath the canopy and around the glowing fire—the only light.

A particularly sound parry of Rostov's shook pain down through Nikholai's body to his knee. He was unable to avoid the limping stride he took. He saw Rostov recognize the weakness. The Muscovite renewed his attack. Nikholai countered. He clenched his teeth against the pain and forced the Muscovite back again to the edge of the canopy.

Shaken, Rostov turned to slice through a rope tie that held the shelter tight. Heavy wet fabric dropped on them. Steam sizzled from the fire. The unexpected weight brought Nikholai painfully to his knees. He held his blade over his head and searched for a way out.

He could hear and feel the movement of the fabric. He sensed another presence. A Muscovite? A Cossack?

Nikholai endeavored to climb to his feet and throw back the fabric. He felt something strike the cloth next to him. Striking back blindly, he drove his blade through the hemp cloth. Metal rang against metal. Then a pistol fired, and a man groaned. Nikholai threw back a fold of fabric to see Rostov clutch his chest and crumple slowly to the ground. Kasyan stood over him.

"I killed him," Kasyan declared. He thrust his smoking pistol into the air in a gesture of victory and shouted, "I killed Rostov. The guilt is mine. The pardon is yours."

Stunned, Nikholai stared at his comrade.

Three weeks later Nikholai halted his Cossacks on the east side of the ford just below Vazka. He looked up at the white cottages on the bluff with relief.

"Looks good, doesn't it?" Bogdan said, speaking Nikholai's own thoughts. The elder rode at the ataman's side and served as his lieutenant now.

"Yes," Nikholai said, twisting around to look at his warriors. Almost a full one hundred rode behind him, some of them from Rostov's streltsy troop.

Others of Rostov's streltsy had escaped into the night. With the realization that their captain was dead, others threw down their weapons. Some of those rode behind Nikholai now. He had not promised them riches, only freedom and adventure.

Others had ridden away with Kasyan, knowing that they chose the life of fugitives. Rostov's loyal streltsy would report the Cossack lieutenant who had killed Rostov. Kasyan was a wanted man.

So they had parted, with Kasyan riding east to freedom and the unknown, Nikholai turning his men toward home. Along the Volga they, too, had encountered gibbets heavy with dead Cossacks. But Bogdan assured Nikholai the pardon was his.

Vazka's Cossacks wanted freedom, but they also wanted to be with their families. Even the hardiest Cossack warrior yearned for a soft bed and a warm woman when the days became short and the nights long.

"There's someone on the lookout," Bogdan said.

Nikholai looked up to see several small figures with a pup at their heels run down the path to the rocky ledge. One boy wore a bright red hat, and for a moment Nikholai thought it was Elise. Then he realized his mistake. The children waved from the ledge. The dog barked a greeting that drifted down from the heights and across the river.

Slowly Nikholai raised his hand to wave back. Elise would be nearing Warsaw by now, he thought. She was on his mind often. He thought of her sleeping at inns, riding in a coach, crossing a river. He hoped she was well, comfortable, safe. He always smiled at the thought of her confrontation with Leopold Polonsky. The vision of the stingy, bewildered man faced with Elise, his uncle's irate widow, was a source of satisfaction for Nikholai.

As Vazka's warriors rode up to the village gates, the wives, mothers, sweethearts, fathers, and children flooded forth to cheer the homecoming warriors. They sang of victory.

As soon as Nikholai dismounted, Natalia flung her arms around him, then grasped his face between her hands and kissed him. He gave her a bear hug that pulled her off the ground. They both laughed. He saw Yergov in the crowd, and Timofe.

Timofe kissed him and, before he could ask, told him, "Kornil Iakovlev is certain the pardon will be granted. The Don Host is working very hard to keep Moscow's retribution under control."

Over Timofe's shoulder, Nikholai saw Thomas Chatham. His heart stopped.

That day of the creek meeting with Alexander Rostov, Nikholai had ridden back to the pirate camp still numb with the realization that Daria was the spy. He found Bogdan, Yergov, and a tall dark-haired, green-eyed man awaiting him. Nikholai knew instantly that this was Thomas. The dark hair surprised him, but the green eyes—there could be no mistake. This was Elise's brother.

Bogdan had been delayed by a lame horse. Then he had been briefly waylaid by Thomas and Yergov. They had traveled as fast as they could, and were still able to avoid the tsar's troops patrolling the Volga.

Nikholai admired Thomas Chatham. The man behaved with the restraint of a saint upon meeting his sister's captor. His countenance was grim as he learned how dire the situation was. But he never blamed Nikholai, never demanded retribution. He only talked of how to get his sister out of Muscovite hands. They had agreed on a plan. Elise was to be rescued from the Muscovite camp before the attack. Then Yergov and Thomas would take her back to Vazka. With Anna they would go on to Cherkassk and home to Warsaw.

As Nikholai nodded a greeting to the tall Englishman, he wondered what had brought Thomas to Vazka. Was Elise with him?

"She is here, Nikholai," Natalia said softly. "She returned with the priest. She took him straight to the babe's grave."

"So the abbot finally agreed to send someone," Nikholai said. He tried to ignore the emotions that threatened his calm. He had not expected to face her again. He had been torn by a sense of relief that he didn't have to deal with her anger and his regret at not saying good-bye. She would be angry, and she had every right to be, he thought. He would want to hold her and thank the saints, the fates, God, Allah, whomever, that she was safe. Then, as he held her close, there would be other things that he would want and need.

"Nikholai," Anna cried. She tugged on his sleeve. "See how Puppy has grown? Elise said we can take him with us when we leave tomorrow."

Nikholai knelt beside the child to examine the puppy. She laughed with him when Puppy tried to lick first her face, then Nikholai's. The villagers around them laughed.

Then, "Elise, Nikholai is home," Anna said, looking over his shoulder.

"Yes, I see."

Nikholai turned to her as he stood. She appeared aloof and composed, dressed in a Western riding habit of brown velvet, her golden curls neatly tucked beneath the sable hat he had given her. Her skin was smooth and radiant, her eyes a clear dark green. She stepped closer. Her apple-blossom scent made him ache for the sweet, tangy taste of her.

"Welcome home, Ataman." She gave him the formal three kisses. Nikholai wanted more.

Murmurs of approval rippled through their audience. Nikholai was suddenly aware of how much of their relationship had been played out before the village. He had never really had her for himself. He resented everyone around them now.

"Where is Kasyan?" she asked, looking at the men behind him.

Anger must have crossed his face, because she shrank back a bit. He clamped a hold on her wrist.

"Nikholai?" Her voice was steady but concerned. "Is Kasyan all right? Does he need help?"

He shook his head. "I want to talk to you," he said, aware that his voice was almost too husky to be heard above the others around them.

"I have some things to say to you too," Elise said. Then to Thomas she said, "I'm going to help the ataman with the horses."

Over Elise's head, Nikholai noted Thomas' watchful look. Behind them, the villagers closed in around the warriors to share their news. Boys took the horses away to be fed and watered.

Nikholai and Elise walked to the stable in silence. His grip on her wrist was almost painful. She said nothing. She sensed his anger, but knew it was only part of a greater turmoil. Around them excited boys led weary horses into stalls.

Slowly she closed the stall door behind them.

"Did you have to let Kasyan kill Daria?" she asked in Polish. In the next stall a boy was feeding Sotnik.

"He asked to do it," Nikholai said, loosening the saddle girth.

"He loved her, Nikholai," Elise said. "Whatever her faults. Now he has to live with her murder all his life."

"Faults?" Nikholai pulled the saddle from the stallion's back and held it out for Elise to take. Surprised, but willing, she reached out, and he dropped it into her arms. She staggered under its weight. "The Gypsy was a traitor," he said, and turned back to brush the stallion.

"You thought me a traitor—and wrongly," Elise said. "You were going to kill me. Worse, you offered me to Rostov."

Nikholai was silent. His back to Elise, he brushed Sultan vigorously. She put the saddle down in clean hay.

"All of the clues of Daria's betrayal were before us for weeks," Elise said, speaking calmly. "None of us saw them. I assumed the obvious. I believed it was Vikola. Kasyan didn't want to believe it was Daria. You . . . you were willing to believe it was me. Why? Because I refused to leave you or because I tried to escape? Why?"

Nikholai continued to brush Sultan.

Elise could feel her anger growing again. She had been over and over this in her mind since she had left Nikholai and Kasyan on the steppe.

"I may have tried to escape several times, but I never betrayed the village," she reminded him. "I never tried to hurt anyone. I only wanted to find my sister."

Nikholai bowed his head.

"Is there no answer?" Elise asked, wondering if he knew himself why he had deserted her to Rostov.

"Yes, there is an answer," he said at last. "Kasyan showed it to me." He paused and took a deep breath. "If I care about you, you will go away. But if you are a traitor, I don't have to care about you." Nikholai's attention was fastened on the brush he held.

What game was this? she wondered. Did he care about her

or not? "It was easier to think of me as a traitor than to care about me?" she asked.

"No, don't twist my words."

"Then what?"

"It was safer," he said. "I denied you because it was safe, and I will regret that the rest of my life." He began to brush the stallion again, slowly. Elise waited. He did not say he was sorry. He did not say he cared.

At last she picked up the saddle. "I'll put this in the tack room." She felt the tight aching tension of disappointment in the back of her neck as she lifted the saddle.

Nikholai was suddenly there beside her. He took the saddle from her. "When do you leave?" He wasn't looking at her.

"Tomorrow morning," she replied. "We were going to leave today, until your scouts arrived last night. I wanted to tell you about the priest's blessing the baby's grave and to say good-bye to Kasyan." She now regretted that decision; she wished they had ridden away as planned.

"Stay."

"What?"

"Stay with me tonight," he asked, meeting her gaze at last. "Just tonight. Just to say good-bye. It's all I ask. Tomorrow you will be free to go whenever you like. I promise."

His eyes were dark, not thunderous, but appealing. She looked up at him, aware of his nearness, his male scent— tobacco and horses. His strength. His tenderness. The stubble of his beard. The little lines on either side of his mustache that became dimples when he smiled.

She nodded. It was foolish, but she wanted one last night with him too.

"Go join the others," he said with a smile, the uncertainty gone from his expression. "I will come for you when it's time." He opened the stall door for her. "Go. Go."

She smiled hesitantly and went.

She did not see Nikholai again for more than an hour. She found many of the elders gathered around Bogdan to ask about the final confrontation with Rostov, about Kasyan and Daria. He told the story several times. Rostov's accusation that Elise was the traitor was never mentioned.

A group of weary warriors lolled on benches near the

bonfire, enjoying their pipes. One pair started a dice game. Another group began to play cards. They invited Thomas to join them, but he refused politely and joined Elise.

"Are you all right?" he asked with a wary glance at her.

"Of course," she said. "What did you expect?"

"Something is going on here," he said uneasily, looking about him again. "I sense a determined effort to keep us separated. Your ataman wouldn't change his mind about releasing you, would he?"

"No," Elise said, and laughed. "He gave me his word we will be free to go tomorrow. But, Thomas, tonight I will stay with him."

To Elise's surprise, Thomas merely nodded. "You don't have to do this," he said. "I can demand we leave now, but I'm not sure he would release us."

"He would if Yergov asked it," Elise said confidently.

"I'm not sure of that," Thomas said. "I think Yergov has joined them."

Natalia brought Elise some food and encouraged her to eat. Timofe stopped to talk with her about Katia and the baby, Sophia. He also expressed his pleasure about the pardon—he had no doubts it would be granted.

Then Yergov invited Thomas to play cards. After a reassuring nod from his sister, Thomas went.

Bogdan and the elders began to gather around Elise and Timofe.

"And Razin?" one asked. "What is heard of him?"

"Rumors fly like the devil at night," Timofe said cryptically. "Some say he has returned to Kagalnik. Some say he has returned to his mother's homestead near the Volga. The forces Alena took with them have dispersed, so he has no real protection. There is much pressure on Kornil Iakovlev to surrender the rebel to the Muscovites."

As the sun dropped lower in the sky and the fire burned brighter, Nikholai reappeared. He was clean-shaven and his mustache expertly trimmed. He wore a clean shirt—a celebration shirt with colorful embroidery at the neck—a red sash, clean trousers, and boots. His wolf-lined burka was draped over his shoulders.

Nikholai was introduced to Vazka's new priest, Father Dimitry. Elise liked him. In Cherkassk, when she had heard from Timofe that a priest was journeying to Vazka, she had insisted she return with him. Thomas had been reluctant at first, but when Elise told him of the baby's grave, he had agreed they should go. Without questions, Father Dimitry had willingly blessed the small grave.

"So it was you, Nikholai Fomin," Father Dimitry said, "who upset the monastery with your request for a priest?"

Nikholai only smiled.

The father was a humble but garrulous man. He did not hesitate to tell the village how one day near Christmas a tall Cossack dressed in uniform had appeared at the monastery gate, across the river from Cherkassk. Once admitted, this Cossack went straight to the monastery's chapel.

Idly he had admired the large, rich icon of St. Nikholas his family had donated to the chapel. Then he told of how his village, Vazka, had no priest, nor an icon so fine. He went on to say he would be very pleased if the monastery could give up the icon since it could not spare a priest for the village. The icon had been a central place of display and adoration in the chapel for years, and the abbot, priests, and monks were reluctant to part with it. They decided to send a priest.

Elise smiled secretly. So Nikholai had been busier in Cherkassk than she knew. She looked across the circle of villagers to see him laugh with one of the krug elders.

Ganna stopped to visit with Elise. The young widow was sad when she spoke of her husband, Filip, killed at Simbirsk. But life sparked in her eyes when she talked of her coming baby. Others stopped to talk, to discuss how Daria's mother had been seen slipping away from the village early one morning after Yergov, Elise, and Thomas had returned to tell of Daria's part in the betrayal.

"She told me once of a son in a work camp in the Urals," one of the women said. Others nodded. "She's probably gone north to Tula, where the Gypsies gather sometimes."

Olga brought her twins to Elise to show how much they had grown. Young Stepan gifted Elise with a bird's nest.

The night was black when Natalia took Anna away. "We'll sleep in Ganna's loft," Natalia confided. "She does not like to be alone."

Elise stood and looked around, wondering where Nikholai had gone. The bonfire had died down to glowing red embers. A place in a loft was found for Father Dimitry. Yergov and Thomas had wandered off with their card-playing friends. Elise hugged herself and shivered.

She did not hear his approach, but she felt the warmth of the wolf fur around her—no dream this time.

"I expected you sooner," she said, closing her eyes while he kissed her eyelids. "I thought you would throw me over your shoulder and carry me through the village for all to see."

"They don't have to see to know," he said, brushing a kiss across her nose.

A bright fire burned in the oven of the Fomin cottage. No lamps were lit. The bed was turned down. Boughs of evergreen freshened the air. Hot tea and cakes awaited them on the table.

## ❧ 29 ☙
## Separation

Elise was unsure of what Nikholai expected of her. They drank tea and talked like a couple long married—how much the twins had grown, how well Natalia looked, what a proud father Timofe was. Elise told of seeing their goddaughter in Cherkassk and of admitting, at last, to Katia some of the truth about their relationship.

"Was she disappointed?" Nikholai asked, handing Elise another honey-barley cake.

Elise laughed. "No, she thought my being your captive was romantic. I don't think she believed I'm going home."

Nikholai said nothing to that. He rose from the bench, paced the room, then stood behind her.

Elise turned. "What are—?"

"I'm just taking off your hat," he said softly. He tossed the sable piece onto the table and began to remove combs. "There," he said, running his fingers through her hair. He began to massage her scalp. His fingers worked from the top of her head to the base of her neck, and she felt all her tensions ease away. She closed her eyes, leaned back against his belly, and sighed. Gently he stroked her shoulders. His hands began to work at the buttons of her military-style riding habit. Once it was unfastened, he encountered her linen shirt.

"What's this?" he demanded softly. Elise heard the impatience and looked up to glimpse the passion he had kept so carefully tethered inside.

"No, don't, Nikholai," she said, pulling at his hands. "Let me." She kissed his fingers and quickly unfastened the buttons of both the jacket and the shirt. He pulled the garments open to stroke her throat. His touch was light and soothing. Elise closed her eyes to better enjoy it. In a sudden movement that startled her, he seized her hand and led her to the bed. There he made no pretense of patience.

He pulled off her boots and pulled at her clothes, tossing them aside as quickly as he freed her of them. When at last she wore nothing, he tried to kiss her, but she avoided him and began to unbutton his shirt. She unwrapped his sash. When it was gone, she helped pull his shirt off over his head. She grinned at him, trailing her fingers down his chest. She kissed his breastbone teasingly and tugged at the waist of his trousers. Nikholai took a sudden sharp breath.

Then, with a chuckle, he took her face between his hands and gazed into her eyes. The intense passion on his face softened into a tender smile. "I never know what to expect from you, Green Eyes," he whispered, and stroked her wild curls. "But you can't be any more impatient than I."

"Don't be too sure, Cossack," she laughed. She drew her fingernails down the valley of his back and pressed her pinked, peaked breasts against him.

He groaned and pushed her away to remove the rest of his clothes. Then he began kissing every part of her. At first she resisted the intimacy, tugging at his hair, but he would not be deterred. When the hot probings were too much to resist, Elise fell back against the down pillow, panting with pleasure. He stroked her belly and teased her breasts with feathery kisses.

The desire to possess her was strong and painful, but Nikholai intended to make the night last as long as possible.

He caressed her slowly and insistently, taking pleasure in hearing her sighs shorten to needful sobs. She put her arms around his neck and rubbed her swollen breasts against him.

She moved her hips in that inviting feminine dance no man could resist. He covered her body with his, accepting her invitation to lose himself in her warm, velvety depths. He matched her rhythm this time. She knew what she needed from him now, and he would give it. When her breathing became more rapid, she arched against him, twining her legs about his. He let himself soar with her.

Afterward, he held her tight, aware of her long legs still tangled with his. While she was awake, he whispered his concerns. "If there is a child of tonight, Green Eyes," he said, "you must tell me. I want to know. If you ever need help of any kind, you must send for me. The Don Host will know where I am. Promise?"

"I promise," she murmured drowsily, and curled up against him, her hand tangled in his chest hair. He did not remove it, but held it in his own and thought more about the future while she slept. Natalia thought he could still persuade the countess to stay with him, but he did not feel he had the right to ask, or to separate her from her brother.

She stirred. "Where are you going?" she asked, nuzzling his neck.

"Nowhere," he said. "I'm staying right here with you."

"No, I mean, why wouldn't you be in Vazka if I need you?"

"Because the warriors have agreed with me that it is time to move east, away from the Muscovites, to Siberia perhaps."

"Siberia?" She sat up, wide-awake. "Like the great Yermak? What an adventure! A land as new and unknown as the New World. A land of riches, of strange animals and even stranger peoples . . ."

"Are you going to sleep?" he asked, eyeing her full breasts.

"No," she said. "This time I want to ride."

And a delightful ride it was, Nikholai thought. Lying on his back, he had a perfect view of those lovely pink-tipped breasts rising and falling with her hip movement. She tossed her head back and closed her eyes as pleasure blushed across her face. He poured himself into her. She tensed and gave a triumphant cry, and he grasped her about the waist as she sagged against him.

She put her arms around his neck and slept. Nikholai held her and dreaded their coming separation. One day another man would come into her life. That man would share with her what had just passed between them—touching her so deeply he brought her life and death.

Nikholai couldn't sleep. His mind ticked off the choices. He could ask Yergov to hold Thomas prisoner and take Elise east. Thomas would never find them in Siberia. But what if she decided to escape? Old fears stirred in his heart. He was a fool. He reminded himself why he had asked for this one last night with her.

He shook her gently. "Green Eyes, there is something I must tell you," he whispered into her ear.

She sighed and twined her fingers in his chest hair. He wasn't sure she was awake, but he spoke his heart anyway.

"I love you, Green Eyes. And I set you free."

To his surprise, she whispered, "And I love you, Ataman. But what I want to know is, am I free to go with you? To Siberia? It will be a great adventure. I want to go too."

Nikholai held his breath. Was she really awake? Did she know what she had asked? "If you go to Siberia with me, it will be as my true wife," he said. "It will be forever."

"I know," she whispered. "I have conditions of my own."

She *was* awake, he thought. "And they are . . . ?"

"I will not be held to all that is properly Cossack," she said. "I will wear my head covering as I wish, and I will continue to sit on the krug and speak my mind."

"I thought that was established."

"I ask for the same rights for our daughters," she said.

Nikholai groaned. "How will our sons defend themselves against their sisters?"

"Our sons will be man enough to manage," she said.

Nikholai laughed. He had not laughed in a long time, he realized. Laughter felt good. He pulled her close. "Is there more?"

"Yes, and the most important," she said against his neck. "I ask for your trust and faith. I have proved my loyalty more than once. You have never accepted it."

"But I did," Nikholai said with a sigh. "True, I should have accepted it sooner. But I did not leave you at Rostov's

333

mercy. Not for long, anyway. When I saw that bruise, I knew something was wrong. Then you said that outrageous thing about a love mark, and your eyes flashed."

Annoyed, Elise brushed his hand away from her jaw. "Will I have to suffer a broken jaw every time you question what has happened?" She pushed him away and met his gaze.

"Not if you vow before Father Dimitry that you are my loyal wife."

Nikholai flashed his most winning smile, the one with dimples and clear eyes. The one she could never resist. The bloody Cossack, she thought. "What about Anna?" she asked. "She adores Natalia."

"Of course, Anna stays with us," Nikholai said. Something flickered in his eyes. His grip on her waist suddenly tightened. "Are you really going to stay, Green Eyes?"

Elise glanced at the window to see the first glow of daylight pale the sky. "I will if you vow before Father Dimitry that you are my trusting husband."

"We'll do it today," Nikholai said. He kissed her soundly several times before he went to make preparations.

Elise thought Thomas took the news well. She found him drinking with Yergov. Great dark circles marked his eyes. "I am not surprised," he said. "The whole village has wagers on it. They kept me away from you all night with their games. You'd think they would at least allow me to win," he complained.

Nikholai promised rematches during the wedding celebration.

Anna and Natalia danced in a circle, with Puppy yapping at their heels when Elise told them of the decision.

Before Father Dimitry, with Thomas, Anna, and all of Vazka watching, Nikholai took the hand-clasped wedding band from his little finger and placed it on Elise's ring finger for the second and last time.

Once again Vazka joyously celebrated the wedding of the ataman and the countess.

# ❧ Epilogue ❧

In the spring of 1671, Prince Boriatinsky's forces found Stenka Razin's family homestead near a small tributary of the Volga. With Alena's nursing, the rebel had recovered enough to go outside to watch his horses graze on the spring grass.

Some said the Muscovites learned the location from spies. Some said the streltsy accidentally rode down on the grazing horses. Others whispered that Stenka Razin's own godfather, Kornil Iakovlev, had revealed where the rebel was hiding.

The tale is told that the giant Cossack fought, but threw down his sword when he saw the soldiers ready to overpower him with only Alena at his side. "Take me, you dogs," he cried.

They left him no dignity. They took away his fine clothes, confiscated his best horses, and chained him in a cart drawn by black oxen. The infamous rebel was paraded before jeering peasants through the streets of Moscow to Red Square.

Stenka Razin was tortured—flogged and branded—to make him beg for his life, but he did not. He did not cry out

335

in pain or beg to be spared. He walked to the scaffold, where the tsar's headsman awaited him. He asked to enjoy two last pipe smokes. His request was granted.

Moscow's brass bells clanged in triumph, and trumpet calls flourished as the ax fell. Razin's body was burned for three days and sprinkled with holy water to exorcise the evil spirit.

But his story, his courage, still lives in traditional Russian songs, and folk tales.

In the decades that followed, greedy men would dig up the riverbanks of the Don and the Volga to find Stenka Razin's pirate treasure. The Cossacks of the Don, Volga, and Yaik would rebel again and again, and eventually be harnessed— their daring and fierce courage converted to Moscow's military advantage.

But some of the Cossacks unhappy with Moscow's growing power and influence would take their hardy independence and courage to the frontier, pushing it farther east.

Nikholai and Elise joined those Cossacks. Many from Vazka followed them. Nikholai became New Vazka's ataman, and Elise continued to be known and respected as "the countess." Anna grew into a lovely Cossack maiden.

Natalia and Bogdan also settled in New Vazka, despite much muttering from both about being too old to start a new life. Yergov wandered away, as was his habit, but returned to visit Nikholai and Elise from time to time.

Kasyan was never pardoned, but on the frontier it didn't matter. He lived to play uncle to many little Fomins, and to love again.